WHERE
THE DAY
NEVER ENDS

A collection of short stories

Francesco Marincola

ABOUT THE BOOK

"Where the Day Never Ends" is the third collection of short stories that includes contributions from my pen pals Yao Lu and Catterina Coha. The title of the collection refers to a trip to Lapland, where the photo on the cover was taken at midnight when the Bifrons sun reflects on the day gone and the day to come at the same time. So I hope that the stories offer the reader's soul an infinite cycle in which past and future merge in the harmonious light of recollections and hopes that comfort us in difficult times and allow us to dream of an unending beauty.

The two stories, "The Tidal Lock" and "The Strange Case of Clara's Eyes", are longer and could be described as novels, the first being the utopian icon of steadfast love and the second a cynical version of the same theme. The reader should choose their favorite. The other stories are short vignettes of ordinary life, often presented as pseudo-autobiographies, a style favored by myself and my contributors because we believe it speaks more directly to the reader's imagination. However, I would like to emphasize that, apart from "To My Father", all the stories and their characters are imaginary. To paraphrase the preface to my novel "The Wise Men of Pizzo", they are cumulative narratives derived from lifelong experiences and encounters, and with few exceptions, every word is pure fiction.

"To ask whether the characters truly existed or whether they were just the fruit of imagination is as vital as asking two centuries from now whether any of us truly existed. Like asking whether the notes of a musical composition are real, such information has no bearing over the appeal of a symphony."

TABLE OF CONTENTS

TABLE OF CONTENTS

WHERE THE DAY NEVER ENDS

I have been to Africa, I have been to Asia, I have been to the Americas, and I traveled across Europe, almost all of it. I have watched the black rhino run free at Ngoro Ngoro, and the lion inhale the scent of freedom at the Serengeti. I caressed tigers at Chiang Mai, and I held my babies when they were born. I prayed to an unknown God at the Temple of Heaven in Beijing and to the Black Madonna at the Pilgrim Church of Monserrate Hill. I kneeled at the mummy of San Carlo in the Crypt of the Duomo and at the bold eagle hovering above the Potomac. I visited strip clubs in California to escape the imposing majesty of the Grand Canyon. I observed ugliness in beauty, and I searched for beauty where there was ugliness. I went through one too many E-ZPasses up and down I-95 and along many other highways of life.

But here, in the land where the day never ends, where only the ultimate travels, here, I wonder:

"What is this abandoned beauty? Why this mute solitude? What's it all for?"

"Perhaps," I marvel, "here is the place where the souls of the rightful come, the longed paradise for the believers in a purity that could not be found in ordinary life, for those who aspired for a beginning without end, for an unending cycle of purity. Maybe they are sitting on that bench, viewing a crepuscule harbinger of a beginning. Or perhaps they are walking along the sandy beach, or across the green meadows. Perhaps they are turning, my departed parents among them, to stare at me wondering whether I will ever join. . . Perhaps."

TO MY FATHER

August 15th, 1924 – December 23rd 2021

Mother was fretting in the kitchen under the gloomy light, and Father was patiently watching. It had been a long day and dinner was more about forgetting than stuffing the stomach. Father thought about the baby, his only child, and he was proud of his boy. He imagined the boy growing into a vague, indeterminable future, something beyond the reach of his imagination. Then he thought that glory was not as important as long as the boy was healthy and self-sufficient. Yet, he could not stop wondering:

"What will become of this boy?"

The dad realized that the baby had been silent for far too long. He judged that it was unusual.

He rose and entered cautiously. The room was illuminated by a whisk of light from the kitchen. He checked with angst the cradle. But the baby was well. He was awake, his eyes wide open, curiously following the movement of his hands that with impertinent movements kept entangling as he intertwined his chubby fingers in front of his nose.

When the dad moved closer, the baby glanced at him and, recognizing him, smiled for the first time. It was a bond that lasted for sixty-eight years.

***

Paolo was not just my dad. He was my best friend, the harshest judge of my actions, and the most benevolent father.

He would say, "You made a mistake. Learn and don't do it again." That's how he taught me to be honest to myself.

"It's easier to amend if you are not afraid of judgment!"

***

Paolo inspired so many characters in my stories, including Giuseppe's father in *Wise Men of Pizzo*, Frank's in *The Impostor Syndrome*, Christian in *The Visit*, or Julius' in *Scrooge 2011*.

I quote here a paragraph from *The Old Boys Academy* that was inspired by an unforgettable conversation between the two of us on our terrace in Pizzo. It was a limpid summer night in the mid-nineties:

. . .Later that night, Luca and his dad were sitting at the table after a simple and cozy dinner. It was not a talkative time and the two sat side by side with the background of the television informing about irrelevant events occurring out there in the vast world.

The dad did not initiate any conversation of substance because he knew his son. He knew that he did not like to talk about failures. . . Of course, Dad wanted to know more to provide comfort, but he let the son take the time he needed.

Indeed, after dinner, Luca seized the remote and silenced the television:

"Dad," he whispered, "of our existence, days are like leaves shedding from the old horse chestnut tree. . . lying on the ground wherever the wind scatters them as testimony of an irrevocable past. The rain, the wind, and the sun mark the passing of the seasons ahead, and the trees will sprout more leaves for them to fall in this meaningless cycle. I am perplexed about what lies ahead. But I will accept what's to come: the joys and the sorrows. . . day after day, as I am expected to do. I will follow the path that you lined up for me, just as other good sons did before. I will; but I suppose that it won't be trivial, and I need your guidance. I ask for your blessing before I embark toward the unknown."

And the dad replied:

"The future! We all obsess over the future and do not live the present! Your Mom ate only rotten fruit to save the good for the next day when it will be rotten, and she could eat it without guilt. Just the same for bread, she only ate bread from the day before. In a lifetime, I could not make her understand that it made no sense! That she could break the cycle just by skipping a single day. When she died, there were so many new dresses left in the closet that were never worn, waiting for the right occasion. In the country, we had two dogs. One came at the gate when it saw my car and waited till the gate was open and I continued all the way to the end of the driveway to park. And he followed me, wagging

his tail day after day for all its life. The other dog, after a few repetitions, figured out the pattern and when he saw me, he ran to the end where he knew that I would step out and greet him. Which one was right? Which one understood the difference between the present and the future? Which one was happier? We will never know.

"In the beginning, life is a journey crammed with hope. Without it, there would be nothing, not even the memory of your childhood so full of fragrance. As a youngster, I had no time to worry about the future. My present was hard enough to distract me from other worries. I just tried to survive the miseries of the war and the collateral damage to our family. Besides, I had nobody to talk to. I had no dad, my mother was too busy making ends meet and my brothers had either died in the war or had gone far to build a new life. . . and you, of course. . . you were not there as yet. So, I learned to carry on without asking questions to others or to myself. But now, you ask your father's advice. You ask questions that I never dared to ask myself! What can I say? Maybe I could tell you what life has been like for me.

"I remember that life begins as a dream when, as a boy, one plays around his mother's skirt. But soon it turns into a troubled battle, and one realizes that, child no more, he is walking a solitary journey fearful of what's to come. And, while one fears the future, the nostalgia of the time past hovers like fog upon a deserted path.

"It is toward the end of the journey that I suddenly see in front of me my son, pensive and hesitant just as I was then, and I wonder what his future will bring. Why would it be any different than mine? One would not know. When I observed you as a child and listened to your loquacious dreams, I said to myself:

- perhaps I accomplished something! –

But now that your life is gradually equating to mine, now that your dreams are resting in the casket of memories together with mine, I ask myself:

- What did I do? –

"But at least listen to this advice: life goes on at its own pace and so will it continue. Do not worry! Live in peace as much as you can, do not hurt anybody, and hope for the best. What is to come is beyond your control and, therefore, the future is not your burden.

"*Soon, a day will come when your own son, on a quiet night like this, will ask the same eternal questions. I cannot guess what you will say, but I imagine that you will recollect this night. . . . Enjoy the moment now, the quiet night appears still, and yet it will soon be gone. Observe carefully because one day you will relish each gesture. . . each word of mine.*

TIDAL LOCK

When by chance two celestial bodies cross paths and the smaller one is drawn into the other's orbit, an eternal bond is established and a marvel occurs: in tidal attraction, both slow their spin to face each other. The gradual process first locks the rotational period of the smaller one to match its orbital pace. Then imperceptibly, the dominant abides by the same fate. It is such a common occurrence in the universe that one pays almost no attention to it. This is how our Moon pointed her seductive face to Earth for billions of years past. And the Earth will have no choice but to reciprocate in the billions to come. . . unless a premature death parts them beforehand, when the Sun, in a giant red explosion, engulfs both in a mass suicide. But till then, the fatal attraction will persevere.

And so will the fate of true love.

This is the tale of Giselle and of her improbable love story.

GISELLE

In the haze of a chilly autumn morning, a door squeaked ahead of opening to let an elder woman out of a gray and rusty hut and from which a languid swell of dark smoke levitated unhurriedly on its way to the clouds above. It was the first commotion since dawn, breaking the majestic silence that hovered over the snow of the steppe. The whisper of a chilly breeze had been playing an inconsequential cadence through the naked trees and was of no interest to a shiny black crow. The crow instead sharpened its beak against the branch upon which it was perched and returned to observe the scene with the indifference of a seasoned veteran. With comparable heedlessness, the bird followed the steps of the woman.

The elder marched nimbly over the slippery mud, her left arm holding a tiny bundle which she zealously covered with her right forearm. The tip of her index finger was dipped into the bundle and gently stroked the tiny cheeks of a newborn girl, who had just come into the world.

Soon, she reached a slightly bigger hut, somewhat less rusty and not as gray—around which a few early riser chickens were scraping the dust under the supervision of a proud rooster. The woman pushed the door with her right shoulder and entered into the darkness. In the penumbra, she walked to an old dresser and with her right hand pulled out the top drawer. She took a blanket from the adjacent bed, wrapped the baby into it, and reposed the bundle in the drawer repurposed as a cradle for the time being. The woman, the baby's grandma, then turned toward the wood-burning stove that was dead cold. She opened the door of the stove, inspected the damper, and sighed. Then she cleared the ashes from the previous day and prepared it for a new fire. She went out to fetch wood, carried it back wrapped in a log canvas, and swiftly piled it into the stove on top of dry autumn leaves.

She searched for a match, and it was that necessity that brought back the events of the previous day.

In the middle of the night, she had brought the matchbox to the other hut to start a fire. It was where the baby's birth was supposed to happen and where her daughter Anna, the baby's mother, was now resting in eternal peace. The midwife had been summoned from the village the day before because Anna's contractions had begun. Her name was Kateryna, an old acquaintance from her youth, who pledged to help at no cost thanks to their enduring friendship.

In the evening, since the delivery was taking its time, Kateryna encouraged the elder to go back home for a short nap and to return to help when she woke up. But instead, as the night was still young, the midwife had rushed in to wake her. There was blood coming from everywhere, the baby was alive, but the bleeding would not stop. The elder hurried back to the hut with sheets and buckets. She searched for wood in the darkness and went back to fetch the matchbox to start the fire. All activities were done with the alacrity of desperation, the fussing that can bring distraction but cannot prevent the inevitable.

She fretted by cleaning, washing, and following the midwife's frantic orders till there was only silence and Kateryna went to close Anna's eyes forever. Then, they remembered the little orphan who, unaware, slept peacefully beside her dead mother.

The dad had died under unclear circumstances just a few months before. He was a handsome lad, carrying Cossack blood and the genuine pride of a horse rider. He had spent most of his life on a horse rather than on land and that had made Anna lose her mind. But Cossacks, at the time of our story, were only a memory of the past. In modern times, horses and their riders were of little use in war and in peace since there was no cause to keep the Cossacks going after their repatriation. So, the valiant spirit of a warrior turned him into a truculent drunkard, and after escalating quarrels, they eventually found him with a smashed head along a brook that ran into the Don a few kilometers East of his hometown. Nobody seemed eager to find the perpetrator and even the police captain shrugged his shoulders: "It was going to happen sooner or later."

And because the body was found out of his district, he turned the case to the other municipality, which, by the time they pursued the incident, found nothing at the scene but an empty pack of cigarettes, a rotten booth, and a dirty sock.

In a slurred speech, the grandma remembered that the dad had once voiced that he cared for his son to be named "the invincible." But he had left no entitlement for respect, nor had he prepared for the contingency of a female progeny.

Anna had died without having a chance to say goodbye to her little baby, without at least giving her a name. But Grandma remembered Anna's affection for the ballerina's Giselle's story, told by a teacher, though she had never been to a ballet. So, she grabbed the baby from the bed and said:

"Come, Giselle, say goodbye to your mom, and let's go to your new home!"

But the new home was cold, the stove was empty, and there were no matches.

Daria, the cat, was sleeping on a chair close to the stove, likely waiting for warmth in remembrance. When the old lady gently shushed her away to move the chair to the front of the stove and sit on it, the cat arched, stretched, yawned, and walked toward the door. There, she sensed the whiff of the cold breeze coming from a fissure and decided better to keep inside. So, she grunted a meow (as much as cats can grunt), turned around, and wandered back toward her master, who was by then sitting on the same chair. Poor Daria! Like the old lady, she had seen one too many days in her long life and had gone through God only knows how many litters. She was a retired cat now, and as such she only coveted her well-deserved respite for what remained of this life in preparation for the ultimate repose. So, she yawned, stretched again, and jumped on Grandma's lap.

Grandma caressed Daria mechanically with one hand while on the other she rested her own chin. She recognized that she had to go back to fetch the matches, but she had no energy. She also could not bear the thought of looking at the body of what used to be her beautiful daughter, so healthy and strong just a day before. That cheerful girl, whom everyone loved! The last of her children, who had chosen to stay by her rather than move to the city like the other ones! Anna, with her smiling dark eyes and black hair that framed the palest skin, had been the only company for the strong widower who never remarried after her husband died and who raised each of her little ones with no money or asset other than the strength of her arms and mind and the loving respect of her neighbors. Now, Anna was gone and had left her alone to rear the baby. But that idea did not falter her for long. Her heart pumped warm blood into her head when she thought of Giselle! An overpowering resurgence sparked the old woman's resolve when she heard a gurgle coming from the drawer. Caressing Daria, she asked:

"What do you think, can we go through another litter?"

Daria burped a consenting meow underlined by a yawn to make it clear that, for both, it was just ordinary business. What's another litter after all?

Encouraged by the unequivocal assent, Grandma turned to the dresser:

"You know, Giselle, you will be the best of all, you will make your mom proud one day. You will see! You shall overcome!"

Having said that, Grandma rose and stepped toward the drawer. She stared at Giselle, then she rubbed her fingers against each other to warm them up to touch the baby's cheeks. The newborn opened her eyes and stared at her with a resilient gaze as if she could already gauge the magnitude of the adversity and was prepared for whatever was to come.

"Yes, you shall overcome!" Grandma repeated, looking firmly into Giselle's eyes.

***

With reinvigorated resolve, she told herself:

"Need to feed the baby, need to warm the room, need to thank Kateryna, need to fetch the matches. . . need to take care of Anna."

She stepped toward the door to return to the hut where they left Anna, then she suddenly stopped. Could she leave the baby alone? She turned toward Daria and said:

"Now you look after Giselle, she is our new girl, you keep her company, and I will be right back!"

Daria, recognizing her name, raised her head skeptically and looked into Grandma's eyes, trying to understand. Then she jumped on the chair once more, at intervals flickered her ears in concentration, and turned her back toward the entrance.

***

Kateryna had cleaned and recomposed the body and Anna was now peacefully resting under a clean sheet. She did not seem worried, and she appeared even eager to undertake the ultimate journey as if she had already forgotten about her baby. Ylia, Ivan's wife, who had dropped by to check on the status of affairs, was now helping too. She was yelling from the front door at Ivan, who appeared from a distant hut, asking to help with the preparations for the funeral. Everyone wanted to help the old lady as she had done for them for decades since they were little, when she was still full of energy.

***

Giselle grew up more of a tomboy than a suave ballerina. When the boys derided her for being a girl, she punched and kicked them, making them laugh even more. And when the girls looked at her dumbfounded, she shrugged her shoulders and shook her head. A boy developed an affection for her and followed her everywhere like a dog follows its master. He was a tiny boy of docile temperament, whose name was Sasha. Soon the two chevaliers bonded, and Giselle walked proudly across the village followed by her minuscule army.

She also soon realized that it was impractical to compete with boys on the grounds of physical might. Hence, she resorted to the power of the mind, and whatever teaching the children received in the tiny hut in the middle of the commons, that was called school, stuck with her and made her stand out among her peers. Anything mentioned by her elderly teacher was inscribed in stone to be rehashed at any opportunity. Soon the teacher, an old man named Borysko, whom most referred to as "Uncle Borysko," began to take Giselle into special consideration.

One day, Uncle Borysko asked Giselle in front of Sasha:

"Giselle, what do you want to become when you grow up?"

With decisiveness, Giselle answered:

"I want to be better than all the boys! I want to be the chief of the village!"

And while Sasha was nodding in approbation, she climbed on a chair and posed as if she was the latest hetman of the Cossacks.

Uncle Borysko smiled and said:

"Giselle, there is a big world out there, nothing will come to you by worrying about the boys of this town. Don't ever look behind but look ahead of you. Pretend that you are the captain of a liner searching for a magic island beyond the horizon. Besides, not all boys are wicked. One day, I am sure, you will meet someone who deserves you and you will fall in love!"

Sasha stopped nodding, while Giselle responded with a skeptical yet inquisitive look.

She also became interested in movement. Nobody knows why, but she decided to stand upside-down against the wall of the barn to impress Sasha and she pushed him to emulate her. She then realized that she could move away from the wall and stand upside down all by herself! Still, to impress her friend, she started to walk on her hands and perform acrobatics such as cartwheels and somersaults. Poor Sasha! After a few tries, he resorted to sitting and watching Giselle perform, particularly when flexibility and strength were required. There were no monkey bars in that village, no rings or other equipment, but there were plenty of trees and meadows, slopes, fences, and other hurdles and none of them deterred Giselle, who took everything as a challenge, climbing and jumping at every opportunity, or balancing over a fallen tree that bridged over the noisy torrent in the rainy season.

But the meaning of motion dawned suddenly when a fiddler came to play in the town's marketplace. He was a short and skinny man with a big nose and severe mustaches that zigzagged like vines up his cheeks all the way to his sideburns. He wore a velvet vest and stained pants. Under the vest was a shirt that must have seen better days. But there was magic when he played. It wasn't just the fiddle, but it was the tapping of his foot and the rocking of his body. Everything else followed! The whole band followed, players and instruments, all juddering after the tapping of that supernatural foot!

Music comes in a script, but what gives it life is rhythm. So, Giselle began to tap her foot too, and then she tapped in turn one or the other and clapped her hands, and because she was light as a feather, she started spinning, and performing pirouettes, and jumping, and running from one side to the other of the little square as if she herself had invented what others have called for centuries in the past —ballet.

She was so fired up that she could not stop, and it was only at the end when the band ended their performance and she saw a few good soul toss one or two kopecks in the old man's papakhas, that she ran home to fetch—in front of her astonished Grandma—a few precious coins that she had accumulated birthday after birthday to be saved for an indeterminate future. She ran out of the hut holding them tightly in her fist and proudly leaned to depose them in the fiddler's cap.

But the fiddler shook his head, and, perhaps in awareness of the little girl's modest means through word of mouth, said:

"Sorry, my magnanimous young lady, we do not accept money from children."

Then, noticing embarrassment from her rosy cheeks, he frowned and, pretending to ponder, added:

"We do not take money but, since you are such a good ballerina, maybe you can help us by coming again tomorrow. That will be Sunday's great performance and you can dance for our band! And, you know what? You can also get up early in the morning and run in the fields to fetch the firstling blossoms of spring that we can use to decorate our humble stage for the occasion."

And so it was that impromptu. Giselle submitted to the fate imposed upon her by her given name and became a weekend ballerina. And she did it in such earnest that the band decided to share with her a few kopeks. This idea resonated with Uncle Borysko, who suddenly realized that some flowers could improve the status of that humble hut called school and, therefore, for a few kopeks he negotiated special deliveries of wildflowers by Giselle for any foreseeable special occasion. All these favors by the elders converge into crumbles of wealth that one day could serve Giselle in that indeterminate future.

Uncle Borysko also took notice of Giselle's performances and with the intent of educating her about what had naturally sprung from his heart, he went through dusty boxes to find a book that, among several obsolete stories, comprised a synopsis of Giselle's celebrated ballet with a picture of a lovely ballerina:

"I want to show you something. . . . Look! This is the real Giselle—a real ballerina!"

The little girl quickly replied with a frown:

"I am the real Giselle!"

Uncle Borysko smiled, then turning serious, looked straight into her eyes with corrugated eyebrows:

"Yes, of course, you are the real Giselle! How silly of me! And perhaps this ballet was made especially for you!"

"And what is the story about?"

"It is the story of a peasant girl who falls in love with an upper-class boy, and she continues to love him even after she dies, protecting him from the evil spirits that want to hurt him!"

And since Giselle was attentively listening to him, he continued:

"But you see, this is not a true story, it was made for a ballet, one of the most famous ballets that only very special ballerinas can perform!"

"Can I do it? Can I see it?"

"Of course, you can! Never put limits on your dreams and aspirations. But not in this village, where nothing happens! As I told you, there is a big world out there where things that you cannot even imagine happen."

***

So, Giselle was nurtured and raised by a community that respected the old Grandma and the granddaughter, who both bore in their veins the blood of a kozaczka.

On a brisk autumn morning, sitting astride a branch of a pomegranate tree, Giselle told Sasha:

"If you want to marry me one day, you must learn to do somersaults."

Sasha looked at her from the ground not knowing how to respond on account of both prospects.

Poor Sasha! He never had a chance, whether he wanted it or not, to reach any of those goals. Just a few days later, he started to suffer nose bleeds that kept recurring ever more often. More days passed and his gums began to ooze. So they took Sasha to the closest town, and when he returned, he was in a coffin.

A well-meaning but insensitive soul convinced Grandma to lock up Giselle in the chicken run to spare her the pain of the funeral. But Giselle did not concede and, piling a few baskets on top of each other and using all her self-taught skills of equilibrium to counter gravity, she managed to reach the top of the fence and jump to the other side where a blackberry bush welcomed her with its spiny thorns. Extricating her bare legs and arms, she searched for the way to the cemetery when she saw one of the village boys, Demetri, approaching her.

Demetri was a handsome young boy against whom she used to fight at any opportunity just for the sake of it, but this was not the moment to be cornered. Giselle ran away from the village and the past that it represented, and she kept running, darting across meadows, leaping over creeks, hopping from stone to stone, climbing fences, and springing over bushes. But the determined boy kept following her and he was faster.

In the end, Giselle gave up and, climbing to the top of a tiny hill where a big oak tree stood, she turned around and, ready to confront Demetri, questioned:

"Why are you following me?"

Perplexed, the boy answered:

"I don't know, because you were running away."

"What do you want from me?"

"Nothing. . . . I just wanted to say something to you!"

"What?"

"I want to tell you that I am sorry for Sasha."

"And for you," he added.

23

Giselle looked at Demetri with suspicion at first, but then with acquiescence. Maybe the old teacher was right, not all boys are destined to be wicked. So, she sat on a rock under the oak tree, hugged her knees, and looking far toward the dawn that could be seen in the distance, she muttered:

"Thank you."

Demetri came to sit by her side and they both stared at the infinite, till Giselle rested her head on Demetri's shoulder. It was their first encounter with the finality of death.

***

Ivanna was attending to the chicken run and the small chest that served as a chicken coop. The hens were shadowing her steps while she kept sweeping and piling the manure into a corner and adding fresh hay to the coop. At other times, it would have been an enjoyable chore, an occasion to have a good time with her loyal friends that reliably produced the eggs that nurtured Giselle. But lately, even that simple routine was turning into hard work—her legs were shaking, her knees made cracking sounds, and her breath had to pay a heavy toll to escape the depths of her lungs. Granting herself an excuse for a break, she stopped the sweeping and looked up and around as if she were concerned about the weather:

"Another good day tomorrow, I tell you! The clouds are high, and the sky is blue. But you know what? We need rain. I cannot fetch water for you anymore, my good girls. And you drink a lot, you know? And you mess up the water. You are so messy! Maybe I should just get rid of you!" And she placed a hand on top of her right buttock, stretching her spine to ease the path for her breath to exit her lungs.

The hens did not seem worried and kept pecking as if they very well knew that the old lady was all talk but no action when it came to inflicting grief on any living being.

Meanwhile, the old rooster had approached and was looking at Ivanna with suspicion, perhaps sensing that something was different. He had been a stern defender of his harem for so many years that no weasel, fox, or raccoon dared to confront them, day or night. At least that was what Ivanna thought at that moment. Indeed, for whatever reason, the hens had been safe in that tiny sanctuary, that parcel of heaven where she had lived her entire life.

The old rooster had indeed noticed the unusual interruption of their mundane activities and cautiously approached as if he was truly concerned. When he came close, he squatted—an acquired habit for a rooster, taught by Giselle, who could not understand why only hens would do it in her presence.

"Why the hens and not you?" she would reprimand. "Squat down!" she would command, pushing him down gently toward the ground. . . and, lo and behold, the rooster managed to figure out what Giselle meant. That poor Oldie, who had a predilection for the little girl, had learned with time to squat and let her pick him up to pet his feathers and crest.

Ivanna, copying Giselle, lifted Oldie, and said:

"Thank you, my dear, for crowing in the morning. If it wasn't for your reminder, I would not get up anymore. These old bones are no longer listening to their master, as well as my legs and arms. But they obey your call out of habit, and thanks to you, each day starts anew! I don't know how much longer we will have to worry about it, do you know? We are both old and tired. You no longer even fly to the top of the fence at sunrise. Do you think that I didn't notice? Yes, I know that you also can't wait to rest in eternal peace! But what about your lovely hens, who is going to take care of them. . . and what about our Giselle if we both go?

"After Daria died, remember her? You are all that is left!"

Out of empathy, Oldie cackled something indecipherable while Grandma released him, intending to resume her chore. But as she was about to reach for the broom, Uncle Borysko's voice called from the other side of the fence.

"Ivanna, are you there? Good day to you. Can you open the door for an old friend?"

Ivanna opened the wobbly gate of the chicken run to find the old teacher standing in front of the hut with a little package in his right hand.

"Where have you been? I have not seen you around much lately. Are you turning into a hen yourself? Anyhow, I brought you some tea. Can you let me in?"

25

"I have work to do; don't you see? I have no time for anything else, not even to worry about anything else. What brought you here, what did Giselle do this time!" said Ivanna as she walked past the old teacher to open the door of the hut.

As they entered, she went to the blackened samovar, fetched the pot, filled it with water, put it back on the top, checking for kindling. Uncle Borysko foresaw her next move.

"Wait," he said. "I can go fetch some woodsticks myself. You wait here."

Ivanna would not have tolerated such an insult to her abilities at other times and would have nailed the intruder to his chair just with a glance, but this time, she took a deep breath and sat on the opposite chair facing the entrance.

"So, what did she do this time?" Ivanna asked when they were both sitting in front of each other, and the water was heating.

"Nothing. . . I mean, nothing bad. You know, now we have a new system, and we send progress reports to families about our students. It is a mandate from the Ministry of Education, and I am responsible for it. We need to document scores and achievements and send the scorecard for signature," said Uncle Borysko casually scanning the premises but keeping sight of Ivanna with the corner of his eyes. Since no reaction occurred, he changed the subject and, looking around, he asked:

"Where is Daria?"

"She is in a better place! She is waiting for me. . . hopefully not for long."

"Way, way, way! What is going on, Lady Ivanna? You are not known for being a sweet mouth, but this is too much! You look better than a spring flower and as charming as you have ever been! What are you talking about? Let Daria sleep in peace and I promise that I can get you another cat that will be just as good, or pardon me. . . almost as good!"

"You don't know what you are talking about! If it wasn't for Giselle, I would have already given up. But I can't. You know that. She still needs me."

And then, looking straight into the teacher's eyes, she asked:

"So, spit it out, what did she do this time?"

"Going back to the reports; didn't you get one from me? Didn't Giselle bring a letter home for you?"

Ivanna stood up and went to the old dresser, opened the top drawer that, once upon a time, used to be Giselle's cradle, and took out a sealed envelope. Returning to the table, she pitched it in front of the visitor's nose.

"You mean this thing?"

"Yes! You didn't even open it?"

"What's the point? My glasses are getting too old and don't work anymore, and I cannot see through them at all!"

"My fair lady, forgive me for breaking it to you but it is not the glasses that get old. Your eyes are! You should get new glasses, at least reading glasses!"

"What's the point? A big waste of money, and who could I leave them to? Giselle can see better than an owl on a moonless night."

"Well, I will read it to you then," said Uncle Borysko, opening the envelope with the shaft of a teaspoon. Then he changed his mind:

"Forget the details, let's get to the point: Your granddaughter received outstanding scores. She is by far the best in the school. Her personality may be challenging sometimes but her brain is as sharp as a Cossack's sword and her will indomitable. You should be proud of your Giselle!"

"I am, I am, I have always been! Others come to report what a brigand she is, but I would kill myself for her, and I know she would do the same for me."

"Well, those were the good news," continued Uncle Borysko. "The bad news is that I think she is wasted here. I know, Ivanna, that she is all you have. But she needs to move on."

Ivanna didn't react. She rose, went to the steaming pot, picked it up, and poured a touch of hot water into a porcelain cup that had been sitting on a shelf for years, drained the water after shaking it a few times and then she added the tea for Uncle Borysko. Then, she went to the bucket close to the stove and fetched an old clay cup, poured more water and tea for herself, and returned to sit.

"Giselle is life, I am death. She is the future while I am the past. She is almost seven now! She gave me seven blessed years of joy, seven years stolen by destiny from her mom. What more could I want? God already blessed me with more than I deserved. What is good for her is all that counts. Now it is her future and nothing else matters. Besides I still have my Oldie to talk to if I feel lonely."

"I have a niece named Maria, the daughter of my sister who lived in Vienna. My sister, remember her? Loathed our place and she ran away as soon as she could. She went to Moscow and married a Jew there. When the Berlin Wall fell, they moved away and went to Austria. Her daughter Maria eventually moved to Milan to study fashion and there she met and married a doctor and they live there now. My sister died a few years ago, but Maria still writes me. I have never met her but she heard about me from her mother. I guess she did not completely forget me. She wrote that she would like to come for a visit sometime. They have no children for whatever reason. I told her about Giselle. I am sure that they would love to raise her. They are well-to-do. Giselle could have a good upbringing."

***

That evening, Ivanna looked at Giselle, at her thick, shiny black hair and the pale forehead below, her pensive eyebrows framing her wide black eyes that were intently staring at the steaming egg and tomato soup. She could not refrain from admiring that young version of herself and reckoned that she was seeking to imprint that image forever in her mind, an image that would soon belong exclusively to the past. While Giselle was eating, Grandma said:

"Giselle, there are moments when a page needs to be turned, when what is familiar turns into precious memories, while new opportunities demand our consideration. When your mom died, it was nevertheless a beginning because things had to continue. And we both made it happen! But now, a new chapter is about to open. Life is like a dandelion puff with seeds that are freed by the breeze to fly away to something new. I am sure this is what your mom would want for you. Uncle Borysko thinks that it is time for you to go where you can bloom into your destiny. A place that is far from this little village. . . and I think that we should follow his advice."

"And what about you, Grandma?"

"I will wait here for you. Each evening I will pray for you and each morning I will look at the sky querying the clouds for good omens. And I will wait for your letters. I will buy new glasses if I must. And you remember to write often, and no chicken scratch! Write big letters, just as big as your heart. Remember Grandma's old eyes."

Nobody had ever heard or seen Giselle cry. But that night, in the darkness, Ivanna heard a soft sobbing.

"Giselle," she asked, "why are you crying?"

"I am sad."

"Don't be sad! You will see, you will have new friends and you will live in beautiful places that you cannot even imagine!"

"I am not sad for myself, Grandma. I am sad when I think about how much you will miss me!"

***

Occasions arise when, upon awakening, it takes time to regain consciousness of whereabouts in space and time. Extremes include rejoining life after a prolonged coma or deep anesthesia. In ordinary conditions, dreams can present themselves so vividly that, upon recall in the morning, they overshadow reality, making it hard to shake off recollections and to reckon that it is inconceivable for one to fly along the open skies like a bird, holding hands with a long-gone mother. The same is true for preposterous delusions. And, like Chuang Tzu, one wonders whether the incarnation of a butterfly dancing from flower to flower reposes in one's dream or if it is the butterfly that, upon falling asleep, lives the illusion of being a human.

Among such extremes was Giselle's awakening in her new home. Nothing around her was familiar and only a vague remembrance of the previous evening lingered to connect her to the past. It was as if she was a different person, while Grandma, Oldie and its hens, Uncle Borysko, Sasha, Demetri, and the fiddler with the big mustache and his tapping foot were just accessories from an ancient period that loitered in the outskirts of a capricious fantasy.

In the stillness of silence, sunlight sieved through the gaps of the roller shutter, projecting faint beams, tainted by busy dust particles, over scattered objects unknown to her. From the soft mattress where she was lying, she could observe a mahogany dresser and a desk. On the desk stood a shiny brass lamp. It was a bankers' lamp with an emerald-green shade. Close to it rested a Royal of Copenhagen porcelain that portrayed the figurine of a little girl in a light blue dress and wearing a white Dutch cap. Her head was reclined toward a doll that she cuddled with her fragile arms. A loveseat stood on the opposite side of the room, above which hovered the painting of a lake with mountains surrounding it and elegant ladies in the foreground holding colorful parasols with gloved hands. The loveseat was coated by silk upholstery of delicate patterns, and weavings of gold and green vines ran up and down its pink pillows and azure armrests. A Persian carpet connected the components of this new world, which was patiently waiting to be enlivened by Giselle.

Such unwarranted beauty held no place next to Giselle's stark previous life.

On a chair to the left of the bedside table, she noticed her open and empty cracked leather suitcase. Giselle remembered that Mrs. Maria had asked the driver to carry the suitcase up and deposit it right on that chair. When Giselle tried to open it to look for the wool nightgown that Grandma had saved for her, Mrs. Maria waved her hand and said in Russian:

"Do not worry! Tomorrow you can take care of your things! Time for you to go to sleep now." And she handed her a flannel Tyrolean nightgown with patterns of red hearts and blue flowers and an eyelet lace trim. That was her last memory from the night before because as soon as she sunk into the soft sheets also made of flannel, her eyes shut and her thoughts, together with her vision, turned black.

***

But then, what happened to her belongings? she wondered.

Life had moved so fast since Grandma accepted Uncle Borysko's advice to send her to Milan, a place she had never heard about. Mrs. Maria had sent a plane ticket just for her, with a provision for childcare during the flight. Uncle Borysko had taken her by bus to the airport in Kiev and strangers had taken her into the plane, made her sit all the way in the back, and gave

30

her soda and cookies. A young lady, who was sitting close to her, smiled and said something that she could not understand. Then the lady fished from her purse a little box of mints and gave it to Giselle. Giselle took the mints and put one in her mouth, returning the rest to the kind lady, never to be seen again in her life.

Other strangers tended to her after the airplane landed until she was out, past customs, and saw a sign with her name written in Russian held by an elegant lady whose name was Maria and who was meant to become her surrogate mother from that day on.

Before letting her go, Uncle Borysko had shaken her hand, like grownups do, and opening an old bag made of discolored and cracked leather, he took the book where the story of Giselle was engraved.

"This is a gift for you. In Milan, many wonderful things are waiting for you. Among them is a theatre called *Teatro alla Scala*, where only the best of the best performs. One day, you will be one of them! You must be the best of the best because you can. This way, you will make all of us proud and your grandma's sacrifice worth it."

Then he added with a conspiratorial smile:

"And. . . I want you to show the whole world which one is the *Real Giselle!*"

Then, he took another little black handbook with an Italian flag painted at the top right corner:

"This is a dictionary from Russian to Italian. You know enough Russian to get by with Mrs. Maria; this will help you with the rest. Carry it with you all the time."

Then Uncle Borysko patted her on the shoulder and quickly turned around. Giselle followed him till he walked out of her sight, waiting for him to turn around for a last goodbye. But he didn't.

***

Now, a new day was dawning and with it, a new life. It was a day that faced the unknown, in which the only sequence to follow were the steps that a little bird takes away from her nest to spread her hesitant timorous wings and fly toward an unexplored world.

And so, Giselle, with caution, put a foot on the floor, listened for sounds coming from behind the closed door, and walked to the suitcase which remained empty even upon close scrutiny. Wondering about her clothes, she went to the dresser to find her modest belongings folded with care, ordered, piled, and organized according to purpose in different drawers. The dress shoes, the first pair in her life, that she had tolerated during the flight with the dignity—and pride—of a little girl, had been stored under a little bench at the foot of the bed with its tips basking under the warming sun rays. And the two books rested on the desk, right under the brass lamp, on top of each other, silently waiting, just like Giselle, for the future to come.

Timorously, Giselle opened the door, jutted her head with caution out of the frame, and looked left and right. There was a long corridor where a runner rug stretched over the marble floor in either direction toward dark and mysterious ends. Tiptoeing barefoot, she stepped out a little further.

It was then that a middle-aged lady appeared at one end and shouted:

"Ma no, signorina! Ma cosa mi combina!? Non coi piedi nudi sul marmo! Si prenderà un raffreddore!" [1]

The lady walked toward her, pointed at an armoire to the side, opened it, and withdrew a pair of pink slippers.

"Ma metta queste, per favore." [2] And without waiting, she bent over and in turn placed over her knees each one of Giselle's feet to tuck the slippers.

Giselle, who did not speak a word of Italian, bowed and looked with wide-open eyes, wondering what she could have done wrong next to upset the lady.

"Io sono la Lori," [3] said the lady pointing at herself and then, pointing at Giselle, she added, "e Lei è la mia nuova padroncina! Andiamo, andiamo a fare un bel bagno e poi la colazione. [4]"

---

[1] "But my young lady! But what trouble are you getting into? No, the feet on the marble floor! You will catch a cold!"

[2] Please wear these ones!"

[3] "I am Lori . . . And you are my new little master."

[4] "Come on, let's go take a good bath and then . . . breakfast."

And, appreciating that Giselle had no clue about what she was talking about, she held Giselle's hand and guided her to the bathroom.

Now, Giselle had never seen a formal bathroom before, least of all the monumental vision to which she was introduced. A dark granite bathtub and two sinks with brass faucets, knobs, and dispensers were bordered with ledges of white marble. These in turn were framed by candid and elaborate stucco sidings, creating patterns on the wall all the way to the high ceiling. The windows' long silky drapes were kept apart by golden holdbacks, and in the center, an armchair faced a huge mirror where Giselle could see a little girl in a flannel Tyrolean nightgown looking at her with wide-open eyes. A warm fragrance of jasmine impregnated the room, stirring her curiosity. But she could see no flowers.

Lori went to the bathtub and turned the faucet, checking every few seconds the temperature, and then went to a closet at the entrance of the bathroom to fetch a plush, white bathrobe of Turkish cotton. Lori came back, and while waiting for the tub to fill, she proudly showed Giselle the golden letters on the front of the bathrobe that read: "Gisella."

"Ti piacciono? L'ho cucite io!" [5] she said, miming the sewing act.

"Su! Provalo!" [6] And resolute, she unfolded the garment around Giselle's shoulders, and tilting her head, she motioned with an encouraging smile for her to slip her arms into the sleeves.

"Un po' grande!" She frowned. "Ma non troppo. E poi tu ci crescerai dentro come una bella signora in un battito d'occhi!" [7]

The next moment, Giselle found herself floating over a cloud of foam while Lori scrubbed her back as if she were grooming a horse for the fair. Then came the time for the hair washing and drying, and then the brushing and styling, while Lori kept adding along each step cryptic comments that could not be deciphered. In the end, when all was said (in an unknown language) and done, a satisfied Lori stood Giselle in front of the mirror, and a completely different girl was staring back at her.

---

[5] Do you like them? I embroidered them!"
[6] "Come up, Try it up!"
[7] "It's a little large...But not too much...Oh well, you will grow into it like a beautiful woman in the blink of an eye!"

It was not that Giselle had never seen her reflection in a mirror before, but she had been too taken aback by other preoccupations to pay any attention to her own looks, particularly when there was nothing special to explore. But now, in that regal environment and all the time at her disposal, those big black eyes, contained within the frame of her braided hair, made a mark.

Yet unsatisfied, Lori made Giselle spin around a few times to underscore the three-dimensional beauty of her gracious person. In the process, Giselle began to be conscious—for the first time in life—of her own appearance. She reckoned perceptions are bidirectional and from that day, like all of us in the process of maturing, she lost the naiveté of the inner person that could only observe the world behind the safety of the eyes. A second person came into her life—the outer Giselle, exposed to judgment by the surrounding world. As for all of us, that discovery molded her spontaneity, turning it into self-consciousness that proved critical in order to hone her skills in the years to come. Often as life went by, she recollected that moment when the carefree Giselle had turned into a rigorous performer.

The enchantment did not last long because Lori, who had stepped out, returned with a set of clothes for the new Giselle. Cute underwear with minuscule red flowers, a cotton undershirt and a short sleeve blouse with a dark V-neck embroidery matching the color of the dark blue skirt with a Gucci logo on the belt. Lori kept piling these ornaments over the little girl as if she was dressing a Christmas tree, till the time came for a pair of cotton socks and the slippers. Then Lori took Giselle by the hand, walked her to the kitchen and showed her to a white bench while she prepared breakfast. A muffled whirring sound reminded Giselle of the burr of the water mill at the end of the village. It was the telephone, another acquaintance of the new life. Lori interrupted her fretting and answered. Then she hung the phone and came to Giselle:

"Era la signora, chiedeva come stai! Lei é al lavoro. Sono tutti al lavoro. Non ti preoccupare, ci penso io a te, fin quando ritornano."[8]

Giselle thought of the dictionary patiently sitting on the desk and felt an urge to go to the room to fetch it, but she didn't dare. She realized her body was frozen, with no resolve whatsoever to make any movement that was not

---

[8] It was the mistress, she wanted to check on you. She is at work; they are all at work. Do not worry, I will take care of you till they return."

directed by Lori. So, she patiently waited, while Lori warmed a croissant in a funny-looking oven that kept beeping. Lori brought it to her in a white plate, together with a cup of warm milk, another little plate with a piece of butter, a Nutella jar, and a silver spreader.

Lori, noticing that Giselle was paralyzed at the bench, took the spreader, sliced the croissant with it, and placed a little bit of butter and Nutella at a corner.

"Prova! Vedi se ti piace,"[9] she intimated.

Giselle put the flavored corner of the croissant in her mouth, cautiously chewed, and then nodded. She would have wished to say that what she really missed was Grandma's eggs and tomatoes, but instead, she waited while Lori spread the butter and Nutella all over the rest of the croissant.

While Giselle was eating, Lori disappeared. Left alone, she slowly chewed breakfast piece by piece, swallowing tiny sips of milk with each portion, and began to recollect as a wall clock was ticking the pace of her new life.

Her last sitting meal had also been a rushed breakfast the day before. Grandma had woken her up when it was still dark outside because Uncle Borysko was already waiting. She handed the fresh clothes and showed the suitcase that she had prepared during the night while Giselle was sleeping. Then Grandma told her to put on the new dress shoes. When she was dressed, Grandma examined her front and back.

"Very good!" she said. "A real lady to please Uncle Borysko!"

Then she sat the plate with the eggs and tomatoes in front of her, and some stale bread to go with them. She poured some tea, added a vein of milk, and stood admiring her.

"Aren't you eating, Grandma?"

"I am not hungry, and I have a lot of things waiting for me to do as soon as you leave. Better get ready for a busy day! Lots to do without your help!" Grandma said, looking at Uncle Borysko.

"Will you feed the chicken and Oldie for me, Grandma?"

---

[9] Try it, see if you like it!"

"I will, don't worry."

"Will you say hi to them for me?"

"Of course!"

"Will they miss me?"

"I think so, but they will be happy to know that you will be in a better place. Do not worry, you write to me, and I will report to them all that you say."

"And I will get new reading glasses for your grandma!" added Uncle Borysko.

***

After breakfast, Giselle returned to her room to find everything in perfect order; the roller shutter raised, the window open, and a fresh waft lulling the curtains. The bed was made, the suitcase gone, the nightgown folded at the foot of the bed, the books moved on the bedside table. A plush teddy bear resting on the pillow and wearing a green bowtie was waiting for her with wide and lucid eyes. Recollecting the mysterious reorganization of her belongings during the night, she could not explain all those changes, and not being familiar with the concept of being served, she began to wonder whether that home was under a magic spell and spirits, albeit of favorable disposition, governed its course.

But Giselle had not much time to wonder as Lori came in wearing a soft jacket and holding a red umbrella, and told her:

"Andiamo a fare la spesa."[10]

Giselle understood that they were about to leave, and she pointed at the dictionary. Observing no qualms from Lori's end, she walked to the bedside stand, held the dictionary, and showed it to Lori. Lori smiled. Then, as if she was suddenly caught by a revelation dispatched directly from the heavens, she slowly enunciated her words.

"Ma certo, mia cara signorina, c'e' bisogno della borsetta!"[11]

---

[10] Let's go grocery shopping.
[11] Of course, my dear lady! We need the purse!

And walking to the armoire in the hall, she took out a mix backpack-purse of red leather that had been specially acquired by Mrs. Maria for Giselle. Then Lori took the dictionary from Giselle's hand, deposited it into the backpack, and motioned for the girl to lift one arm at the time to be vested with a final touch of Milanese vogue.

***

June had just begun; the air was crisp and warm at the same time. It seemed like a breeze of bipolar temperament pleased itself by frolicking with the passersby. A few clouds were scattered over Piazza della Scala, but posed no threat, and Lori's folded umbrella hung from her left forearm, while the right hand kept a tight grip on Giselle's. Coming from via Manzoni, where they lived, the two ladies crossed the Piazza, walking around the severe statue of Leonardo da Vinci encircled by disciples to reach the Galleria, marched through it, entered Piazza del Duomo, crossed it all the way toward via Torino, and turned right to via Spadari, where Peck stood since 1883, the zenith of high-class Milanese indulgence.

Innumerable scenes had passed through Giselle's eyes along the path as if a dream had taken control of her mind. That sensory overload had shut her reasoning and she passively accepted the kaleidoscope of impressions imposed upon her by innumerable colors and denominations, from exotic tourists who took pictures of everything, to elegant businessmen in dark suits and gaudy ties, from carabinieri with red feather plumes on their bicorn hats to elegant ladies wearing the latest fashion, and mischievous children, and artists sketching portraits in front of jeweler shops and the fashion windows of Prada, the restaurants and bars teeming with solicitous waiters, and the newsstands adorned with colorful flags of the soccer teams and the respective shirts, together with golden statues of La Madonnina, and models of the Duomo, and the pigeons in front of the Duomo scouting charitable souls that would buy corn grains from improvised photographers for their grateful consumption.

By the time they entered Peck, Giselle had been exposed to more newness in the fraction of an hour than in her entire previous life.

At Peck, an endless chain of crystal-clear display counters featured exotic delicacies and emitted overbearing fragrances. Chocolate wonders on one side, collections of wild mushrooms and truffles on the other, coming from

God knows where, whether in season or not. And the meats, arranged to look like blooming flowers, and pastas in all rainbow colors and unthinkable shapes, freshly made or imported dry from the surrounding towns of Modena, Parma, Bologna, and hundreds of cheeses paired to exotic dry fruits to compose still-life worthy of the Poldi Pezzoli.

Lori proceeded resolute to the delicatessens display. From there, Giselle glimpsed the busy kitchen in the back of the store with chefs fussing around flaming stoves that incessantly erupted fresh delights to be ferried to the counters in silver plated serving trays. In those, there were Cornish hens stuffed with aromatic herbs, slices of sear-roasted beef dressed with caramelized onions, compositions of skinned animals, fish, vegetables and bottles, gelatin-covered lobster tails floating on pink mayonnaise, quenelles, seafood salads, Russian salads garnishing pink salmon trout, veal in tuna sauce and capers, sardines in vinaigrette sauce, caponata and parmigiana eggplants, and so much more.

 A server from behind the counter greeted Lori. It was a young man wearing a white uniform, a chef beanie, and a black bowtie:

"Buongiorno, signora. Cosa posso offrirle oggi? Abbiamo dei cappellini farciti con morelle fresche e vengono con una salsa di salvia da aggiungere a fine cottura!"[12] As he was describing the latest options, a lady came to Giselle's side and greeted her:

"Ma che bella bambina! Da dove vieni? Non ti ho mai visto prima."[13]

It was Mrs. Rossi, the store manager, who knew Lori quite well and enjoyed gossiping in the mid-morning when the traffic in the shop was at the nadir.

Giselle looked at the lady, also dressed in a white coat, and tried to smile, but even that effort was unsurmountable . It was Lori who answered:

"Questa è Gisella! La mia nuova padroncina. È appena arrivata a stare con noi e non parla Italiano ancora. Gisella, saluta la signora Rossi. Dille: piacere di conoscerla!"[14]

---

[12] "Good morning, ma'am, what could I offer you today? We have cappellini stuffed with fresh morels. They come with sage sauce to be added before serving."
[13] What a pretty girl! Where are you from? I've never seen you before!
[14] "This is Gisella! My new little master. She just joined us and she does not speak Italian. Gisella, say hi to Mrs. Rossi! Tell her: nice to meet you!"

The confused Giselle instinctually tightened her grip on Lori's hand and approached her flank as if to hide, an innate reaction that surged for the first time in her life, since she never had a mother to hold hands with and Grandma almost never left the hut.

But Mrs. Rossi was not the one to let the conversation languish:

"Ma si capisce benissimo solo a guardarla che è una bambina intelligente e graziosa."[15]

Then posing the right hand as if she was holding a fork, she asked:

"Che cosa vuoi da mangiare?"[16]

Giselle shrugged her shoulders in response.

Lori had a constructive idea and pointed at items sitting behind the glass of the display counter.

"Quale ti piace? Dai, aiutami a scegliere!"[17]

Giselle, who had finally figured what all the turmoil was about, came up with an even better solution: she slipped off her backpack, dug into it, brought out the dictionary, and when she found what she was looking for, showed it to the ladies.

"Mm. . . Uova. . . pomodori,"[18] said Mrs. Rossi. Then perplexed, looked at the server behind the counter. "Ma io non credo che prepariamo questo piatto."

There was a tense moment. Then, as Lori was about to suggest that it did not matter, the servant with the bowtie said:

"Un momento!"[19] and he went to the back kitchen.

When he returned, he announced triumphantly:

"Se questo è quello che madam vuole, questo sarà!"[20]

---

[15] "But everyone can tell, just by looking at her, that she is a smart and gracious little girl!"
[16] "What would you like to eat?"
[17] "Which one do you like? Come on, help me choose!"
[18] "Eggs, ...tomatoes" ... "But I don't believe that we prepare this dish."
[19] "Just a moment!"
[20] "If this is Madam's wish, then so be it!"

And in fact, moments later a sous-chef came from the kitchen, ceremoniously presenting a soufflé of eggs and tomatoes in an improvised pie crust garnished with sage leaves.

And so it was that from that day on, among the hundreds of delicacies, Peck began to serve the famous "Giselle's quiche."

***

That evening at dinner, Giselle ate servings of the quiche that had gained popularity even among the other family members. Not much was said at the table that is worth reporting save for a comment made by Mrs. Maria that changed Giselle's life.

Casually speaking in Russian to involve Giselle, Mrs. Maria told her husband:

"Uncle Borysko mentioned that Giselle wants to be a ballerina. I have a friend who moved from Moscow a few years ago. She was an instructor at the Vaganova Ballet Academy, and she now trains for La Scala Ballet School. She successfully prepared many girls. She has a studio nearby and she said that she would be happy to meet Giselle."

Professor Federico, posing just exactly as his great grandfather portrayed in the painting on the wall behind him, turned toward Giselle, gestured toward her and asked in broken but understandable Russian:

"Let's ask Giselle what she thinks. Do you want to give it a try sometime?"

Giselle's cheeks flushed red as she kept staring at the plate in front of her. Then, she shook her head:

"It is not true; I don't know how to dance. Nobody taught me."

"Well, that is what schools are for! You will never know if you do not try!" said Professor Federico with a provocative smile.

***

Back in her room, Giselle set the teddy bear aside so as not to disturb it. She opened the book to the page with the picture of Giselle and she heard destiny knocking at her door. She remembered Grandma's last words:

"Bye, my dear Giselle! Be happy! I did my part and now it is your turn. And I know: you shall overcome!"

Giselle reckoned that it was not up to her to choose; from the day of her birth, life had chosen for her.

THE DARK SIDE OF THE SUN

Irina Petrova nodded, index finger pushed the bridge of her spectacles upwards to rub the glabella between her corrugated eyebrows and, to confirm the end of the audition, completed the ceremony by rubbing her eyelids with her thumb and middle finger. Then she spoke to Signora Maria and Professor Federico, who had been patiently waiting for the verdict.

"The girl does not have any fundamental knowledge about the fundamentals of ballet. She runs, she jumps, and she has a great sense of rhythm—and great equilibrium! Definitely! But no awareness of positions, no appreciation for the discipline of movements. Obviously, she was never formally trained."

"Well, this is why we brought her here! There is always a beginning for everything!" rebutted constructively Professor Federico with undeterred optimism.

"Soon, she is going to turn seven, that's a late start for a ballerina, whether in Moscow or Milan."

After a calculated pause meant to test the effect of her ruling, and acknowledging the determination in Professor Federico's inquisitive eyes, Madame Petrova, to break the silence, added:

"But if one lowers one's expectations, I don't see why we couldn't try."

Almost apologetically, she then added:

"I just don't want to embarrass her in front of the other girls. . . I guess I could give her private lessons, and she could come to observe the girls practice to learn by mimicry till she feels ready."

Turning to Giselle, she then mumbled:

"I like her, she is driven! She is smart, quick to catch up, and responds immediately to my instructions. . . this is the most important path to success. And she is of an astounding beauty.

"I am sure she can be a fast learner," continued Madame Petrova, dazed by the spell of Giselle's charisma as her own impressions rapidly morphed.

"She speaks Russian already, but she may need to learn French. . . and English nowadays. . . and of course Italian. That's a lot to ask from a little girl. Let me talk to her."

Madame Petrova did not mind reverting to her mother language on occasions. It allowed a fleeting respite to a brain bruised by a mix of French, Italian, English, German, or whatever else would come through the door of the studio. She turned toward Giselle, who was silently looking at her own reflection in the mural mirror. It was a wall-to-wall, ceiling-to-floor reflection through which she could constantly examine the position of the body as it would be seen by an imaginary audience. An urban intrusion into the carefree life of the village; a reminder that there were two Giselles now, as she had discovered in front of the bathroom mirror on her first day in Milan.

With a simple gesture, Madame Petrova summoned Giselle, who walked straight, inadvertently defiant, giving no impression of being intimidated by the unfamiliar circumstance. As Giselle directed her innocent dark eyes toward the teacher, Madame Petrova felt a buzzing sensation down her spine, and in a complete reversal of her previous thoughts, she said in front of the dazed adoptive parents:

"Giselle, you are very smart. If you really want this, and if you work hard, I commit to make you succeed. But before that, tell me: why do you want to become a ballerina?"

"Uncle Borysko told me that I should. . . to make him and Grandma proud. He also told me that I should give beauty to the world. But how can one give beauty?"

Madame Petrova smiled, squatted to match the stature of the little girl, held Giselle's chin up, and said:

"That is an interesting way to put it! But I think I know what your uncle meant."

***

Giselle was a natural. She could be spontaneous and rigid at the same time. She possessed a combination of strength and graciousness. Her neck and arms could flow with elegance around a flawless and disciplined posture, while her ankles and toes carried her weight, and her torso and legs secured her balance. Steps and routines came effortlessly as soon as her brain absorbed them by observing the teacher and the students.

But special was her passion for the rhythm that started in the old village. Music in the studio was different from the cadence that enlivened the fiddler's tapping, not as intuitive perhaps, yet, overpowering. Enchanted by the miraculous power of music, she asked to take music lessons. She cared more about the scripts than the playing. She liked solfeggio. Her right hand would dance over the reposing left, with the discipline of the torso, while the fingers played artistic games following the encouragement of a measured voice.

At the beginning, class was once a week, but that soon changed as Madame Petrova became increasingly demanding. Every other day, when she entered the class, she was greeted with a serious glance by the austere teacher, and with silent acceptance by the established disciples. When she turned eleven, she frequented the studio daily. By then Madame Petrova judged that Giselle's feet were ready for pointe. She was light like a feather, yet her muscles boasted the elegant strength of a cheetah.

She made no friends, but she had no foes. She danced according to ordinance. She listened and executed, challenging herself against the mural mirror. At home, under the sound of music and in front a mural mirror that had appeared in her room, she resumed with strength exercises and stretches, splits, sitting with legs parted and chest on the floor, holding the foot with a leg straight and outstretched.

Gradually she became the best for her age. Later, she was the best of all.

Around that time, she started recitals in preparation for public performance. She also began to partner with other girls first and then with boys from the adjacent studio.

It was also around that time that Madame Petrova approached Giselle, who was gathering her belongings into her purse after class. She sat on the floor close to Giselle and said:

"Giselle, you are perfect. You are a teacher's dream. You are smart and disciplined, from following the diet, to studying the scripts, memorizing the steps, governing your strength; I could go on and on chanting your qualities. . . and I believe that you are ready to perform.

"You are a good ballerina. But there is something that you lack to become a *great* ballerina. There is something, that your heart, not your body, misses.

"What do you feel when you dance? Who is dancing? Is it Giselle or is it another person portraying an unfamiliar character? What kind of beauty do you want to give? The beauty of your figure or a deeper beauty rousing from your heart? The elegance of movements that expresses the mysteries of the soul.

"All these years, I barely saw you smile, I never saw you happy or upset. Your peers admire you, but they don't get close to you. Even the boys, they like you, but they do not dare to partner with you because they are intimidated.

"You had a very difficult childhood without a mom or a dad. Then, you were taken away from home. Perhaps, to cope with the uncertainty of life, you imprisoned yourself in a jail of discipline; perhaps to please those who cared for you so they would not abandon you again and again. And I admire you for this resolve.

"But now, it is time to be a little selfish. You want to make your grandma proud, and your Uncle Borysko, and Mrs. Maria and Professor Federico, to show them gratitude for raising an orphan. But none of them did what they did without expecting something in return. They do not expect sacrifices from you. I am sure that all of them want, out of anything, for you to be happy.

"Do you miss your Grandma? Do you miss the village?"

At first, Giselle did not reply simply because she did not know what to say, but as Madame Petrova was about to walk away, she murmured:

"It is difficult to feel when one is overwhelmed by emotions."

To which Madame Petrova replied:

"This may apply to words, but dance can liberate your emotions one by one from your heart. . . and that is when you will become the principal ballerina."

***

A few years earlier, about a year after her arrival in Milan, on a dark and rainy morning, Giselle woke up under a gloominescent light. It was Sunday, and her routine demanded a walk with Professor Federico. By then, the little girl had become attached to the kind and cheerful man, while Mrs. Maria had relinquished all maternal duties onto Lori. Mrs. Maria was not a bad person. She was earnestly devoted to the upbringing of Giselle. She had given into her husband's desire for adoption since she could bear no child, and she honored the commitment without the presumptuous expectation of a maternal relationship. However, empathy did not come naturally, and her relationship with Giselle was limited to the assurance that Giselle would have all that she needed for a comfortable life. On the contrary, Professor Federico adored Giselle and holding her hand on Sunday morning along the busy sidewalks, snaking between tourists and churchgoers, was pretty much the only purpose in an otherwise meaningless life.

A chilly autumn sun timidly touched Giselle's cheek as they walked out of the house in via Manzoni and headed for Piazza San Babila. By then, she had learned to tolerate the privileged life, in which she had been engrafted. Although life was not as carefree as the simple routines of the village, her multiple activities kept her busy and provided satisfaction at the end of the day. She was learning Italian by listening to Lori and her friends, or listening to the television, or catching conversations in public transportation, or by interacting with strangers or peers at school. And she managed to balance her tongue over the precarious path of wild Italian diphthongs, double diphthongs, triphthongs, with the grace and agility of a ballerina on stage.

Since she was sent to an American school, she learned English, while the ballet school were the venue for private French lessons.

She still thought with nostalgia of Grandma's eggs and tomatoes. But she had learned to appreciate the fancy Milanese cuisine, and the proper manners demanded by such privilege. Lori had been her teacher and advocate. She never had to apologize for any inappropriateness because Lori took on the blame for the maleducation and defended the little girl as a tiger would do for her cubs.

Thus, what made Giselle's life tolerable were the relationships with Lori, who became her surrogate mother, and with Professor Federico, who had become her unspoken, *de facto* father.

Professor Federico was the nicest of men and he treated Giselle with respect and affection. He tried very hard to act stern and serious like a good dad should be, but in the end, their relationship thrived in flirtatious jokes, benevolent treats, and the unspoken understanding that whatever Giselle wished would concretize within the blink of an eye. This, in turn, did not spoil Giselle, who, despite the privileged life, maintained a simple ethic as a remnant of the nurturing and candid teachings of her frugal youth.

Professor Federico, however, was not perfect and in fact, he carried a momentous problem. He was an incoercible liar. Unbeknown to him, life had been an immense lie, a desolate world of emptiness hidden behind jaunty optimism; a façade that covered his other dark side. Yet, his radiant smile served his daily routine well, and made life, if not rewarding, at least tolerable.

The Professor was earnest in matters that affected others. He would not deceive for personal gain and his actions were as pure as spring water. He just could not be truthful to his own emotions. When honesty could lead to confrontation with parents, relatives, friends, and most importantly, his wife, he swerved toward broader topics. That worked well for his career, where he was respected for his constructive nonbelligerent demeanor. And it worked well with relatives and friends, who felt comfortable with someone who preferred not to challenge them. And it worked well with his wife.

Professor Federico and Signora Maria married when they were both too young and inexperienced. He was thrilled by her exotic background and professional ambitions. But he soon recognized that he had married a dream. After a few disagreements, being rebuffed by condescendence and dismissal, he gave up arguing with a strong woman uninterested in others' opinions and feelings; a woman who couldn't interpret silence; a mind sternly certain that preferences were founded on granitic logic rather than subjective inclinations and, therefore, were not negotiable or amenable to challenge. As we said, this worked well save for the collateral damage of turning Professor Federico into a lone wolf that roamed as an invisible ghost through the noisy avenues of the upper-class Milanese society.

Gradually he realized that choosing to put others' preferences over his own aspirations was a path to unhappiness. But, instead of amending the cause, he tuned the effect by training his mouth to smile in front of the mirror as a testament to fulfillment. He reassured himself that rather than spending Christmas with the aging parents, as a decent son would do, it was more reasonable to enjoy a vacation in a fancy resort in the Seychelles; that going to his sister's commemorations was not as crucial as taking his wife to the theater; going to the stadium to watch a football game was not as productive as spending the afternoon with his wife's friends drinking tea and discussing the value of minimalistic painting. When his wife started a strict diet, furtively checking the fit of the adherent cocktail dresses in the mirror, when calls came frequently late in the evening, to which she answered with monosyllabic whispers before hanging up and stating "They are driving me crazy at work nowadays," when she came late and did not bother apologizing to the little girl who stubbornly waited for supper, Professor Federico considered how lucky he was to have such a wonderful girl as an addition to the family, and without questioning, he wished everyone a good appetite.

When occasionally at night his conscience woke him like a buzzing mosquito, he shrugged his shoulders and scolded himself for indulging on afterthoughts of commiseration rather than gratitude for a fortunate existence.

With Giselle, however, Professor Federico felt differently, and while his manners reflected the deceitful temperament when dealing with the rest of the world, his mood quickly turned into a genuine and radiant demeanor, encouraged by Giselle's dark eyes that never blinked when looking straight into his. And he developed a paternal attitude. Without imposing himself as a father, he took it upon himself to learn the art of parenthood, following a trial-and-error tactic responsive to Lori's benevolent criticisms.

***

As we said, such deception had worked perfectly for decades against the big world out there and, therefore, it came as a cold shower when, as they were walking along that memorable morning toward via Santa Redegonda to fetch Giselle's favorite panzerotti at Luini's, he heard a little voice questioning:

"Why are you always sad?"

To confirm the source of the voice, he looked down to catch Giselle's big black eyes staring at him unflinchingly, her corrugated eyebrows firmly demanding an answer.

"I am not sad! I am the happiest person in all of Milan! What makes you think that I am sad?"

"Because you smile only with your mouth but not with your eyes."

"I didn't know that one ought to smile with the eyes too! The mouth is good enough! I am just trying to save energy, I guess," Replied the Professor, looking away.

"See, you do not even look at me when I ask you whether you are happy or not. You do that with everyone when you are not happy, you do not look into people eyes!"

Professor Federico was not prepared for such an inquisition and did not know what to say.

For a few moments he blabbered to himself: "I know," which meant: "I know that I don't know." But then, he wondered: "What is it that I don't know that even a simple girl knows? And how do I know what I don't know?" And he thought of the reflective mirror that had haunted him for decades wherever he went, because it told him that there were hundreds of him, or thousands, who vaguely knew that they didn't know. Thousands of him, who did not question life, perhaps they did not dare to know; did not dare to question what happiness was.

The little girl was still piercing his brain with her determined eyes, and he realized that he had to give her an answer. And, as all grownups do in such circumstances to alleviate the concerns of a growing mind, he shook his head and placatingly stated:

"You are too young to understand. One day I will explain it to you, but now, let's go to Luini to fetch our panzerotti!"

We cannot gauge to what measure that answer satisfied Giselle, but something extraordinary happened at that moment. Giselle learned that appearances are not necessarily mirrored by reality and even Professor Federico's life, while wonderful on the surface, carried a dark side. She learned that happiness comes from the depth of one's feelings. Happiness was not linked to a luxurious home, professional success, and social status.

"Perhaps," she thought, "I have not seen the face of happiness since I left Grandma with her grunts, or uncle Borysko's arched eyebrows while checking my homework, or the fiddler's lively tapping while examining my steps. Perhaps, this is what uncle Borysko meant when he said that I should give beauty to the world. It is the beauty of kindness that he was talking about." Suddenly, Giselle felt rich, more than anyone around her. She felt that her chest was too tiny to let in the fresh new air, the breezes of gratitude, the desire to reciprocate, the joy of giving. And she squeezed Professor Federico's hand tightly.

From that day on, Giselle nurtured a maternal attitude toward the Professor. In a role reversal, she began to defend his silence against those who did not know how to listen; in particular, she resisted the insensitive choices of Mrs. Maria and gradually, gained an influential role in the family mediating difficult conversations with her calm yet determined demeanor.

Surprisingly, Mrs. Maria welcomed Giselle's confidence. Being a person of little feelings, Mrs. Maria governed her dealings according to logic rather than empathy. So, she much preferred the constructive exchanges with Giselle over the inscrutable silence of a weak husband. Soon, those discussions between the two ladies of the house rose to a cherished routine that kept both busy and even amused. And so, through logical reasoning, Giselle opened a door into Mrs. Maria's heart, who clung to her to translate her husband's clandestine feelings into words. Gradually, theater and friends became less essential for Mrs. Maria compared to Federico's parents and siblings.

Among the various changes dictated by the new Giselle was the preference to introduce into family conversations Italian or English rather than

Russian, a change that of course helped the debating skills of Professor Federico.

So, it was many years later that Giselle, who just turned fifteen, stated in Italian during dinner:

"I do not want to become a professional ballerina. I want to become a doctor. I want to be a surgeon like my dad."

By then, Giselle had decided to call Professor Federico and Mrs. Maria Dad and Mom respectively.

Mrs. Maria looked up at Professor Federico, who reciprocated with a defensive smile and questioning eyebrows.

At fifteen Giselle was performing regularly in the corps de ballet and was given soloist roles. Madame Petrova had already started to treat her as the next principal ballerina and already pulled her connections to identify small cities around Milan for Giselle to perform in. Cities like Parma that were small but breathed the sound of music. Cities where stars were born.

Therefore, Giselle's comment poured on the two parents like rain on a sunny day.

"But Madame thinks that you have a great future ahead, that you are made to become a great ballerina. What made you change your mind?" said Mrs. Maria.

"I never wanted to be a ballerina. It was decided for me by others since I was born, and I did my best, but I never really wanted to become one. I think it is too risky. Others chose a safer path, none in my school wants to be anything like a ballerina. All doctors, engineers, teachers. I like what dad is doing. I think I can do it. I like going to the University with him. I like it and it is useful."

Who could argue with this logic? And truthfully, that was what both had been thinking since the day Giselle entered their life. Ballerina was a good dream; it offered a purpose and a way to integrate into her new life. Giselle was right; now that she was perfectly adapted to the Milanese life, more substantive propositions should be considered. Besides, both parents felt strongly that Giselle had the right to choose her own future. Thus, Mrs. Maria said:

"Giselle, this is your choice, but what do you want to do now? Do you really want to quit ballet? Do you think that you cannot continue anymore? Is it too time consuming? Why are you bringing this up now?"

"Just wanted to give a heads up. I can continue for now, school is good, and I manage my homework. But after high school, I will go to medical school."

Then with a supportive smile, Professor Federico veered the conversation to other topics.

***

But Giselle had addressed the wrong audience. She did not consider destiny, whose attitude is far less malleable than the bidding of adoring parents, and other events out of her control were about to happen that would turn her into a most famous performer.

THERE IS NO SUCH THING
AS EVERLASTING LOVE

Hesitant, Paul scanned the surroundings. The tables were taken by a mob of youngsters, a noisy crowd of students enjoying a break in the cafeteria at the Accademia del Teatro alla Scala. He had managed to carve a tad of free time out of an intense schedule imposed upon him by the schoolmaster of the music department. The latter was eager to introduce the renowned composer to the disciples, in a succession of enthusiastic but chaotic interactions with aspiring musicians, conductors, and composers. It was Paul's first time in Milan, part of a tour organized just for him by the Italian Ministry of Public Education. The visit resulted from an abrupt acceptance of a long-standing invitation in a quest to distract himself from current predicaments.

Back home in New York, Paul was worn by the suffocating routine to which celebrities are subjected. Not a place to walk or dine without interruptions by zealous admirers, most often mischievous and aggressive women descending on the charismatic musician like flies on a cake.

His music spanned a wide range of genres centered around rhythm. As a youngster, while receiving a classical music education, he enjoyed listening to rock music, and watched with envy as iconic drummers and soloists led crowds in the largest arenas. He relished the interactions between musicians and the crowd, something absent in the sterile environment of classical performances, where a sneeze or a coughing spell resonates like thunder in the auditorium, like a memento of human vulgarity.

Soon, although his career developed from classical compositions, it deviated into a mix of eclecticism and rock, a sound that is better heard than described. Because of this, Paul's music was choreographed into ballets. A mix of African, Western, and Asian themes creating a modern version of Shen Yun that conquered theaters across the world.

But the professional success clashed with his personal life. As a withdrawn character, Paul did not enjoy his celebrity save for the satisfaction of seeing his work performed. Everything else was a burden. Soirees, dinners, tours in which he had to trumpet a jovial demeanor were not part of his nature and he subjugated to them only in deference to Jerry, his agent, who wanted him in the front line because of his good looks and charisma.

Privacy was extinguished from the life of a solitary man who had chosen music as a liberation from societal conventions that prescribe words to package emotions like sardines into a tin can. Paul reserved contempt for words and favored the universal language of music that is understandable by all souls independent of race, culture, and geography. But social interactions required a dialectic discipline that he abhorred, much preferring the silence of his apartment to the mundane New York life.

Thus, Paul's personal life had been a complete blunder. And this extended to matters of women. Part of it was due to paranoia inherited from a young age when, at the dawn of success, he was raped by a few admirers. Sex had turned into a social responsibility. When a groupie lured him in a hotel room after a few drinks, he docilely succumbed to kisses, caresses, and moans, and performed as he felt obliged. Yet, in those intimate moments of passion, his mind strayed into another world, where a distant echo evoked a fragrant and cheerful voice. It was a melody reminiscent of the thrilling calls of his young mother, who from the balcony summoned him for dinner from the courtyard where he was playing with friends, or the shrill of a girl calling his name from the stairs of the elementary school, and her giggles when he turned around to look at her. It was a call from ancient memories that had evaporated with the innocence of youth.

The morning after those empty nights, when he searched for himself in the mirror, he felt a longing for something vague. It was a void that occupied large spaces, an overbearing emptiness that weighed more than the mass of a star, an invincible horizon whose unforgiving claws dragged his soul down into a massive black hole.

This paranoia was amplified by the agent, who worried that women tempted him to exploit his fortune. They might turn the table around to accuse him of actions they initiated. Most of it was probably not true, but it contributed to his quest to distance himself and find refuge in solitude.

A psychiatrist, after giving up trying to understand the intricacies of Paul's obsessions, offered a simple solution. He prescribed anti-depressants that made life more bearable but dampened those same emotions that inspired his work. So, the remedy did not last for more than a few weeks.

There had been better moments. In the recent past, he cherished a relationship with a beautiful woman who lived in the West Coast. For whatever reason, that woman had touched his soul with her gregarious demeanor and for the first time, he felt the thrill that others call love. But he hesitated to use that word.

"How would I know whether I am in love?" he asked himself.

Indeed, the subject was not included in the conservatory curriculum.

It was a long-distance affair that needed nurturing, but he did not seek her company as much as he should have. It became a unidirectional effort, with too many red eye flights toward the East that were seldom reciprocated. Thus, the relationship stalled, suffered, and dried.

In the end, frustrated and hurt, the beautiful woman said on the phone:

"Come see me this weekend, otherwise I will move on!"

Misinterpreting her words as an ultimatum, he thought:

"Me or someone else. She is asking for permission to go on another date."

So, he did not go.

"Love should not be subjected to ultimatums."

Next time rumors reached him; it was said that she was dating someone else. He wished her all the best. But a bitter taste spoiled his nights. To cope with the rejection and shift the weight of responsibility onto the poor woman, Paul's subconscious used the incident to reinforce the conviction that there is no such thing as true love.

Therefore, just a few days before his visit to Italy, he confided to his beloved cousin Laura:

"There is no such thing as everlasting love. Love is a conditional proposition. It works till it works. Till one abides by expectations." And he shared with Laura the story of the beautiful woman, who had moved on.

"Love is bartering of goods, a trade where one worries more about receiving than giving."

They were having a drink in the balcony of Laura's apartment overlooking the Northern side of Central Park. The younger cousin, a descendent of an ancient aristocratic dynasty, was his only shelter from the New York crowds and there he retreated when he could bear solitude no more. Thus, like many times before, the doorbell would ring, and Paul would appear unannounced.

With maternal devotion, Laura admired her handsome cousin, who was staring at the indifferent clouds that hung over Central Park. Then she interrupted the silence:

"You are like an onion, Paul. So many layers cover your heart. No one, not even you, knows what is at its core. *There is no such thing as everlasting love.*' What about me? I loved you and will love you forever. Nothing could change my devotion to you, and you very well know that. But love, like happiness, is reciprocal, you need to give to appreciate receiving. It is not a venal barter; it is the beauty of giving that makes one value the returns. You take love for granted and do not fight to conquer it, which ironically makes me feel good. I am spoiling you, and I love it. I cherish being just the Talking Cricket on the wall of your life.

"But you are a spoiled child, who cannot appreciate a gift. *'Love is bartering of goods, an exchange when one worries more about receiving than giving?'* Look who is talking! This is exactly what you do. Do you ever consider giving? Why would you expect unconditional devotion when you do nothing to encourage it? Are you afraid of exposure? Do you feel more comfortable commiserating than risking rejection?"

Then, to alleviate Paul's surging anxiety, she continued in a jovial mood:

"Real men don't cry even when they chop onions!"

"You are the product of an awkward mix of machoism and diffidence. You suffer in isolation, but you would not admit it. And only the one who could break the shell will expose the hermit crab! But in the meanwhile, you cannot recognize love even if it is sitting like an elephant in front of your nose, and this is your curse. You will never find love on your own. If you are lucky, one day, love will find you."

***

And this explains why Paul jumped into this tour of Italy, to breathe fresh air and forget New York and all qualms about his chaotic and meaningless life.

But fame follows wherever one goes and even now, in the cafeteria, as he was scanning for an open seat, where to chew the apple and drink a San Pellegrino, he sensed that a myriad of eyes were following him.

Finally, he rubbernecked an empty space at a corner table and, upon approaching, asked a young woman, who occupied one side of the table and was focused on a tomato salad, whether the seat was free. As the woman turned around to confirm with a cordial smile, he held his breath. She wasn't just beautiful. She was the faultless depiction of beauty. Most striking were her black eyes that could swallow a man's emotion in a snap. They were so black that one could not sort the pupil from the iris, and they blended into dark fawn's eyelashes, which gently flapped with naivete and wonder like those of a little girl who stares with trust into her father's eyes.

Recovering from the trance, Paul said:

"Grazie."

Then, the woman returned to her salad and flipped open a book, in total absorption.

He had barely settled when a pair of women came to ask for an autograph. As usual, he tried to decline stating that he had no paper or pen. But of course, they had the ammunitions ready, and, in a few seconds, he was surrounded by enthusiastic fans, while the woman at his side continued to chew one piece of tomato at a time. At last, the locusts left, and he could focus on the apple. But the corners of his eyes could not refrain from turning to the pretty lady. She was indeed a woman of perfect beauty, the simple and natural beauty that appealed to him. She wore no make-up, her clothing was elegant but unpretentious, her demeanor was humble, her silence enchanting.

So, before he knew it, he asked in English:

"What is your name?"

Without smiling, the woman turned and said:

"Giselle!"

"Nice to meet you, Giselle. My name is Paul."

"I know!" replied Giselle.

Then the conversation stalled, until in a spark of geniality, Paul's mind found an opportunity to further the conversation:

"What do you do, Giselle?"

"I study."

"Study what?"

"I am going to classical high school."

Surprised, Paul asked:

"But how old are you?"

"Fifteen."

"You look much older," and realizing the ambiguity of the statement, he added: "I meant it as a compliment!"

"Thank you," replied Giselle.

Contrary to his natural disposition, Paul at this junction felt at ease with words and persisted in the inquisition.

"So, Giselle, what do you want to do when you grow up?"

That question froze Giselle. She did not know what to answer. It was only a few days before that she announced to her parents that she wanted to attend medical school. But that was not what came out of her mouth:

"I want to become a principal ballerina."

"This is wonderful!" replied Paul with condescendence, while thinking: "What's the chance of that happening?"

"I've been studying dance and music since I was seven, and I perform as a soloist for our company. But I also think that this may be a risky choice. Perhaps, I should go to medical school and become a surgeon like my dad."

Here, Paul recognized that, far from the casual intentions that originated the conversation, he had been caught deep in a serious exchange. He also recognized that Giselle's dream was not as far-fetched as he first assumed and she probably bore the credentials to pursue her dream. Moreover, her quandary resonated in his heart. Didn't he experience the same dilemma when, as a kid, he had to choose the uncharted over the safe path? Music versus common-sense degrees? So without further hesitation he said:

"Do what you want to do, not what is safe! Follow your heart and not your mind. I did the same long ago."

Upon reflection, Paul then constructed a sentence more complicated than any he had ever elaborated:

"You see, we live two lives. There is an inner life that belongs to us and only a few can share. Then, there is the outer life, one that carries us along, provides food, distracts us from the gravity of existence and keeps us going. We allocate brief moments during the solitude of the night or other fleeting alcoves of introspection to the former, while the latter gets most of our attention. And we abide by the safe choices that the outer proposes while we forget the inner one."

"So, what made you decide to become a musician?" asked Giselle, who obviously knew whom she was talking with.

"Because music was there! Inside of me! Like the summit of Everest was inside George Mallory, and he couldn't resist the compulsion to climb it! No reason to rationalize why we do what we do. If we followed logical thinking, we would do nothing. We would sit on the fence, from dawn to sunset, waiting for time to pass and for death to relieve us of the burden of life. In the end, I had no choice. Whenever I listened to my inner self, becoming a musician was the only option."

Then, after a few moments of reflection, he added:

"Therefore, if being a ballerina is what your heart tells you to do, just do it! I am sure you will become a great one."

Giselle looked at the illustrious stranger that chance had placed in front of her. Looking into his eyes, she recognized Uncle Borysko, the fiddler, and Professor Federico, all combined in a younger and attractive figure, and she heard herself saying:

"Yes, I should do as you say. . . I will work hard so one day I shall be as great as you are!"

To which Paul, smiling, replied:

"No, Giselle, my dear new friend. You do not want to be like me or anyone else, you want to be better than me, you shall be the best of all. Do not put limits to your imagination."

And because the apple was wiped to the core and the bottle of San Pellegrino empty, Paul rose, tapped Giselle on the shoulder and said:

"Good luck to you, Giselle! Remember, never give up!" and he left.

***

That night Giselle could not sleep. She sat up in the darkness, looked straight into the future, and told herself:

"I will become a principal ballerina; I will see him again and I will marry him."

Yes, that was our naïve and stubborn Giselle!

***

In the hotel room, just a few blocks from Giselle, Paul had forgotten about her and was finally resting after worrying over an overdue script, when Giselle's eyes came to visit.

"What a beautiful young girl, that Giselle! Maybe I will see her again. I wish her all the luck! A ballerina? Why not? I can see her up on stage!"

In the middle of the night, Giselle pierced into Paul's dreams. She was dancing and moving in a way he had never seen before, something adapted from his scripts, and she kept smiling at him while she performed as if she could see him from the stage.

In the morning when he woke up, recollecting the dream, Paul told himself:

"She must have put a spell on me!" and with a smile shrugged his shoulders, prepared his belongings, and walked down to the car that would take him to the next stage of the tour.

***

Time flows and corrodes emotions; soon the fresh gardenia will wither. Few things are everlasting, if any. Paul's tour was packed, the schoolmasters eager, the fans demanding, and Giselle and her spell vanished.

BACK WHERE WE BELONG

In the modern era, all problems seem solved. It is unnecessary to go to stores to shop, no need for bookstores, car dealers, or restaurants; everything is delivered. Virtual visits to the family doctor are good enough, who needs a photographer when selfies can be taken with semi-professional lenses by a phone controlled by a paired watch? Hitches? Solutions are waiting in the magic of cyberworld. And why stress over choices: which songs, movies, shows? Virtual assistance technology preempts wishes better than the percipient's own desires. Cars and flying objects govern themselves; robots clean homes and take dogs for walks! Motion-activated cameras catch racoons daring to grab a snack from the garbage bin, and they sit alert everywhere to assure that not even a banana is stolen at the supermarket! Smart phones and their Apps take care of everything else, gratifying dopamine addition while keeping innovation in complete harmony with the expectations of consumerism. Marketing and advertisements keep the rest in motion, rain or shine. Perhaps, the only emerging concern may turn out to be the extinction of problems. What will the next opportunity be for tech valley? Even this is no problem! Artificial intelligence will create now unforeseen problems and necessities to allow the industry to thrive.

Thus, all seems solved. . . except of course for real problems like climate change, capricious wars, poverty and hunger, homelessness, lost children, preventable and chronic diseases. Misinformation, callousness, cynicism, depression rule lives, hidden behind the shine of prepackaged routines. All of these are here to stay. But who cares? All rests in the cozy slumber of mundane indifference.

Giselle, from her privileged life, had not forgotten her old village and the poverty from where she came, that frugality full of life and passion, where even an egg could make a difference. The modern world and its perks bore a negligible impact on her stubborn mind that frequently returned to lost characters and moments. The past was more concrete than the present and stood the ground against frivolous distractions. She missed Grandma and Uncle Borysko. Each evening before sleeping, she vowed to give purpose to their sacrifice by making them proud.

Giselle wanted to return beauty to the world where she belonged, share the grandeur of opportunities unknown to the lethargic village, and inspire hope and confidence in horizons broader than their imagination. Her decision to go to medical school was stirred in fact by the motivation to share with that forgotten world the luck bestowed upon her by destiny, to return home to treat children with cancer, inspire little girls to believe in their dreams. She felt that Uncle Borysko would support trading a gracious ballerina for a more useable physician.

Each summer, she returned to the village accompanied at first by Professor Federico or Lori, since Signora Maria was too busy, though she joined them eventually. In time, Signora Maria had changed, she mellowed, her heart learned to listen, and her face gained new expressions. One parent would take Giselle to the village and the other would take her back home. Attempts were made to upgrade her lodging, but it was unnecessary. Giselle was happiest when she could lay on the wooden bed close to Grandma, eat eggs and tomato soup, feed the dwindling chicken population, and wait for the crickets to liven the silence of the night. In time, Oldie joined Daria and only a few hens remained. Everything else, however, stayed unchanged, patiently waiting for her return. Italy had been wonderful, her adoptive parents grand, but the village was the place where she belonged.

So, once she asked Grandma:

"When I move back to stay with you, can we get another Oldie and another Daria?"

Grandma smiled and jokingly said:

"Yes, of course! And maybe another Grandma!"

***

After Giselle moved to Milan, Uncle Borysko often joined Ivanna for dinner with the ambitious intent of turning the grumpy lady cheerful. He would bring a bag of beans for soup and a bottle of vodka. Refusing help and holding onto her walking stick, Ivanna would wobble out of the hut into the garden to collect a few leaves of lettuce. And while she shunned him away with her free hand, Uncle Borysko waited at the doorstep, shaking his head and thinking:

"What an obstinate lady! More stubborn than a mule! I know of only one who can be even more stubborn." And that thought carried him to Giselle, that determined little girl, whom he loved so much.

Then, Ivanna would pour the gifts and the harvested goods in the boiling pot, while Uncle served a generous portion of vodka and sipped with patience. Before setting the table, and while the soup was bubbling, Ivanna would fetch a pile of envelopes from the drawer that used to be Giselle's first cradle and set it in front of Uncle.

"Read while I cook. Time will go faster," she would say, squeezing his shoulder.

They were Giselle's letters chosen at random and rehashed anew each time.

In the beginning, Giselle's style was dry, her sentences were short. Luxury, success, privilege, were dealt as given constituents of a remote existence, where things were no better or worse, just different.

It was telegraphic journalism meant to offer Grandma a sense of involvement. She would write:

Dear Grandma,

Milano is very big, much bigger than the village. So many people here, who do not know each other. They walk around and they do not say "good morning" or "good evening." There is no chicken here but only pigeons. People feed them even though they do not lay eggs. There are no horses or mules but trams. I really like to ride them with Lori. And they do not have eggs and tomato soup, but they made a special pie for me. I like it, though it is not as good as your soup. Children here use shoes even when the weather is good. I must wear them too. Girls are prettier here, and boys nicer; they don't laugh at me because I am a girl. At school they wear uniforms. I have one too with my name embroidered. Each evening I take a bath before going to bed. Lori scrubs me as if I can't do it myself and then she dries me with a big towel and puts on a robe with my name embroidered! She does not speak our language or even Russian, but I understand her easily. She is very nice, and I hope that one day you will meet her. Maybe, she could also give you a bath. She also makes my room while I eat breakfast. At first, I thought the house was haunted but one morning I followed her, and I saw what she was doing. Professor Federico is also very nice and takes me out for walks and treats during the weekend. I really like panzerotti—they consist of fried dough with melted cheese and tomato sauce inside; really, really good! We do not have them at the village. I wish I could send some for you to try. Signora Maria is also very kind but is seldom home. She works very hard.

I forgot to tell you; eating is very complicated here. One cannot use hands to grab food. The napkins, knives, and spoons should be kept on the right side of the plate, forks on the left. Plates have golden rims, and I should be very, very careful not to drop them. Before eating, the napkin must be unfolded and should sit on my tummy the whole time. Each person has many glasses—one for water, one for white wine and one for red, and a cup for coffee or tea. But they do not have vodka in Milano. It is very important not to make chewing noises and one must eat with mouths closed. Also, elbows should not be on the table. This is very important in Italy."

And on and on she went with a compilation of details trivial for anyone except the recipients of the letter, who drank each word with the avidity of desert thirst.

Then, she would conclude:

I miss you, Grandma, very much. Say hi to Oldie, and the Chicken. Say hi to Uncle Borysko. Tell him that I use the dictionary often. Tell him that Madame Petrova thinks I could become a ballerina.

Love, Giselle

P.S. Madame Petrova is the dance teacher.

When the daylight dimmed, and the soup was on the table, Ivanna would light the candle and with her caved hand, she would encourage Uncle to read more, as if she were scooping words out of his mouth.

As time passed, letters adopted a more substantive tone. Giselle reported academic achievements with modesty, with the intent to reward Grandma's sacrifice. She conveyed agreeable news about her adoptive parents and Lori, and the world where she lived, her teachers and peers. The positive coverage was earnest yet motivated by the concern of assuring Grandma that everything was fine. At the end, she always mentioned Uncle Borysko and reserved details for him about her progress as ballerina.

"Madame Petrova said I could be a principal ballerina one day, she said that I am the best student she's ever had. Thank you, Uncle Borysko, for encouraging me."

***

When Giselle was back at the village, things took a different tone. No need to read letters, of course. The news was fresh and alive, crammed with energy and wonder. Incredible stories about elegant ladies with parasols and white gloves that made no sense to peasants were absorbed without qualms by the admiring audience. Once, Professor Federico brought a battery-operated music player. Turning the music on, Giselle danced in front of the cheering admirers. On weekends, she went to the village square and, if the fiddler with the band was expected, in remembrance of the old days, she would get up early in the morning to fetch flowers for the makeshift stage. She would then dance together with the peasants, encouraging boys and girls and people of all ages. Among the boys, Demetri was always there, waiting for his turn to dance with Giselle. He had turned into a quite handsome young man, manly and courteous. Giselle would smile at him, remembering the day when she rested her head upon his shoulder.

Uncle Borysko convinced Ivanna to come to the square, where everyone clapped to sustain the rhythm above which Giselle's figure soared. Then with the thumb, he would stretch out one of his suspenders, released it to let it smack against his chest, and he would proudly tell the closest listener:

"I always knew it! I knew that Giselle was made for another world. She is not just the best at school, but she could also be a real ballerina."

CATHARSIS

But love is an arrogant proposition, a capricious and omnipotent god. What made sense before, doesn't anymore, and what didn't, now does. Fantasy turns into reality; gratification comes from dreams that hoard infinity mirrors and cloud the mind. What made Paul's sophisticated mind hesitate for a lifetime, was clear to the young Giselle: love is an incoercible desire to see someone again, an impulse to unravel the mystery of happiness by unearthing treasures buried in the promised land. In the impulsive infatuation of a fifteen-year-old, Giselle nurtured the yearning to close a conversation prematurely interrupted and the pride to fulfil the promise of becoming a great ballerina. All the positive influences that inspired her youth converged into the image of Paul, who, with his charisma, elevated her dreams to ultimate altitudes.

Thus, at age fifteen, the village took a backseat, so did medical school. A poster of Paul substituted the painting of the elegant ladies in her room and the piano resounded with Paul's music. Since Giselle was not a skilled instrumentalist, she repeated the pieces over and over till, upon satisfaction, she recorded her own performance, and choreographed a dance in front of the mirror, imagining that Paul was there watching. In her mind, her interpretation of Paul's music, though imperfect, was more melodious than its commercial versions, and more suitable for ballet.

***

A few months later, Giselle was walking along Corso Vittorio Emanuele when she heard Paul's music played from the distance. As she approached, she saw a young drummer, rolling and juggling the drumsticks in between beats, his rhythm complementing the melodies and harmonies coming from a soundbox. She stood entranced at the margins of the crowd. Then a foot began to tap, and then both did. Then her body moved, and twisted, and rocked, and jumped, and flowed from pirouette to pirouette as if she was still the little girl in front of the fiddler and his band at the village. She forgot about classical moves and positions and danced with spontaneity. But the body, the legs, the arms, the torso, and the neck did not forget the hard-learned discipline, and the improvised pantomime revealed the talent of a master. The people around started to pay more attention to Giselle than the drummer, who kept playing harder and faster while smiling at Giselle. When the piece was done, Giselle was surrounded by an admiring crowd. Coins poured into the drummer's hat together with compliments to both, as passersby assumed they were a couple.

Then the drummer asked in English:

"Do you like this music? Isn't it a perfect blend of everything; classical, pop, rock, African, Asian, Western? And the rhythm makes it alive. I love Paul Vincente's work. He might be crazy, but the music is magnificent."

Giselle stood in silence. She looked at the handsome young American drummer, blond and blue-eyed. He was so different from Paul, yet she felt close to him.

"Yes," she answered. "I like his music and I love him! Do you know him?"

"Of course, I know him! Who does not know Paul Vincente?"

"I mean, do you know him personally?"

"Of course, I don't! If I knew him, I would not be playing for a few coins in a foreign country! This is a poor man's tour! I am no Credence Clearwater Revival and definitely not a band recognized by Master Vicente!"

"But you are good! You are very, very good! I really like your interpretation of his music. I play it myself at the piano, but I am not that good! I want to buy your recordings."

"Anyhow, nobody knows him as a human being. Probably, not even Paul knows himself. People say that he is a lunatic. Rumors are that he is depressed and on drugs all the time. He is rarely seen in public. They say he moved to California and lives in seclusion in the redwood forest like a mountain lion."

That last comment resonated with the power of thunder in Giselle's heart. Now, it was not she who needed Paul. Paul needed her! As with Professor Federico before, Paul's dark side stirred her maternal instinct. She was now bestowed the mandate of finding and saving her hero. She knew with certainty that the nice man she met and who looked straight in her eyes with paternal affection could not be a lunatic or a junkie. Paul just needed someone; someone who could show him true love.

=Giselle, Giselle, how could you be so naïve and correct at the same time? What did you know about life then? What intuition kept alive the shadow of an occasional encounter? What instinct determined a future that was not meant to be otherwise?

***

A few evenings later, Giselle announced at dinner:

"I changed my mind. I will become a prima ballerina."

Reacting to such assertion, Professor Federico and Signora Maria looked at each other. Then Professor Federico felt that the minestrone was in substantial need of salt. He reached across the table with his stretched arm for the salt cellar and poured the precious mineral into the palm of his other hand. Then, he sprinkled the ingredient over the soup, mixed the concoction, tasted it, and decided that more was required. After several repetitions, satisfied with the outcome, he looked at Signora Maria and asked:

"Do you need salt, Maria? The minestrone tastes insipid this evening."

Signora Maria nodded, extended her hand, and mimicked Professor Federico's ceremony.

"Would you like some salt, Giselle?" she then asked.

But Giselle was content eating her soup without qualms.

Having bought sufficient time to reflect upon the current predicament, Signora Maria addressed Giselle.

"And what made you change your mind, Giselle?"

Giselle continued to chew with composure as if the matter had been settled by her opening statement and answering Maria's questions was superfluous.

The truth was that she could not articulate why and how things evolved so abruptly. Isn't this the beauty of youth? Like a kitten chasing a butterfly, at this stage of life, the mind can fly over the pastures of haven lifted by capricious breezes disregarding the boundaries of accountability.

"Seriously, Giselle, what made you decide to become a professional ballerina rather than a doctor?" insisted Signora Maria.

"Because I met Paul at the school cafeteria. He asked me what I wanted to do when I grew up! At first it felt like a silly question, and I did not know what to answer. It was like being caught in a math test unprepared. I needed to think about it. But, before I knew it, my mouth had already spoken:

- I want to become a ballerina – so I told him.

"He then told me that if that was what I wanted, then I should do it, like his choice to become a musician. So, I vowed to be a prima ballerina.

I realized, when our eyes stared into each other's, that an eternal bond was established; a marvel had occurred, and my destiny was locked to his. I cannot forget him, and I want to see him again."

"And who would this Paul be?"

"He is a very famous composer. He came and sat by my side because it was the only open space. He told me that I should put no limits to my imagination."

"I thought you wanted to become a doctor. Isn't what you told us just a while ago? I thought you did not want to become a ballerina. In fact, you felt that it was an imposition bestowed upon you since birth. Isn't it what you told us? So, if you should do what you want, you should become a doctor, or am I missing something?" hammered Signora Maria with aggravating logic.

"The thing is, Mom, I love him. And becoming a ballerina is the only way I can see him again."

"You love someone whom you just met in a cafeteria? And how old is this prince charming?"

"I don't know, maybe forty? I can look it up if you want me to."

"Don't you think it inappropriate for an adult man to come onto a young girl? What else did he do to you? What else did he say?"

"Nothing, he patted me in the shoulder and told me good luck when he left. He told me to never give up."

"Have you seen him again?"

"No."

"Did he leave his contact information with you?"

"No."

"Did he say that he wants to see you again?"

"No."

"And why do you think that he loves you?"

"I never said that he loves me. I love him. And, one day, he will love me."

"And what if he doesn't?" continued Signora Maria, almost amused by the grotesque conversation.

"I think he will! I know he will! They say he is depressed, drinks too much, a junkie, and he hates being with people. So, I think he will be happy meeting someone who truly loves him."

"And my dear Giselle, why would you love someone who is much older, who barely knows you, and who has all possible drawbacks a man could have?"

"Because I know that deep inside, he is a wonderful man. I remember the way he looked at me, I recall his gaze, how he listened to me carefully, and how he talked to me as if I was a grown up. I felt that he was very sincere, and he cared for me—just for a few moments, but he really did. And I felt a warmth inside my heart that I'd never felt before. And then I knew—I know—Mom, that he is the man of my life."

***

There was absolutely no way, that one could add more salt to the minestrone. Professor Federico could not think of anything else that could help navigate the conversation, even for a few moments, just enough to take a deep breath at least.

Life had been perfect since Giselle entered his life. This beautiful, thoughtful, caring girl. But suddenly, he was afraid Giselle was turning mad. Being his first time to navigate the turbulent waters of teenagerhood, this interaction was, to say the list, disturbing.

He, therefore, called:

"Lori, can you come here, please?"

"What can I do, Mister?"

"If I remember correctly, I bought tiramisú yesterday and we forgot to eat it. Should we have it this evening?"

"Certainly!" replied Lori, concerned.

"Something wrong must be going on." she thought.

"Should I bring grappa for the tiramisú, or maybe brandy?"

"Grappa, please. This is a great idea!"

Meanwhile, Signora Maria's deductive thinking was making progress. To guarantee maximal accuracy, she switched to Russian:

"Okay, Giselle. Let's think it through. We are facing two different issues here: The first is that you are in love with someone whom you don't even know, who does not know you, who lives God knows where and may be crazy. That is just fine! Time will tell. But the pressing predicament is your schooling choice. Even for this, you have plenty of time to decide. Federico and I will not try to persuade you one way or another, but don't you think that a career as a performer is too risky? Are you sure that, for whatever good or bad reason, you want to follow such a difficult path? What if you cannot make it as a professional ballerina? Will you be a ballet teacher for the rest of your life? Don't you think that it would be most reasonable to consider a plan B?"

Maria's words made perfect sense. Professor Federico nodded. It was obvious that there was no point arguing against farfetched circumstances. The infatuation with Paul would soon fade and everything would return to normal on that account. But what if Giselle's impulse resulted in irreversible damage to her professional career? It would be a decision she might regret for the rest of her life.

It was then that Federico, the *"cunctator,"*[21] interjected:

"Perhaps, it would be best to talk with Madame Petrova and test her judgment. If she believes that you have the potential to become a successful ballerina, so be it. If she discourages such a choice, you will never find Paul through that path anyway, and you might just as well follow a mainstream track. What about that?"

That reasoning settled the exchange for the night since Madame Petrova was not there and the only option was to switch the conversation to Federico's liking and enjoy the tiramisú, with grappa for the Professor and tisane for the ladies.

***

And so it was that a few evenings later, Madame Petrova sat at the dinner table with Signora Maria and Professor Federico, while Giselle had been encouraged to spend the evening with friends at a local trattoria.

Signora Maria had prepped her husband, suggested they start with a casual conversation without mention of the current quandary to avoid prompting Madame Petrova's judgment.

Therefore, Professor Federico, after the customary pleasantries, started:

"Well, it's incredible to think how far we have gone since the day we brought Giselle to your studio. I remember that you were quite skeptical. Is my recollection correct?"

"Well, it is true that Giselle was quite advanced in age when you brought her, and I was worried about her ability to cope with the new place. Everything was new—the environment, the people, the language, and the rigor of dancing. I didn't feel it was appropriate to put her though such stress. On the other hand, if we had to give it a try, there was no point procrastinating.

"But then, I remember looking straight into her eyes. I remember her humble confidence, or I dare say, her humble arrogance. She looked at me

---

[21] Latin for: *procrastinator*, by name of Quintus Fabius Maximus Verrucosus, the Roman military commander whose cautious delaying tactics during the early stages of the second Punic War (218–201 BC) gave Rome time to recover its strength.

as a tiger focuses on her prey, as if I was the apprentice, and she was the teacher. And she maintained that demeanor day after day. Not a moment of hesitation. She would come to the studio on time, never a minute late. She would listen and absorb every word I'd say. She rarely talked unless asked. I never had to repeat myself twice. And she performed with the precision of a natural; as if dance belonged to her, and we were just accidental bystanders.

"In a short period, she was on a league of her own. Not just because of her physical performance, but because of her poise, focus, self-confidence, the control of her body and spirit, her charismatic presence. I had never observed anything like that. I guess that this is the footmark of legends. Soon the other students looked up to her in awe. And yet she maintained her humble and reserved demeanor. Beyond the dance, she was a simple, quiet, and unpretentious foreign girl, thankful to be accepted. At the end of each lesson, she would return to the bench, collect her garments, put on street clothes over her leotard, and leave without a word. When the other girls tried to lure her into a conversation, she smiled, listened politely to a few words before saying, 'Sorry, I must go home. I have homework to do.'

"I felt sorry for her at times, she seemed to be skipping youth, but at the same time, she thrived in determination, she seemed happier than the other students, simply because she had a clear path to follow.

"We mostly float by our existence rather than living our dreams; that is what happened to me. I wanted to be a ballerina. I became a teacher instead. Maybe I would be nothing now, but maybe not—I could have lived my dream. The sad thing is that I will never know. I fell in love with a great dancer, I worked hard to impress him. But he never noticed me. When I realized that I was not doing it for me but for this fatuous dream, I gave up. That's the story of my life.

"I have observed Giselle for years now. She is the best student I've ever had in all accounts. She is kind, compassionate, thoughtful, and respectful. She is clever, and on the dance floor she is impeccable. Every movement, every posture is natural and perfect. She outperforms expectations by combining soul with teachings. There is no hesitation in a single fiber of her body, and most recently, she added something she lacked before—a melancholy in her gestures. It seems that her arms are reaching for something missing, that her eyes scrutinize horizons beyond the horizon. Her dancing furthers perfection, with subtle deviations from the prescribed geometry that gives spontaneity to the scripted moves."

And then she added in French as if to underscore the significance of her point:

"Il y a toujours un mouvement au bout de ses doigts comme une prémonition pour le suivant plier, etendre, relever, sauter, tourner, glisser, et elancer."

Returning to Russian after the trance, Madame Petrova continued:

"Of course, it is easy for me to be biased. I am in love with this girl, and I may not be objective enough. That's why, I asked the Maestro at La Scala to take a peek at her performance. He told me after just a few instant:

- I know a rising star when I see one, that girl is made for the big leagues. You give her to me, and I will take care of her. I can make her a prima ballerina. -

"And with his connections all over the world, I guarantee that if someone can make her prima ballerina, that is the Maestro."

By the time Madame Petrova was done with her soliloquy, her eyes were shiny. In the absence of a handkerchief, in an unorthodox move, she dabbed her cheeks with the napkin, leaving makeup stains on it.

***

Madame Petrova's statement settled the conversation. No question remained about Madame Petrova's expectations of Giselle.

Yet, Signora Maria was compelled to raise a most reasonable concern:

"But what are her chances of success in such a competitive environment? And what would become of her if she fails?"

"She will succeed in one way or another. She can be a soloist, she has shown it already, and she is quite ready for *pas de deux*. She performed quite well in a rehearsal of the *Swan* and *Giselle*. She memorized everything perfectly. She can already transition from entrée, to adagio, variations, and the coda. She has not tried it in a public performance yet, but she is ready for it, and she has the confidence to go for it. She will be ready to be hired by several companies soon or simply grow from our *corps de ballet*. In any case, she will have a career for sure. The question is how far she will go. That I cannot predict. There is politics in ballet just as in anything else. There is luck, opportunities, or most often the lack of them. But it is promising that the Maestro is on her side. With him behind her, she will have a head start. In the worst-case scenario, she could become a lead dance teacher in a high-level studio. She will have a job and if this is what she wants, she will be happy."

"But the real question remains, does she really want to follow this path?" continued Madame Petrova. "Just of late, she told me that she wanted to go to medical school."

"Yes, this is what she told us too. But then she met this musician. She said his name is Paul Vincente. He encouraged her to pursue her dreams, and since then she seemed to have changed her mind."

Professor Federico, realizing that, besides the overture, his wife had carried most of the conversation from the family side, reasserted his relevance to the conversation by asking:

"Would you like some wine? We have this Pinot Nero that goes magnificently with the swordfish."

Madame Petrova smiled, approached the glass, and continued to converse with Signora Maria.

"Paul Vincente is a great modern composer. His work has been choreographed into modern dance all over the world. He visited Milan recently and met with students. I am not sure what this has to do with Giselle, but she also mentioned him to me. In fact, she asked whether she could transition to modern dance. I told her that it is her choice, but if she decided to continue with ballet rather than medical school, the best chance would be to first establish her reputation in classical dance, since this is what she has been building on and she already has a path ahead. Modern dance is fun, and I would support her if that was what she wanted, but it is less structured than classical and more susceptible to the capriciousness of choreographers. It is less competitive, or the competitiveness is less based on technical skill. She is more likely to succeed within the rigorous boundaries of classical ballet where standards are too high for most."

"And what do you think about this Paul infatuation?" asked Signora Maria, who could not control her angst.

"Dreams are dreams! As I told you, I was young and naïve too, and I also fell in love with a famous dancer who inspired my career. He never noticed me even when there was a chance. It was a nice dream that never materialized.

"I think for her, Paul represents something she can own. A dream that was not imposed upon her by circumstances. We all need dreams, don't we? No point killing a young person's dream. I would let her be. He is a charismatic and attractive man. But she will get over it soon. Besides, he lives in America and rumor is that he is married to his cousin."

"So be it!" exploded Professor Federico. "Let her do what she wants! That girl already gave us more happiness than we could have ever dreamed of! And, you know what? Screw medical school! I never wanted to be a doctor myself! My parents made me become one and I can't complain, but I will never know what could have been if I followed a dream!"

The "screw medical school" concept did not go unnoticed by Signora Maria, who looked sternly, but at the same time admiringly, at her meek husband.

"Is Federico becoming a real man in his old age?" We suppose she thought.

***

Thus, at age nineteen, Giselle was a prima ballerina. Madame Petrova became her *de facto* agent and the Maestro her guardian angel in the formidable circle of the performing arts.

***

Inexorably, time passes. Sometimes it flows calmly down the watershed of life towards uncharted dark blue seas, other times it flies as an unreachable eagle. Little can be done to capture each moment as life freewheels like a whimsical butterfly. Yet, in rare circumstances, time solidifies into a vivid memory that sculpts the rest of one's life. So was that night at the veranda of Ristorante Belvedere at the Isola dei Pescatori.

A lazy breeze was stroking what few trees there were in the tiny island, rippling the surface of Lake Maggiore, and caressing the cheeks of the patrons as it carried the scent of nearby gardenias. Giselle was splendid, donning with unpretentious elegance a colorful cotton dress that delineated the exquisiteness of a perfect figure. Her black eyes shone through long dark lashes that contrasted with the pallor of her face. Her glistening black hair was tightly twisted into a floral bun where petals of a white camelia danced at the rhythm of the zephyr. But it was Giselle's smile that, whenever it shone like a sunray through the clouds, made the Maestro's heart shiver.

Years had passed since the Maestro had first met Giselle at the audition organized by Madame Petrova. With his help the student had turned into a legend. In contrast to Giselle's, the Maestro's silver hair set a tone of distinguished elegance, compensating for a few wrinkles that altered the physiognomy of what used to be a handsome face. Like any other man endowed with eyes to see and a heart to feel, the Maestro was in love with Giselle. That night he had finally gathered the resolve to invite Giselle out to dinner following a memorable day at Isola Bella, where Giselle, as guest of honor, had received a prestigious award.

Giselle, on her end, adored the Maestro. Never having experienced malevolence in her life, she was inclined to trust and follow his guidance. As for other paternal characters that had shaped her past, the Maestro had gained her total confidence in the last four years. Thus, that unexpected dinner invitation with the powerful man was welcomed as a joyful token of achievement. As usual, when she was not performing, she did not wear makeup or other enhancements, and her natural beauty offered that sense of purity and naivete that attracted mature men.

The Maestro had ordered a bottle of aged Barolo d'Alba and as the waiter was pouring the drink into their glasses, Giselle initiated the conversation:

"Thank you, Maestro, for all you have done for me. Without you, this day would have never happened."

"Giselle, this is just the predictable consequence of your hard work. It is true that I opened a few doors, but you must take credit for all that you have achieved. I am sure your parents must be very proud of you."

"They are! Mom and Dad were worried at first about my choice, but now they come to every performance and my dad acts like a ballet scholar, chanting praises to anyone he can pin down! And so does Uncle Borysko, and even Grandma at the village. They all believe that the only thing that matters in life is to be a ballerina! I am happy that I did not disappoint them, and I have to thank you and Madame Petrova for believing in me."

As dinner progressed from a serving of pumpkin gnocchi in a light ragu sauce to a grilled perch dish with porcini mushrooms, the Maestro interjected:

"Do you know, Giselle. . . You are the most beautiful person that I have ever met. I wish I could have met you a long time ago, when I was young and unattached! You must have a lot of suitors; I wonder who the lucky man will be, whom you will choose one day."

Observing a light blush in Giselle's face, the Maestro paused for a few seconds. He held the glass of wine with splayed fingers, gesturing for Giselle to do the same. He clinked with the rim of his glass to the belly of Giselle's to demonstrate his submission to her majestic beauty.

Then, unable to restrain his curiosity, he continued:

"Madame Petrova told me that your heart is already taken, though she did not disclose who the lucky man is."

After taking a sip and resting the glass on the table, Giselle's eyebrows furrowed and lowering her eyes, she answered:

"I used to love a man when I was young. He is the reason why I decided to become a ballerina. I wanted a chance to see him again. But I do not know how I feel anymore. He lives far away, he must have forgotten me, and about a year ago Madame Petrova told me that he is married to his cousin. My grandma wants me to marry someone from our village; a man I have known since I was a little girl. His name is Demetri. He is a very handsome man, a little older than I am. He is a good person. He is studying business at the University in Kiev to become a tour manager. Last summer, when I went back to the village, he took me on a walk along the Don and gave me a kiss. He proposed to marry me when he's done with his studies. But, although I like him as a person, I could not kiss him back. Something made me resist his fervent hug and I pushed him away. I told him that I would think about it when the time comes. I have been thinking of him though. He is a good man. Everyone likes him at the village, even Grandma and Uncle Borysko. Maybe I should yield."

"It seems to me that you do not love Demetri, and let me tell you something, life with another person is a very tricky proposition, trust me. At the very least you want to start with love. It may not be all that it takes but it is an essential step! You do not want to carry life the way I did, following a collection of haphazard interactions that in retrospect one tries to weave together into a wicker basket of memories to compile a narrative that would not otherwise exist."

Giselle's wide-open eyes were glued to the Maestro's lips. Against the Italian etiquette, her elbows were resting on the table, her fingers intertwined, providing support for her chin.

Then the Maestro continued:

"But what about the man of your dreams? How did you fall in love with him? What was special about him?"

"I met him when I was fifteen in the school cafeteria. He was visiting from America, from New York. He is a very famous musician. He sat close to me by accident because there was no other open seat and he asked me what I wanted to be in life. I do not know why, but I told him that I wanted to become a prima ballerina. Then he looked deep into my eyes as if he could read my mind and he told me:

- If this is what you want; then do it! just as I did! –

But I never saw him again, and those who know him say that he is a bizarre person, a loner, a drug addict, and now I also found out that he is married."

Giselle locked eyes with the Maestro, as if she was soliciting sympathy. They were pensive, even sad, and her smile was gone.

And the Maestro replied:

"Giselle, it seems to me that you are still in love with this man or whatever he may represent for you. Maybe, you are in love with a dream, and the wonder is still there. May ask you, who is this famous composer?"

"His name is Paul Vincente. He used to live in New York but he is not there anymore. I even wrote to him a few times, just to ask if I could see him again, but he never responded."

"You kidding? Paul? I know Paul Vicente very well! He is a wonderful man. He is a good friend of mine. I am the one who invited him to a tour of Italy at that time. It is true that I have not heard much from him lately. And, by the way, he is not married to his cousin. His cousin's name is Laura. She is a princess, a delicate, sensitive, and wonderful lady. She is one of the sweetest persons I have ever met and of course Paul is attached to her. Paul's introverted personality craves Laura's safe haven. But they are not married, not that I know of."

Giselle was looking at him with incredulous eyes, and the Maestro continued:

"You know, I understand now why you love Paul! Because you are his twin soul! Looking at you, it feels like looking at him at our favorite Italian restaurant in Greenwich Village. The same intensity, the same purity, the same considerate determination, the same convoluted simplicity, the same charisma. Talking to you, like talking to him, is absorbing! One forgets the rest of the world! It does not feel like a waste of time but rather drinking the essentials of life.

You are both beautiful souls."

Taking a deep breath and taking another sip of wine, the Maestro continued:

"…Now I know why you love him! It is because he is your other half. Maybe that encounter was not serendipitous. Maybe it was meant to be. Maybe each one of us carries a magnet that attracts only one other soul in the universe. And when the magnetism is overpowering, destiny will abide by the inescapable force just as celestial bodies abide by the law of gravity."

"But what about the drugs and the drinking?" asked Giselle.

"People say a lot of things in our world; rumors are food for business to prosper, for the paparazzi to thrive. Epicaricacy gratifies the mob, and celebrities are their favorite targets. Magic Hollywood! East or West! Kingdoms that have no soul, no stories to tell, only stories to sell. I would not pay any attention to what the so-called people say. I admit that I do not know what Paul's private life is like, but I doubt that he can be as productive as he is by wasting his time in self-destructive deeds."

***

After dinner, the couple strolled around the island in a pensive mood with the pretext of facilitating digestion. The maestro offered his arm to Giselle. She rested one hand on it, listening to the soothing splash of waves that caressed the shore. Then the Maestro stopped and embraced Giselle gently. He held her shoulders and, looking into her eyes, said:

"Giselle, you are the most beautiful person I've ever met. As I said before, If I was not old and committed, I would be standing on my knees with a million-carat diamond in my hands! Don't sell yourself short. Do not let anyone interfere in your life. You are an independent individual. Why should you marry a stranger to please your relatives? It's disgusting. You should be the only owner of your life. Do not go for something you don't love. Do it for yourself, in respect of your dream. You do not have to do it for anyone but yourself, not even for Paul. He might not even know that you exist, and he may continue to wander along the path of loneliness. I suppose he is not expecting anything from you and maybe from life. You owe him nothing, but you owe it to yourself! Do not throw away a dream. Do not marry a compromise! If it's not Paul, let yourself fall in love with someone else. You are too precious for anything less.

"And, if you want me to, I can arrange for you to meet Paul. I can arrange for him to discover you. I can introduce you to the glamour of Broadway."

After that, they returned to the hotel to spend the night, and, as they walked, Giselle leaned her head on the Maestro's shoulder.

THE PERFORMANCE

In her entire life, Ivanna Yvanova had never met defeat. That was because she had full control of her territory, where no one would dare challenge the stern lady. Odds changed when the game strayed from familiarity.

New York is enough of a big and scary city to intimidate people unaccustomed to foreign ways and jargons. But a far greater challenge of intercontinental proportions rose from two formidable ladies just as stubborn as Mrs. Yvanova. The ladies had taken upon themselves the daunting task of proving to the world that Ivanna Yvanova was not as old and shabby of a lady as she seemed to be. Thus, New York became the battleground where Ivanna had to refrain from shopping in Fifth Avenue— high heel shoes, Prada and Gucci purses and wallets, Max Mara camel hair coats and silk blouses, and other related accessories that she had never seen before. She also had to undergo manicure, nail polishing, hair dyeing and styling, makeup sessions, and massages at elegant parlors under Lori's firm supervision.

Soon Ivanna realized that it was futile to argue with someone who could not understand a word of what she was saying. More discouraging was the realization that having a language in common was also unhelpful. In fact, when she rebelled by trying to convey her disapproval to Signora Maria in her native language, the latter seemed struck by a mental block that temporarily prevented her from understanding Russian. Signora Maria would rather shrug her shoulders in response to Ivanna's objections and redirect her complaints to Lori, who, unperturbed, executed the predetermined plans. In the end, Ivanna surrendered.

Moreover, in the commotion, she forgot about her shortness of breath, her joint pain, her hesitant wobbling, and all other more or less genuine ailments that had kept her busy in the past. When the cane was also removed from the equation by a negligent Lori, who by coincidence had forgotten the decoration at the hotel, Ivanna had no choice but to appear as an elegant and quite attractive lady in front of Uncle Borysko who in response raised his eyebrows and bowed his head.

Therefore, Ivanna was sitting on the front row of the box at the first tier of Carnegie Hall, tightly holding the new Gucci purse that Signora Maria had bought for her. Behind her, Uncle Borysko was standing in a statuary position, his hand on the half-naked shoulder of Ivanna, who did not seem to notice or, if she did, didn't seem bothered.

Signora Maria was also sitting in the front row. With experienced eyes, she had been following Uncle Borysko's maneuvers, pointing out each progress to Lori by raising her eyebrow, which Lori acknowledged with an acknowledging smile. It was clear that their efforts were converging into its desired effect.

Signora Maria would then turn her attention to her clueless husband, who instead kept staring at the front row of the parquet, where the Maestro was sitting, Madame Petrova to his left and to his right, beyond an empty chair, Paul's cousin Laura. Madame Petrova took out a box of peppermints from her purse, opened it, and offered the contents to the Maestro. The Maestro picked one and in turn extended his arm across the empty seat toward Laura, who nodded, smiled, and took a lozenge before returning her attention to the stage where the show was about to begin.

Professor Federico reserved admiration for the Maestro, who in a short time had done so much to support Giselle. The Maestro was also responsible for reserving the box for Giselle's cheering crowd and for organizing a dinner after the performance in her honor. In other words, a magnate of good old-timey caliber. In addition, Professor Federico had followed the Maestro's encouragement to visit the village and bring a renitent Ivanna to the trip of her life. Ivanna in the beginning refused the invitation with the lame excuse that there were a few more chickens that expected to be fed on a regular basis. She later accepted when Uncle Borysko emphasized that the point of the trip was to coronate the hardship of raising the little orphan into a bona fide kozaczka.

As a veteran, the Maestro had gone through innumerable premieres, but this was different. Since the magical night spent with Giselle, his life's purpose had flourished into nurturing the student and her dream. Thus, the student's debut at Carnegie Hall was making his heart throb. That night at the Isola Pescatori, the Maestro had realized that he loved Giselle in the purest way a man could love a woman. It was beyond paternal affection. It was a bittersweet combination of fondness and passion for a forbidden dream. But he was content to accept the bitterness to relish the sweetness. Therefore, he had honed his efforts to reroute destiny along the unfinished promise of returning Paul to Giselle. He had contacted a friend, a well-known choreographer in New York, who invited Giselle to join a residence company as a guest artist. From there, things moved fast. Soon a top tier company took her in as one of their principal dancers.

While in New York, in her free time, Giselle wandered the streets. Awe for the big city was tainted by disgust, admiration by confusion, attraction by repulsion. It was as if Baudelaire had written Les Fleurs du Mal to remark on the dissonance of metropolitan life. She absorbed all that New York's kaleidoscope could offer, high rises, graffities, horse-led carriages and homeless beggars, street performers and businessmen, elegant ladies and pigeon feeders, timid concerts emerging from the corner of streets, parks, or subways through the clanking traffic: trumpets, saxophones, violins, drums played for a few cents; all types of music from Bolivian flutes to Caribbean steel. And she watched, observed, listened, and studied the street performers that created a tapestry of styles from the variety of cultures in New York. In her subconscious, she compared those scenes to the tales of classical ballet, where women turn into swans, or princesses love implausible heroes, delusions that could not be reconciled with the reality of the streets. She gifted beggars and street performers that were putting up a show for her, wondering to whom her performances were directed? To the conceited upper-class society or the street walkers, the unpretentious everyday crowd that breaths the asphalt of New York avenues?

And she recollected Uncle Borysko's words:

"I want you to give beauty to the world!"

But what world was he talking about? The world of Giselle and the dying swan, the world of princes and princesses, or the unprivileged world of the New York streets?

When the Maestro was in town, she strolled along Central Park with him, discreetly musing at imperfect performances. But she also made a few acquaintances of her own; among them a dancer and a musician. They roamed the streets together, they went to bars, to nightclubs, to live performances. She absorbed it all and she translated everything through the filter of motion into her own ballet style. It was a subtle rebellion that could only be sensed but not seen. Subliminal deviations from the prepackaged scripts that could not be verified but only admired.

New York had changed Giselle. The skills were the same, the rigor the same, it was just the audience that differed. She was now performing for the poor, the lost, the unfortunate, the confused, those in the streets, rain or shine. She forgot the theater spectators. There was no more reflective mirror, but thousands of infinity mirrors inside of her reflecting into myriads of voices that could not be heard.

At rehearsals she built a role of her own. That was when a fortuitous partnership propelled her career. The top male dancer saw her and chose her as his partner. Ballets were choreographed and created just for them based on their technical skills and acting talents.

Many at rehearsal wouldn't understand what they were doing, but the Maestro and the artistic directors did. The ballet was crafted for them and was not a coincidence that it was based on Paul Vincente's music.

***

That is what the Maestro was thinking at the time when the curtains of the stage were about to be raised. It had been the masterpiece of his life. Giselle was at the summit of Mount Everest, and he had been the mastermind of her success. This evening represented the coronation of a lifetime of aspiration and rigor by a wonderful woman, and all was set for this celebration. Professor Federico and Signora Maria had brought all of Giselle's past to New York and the Maestro had orchestrated the evening to be the joyous culmination of an impossible dream.

And this is what happened.

At the end of the performance, the spectators stood up. Several rounds of encores were requested. Flowers were thrown to the stage at Carnegie Hall. A bouquet was thrown from the first row. It was from the Maestro. And Giselle picked it up and held it as one would hold a baby. Just as Grandma held her on the first day of her life. That had been Giselle's best performance. Everyone knew that she was an established star, and everyone was excited. . . everyone except Giselle, who wondered what Paul's impression was of the performance.

The Maestro told her just the day before that Paul was supposed to attend the premiere. She sensed that Paul, more than anyone else, could appreciate the soul of her motion that reverberated through the fervor of his music. Just before the performance, in the dressing room, she saw the fifteen-year-old Giselle, dancing in front of her bedroom mirror in Milan. She recalled her amateurish choreography of Paul's music. Who would have guessed that in a few years the implausible dream would turn into reality at Carnegie Hall?

***

Backstage, after the curtains were lowered, she sat on a bench because she was tired. It was not physical exhaustion, but a spiritual fatigue that had accumulated over the years. Now that she had reached the peak, and she could divert her attention from her coveted goal, she could pause and recall the journey. She thought of Daria, and Sasha, and Oldie, and the fiddler, and the village. And she thought of her mother and her father whom she never met. Would they be proud of her? She thought of Uncle Borysko, and Grandma of course, and her benevolent stepparents, and the attentive Lori, who had shaped her growth day after day. And Madame Petrova's and the Maestro's unconditional support. She felt the weight that she had carried in her subconscious all along and was tamping on her all of a sudden.

Then she remembered that she was about to meet Paul, the man who prompted it all. And she realized that she did not care that much anymore. Was he real, or just an illusion as the characters of the ballets? Was he just as imaginary as Giselle's lover in the scripts? Was he just the fruit of her imagination? She thought that it would have been better to leave the dream immaculate. What if the reunion turned into mutual disappointment? Why spoil a wonderful tale with the frailty of reality?

***

But these reflections were soon interrupted. A crowd was approaching. It was the Maestro, and Madame Petrova, and Professor Federico with Signora Maria. . . but what? Wait a moment! It was uncle Borysko. . . wait a moment, was that elegant and pretty lady Grandma?

"Surprise!!!!"

Giselle was stunned and barely reacted. She went from hug to hug, kiss to kiss, handshake to handshake without understanding. Her happiness was too deep to be expressed. It was as if the performance was just about to start. As she was accepting their praises, she remembered that Paul was also supposed to be there. She searched for him but there was no Paul.

The Maestro caught her inquisitive look and approached her. He looked into her eyes and told her:

"I am sorry. Paul did not make it. I guess you could not see the empty seat beside me from the stage."

"It's okay," answered Giselle. "It does not matter. I was just curious to meet him. Maybe another time."

***

Back in the dressing room, Giselle was clearing her makeup, and preparing for dinner while family and friends were waiting downstairs; a wonderful and unexpected celebration with those who made the improbable happen.

And she thought:

"Uncle Borysko and Grandma here? What an incredible surprise; all this love culminating in a faraway place. How did they make it all the way here? And how handsome Uncle was! And what about Grandma? She looked beautiful! What happened to the country lady? Is Grandma proud of me? We barely exchanged a word in the excitement. And what about Uncle Borysko? Is he proud? He is the one who had the foresight to send me abroad to achieve what was unthinkable at the village.

"And what a relief that Paul did not come! Paul has been a spell; a curse that suspended my personal life. Now it is finally over! Yes, Paul has been a dream, an inspiration, a virtual character that appeared once, a *deus ex machina*, a prince in the ballet stories that vanishes after the curtain is lowered. I am free, finally! Free to live my life, to love and be loved!"

As she was looking in the mirror at the new, free Giselle, she heard a knock at the door:

"May I come in?"

It was a woman's voice.

"Am I disturbing you? I am Laura. I am Paul Vincente's cousin."

The woman entered. She was a slim, elegant middle-aged woman, with curly black hair and tanned skin. Her black eyes were smiling, just as her mouth, in a semblance of kindness.

"I am not going to take much of your time. Sorry for bothering you. But Paul asked me to apologize for him. He is sorry that he could not make it."

Giselle looked at the pretty woman, the famous Laura! The one against whom she had been competing in her dreams! She was pretty but not beautiful. Yet she could see why someone like Paul would like her. She seemed so gentle, and she felt good that Paul was close to a woman like her. It spoke well of him. At least Paul would be happy in his life, while she would go on with hers.

"Thank you," answered Giselle. "I know who you are. The Maestro talks very highly of you. Thank you for coming to the show. And please relay to Paul that it is okay. I totally understand. It could be for another time."

"I know that you care," replied Laura. "I know that Paul is important to you. The Maestro told me. And therefore, I am here. Paul did not come because he is sick. It is not an excuse; he is very sick, and he could not leave California. He truly apologizes. He knows who you are. He remembers you. He wanted assurance that I would convey his sincere apologies to you."

Giselle's heart was not prepared for this:

"What do you mean he is sick?"

"Well, it is a long story. You must go to your dinner now. They are waiting for you. If you like, I can tell you when there is enough time. It is in fact a long story. You are very welcome to come to dinner at my place any day and I can tell you all about Paul if you are interested."

"Of course I want to know! I love Paul!" came out of Giselle's mouth and then she quickly corrected:

"I mean, I used to love Paul—I mean I used to love his music of course! Of course, I still do!"

Laura smiled with imperceptible condescendence, and looking into Giselle's eyes concluded:

"I know. I understand everything. See you at my place then."

After Laura left, Giselle returned her attention to the mirror. The fifteen-year-old Giselle was staring at her:

"So, you wanted to get rid of Paul? Is this what you call everlasting love? You know that you still love him and only him! Do you need a teenage girl to teach you about life?"

It was a fifteen-year-old strangely scolding a mature woman. But Giselle understood what the severe younger self was telling her.

Yes, she was not free after all. Her life had been locked forever with that of Paul.

AN UNFORGETTABLE EVENING

Giselle arrived early at Laura's place since she had not realized that there were only two blocks between Carnegie Hall, where she was for rehearsal, and 59th street where Paul's cousin resided. Maria received her at the door. She introduced herself as the house stalwart and announced that Laura was going to be late. She then escorted Giselle to the living room and offered a drink. After Giselle declined, she excused herself to return to her chores.

Alone in unfamiliar territory, Giselle was compelled to explore. A perfunctory inspection of the place revealed Laura's aristocratic simplicity balanced by grace from family memorabilia with contemporary add-ons, the latter collected in large part from Laura's exposure to the New York highlife. Giselle felt useless in the silence of the empty room. It seemed that time, in synchrony with the tick tock of the wall clock, was in turn taking a step forward and backward, indefinitely suspending its progression. She was breathing an atmosphere of controlled unease, and for a while she stood still in the middle of the room as her steps, like those of time, hesitated to follow the unfamiliar script. It was as if the Devil had choreographed a dance without motion.

Among the antiques, and on top of a Persian carpet, a grand piano sat close to a French door that opened into the terrace overlooking Central Park. The piano was an old Steinway of exquisite marquetry, with the spruce soundboard and keyboard inlaid with carved statuettes and tessellated with fancy stones.

On top of the soundboard, three standing frames caught her attention. Giselle approached to discover that they contained pictures of Paul and Laura. In the first, Paul stood center stage with Laura on one side, the orchestra director on the other, and the instrumentalists behind. In the second, Paul was smiling, holding a glass of wine, his head turned towards Laura who, in an elegant soiree gown, was returning the smile. The third picture portrayed them in casual attire walking barefoot at sunset along the seashore with a seagull flying in the background. She took the frame in her hand to take a closer look. Paul appeared cheerful, even ecstatic, and Giselle forced herself to feel happy for the beautiful couple. But then she wondered:

"What am I doing here? She brought me here to show how happy of a couple they are! She made herself late on purpose to give me a chance to explore the evidence of their intimacy. What am I doing here? I should have thought before accepting. . . . It is okay. I have no right to intrude into someone else's life. What am I expecting? I have never been part of this man's life! He barely knows I exist. . . if he even does! But now. . . what am I supposed to do? Spend the evening listening to Laura chat about her wonderful man?"

***

"It isn't what you think. Paul adores me like a little sister, but he does not love me," Laura's voice interrupted the silence. "I know there are lots of rumors about us. People like to talk, they cannot shut their mouths. But none of these rumors are true. Do not worry, Paul is a free man, perhaps he is too free, which could be another way to say. . . a lonesome man."

Then Laura continued:

"Thank you for coming, my dear! You are a superstar now! What a great performance the other night. I heard only wonderful comments! You made it where only few can't even dream of. You are a Broadway star! And you are so beautiful! Breathtakingly beautiful. Sei bellissima! E' un piacere di averti qua.[22] Should we speak Italian? Maybe not! I have been in America far too long. It comes easier to speak English if you can believe it."

Giselle assented:

"Thank you for inviting me. It's so elegant, so beautiful here, and what a great view of Central Park. May I look out?"

---

[22] You are beautiful. It is a pleasure to host you here.

Laura moved ahead, anticipating Giselle's steps. She opened the French door and walked out first. Then, she leaned through the threshold of the door into the apartment and called:

"Maria, bring us the Prosecco and the appetizers." Then, turning to Giselle: "We can eat out here if you prefer. It is a pleasant evening."

Waiting for the Prosecco, Giselle looked down.

At the close margin of Central Park, a queue of horse-drawn carriages waited for costumers. Behind it, there were stands improvised for some special event. A mosaic of tourists fretted like a colony of ants around the stands, examining deals and selecting grubs. A melee in the distant meadow turned out to be caused by children fighting over a soccer ball, while, at a closer distance, unperturbed ladies practiced tai chi. At another corner, a violin's lament ascended over the crowd and traffic, reaching for angels in the sky.

Laura rested on a wicker armchair and Giselle sat in front of her, in Paul's favorite spot.

Referring to the Maestro as Giovanni, Laura continued:

"Giovanni is right. You and Paul are identical! It is difficult to explain, but your behavior is so similar. It is as if the same soul split into two persons; confident posture. . . mixed. . . I guess, with inquisitive reticence; minimal loquacity, waiting for others to start the conversation, intense engagement, no small talk, no frivolous giggling. I do not know about you, but Paul detests small talk; it is either a conversation of substance or silence. This is why he likes my company. With no expectations from my side, spontaneity can flourish and every word, expression, and gesture is genuine. Yet, his— how should I define it?— his magnetism! Yes, his magnetism can be exhausting at times. I hope that you are not as bad!" concluded Laura with a smile.

"I barely know him," acknowledged Giselle. "I met him once for a few minutes in a cafeteria in Milan; a fortuitous encounter, he just grabbed the only open seat, which happened to be at my side. But you are right, each word, each eye movement, each expression, drew me into the center of his life, at least for those few moments. It was as if the rest of the world had vanished and only the two of us existed. With a few words, he shaped my life. For a long time, I believed that I loved him. Can you believe I loved someone I barely knew?"

With a reticent expression Giselle concluded:

"Do you think I am a fool?"

"Not at all, my dear. Not at all."

"I even tried to contact him. I felt that our conversation had been cut too short. I needed some sort of closure. And I wanted to see him again. But he never returned my mail."

"Of course, he didn't. He probably never saw it. His agent most likely discarded it. But I can tell you that if he had, he would have responded. Can you guess how I know?"

Giselle kept staring wordlessly into Laura's eyes.

"When he came back from Italy, he mentioned you to me:

– I met a young woman; her name is Giselle. She acted mature, but she was only fifteen. She knew who I was but did not behave like a fan. No small talk, no ass-kissing, no pretensions, no attempts to impress; I only recall spontaneity. She opened herself to me and shared her dreams and uncertainties. She told me she wanted to become a principal ballerina. At first, I laughed inside, but then, when her big unflinching eyes pierced into mine, I sensed her determination, and I encouraged her. God knows what will become of her, but my intuition tells me she will succeed in whatever pursuit she chooses. I wish I could help her, but I did not even ask for her contact. Who knows, maybe one day I will see her again, perhaps performing somewhere. –

"So when Giovanni mentioned you to him, Paul smiled, he seemed to remember, and agreed to attend the performance."

"But what happened then? Why is he sick?"

The prosecco arrived with the appetizers, an Italian charcuterie with meats and cheese. Enough for a complete meal. Hot bruschetta with basil and chunks of fresh tomatoes and burrata slices. An Italian feast in Giselle's honor.

"I know that you are from the North, but I am sure that you would appreciate a little spiciness from the South!"

Laura spread a layer of velvety 'nduia[23] on the bruschetta and offered it to Giselle.

"This is imported straight from Italy! Do not ask how!"

Giselle was not hungry, and every crumble of energy was concentrated on Paul's life. It was as if their encounter had appended just the day before. She crunched a few bites of bruschetta and listened.

***

"Paul's story is unusual. His youth was not privileged like ours. You come from an upper-class family, living in one of the capitals of fashion and culture. You probably do not even know what poverty means."

Giselle did not interrupt; there was no point explaining to Laura that she very well knew firsthand what poverty meant.

"As for myself, I had all that a person can hope for, a supportive family, the best education, and all the frills one could ask for while growing up. But Paul's life is different. He is an orphan. He is the son of my mother's older sister. She was the family rebel and refused to marry a distant cousin. Rather, she got pregnant after an anonymous affair and ran away. Nobody knew what happened to her and the baby. Later, a nice Italian man from the Bronx named Arturo married her and adopted her son. But soon she disappeared again till she was found dead thousands of miles away. Paul retains only vague memories of his mother. He told me he remembers her voice that sounded supernatural, like the chimes of an angel.

The poor man raised Paul the best he could. Being totally unfamiliar with the concept of fatherhood and discipline, he raised Paul more as a pal than a son. So Paul never became acquainted with childhood. Instead of playing with toys, he would stand on a chair close to the sink at Turo's side to wash and dry the dishes. Paul became Turo's ambitious sous chef and learned to master techniques including the knuckle rest to protect the fingers from sharp knives. And if his eyes watered chopping onions, Turo would say, -

---

[23] Very spicy and spreadable sausage from Calabria

Come on, Paul! What is that! Don't you know? Real men are not supposed to cry even when they chop onions!

With Turo, Paul would go to the laundromat each weekend. Still standing on a chair, he pushed buttons at the cash register in Turo's store and listened to the ring, while the grandmothers, who had come to buy fresh dinner ingredients, praised him, and congratulated Arturo for benefitting from such great help. And they frequented a bar protected by a local mafia family, where Turo bought ice-cream for Paul while he poured sambuca in his coffee and exchanged intelligence with friends in Bronx-Italian slang. This educational method, though not recommendable from a pedagogic standpoint, created an indelible bond between the two, while giving Paul the illusion of being a pocket-sized man rather than a child.

Indeed, Arturo was a simple man content with a frugal life. They lived on modest means provided by a faltering business; a small convenience store at a corner of a street that could just about survive the competitive intrusion of chain markets. Prices had to be lowered to adjust to the competition, reducing the margins to centesimal proportions. Yet, several loyal clients continued to visit out of habit or even social obligation, and they paid when they could or deferred when they could not since Arturo had no notion of keeping track of the balance sheet.

Arturo was also a wannabe musician. So, most of his free time was spent playing in improvised and unpretentious bands. He and his friends would play in parks, street corners, bars, or nightclubs in the neighborhood. Since Arturo saw Paul as his mirror image, he taught him what he knew best. He purchased a secondhand violin for Paul's birthday and showed him how to move his fingers up and down the strings with one hand and holding the bow with the other. That was when Paul was four years old. Paul complied out of good nature, but soon developed affection for the instrument and the teacher. It felt that for the first time in his life he held something concrete in his hands. He was soon inducted into the band, which in turn attracted listeners, more amused by the presence of the sweet boy than by the music. Coins poured in the hat and were used by the jovial group to buy hot dogs, drinks for all, and ice-creams for the boy. In truth, that money was not needed for a carefree life rooted on simple necessities but it gave Paul the satisfaction of contributing to the family business. In the shabby nightclubs, Paul was adopted by dancers, singers, and strippers, beautiful women that reminded him of his mother's image as described by Turo. It made him wonder if any of them knew her.

So, for a few years, life proceeded without worries for the two comrades. But good things are not meant to last forever. As the business was failing, Arturo tried to find a paid job with the intent of selling the store. Yet he remarried instead. She was a Jewish immigrant from Eastern Europe. A tiny and pretty woman, who carried iron bones under a soft skin.

The carefree life soon dissipated. Paul was confronted with the preposterous concept that school is not about survival but excellence. He had started going to a public school because each day, before opening the store, Arturo would walk him there, holding his hand. Arturo also explained that this was what children are supposed to do and it seemed reasonable to try to learn something since one had to be there anyways. But learning was more about pleasing the teacher than for any long-term purpose. He was a decent student, liked by the teacher most of all because of his agreeable temperament. But when Naomi took control of the household, expectations soared. Even playing with the band depended upon performance. Good grades, one could play; bad grades, stay home and study.

It turned out Naomi was a well-educated pedagogue, who taught education to future teachers in her original country. For her, Paul, whatever title he held in the family's organizational chart, became, whether he liked it or not, her *de facto* son. To better appreciate the woman's mindset, I should tell you that she once had a son of her own, who would have been a little older than Paul but died of leukemia. Perhaps that was the cause of her migration from a forlorn past towards the New World.

Although, her credentials could have paved the way to become a teacher in New York, she thought it was better to fix her husband's business. Having a great deal of common sense, she came up with the stupendous idea that as a starter one may want to keep a balanced sheet, for example, requesting debtors to become solvent, independent of any personal relationships with Arturo, who with his leniency had accumulated more friends than he could afford. In addition, with her bones made of iron and despite her tiny figure, she could negotiate much better deals with vendors than Arturo could have ever dreamed of. She also promoted a differentiation strategy expanding the offerings of the convenience store to target ethnic preferences in an evolving neighborhood; nimble adjustments not easy to match by the bureaucracy of big corporations. In summary, with Arturo following her marching orders, and Paul helping behind the counter, it took little time for Naomi to turn the business profitable and even prosperous.

One day, Paul, in a peaceful moment spent with Arturo at the nearby park, asked:

"Turo, do you think it was a mistake to marry Naomi?"

To which Arturo replied:

"My dear Paul, I didn't do many things right in my life, and I made many mistakes. Therefore, marrying Naomi must be one of them. But if it is, it is the best mistake I have ever made!"

And then he asked: "Why did you ask? Don't you like her?"

"She is too bossy, not only with me but with you as well. She acts as if she is the man of the household, and we are a bunch of little girls. She also wants me to study more than I already do. But I do not want to. We were happy, we have all that we needed, what is the point of these changes? Don't they say, if it is not broken, don't fix it? The teachers are happy with me, and I pass my classes!"

"Yes, but there is more to life than just passing. Look at me. I barely finished high school and I am not for sure a beacon. Don't you want to be more ambitious than this? Do you want to spend your whole life in the Bronx like me? Don't you know that there is a bigger world out there?"

"What is wrong with your life, with our life? It is just fine. I can work in the shop, I love working there, and I can deliver the goods, I can take care of the displays, I can tell my friends to buy stuff at our place. And then in my free time, we can play as much as we want."

Who could argue with that? Why would one want to fix something that it was not broken? That argument resonated well with Arturo. . . but bore no chance with Naomi.

"Paul, life is bigger than the Bronx," she would say, "and you are a pensive boy. You must explore! Besides, trust me, education is not that daunting. Your teachers think highly of you, and they think that you could do much better if you just apply a little more ambition. They say that you are great at math. Come on, Paul, in your dreams, what would you like to be one day?"

"I want to become a musician" was Paul's first response, perhaps in retaliation to the anti-band curfews that, according to his account, he had to endure way too often.

"But this may not be very practical, it is difficult to make a living as a musician."

He didn't respond, so to honor Paul's answer to her original question and demonstrate appreciation for his effort, she continued:

"I tell you what, why don't we start with some music lessons then? This way we can test whether there is a future. And don't worry about tests or grades, take the lesson just for fun without any exams ahead!"

"But I already know how to play."

"That makes it easier, but still, it would not hurt to learn from a teacher."

As so it was that a few weeks later Naomi had movers carry a secondhand piano in very much need of tuning into the tiny living room.

***

In the beginning, Paul looked with suspicion at the piano, wondering how one could carry that mastodont into parks and streets. Soon, however, the instrument roused his curiosity. Teasing the keys, he discovered that it was out of tune. This observation, rather than displeasing, intrigued him. He was fascinated by the consonance implied by the ordered succession of intervals, chords, and scales and the dissonance resulting from the plentitude of wavelengths that lived in between; sounds discarded by the harmonic system that still thrived in the realm of nature. Paul envisioned the keys of the piano as rigid integers as opposed to the analog flexibility of the violin's nodes.

When the technician came to tune the piano, he followed each movement like a kitten tracking a moth across a window, pricking up the ears to the tuning fork. Since that mystic experience, Paul spent whatever time he was allowed listening to himself playing the piano and the violin in turns, circling analog vibrations around integers to better represent the continuum of nature's voices. This did not result in sloppiness but rather honed Paul's appreciation for tonal music with its melodies and harmonies, cognizant, at the same time, of deviations that belonged to the singing of birds, the whisper of the wind, the rumble of thunder and seas: experiences that could not be controlled but only imitated by scripts.

The piano became his battleground; ten fingers created infinite harmonies around a violin's melody turning him into the accidental conductor of an imaginary orchestra. When the teacher came equipped with books written in a foreign language and consisting of symbols rather than letters, Paul, who till then had played by ear, was introduced to the logic of music. He soon realized that music was the pleasurable interpretation of mathematical concepts, and compositions could be crafted through the exercise of the mind without need for instruments; this was Paul's encounter with composing. From then on, there was no more need for Naomi to motivate Paul; his ambition had taken off like a chick that has learned to fly.

Then, serendipity brought the final touch. It came from the basketball courts in the Bronx, where Black and Latino children hung out rain or shine. Like most tramps growing up in the Bronx, Paul boasted an athletic built and a confident attitude that prepared him for any competitive challenge. In the courts, he was good enough to be tolerated and even accepted by the street gangs, to the point that his Caucasian friends dubbed him "*El mestizo blanco.*"

There, Paul was introduced to hip hop music and culture. Though he did not think much of the stylized repetitiveness of rap, the environment attracted him, the mixture of physical and mental activity and the communion between a simple script and creative alliterations, discursive singing, and sportive dancing under the absolute governance of rhythm.

Among members of a gang, an older black boy maintained a special affection for Paul. Paul observed the boy staring at him much too often. Whenever their eyes met, the boy would smile, showing a bright row of white teeth. In the beginning Paul was unnerved and avoided interactions, but one day he confronted the older guy:

"Why do you stare at me all the time?"

The boy seemed embarrassed but, after recovering, he rebutted:

"I like you, man! I have seen you play in the park. I think you play the violin well! The fingers know the hell where to go; but the rhythm; the rhythm is what you need. You worry too much about the melody. . . but what gives life to music is rhythm. It looks, when you play, that you are walking on scorching charcoals rather swinging on a dance floor! What are you afraid of?"

Two gang members circled around them, while the boy continued:

"You should play with us." And turning to the newcomers:

"That's the chico in the park! The violin player. He plays the violin well and that could go well with my steelpans! We never tried that. Worth giving it a try. We can make it good."

Since Paul seemed hesitant, the boy reached out his hand:

"Hi, my name is Wayne, moved here a year ago from Jamaica. Nice to meet you."

It was a bond that lasted a lifetime; perhaps the only friend Paul ever had.

***

Dinner was served: grilled seabass dressed in fresh basil, a touch of virgin olive oil, roasted slices of garlic and arugula.

"I was unsure about how to fix a ballerina's diet. I assumed that you prefer light food during the performance season. I hope that you like it."

But Giselle was speechless. Every word originating from Laura's mouth resonated in her heart as if she was raised in the Bronx and had lived each moment of Paul's life.

Laura, recognizing Paul's intensity in Giselle's, smiled and, cutting the small talk, continued:

"But Wayne lived in his own world split from reality. Percussions of any kind or shape were the sole heartbeat of his planet; other facets of life did not exist. He could not keep his fingers still for a moment, or his hands and arms. He would drum on subway rails, take plastic bins to the park, and juggle self-made drumsticks while grocery shopping."

"Crazy Wayne," that's what they called him in the neighborhood. He was a legend, and everyone loved him because of his talent and sweet demeanor.

In the wake of Wayne's popularity, the two formed a band, "The Oriundos," that played at parties, bars, and later, clubs. The eleven-year-old Paul gave up the violin to take on electric guitar and keyboards, to become the band's mascot. He never became a virtuoso like Wayne and the other band members, but compensated with creativity. He composed in support of Wayne's mastery till his compositions took a life of their own and the Oriundos became recognized not only for technical talent but also originality. The band became popular in adjacent neighborhoods, and for the most part, colored communities.

Paul's success made him popular and established him as a weekend child prodigy. . . but in Naomi's eyes, "he remained a big fish. . . in a very small pond."

Therefore, toward the end of eighth grade, Naomi, reacting to the feedback of teachers and friends, and acknowledging Paul's potential, addressed the boy in front of Arturo:

"Paul, you told me years ago that you aspired to be a musician and you proved that you have the potential. Now is the time to fulfill your dream. I talked to Arturo, and he agrees with me.

"There is a prestigious high school in New York called Fiorello LaGuardia. It is for children gifted in math and music. Auditions will come soon. But—there is a but—you need to be a resident of New York City. I talked to your aunt, your mother's sister. She lives in Manhattan. They are a very wealthy, upper-class family. They would be happy to take you back into the family where you belong. . . . It is complicated, Paul, but you have never been formally adopted. Arturo never thought about it before or after your mother died. Neither did I. We took it for granted that you were our son. Technically, you are an orphan, and you are up for adoption. Here is a wealthy family related to your mother willing to take you. You can live with them during the week and return home on weekends. Nothing will change; this is the chance of your life."

"But what about you? Who is going to help out in the shop?"

"Do not worry about us, we will be here as usual, happy to know that you have a better home. We will be here waiting for you. And the business is doing well. We can pay for your studies."

This is how an estranged cousin became my stepbrother. I was four years old then, about ten years younger than Paul, yet I remember the day I met him as if it were yesterday.

He came with Arturo and Naomi; it was an awkward spectacle. They came dressed for a wedding: dark suit and tie for both Arturo and Paul, dark silk blouse and high heeled shoes for Naomi, who held a tight grip on her purse with gloved hands, demoting her looks to that of a grandma's.

Paul sat still at the far corner of the living room couch, stiff like a marionet. He was pale and his face was rigid. His neck did not turn but he rolled his eyes to explore the surroundings. Then, when he noticed me, he relaxed, turned toward me, and smiled. I fell in love with him on the spot, if it is appropriate to use such a term for a four-year-old. I will never forget the contrast between his weary expression before and his smile, like a sunray in an overcast day.

Words of support were offered by my parents, who tried to make the humble couple comfortable.

According to my mom, Naomi, being the practical lady, insisted on covering the costs of schooling and boarding. She proudly explained that the family business was doing very well, and they saved plenty of money to be used for Paul's education. They were just thankful for the hospitality at a suitable location.

My mom recollected that my dad was about to decline any support; they could have easily taken care of Paul's needs, but she squeezed his shoulder. She did not want to humiliate the foster parents. They had earned the right to take care of the boy as much as they could afford. If needed, of course, they could always help.

When Arturo's eyes watered and became too red to hide, my mom smiled and said:

"Your Paul will always be your Paul; we are just happy to help."

***

Paul flew through the audition, his theoretical skills were fine, and his musical talent way above expectations. He could play several instruments with proficiency, understand and discuss different styles of music, interpret and perform unfamiliar pieces after taking a perfunctory glance at a script, and the compositions crafted for the Oriundos denoted a gift for creativity that could benefit from formal teachings. It was obvious that the boy bore a natural talent.

So, Paul lived a parallel life as a model highschooler during the week and a street player during the weekends.

***

"Are you okay?"

Laura hesitated, interrupting her narrative. She saw tears in Giselle's eyes.

"Is everything okay?"

Giselle dried her eyes with the paper napkin and nodded with a subliminal smile.

"Yes, I am fine. It just feels strange. I feel like I lived each moment as if you were recounting my life rather than Paul's. I am an orphan too. Federico and Maria adopted me. I lived all my life as a guest. My adoptive parents are wonderful to me, but. . . it is difficult to explain; it is difficult to explain how it feels to have never known your own parents; one always longs for acceptance, like an immigrant feels in a foreign country. I remember looking into Paul's eyes on the day we met. It may be my imagination, but in those brief moments, we read into each other eyes, just in a glance, our untold story.

But please, don't mind me; go ahead."

High school was the best in Paul's life—and mine. I had the big brother I had never even hoped for. Perhaps because of his experience with Turo, Paul treated me as a peer rather than a little sister. Whenever he could, he would take me with him. During the weekends, I frequented his modest place in the Bronx, had quasi-Kosher dinners mixed with linguini, salami, and prosciutto. Naomi made Matza ball soup, which was my favorite, and introduced me to gefilte fish. I was the only one who shared enthusiasm for it, while both Turo and Paul developed undiagnosable abdominal irritations on such occasions that prevented them from eating. And I followed the band to performances in parks and clubs, Turo and Naomi accompanying me. Once, Turo told me:

"Figure, we thought that we were going to lose a son, instead we gained a daughter."

The Oriundos elected me as their mascot and taught me how to sing. I sang in the streets or square concerts, just one song to warm up the audience, while Wayne smiled at me and winked at the pace of the rhythm. He would nod his head before each measure to prime me. He then taught me how to play the drums, or at least he tried with the patience of an angel.

Those were magic years. Then, Paul's graduation day came, and my parents organized a party at the Empire State Building. Paul was very emotional in the preceding days.

I remember that I was sitting on his lap in Central Park, and I asked:

"Why are you sad? Aren't you happy that school is over?"

"You know, Lauretta, I must tell you a secret: I am not a good person. My mom died because of me. One day, a long time ago, I threw a big temper tantrum, making her very upset. In the end she said: 'If you continue to be such a brat, I will leave you.' And so she did. The next day she disappeared for good, and sometime later they found her dead. Now I wonder if she would be proud of me, but I will never know."

I was only eight years old then. I did not know how to react, and I just cried:

"No, Paul, you are not bad, you are my big brother. You are the best brother that a sister could have!"

I felt embarrassed for crying.

"Come on, come on, Lauretta, don't cry," said Paul. And I resented being treated like a little girl. So, I rebutted:

"Why don't you cry, if you really miss your mom?"

To which Paul replied with a rare smile:

"Because, as Turo says, real men are not supposed to cry even when they chop onions!"

You cannot imagine how many times I reflected over that moment; how many child psychologists I consulted. None of them believes that Paul's recollection is accurate. It is only a subconscious reflection of guilt. I talked to Paul about it so many times to console him. But he is stubborn, and he swears in earnest that this is what happened, and that he is the cause of his mother's death. A burden that he has been carrying all his life and has shared only with me.

But going back to that fateful day in Central Park. . . Paul continued:

"You know, I am also selfish: I never acknowledged all that Naomi did for me. I never thanked her for taking me under her wing as her own son and for

standing by me day after day. Instead, I only resented her for bossing me and Turo around. I have been so self-centered. But I am looking forward to recognizing her and everyone else for the help that turned me into what I am. I prepared a speech for the party. Do you want me to read it to you?"

***

But the party never happened. . .

The night before graduation, Naomi and Arturo were crossing the Washington Bridge towards Manhattan when a truck deviated from its lane, flipped, rolled over, and smashed them. Paul did not have a chance to thank Naomi, and that regret sculpted his life.

***

After graduation, my relationship with Paul faded. He rarely came home from college. Then, my parents chose to repatriate in Villaricca, near Naples, where, in our absence, properties had been tended to by loyal managers, farmers, and ranchers harvesting exotic fruits, making delicious wines, and raising water buffalos to produce mozzarella. My parents wished to raise me according to our culture.

After the move, letters from Paul also lessened till they ended altogether, save for the customary greeting cards around the holidays. We invited him several times for a visit, but he never seemed to find the time. Preoccupied by the vicissitudes of teenagerhood, I then forgot about him.

Then, I was accepted at Cornell University for graduate school. My parents encouraged me to return to New York to complete my education now that they were confident in my devotion to our ancestry. I returned to this apartment, where we are dining now, which is also where Paul grew up. That is his piano! My parents used the apartment for occasional visits to America to check on our business here and kept everything unaltered and pristine.

When I entered the apartment after so many years, everything came back as vivid as when I left, and with it, Paul's ghost returned. Nothing had changed, including my little girl's room. So was Paul's room with the pictures of us and his friends playing around in the Bronx.

In New York, I had the impulse to reach out to Paul, but I had no idea where he was and feared his reaction. I dreaded a rejection; I could not bear the

110

thought of him not caring about me anymore. Also, I was busy enough developing new acquaintances at Cornell.

I kept postponing till one day I saw Paul's photo on the front page of the newspaper. It was a good picture, where he appeared just as I remembered him; my handsome lowkey stepbrother, with his typical stern and inquisitive demeanor.

The article mentioned a premiere at Carnegie Hall, just two blocks from here.

With my heart throbbing, I texted his old phone number:

"Hi Paul, this is Lauretta! Do you still remember me? I am in New York. Moved here a few months ago for graduate school. I just saw your picture in the newspaper."

I sent it without expecting a response. And yet, after a few seconds:

"My Lauretta! Of course, I remember you. I missed you. Where are you? I want to see you."

And so, that evening the doorbell rang and Paul was back home after fifteen years. He had cancelled all commitments and yet he sat in front of me in this terrace, right where you are sitting now.

We talked about my troubled teenage experiences, my failed marriage that lasted only a year, my decision to come back to America to further my education and start a new life. He recounted his experiences in college and graduate school. He flew through classes and by graduation he was well-known in music circles. Hollywood noticed him first and he was contracted to compose music for shows, documentaries, and movies. This is how he met Jerry, who became his lifetime agent.

With that head start, he was noticed by other circles and his compositions were acclaimed, recorded, and choreographed across the country.

After hours, he dwelled and thrived in Wayne's honky-tonk world. When school allowed, he joined Wayne to New Orleans where they lived in the French Quarters absorbing the subtleties of jazz, or Nashville, at Lower Broadway, and the Grand Ole Opry. There, Wayne's band had broken in with a combination of country and rock 'n' roll music. They made many friends.

While Paul never achieved the technical aptitude to perform at that level as an instrumentalist, his compositions made it. Paul and Wayne dwelled in rock 'n' roll in Memphis, and lived in Austin, and Motown, and Chicago. But the sweetest was the Bronx, where they returned to play in bars and nightclubs. By the end of graduate school, Paul was well-known for classical and modern composition while Wayne, without receiving formal training, had become, with his band, the hitter that we all know.

Later, Paul and Wayne decided to move to Paul's old apartment in the Bronx. Paul bought the entire building, remodeled it, and created two upper apartments for him and for Wayne. At the lower level were servants and security guards. Everyone knew them in the neighborhood and tolerated the noise and eccentricity that occurred behind those walls with pride.

Life was active with people going in and out. Among the frequenters, beautiful strippers were hosted. Wayne enjoyed women and the temporary entertainment that casual relationships can offer. For Paul, it was different. He was interested in their stories, their dreams and disappointments, their philosophy. He was searching for his mother's story through their smiles, sighs, and tears.

But their relationship had faults. Whether because of his mother, or Naomi, or organic depression, Paul lived at the boundaries of angst, in the twilight of dejection. What drove his music to greatness were the pains of his heart. Even music was a distraction to alleviate his solitude. When composing was insufficient to mitigate the angst, binges with Wayne sufficed. Crazy Wayne lived to enjoy life, beating his drums till he was tired and turning into women, alcohol, and drugs afterwards. That influence caused Paul's dependence on an alternate life. What was fun for Wayne, became for Paul a necessity to quench a vague and rootless sense of guilt.

He also had no romantic relationships, only casual encounters tainted by the fear of disappointing them. In each woman he saw his mother, or Naomi. Both asking him: "Why didn't you care for me when I was alive?"

He told me:

"Truth is, love doesn't sound like the wind going through reed pipes. It sounds like the dullness of an empty tin can drifting down the street at the flightiness of winds."

***

That evening, after spending hours exchanging the stories of our lives, Paul slept over. If he were a kitten, he would have purred all night. He fell asleep with his *head on my chest as if we were children again. Since then, Paul returned often and unannounced. He took me for granted and I let him because I knew that I was all that he had. I gave him the keys to the apartment, but he always rang at the doorbell. Never used the keys.*

I helped him but not enough. His self-destruction continued. The greater his success, the more detached he was from it and the more he resented it, the deeper he retreated into a solitary life with Wayne in the Bronx. He resented his agent, Jerry, a scrawny guy, who talked too much, could not complete a sentence because he nervously laughed at his own words before he could deliver a punchline, which made no one laugh. You can imagine, knowing Paul, how much that behavior irritated him. He would say about Jerry:

"Why can't Jerry be normal? Why does he have to piss in his pants when he talks to me? Do I look like a freak?"

Despite the wealth, they lived in the old building from which each morning Paul could look down through the window at the shop across the intersection, expecting to see Turo and Naomi open to the customers.

About three months before your performance, Wayne died of an overdose. Paul found him lying in the living room, with eyes wide open and a drumstick in his hand. Paul recollected the warnings from his friend's therapist:

"You've got to do something!"

But he had done nothing. Once again, he felt he had failed his loved ones through his negligence.

Within a few days Paul sold the building of his youth to the first offer and moved to California, to a small community on the Pacific Coast just South of San Francisco, called El Granada, where the foghorn cries every eight seconds, and the sealions complete the melody. Years before, he had bought a home in El Granada with a view of Pillar Point Harbor. It was a retreat where he and Wayne dwelled at the Dynamite Society in Mirámar and other similar clubs. Paul loved the Ocean front, the power of the winds that silenced the pain of the soul. A lowkey community, a mixture of farmers, fishermen, hippies, and Silicon Valley nerds.

Three days before your performance I received a call from Stanford Hospital:

"Are you Laura? Paul recorded you as emergency contact! He is in the ICU, unconscious. Just needed to let you know."

113

"What happened?"

"He was found unconscious in his home by his agent; it could have been a suicide attempt with benzodiazepines. It must have just happened. The paramedic resuscitated him and with a gastric lavage and respiratory support he should be fine. The EEG is active, but consciousness has not returned. We must wait and see."

By the time I arrived in California and went to the hospital, Paul was recovering. He denied the suicide intent but agreed to suicide watch.

Jerry had saved his life. The night before the accident, Jerry was distraught by a conversation they had. Paul was drunk, his speech was slurred, his words made no sense except for the recurring theme that life was not worth a penny.

"Sell Wayne's and my copyrights and use the money for the homeless," he told Jerry before hanging up.

So, Jerry jumped on the first flight from New York to San Francisco and, when he opened the door in El Granada, found Paul lying, barely breathing on the couch of the living room.

I asked Paul:

"Did you thank Jerry for saving your life? If it wasn't for his devotion, you would probably be dead now."

"Yup! And he would have to find another client!" answered Paul.

As much as I adore him, I was really upset by the cynical remark, and I could not control myself.

"Paul, Jerry cares about you, he has been taking care of you and Wayne for years. He is the reason you have a stable income and you have not squandered your fortune. He protected both of your baffled souls. Jerry loves you. Your cynicism is totally inappropriate."

Paul looked at me with astounded eyes. Then to justify, he said:

"Sorry, it was just a joke."

"Yes, but it was not funny!"

"Well, Jerry would probably laugh!"

"Paul. . . " I continued. "You can destroy yourself, kill yourself, if this is what you wish, but that is not going to change what happened to your mother, Naomi, or Wayne. If you want to make amends, think of those who love you now. Do not disappoint more of us. We are asking nothing more than for you to be happy. You have all that a man could have, talent, money, and a most interesting soul. Your regrets are unfounded. You did not do anything terrible to anyone. Yes, you could have done better. We all could have done better. Myself too, with my marriage, with my friends, my parents. But this is all in the past. It is the future that counts. Here, is your opportunity to make amends. Stop that worthless machoism, that senseless, contrived, and unproductive self-pity. Get back to real life. Accept that there is nothing wrong with saying "Thank you" to those who love you. There is nothing wrong with crying whether you are chopping onions or not."

***

"For this reason, Paul could not come to your performance. Yet, as I was about to leave his hospital room to go back to New York, he called, 'Lauretta, please tell that young woman that I am sorry for not being able to make the premiere.' See? He remembered and cared for you!

"And now you know Paul's story. I made it as short as I could. Are you sure you still care for him now that you know what you are getting into?"

And Giselle replied without hesitation:

"I love him. Even more now than before. I feel Paul inside of me. I understand his soul."

"Then, let's give him a call!"

***

"Paul? How are you? You sound good! Are you home? I have an admirer of yours sitting in front of me, at your place. It is Giselle, the ballerina! She is so great but, even more important, she is so nice! She is a Broadway star just like you! Do you want to say hi to her?"

The phone was passed to Giselle's shaking hand.

"Hi, Paul. I am Giselle, the girl you met in the cafeteria in Milan. I know that you will not remember but I want you to know that in those few moments you shaped my life."

But Paul said:

"Giselle, I remember you. I remember your name, and I remember your eyes and I remember that you wanted to be like me, and I remember that I told you that I wanted you to be better than me! Now you are! I heard about you and not only from my cousin. You are making history and I thank you for liking my music. Maybe, one day, when I am better, we could see each other again, if you would like."

"I would very much like it."

***

By the end of the narrative, dinner was over, darkness had descended on the park and the two ladies looked at each other while enjoying a glass of Amaretto di Saronno.

The night was getting old, their emotions had taken a toll, and Giselle accepted the offer to sleep over at Laura's place. Laura made her sleep in Paul's room.

As she laid down in Paul's bed, she hugged his pillow that destiny had preserved for her. She recollected the chain of events from the day she met Paul till this unforgettable evening when she spoke to him again. All seemed natural and logical. Everything was predetermined since the day of her birth. Someone had been watching them both from a distance.

SERENDIPITY

"Mustikka."

Paul searched the dictionary.

Bilberries! That's the English translation. . . not to be confused with blueberries. ...*Vaccinium myrtillus*, also known as European blueberries (though they aren't blue at all! In fact, they are yellow). That doesn't help either. . . . What about this—it is a Finnish fruit called mustikka. In other words, mustikka was what was in front of his nose, and the only way to deepen one's knowledge was to buy a basket and taste them.

It was summer in Helsinki. The days were long, the nights short, and anticipation pervaded the atmosphere, lulled by a temperate breeze, softened by the cordiality of people, and cheered by the mewing of seagulls. An orderly mix of locals and tourists enlivened Market Square. Among them was Paul. He was a different person from the one we left in the previous chapter. His brain was clearer, his anxieties controlled, his soul content and appreciative.

The catharsis is credited to Laura. He had never been scolded before. Turo was a pal; nothing Paul could do to displease his adoptive father. Naomi was a strong-minded woman, who never raised her voice but entrapped Paul's mind within the intricacies of logic—a Socratic awakening that demanded her presence and vanished with her departure. His second generation of adoptive parents had also been supportive, never questioning Paul's whims.

For the first time, Lauretta had confronted his emotions with a stern and direct reprimand. Whatever Paul hid under the rug of the subconscious, was uncovered once and forever. She made it clear: he had to move on. It did not help anyone, dead or alive, to dwell in regrets and self-commiseration as Paul's essence went beyond that of the lonely character dwelling in the darkness of his living room. He was a much bigger person, part of a greater community of friends, acquaintances, and fans, who cared and cheered for him and deserved appreciation:

"*It is time, to give the future a chance; life is not meant to be perfect, but it is worth living to the best of one's capabilities,*" she concluded.

And so he did; buying the mustikka and wandering carefree through the colorful stands served as the assertion of a new life.

Jerry and his boyfriend, who was from Finland, had organized the trip for Paul. They encouraged him to experience the limpid beauty of the Northern summer, among peaceful and refined people living manageable lifestyles across the majestic harmony of forests and lakes.

The tour minimized scheduled activities and encouraged introspection. A few local acquaintances were recruited to check on him when necessary and offer guidance, but most of the time was left for him to explore.

Among planned events, however, a soiree was to be performed at the Musiikkitalo, featuring a ballet based on Paul's music. Paul was used to performances of his work and would not have considered attending if it wasn't for Jerry's insistence:

"The music hall is beautiful! A Finnish architectural landmark! Great acoustics! Great orchestra. You cannot miss it!"

We will never know whether it was genuine serendipity to twist destiny's arm or (more likely) the result of Jerry's and Laura's plot.

To distract himself from the cacophony of the tuning and noodling of the orchestra, Paul scanned the libretto while waiting for the curtains to rise. In it, he discovered Giselle's picture that introduced her as the guest principal dancer. In this performing version, she looked quite different from his recollection and not as attractive. She was missing the freshness that had enchanted him. Her expression was stiff, trapped by eyeliners, lipliners, lipsticks, blushes, shadows, and glitter; she looked more like a Venetian mask than a human being.

Yet, when the ballet began, she was enchanting, and Paul forgot about everything else. One had to admit that, as a dancer, she was perfect. But other thoughts distracted him. He could not separate the performer from the girl, who looked straight into his eyes in the cafeteria of Milan.

Her voice echoed:

"I want to become a principal ballerina. . . I will do what you say. . . I will work hard so one day I shall be as great as you are!"

And here she was! She had delivered on an unreasonable promise. It was as if Giselle had leaped on the table of the cafeteria to perform just for him and prove that perseverance can overcome any obstacle.

He recollected his original skepticism and how Giselle's naive determination had erased any doubt. And he remembered those eyes looking straight into his for a few unforgettable seconds to establish an indelible bond. For years, in peaceful moments, those eyes resurfaced unprompted, and he marveled at the meaning of the apparition, incapable of wiping it away. It had been a recurrent remembrance that claimed no further action, at least till now, when here she was, in front of him, flesh and blood.

"How did she foresee something that not even the Devil could have guessed?"

***

After the show, Paul was escorted to the reception in honor of the performers. First thing he saw as he entered was Giselle. The make-up was gone, her face was natural, and her hair freed from the grease and the tight braids. That was his Giselle, the one he remembered! She was smiling, shaking hands, and listening with grace to praises. Then, she turned and saw him. She did not seem surprised but, with a candid and welcoming smile, acknowledged his presence as if she had been waiting for him. As he approached, she said:

"Paul! Are you the Paul, whom I longed to reencounter for years?"

Everything vanished; not just the guests at the party, but the people of Helsinki, and those of Finland, and the rest of Europe, and those of Earth.

The universe had collapsed around Paul and Giselle, who in tidal lock were spinning around each other.

Paul felt obliged to ask Giselle for a dance. She graciously accepted. But Paul was a clumsy dancer, and he resented each step. Besides, how can one stand up to a prima ballerina? After stepping on Giselle's toes a few times, at the zenith of embarrassment, he muttered:

"Giselle, I really hate to dance. I am sorry."

To which Giselle answered with a mischievous smile:

"Me too, I hate dancing. Why would anyone assume that I would care to dance?"

What a sweet and elegant liar, that Giselle! But how could one blame her? She was finally, after so many years, in the arms of her beloved. That was all she had yearned for. Dance had only been a conduit to him.

So, they walked to the buffet to grab few delicacies and sat on a sofa. They talked all evening. Giselle knew much about Paul's life thanks to Laura and the tabloids, while he knew little of hers. So, he listened to discover their similarities; from the humble village with Grandma, her chicken, and Uncle Borysko, and the fiddler with the tapping foot, to the metamorphosis into a life of privilege and opportunity with her adoptive parents, the good-natured Professor Federico and the logical Signora Maria. It was a déjà vécu reminiscent of the humble life in the Bronx with Turo and Naomi and the twist of fate that brought him to the embrace of wealthy relatives that gave him the opportunity of a lifetime. And how heartwarming it was to hear about the omnipresent Lori, who raised Giselle as a daughter; and Madame Petrova and the Maestro, who orchestrated their reunion. In retrospect, it seemed a natural progression imposed by destiny over uncontrollable chances, like the foreordained flow of water that docilely follows gravity along creeks and riverbeds till it reaches, from its birthplace, the sea.

Then Giselle recollected their encounter. The rendering was pure and honest. She had no qualms describing her first impression as she had confided to others many times before.

"I felt that when our eyes stared into each other's, an eternal bond was established, a marvel had occurred, and my destiny was locked into yours for better and for worse. I could not forget the way you treated me like a grown up and encouraged me. I wanted to see you again to complete a conversation prematurely interrupted. And now I am here, in front of you despite all odds! I know what happened to you. Laura told me everything, and I am glad that you feel better. I always knew that I would see you again, but I did not expect that to happen tonight."

"Me too. I think it was Laura's and Jerry's scheme. You know, I wanted to see you again. Two weeks ago, I was in New York, and I asked Laura about you. Now I recall her impish smile when she said she didn't know where you were and encouraged me instead to take the vacation in Finland following Jerry's suggestion. I understand now that she had better plans. I guess she thought it preferable to surprise the two of us." And then he continued:

"You know, I remember our meeting too, though so many years have passed. I just could not forget your eyes and I always wondered why."

***

As guests began to depart, Giselle shook a few hands with admirers to compensate for the evening-long egotism.

A flamboyant young man dressed like a butler stepped in front of Paul to congratulate Giselle:

"Your dancing makes Vincente's music look better than it sounds!"

In response to the trite comment, Giselle was about to introduce the stranger to Paul, but the latter, interrupted:

"I agree completely; that is what I have been thinking all night."

And, squeezing Giselle's arm, he bade goodnight to everyone and encouraged her to follow.

They walked into the endless sunset. Giselle intertwined her hand with his. He responded by squeezing hers. He reckoned that he had never held hands before, not his mother's, Naomi's, nor any woman afterwards. He thought of the kind Lauretta and how close they were. Yet, they never held hands. He never thought of it. And now, walking with someone, who was just a little more than a stranger, he felt his heart pumping blood into his brain in response to such a simple gesture.

They sat on a bench at the waterfront as the sunset dragged into the night. The conversation languished under the first stars that timidly peeked in the twilight.

He reckoned that he was attracted to Giselle. She was the perfect depiction of beauty. He felt an urge to kiss her but hesitated. All-previous interactions had been with experienced women, who do not care for corny preambles. But Giselle was different. She kept staring at him, with naïve and trusting eyes, and he felt hesitant like a kitten learning the hunt, teasing the mouse with its paws, or pushing it around, holding it into the mouth without hurting it to let it go, incapable of the kill. He did not know where to start.

In the end, Paul kissed Giselle on the cheek.

The kiss was well received and from the cheek, Paul's lips proceeded toward her mouth. It was a breathtaking moment when their lips touched and for a few eternal moments Paul forgot to breathe. An attempt to a French kiss followed. Giselle reciprocated but, unaccustomed to it, twisted and twirled her tongue against Paul's with the energy of a food processor whipping a bowl of cream. That distracted Paul:

"Why are you doing this? Why are you moving your tongue so hard?"

"I don't know, isn't it how one is supposed to kiss? Isn't it what they do in the movies?"

"I do not know; I think it is too much work. We can just kiss touching the lips and stroking each other's tongue. I think it is more natural. But it is okay if you prefer this way."

It was obvious, that the two lived in different planets when it came to romance. Nevertheless, being both quick learners, after a few kisses, they reached a compromise, the mood relaxed, and the magic returned.

Then, Giselle began to shake. She clinched on Paul and thrust her head under his armpit till the shaking ended.

Paul asked:

"Are you okay?"

"I think so," she replied, and then she added:

"I think I just had an orgasm."

Paul did not know how to react to such an unusual predicament and, therefore, kept silent. So, Giselle asked:

"Do other women have orgasms when they sit close to you?"

Paul thought it over and could not think of any previous instance.

"I don't know, not that they would tell me, I guess."

"Is it a bad thing?" asked Giselle.

"Probably not, I guess. Certainly, it is not illegal. . . at least in the US." And then he pondered: "I do not know about Finland though."

The conversation stalled again. Paul was at a loss. Giselle was stirring too many emotions for which he was unprepared. The only resort was to hold her tight against him.

After a while, Giselle began to shake again, this time without provocatory kisses.

Worried, Paul asked:

"What now? Are you having another orgasm?"

"No, I am just cold."

In fact, a breeze was rising, and the feathers of a bystander pelican, that was looking at them with contempt, were ruffled.

Paul put his jacket on Giselle and offered to escort her back to the hotel.

They held hands till they arrived.

As Paul was about to wish her good night, he heard himself saying instead:

"Do you want to spend the night together?"

To which Giselle responded:

"I was hoping you would ask."

So, Paul took Giselle's hand again and they proceeded to his hotel, just a few blocks away.

One may ask, why didn't they stay at Giselle's place? It is difficult to say. Perhaps, Paul did not think about it. Perhaps it was most practical to offer rather than receive hospitality. For Giselle, it did not matter, she had

decided that in any case she would follow Paul wherever he asked her to go.
. . and not only for that night, but for the rest of her life.

***

In the hotel room, Giselle realized she was still in party attire without any night garments. That did not matter. She went to the bathroom, took a quick shower, undressed, and appeared in front of Paul, topless. Raising the sheets, she joined him. Paul had not thought till then of Giselle's physical appearance beyond the enchantment with her eyes and smile, but when he confronted up close her majestic beauty, he had to gulp down a generous portion of saliva.

Paul embraced her and drew her close, hugged and kissed her. Gently, he caressed her shoulders and flanks, till his impertinent hand reached her breast.

Giselle, who till then had been passive and receptive, started to moan and her body began a delicate rocking motion. She tightly hugged Paul till, suddenly, she jumped out of bed.

"I can't do this; I am losing control." And she went to the bathroom.

When she came out, she was dressed.

"Paul, I want to go back to my hotel. I cannot do this."

"What did I do wrong, Giselle? I am sorry."

"Nothing, you did nothing wrong. It is just me. Let me go, for tonight, please."

Paul rose, hugged her, and gave her a kiss on the forehead.

As soon as Giselle was gone, Paul panicked.

"I can't let her go back by herself in the middle of the night!"

He put his clothes on and jumped in the elevator to catch her.

At the lobby, as the elevator door opened, Paul found Giselle in front of him. Behind, and unseen by Giselle, a stern Russian-looking lady was also waiting for the elevator.

Paul looked at Giselle with an inquisitive expression.

"Paul, I am a virgin, I do not know how to make love," stated Giselle.

Paul looked at her and at the lady, who maintained an impassive expression. It seemed obvious that the latter either did not speak English or was deaf.

"That's okay, Giselle! Nobody is perfect and there are worse things in life. I can teach you sometime. Come up and let's go to sleep. I am glad that you waited for me, I was going to walk you to your hotel, but it will be so much nicer to be together. We do not have to make love."

Both Giselle and the lady entered the elevator. Giselle held Paul's hand while the lady maintained the stern expression of a general at a parade. The elevator door opened at a lower floor to let the lady out. Upon exiting, the lady turned around and, with a naughty smile, she stated in perfect English:

"I wish a most delightful night to both of you."

Back in the room, undressed again, they laid close to each other. Paul, now ready to sleep, said:

"Good night, Giselle, I am glad that you are back."

With his eyes closed and about to drift into Hypnos's arms, Paul felt Giselle's hand caressing his chest and slowly moving toward a man's area that she had never explored before. This had a predictable effect on the target within the region of interest.

"Paul."

"Yes?"

"I want you to make love to me."

By then Paul had made up his mind that at least for that night nothing was going to happen. He was not going to take advantage of an inexperienced virgin, on a one-night stand. As they say, if they are roses, they will bloom at the right time. But for tonight, nothing was going to happen. According to Jerry's coaching, he was not going to take any risk! Besides, it would be unfair to Giselle. She was too naïve and inexperienced. She needed more time to mature from the remnants of a young girl's infatuation into the resolve of a woman.

And we must admire Paul for this noble resolution that persisted for at least thirty seconds, perhaps even a minute, before he found himself on top of Giselle.

Not knowing how to deal with a virgin (who is a virgin nowadays?), he proceeded as delicately as he could till Giselle seemed comfortable and pleased.

It did not take much for Giselle to respond with passionate groans to his moves, and that embrace, that passionate welcome, made Paul appreciate for the first time the difference between sex and love. He was not performing to please someone, he enjoyed every moment, because he was happy to hold Giselle, who, abandoned into his arms, was asking nothing more than to be loved.

Passion does not know control. Soon Giselle was moaning and screaming to the point that Paul worried about the neighbors! And that thought brought him to the general in the elevator and he burst out laughing. Giselle opened her eyes and asked:

"Why are you laughing? Am I doing something wrong?"

"I am so happy, and I was also thinking of the woman in the elevator. You remember her? The one that looked like a cop. I wonder what she would think if she could hear us. I imagined her giving the thumbs up and that image made me laugh."

Paul's laugh was contagious, and Giselle could not refrain from laughing as well. They laughed till their bellies hurt. Tired of laughing, they returned to the original occupation till, after a few more orgasms, Giselle announced that she was sore. Therefore, Paul laid down, enveloped her in his arms, brought her close to him, her head over his chest, and as he was about to whisper good night, he heard a soft and rhythmic murmur out of Giselle's mouth that made the wish superfluous.

Paul closed the eyes and prepared to sleep, caressing Giselle's shoulder. It did not take much to fall into a light sleep, where he found himself holding Giselle at some oceanfront. But as he was about to kiss her, he noticed that Naomi was in his arms instead and she was shaking her head. As he was about to explain, Naomi turned into Jerry. And Paul was now sitting across the desk in Jerry's office. Jerry, as when he was trying to contain his anger, stood up and walked to the samovar to fetch hot water for the green tea. Restoring some control by holding the teacup, he clinched his jaw before exploding:

"How can you do this? Taking a virgin in your hotel room after a party? And a colleague, just for a one-night stand? A fling? Are you crazy? And she had wine at the party, you know that aggravates the facts."

"I did not initiate anything," replied Paul in the dream. "She is the one, who stalked me for years, she is the one who touched my hand first. She did not refuse to be kissed! In fact, she even had an orgasm! And when I suggested we spend the night together, she said that she had hoped I would ask! And she is the one who asked me to make love to her!"

"Nice story, but who is going to believe it?" asked the least welcome of the intruders in Paul's dream.

Paul woke up in angst, but, as he heard Giselle's rhythmic snore, relaxed, and recollecting Turo's assertion about Naomi, he thought:

"If it was a mistake, it was the best mistake of my life" and he squeezed Giselle even closer.

Then another thought intervened:

"She is just too young and immature for me. I cannot be bound to a young woman. God knows what she is expecting: children, grandchildren, pets, cats, dogs, maybe even a parrot or a fish tank, and God knows what more. I am the mature one with common sense. This went too far, and I must stop it before it gets out of control."

Therefore, Paul conceived the dumbest idea that a man could consider after spending a night with a woman:

"Tomorrow morning, I will apologize. I will ask for forgiveness. It was just an impulse because she is so attractive, but it did not mean anything serious or permanent. Just a fling, a one-night stand. A beautiful memory for both of us before moving on. A way for her to grow into a mature woman."

Maybe it was exhaustion, maybe reassurance offered by this most unreasonable thought, but relieved, Paul was ready to sleep. He held Giselle tightly one more time, as he did with his beloved violin as a child, to be sure not to lose it. Then, he joined Giselle in an improvised yet remarkable snoring duetto.

***

Through the thick shades, Paul sensed that the sun was high in the sky.

Giselle was still sleeping in complete peace. He shook her gently to wake her up, but in response she yawned, open the eyes for a moment, then turned to the other side and continued to sleep just as contentedly.

After taking into serious consideration the details of the hotel room, from the humdrum art to the safety alarms, the sprinklers, and the reflection of skinny sunrays on the wall, Paul realized that he could not lay down any longer. Thus, he rose, went to the bathroom, washed his face, brushed his teeth, and returned to Giselle.

She was so beautiful even with the eyes closed. He was incredulous that he was staring to a causal acquaintance of a decade before. The young girl from another country, who shared with him an improbable dream. Yet, she was there now, in his bed, sleeping and trusting him as a puppy would with the master.

Since he did not want to wake her up but was too anxious to wait for her to wake, he wrote a note, left it on the bedside table, and walked out.

About half an hour later he returned, holding two cups of coffee.

Giselle was still sleeping but responded to his touch. She opened the eyes, looked at him, and, reassured that the evening before had been more than a dream, smiled. Then she jumped out of bed and went to the bathroom. Paul heard her fretting, washing her face, and brushing his teeth till she returned to sit with her back prompted against the head of the bed and smiled at him.

When she seemed settled and ready to listen, Paul started:

"Giselle; I did something impulsive that I should not have done. I hope that you will forgive me."

Giselle looked at him worried.

"While you were sleeping, I went down to the concierge, and I reserved an RV for us to drive around Finland for two weeks. I know that I should have asked you before, but I could not resist. We can go all the way up to where the day never ends, past the polar circle. Past the home of Santa Claus."

"Perfect! I cannot wait to go."

"But what about your company?"

"Do not worry. We have a summer break; in any case, I do not care. From today on, I will go wherever you want me to go for the rest of my life. Forget ballet and all else!"

Then Paul said:

"Giselle. . . I need to tell you something. . . I think. . . I mean. . . I just think. . . I am not sure, but I think. . . I think. . . that—"

After taking a deep breath:

"That. . . I love you. Last night was not just an impulse. I could not stop myself because I felt so happy being with you. I was happy for the first time in my life. In fact, before last night, I never knew what it meant to be happy."

Giselle smiled; tears fell from her eyes as she responded:

"I know, Paul, I always knew that you would love me. And I love you too. . . and I am sure of it."

***

They went to places they never imagined. Through the crystal-clear air, they drove along deserted and dusty roads that flanked glittering blue lakes. They picked wild mushrooms visible from the roadside to make risotto. On other evenings, locals offered hospitality. To Paul's and Giselle's relief, most did not recognize who they were, and were kind to them. They shared simple dinners serving fish caught in one of the thousand lakes. They rented cabins, where they could enjoy the sauna experience.

As they progressed north, they observed crossing signs with a moose icon, but not a single moose was ever to be seen. Perhaps they were remnants of an ancient civilization meant to protect an extinct species. Perhaps one might consider mammoth signs along the roads of North America to warn the traveler against the possibility that one of them would suddenly wake up from thousands of years of hibernation and decide to cross the road.

And they drove through the wilderness.

Their first encounter with a reindeer was remarkable. They had stopped for the night, rented a cabin, and took a walk along the lake. There, at the border of a meadow, they saw the reindeer grazing in peace. Paul, recollecting boy scout experiences as a trapper, to impress Giselle, decided to demonstrate how to stalk a wild beast; with stealth and against the wind to dissipate the human scent, armed with a zoomed camera, step by step, he proceeded with caution, followed by Giselle's graceful movements. As they approached, he took innumerable pictures to catch the reindeer before it could run away. But partly because of his talent, partly because the reindeer must have had more pressing things to worry about than indiscreet tourists, soon they found themselves with the camera stuck to the nose of the reindeer, which was looking at them with measured interest.

Judging that they had taken enough pictures of a retarded or handicapped beast, Paul turned around, followed by Giselle and by the reindeer, that had developed a special affection for the clueless couple. When they returned to the cabin, the reindeer stood there waiting, till Giselle had the bright idea of fetching an apple and offering it to the animal. That pleased the wild beast very much and afterwards it continued her grazing back in the forest. It was only on the following day, when they had the opportunity to visit a farm, that they learned that reindeers, just like goats, are tamed fauna, and very much appreciate the company of strangers.

This and similar wild adventures kept the couple busy in the interminable summer days of Finland till they crossed the polar circle, visited Santa Claus's homeland, bought a few souvenirs, and rested their RV for the night just a few miles south of Rovaniemi in the middle of Lapland.

At midnight, the sun grazed the horizon and for a while stood still to oversee, like Janus Bifront, the passage of a time, by brightening toward the West the day past while lighting toward the East the day to come.

They sat on a floating bench watching the wakening of the next day. Trepidant, they wished that the new day, the harbinger of the future, would carry their past dreams toward fulfillment.

The best parts of the trip were the long hours spent driving along empty roads. Paul did most of the driving, while Giselle took care of the entertainment. She sang all sorts of songs as loudly as her lungs allowed, prompted by lyrics displayed by the phone. It was as if a Southern hurricane had filled her lungs like an accordion, to release the winds, out of Aeolus bag in all directions, for the entertainment of the world. Her chest, inflated like that of a proud nightingale, let out messages of love to be heard across lakes and forests. Her singing was charming, and even Paul's sophisticated ears had to admit that charm overpowered imperfections. Saving technicalities for other occasions, and appreciating that just like Nature, Giselle's voice was unrestricted from the rigid constraints of tonality, he very much praised Giselle's performances and enjoyed every minute of it. On other times, particularly in the evening, Giselle performed on her terms. She improvised ballets at the sound of music streaming from the phone. Silly and yet memorable performances; you should have seen her rendering of the moon dance in Billie Jean! Even Michael Jackson would have been jealous!

***

Then the vacation ended, the RV was returned, and the plane took them back to New York. Giselle was home, while Paul had to continue to San Francisco. After customs, Giselle accompanied Paul to the security check. There, they said goodbye. Giselle waited for Paul to go through security and wave one more goodbye, but Paul did not turn and disappeared in the crowd.

ECHO'S CALL

I hear the breeze through the wind chimes.
I imagine how the sun looks like through the shadows under a tree.
I feel the rain by stretching my eyes
over the blooming flowers of the desert.
I know that you are out there
because your echo resounds in my heart.
So, I know that I love you and long for you
for there is a hollow inside of my soul.

***

It was just another perfect California day. To the South, the mist blunted the brightness of the ocean to make it mysterious. To the East, the hills soared over the creeping clouds and shone under the sun. The horizon spoke infinity from the West, and a northern breeze refreshed the soul.

Paul had climbed Pillar Point to scout Maverick's beach from the cliff. The sea was high for summertime, and, from a distance, the surfers paddled on top of their board bobbing up and down like penguins against sixty-foot waves. Formations of pelicans enlivened the sky, while an eagle glided above them. Sealions barked from the rocks below and, in the distance, the humpbacks were breaching. Everything was harmonious. Paul imagined Giselle at his side. He felt her head resting on his shoulder while she stared at the horizon. She had never been to California; never tasted the majesty of the Pacific Ocean.

A call floated above the mewing, cawing, and squawking of the seagulls, the barking of the sealions, the whistle of the gale, the roaring of the waves. It was the echo of Giselle's voice from their Finland days, inerasable by the winds of time. Bizarre runs of offbeat syncopation crowded the musical mind, and he imagined Giselle dancing on the precarious terrain of irregular heartbeats. He even checked his pulse. The rhythm was regular; it was all just in his imagination. In the melody, lyrics recapitulated the moments lived together:

"I want to become a principal ballerina so one day I will be as great as you are" or:

"Paul! Are you the Paul, whom for years I longed to reunite with?" or:

"Me too. I hate dancing. Why would anyone assume that I would care to dance?" or:

"When our eyes stared into each other's, an eternal bond was established, a marvel occurred, and my destiny was locked into yours for better and for worse" or:

"Paul, I am a virgin, I do not know how to make love," or:

"I want for you to make love to me," or:

"From today on and for the rest of my life, I will follow you wherever you want for me to go," or:

"I know, Paul, I always knew that you would love me. And I love you too. . . and I am sure of it!"

His mind evoked those words over and over and Paul could not refrain from smiling.

After returning from Finland, Paul enjoyed the hums of solitude echoing in the emptiness of the oceanfront. Giselle had changed him. Unpretentious, she had turned the concept of love into reality. Paul's life was now simple, meaningful, and rich. Clear was its purpose: love someone and be loved. Long for the reunion in the absence of the loved one, enjoy each moment when together. Certainly, there was passion and attraction for this most beautiful among women, and there was respect and admiration for her strength and determination, but what carved the depth of his heart was companionship. Giselle was inside of him; she was part of his bones and flesh. It was as if his soul had multiplied, and a deeper self with the most soothing voice was culling his worries, anxieties, and pains; someone was now there to share what was to come for better and for worse. For the first time in his life, he was not alone.

However, a void underscored her absence; that was a new experience! Lonesomeness before was a self-contained given. He had lived in a crystal ball that protected him from the rest of the world. But now the crystal was broken, the shelter was gone, and the contentment of solitude was confronted by the reckoning that an alternative, named Giselle, was out there. He wondered where she was, what she was up to, whether she was happy or sad, if she was thinking of him or had moved on. Memories of her had built confidence and reclaimed a foregone existence but could not compensate for the absent smile and the dark black eyes. Those contrasting sentiments kept Paul absorbed; the longing heightened the scent of his cherished moments.

Yet, he had not called her. He rather waited for her to call. He felt that a coveted long-term relationship with that young woman made no sense, or, if it did, it should be solicited by her and not forced upon. He suffered a delusional conviction that the sacrifice of an older man was indispensable to protect the future of a gifted young woman. He was just too old. The fact that she had not called reinforced that concept. She had already passed on him, demonstrating, like several women before, that there is no such thing as everlasting love. Now that the anticipation of the reunion was satisfied and the curiosity quenched, she must have realized that there were better choices waiting out there and who was he to trap her? And even if she still loved him now, how long would it last before she realized that she had chosen a used toy, a secondhand car? She would sooner or later grow tired of him, and he was not prepared to experience another rejection.

One cannot blame Paul for such insecurities. His life had been tainted by tragic abandonments, and his best protection was assurance that peace and wellbeing were not dependent upon the whims of anyone else.

Yet, deep inside, he knew that Giselle was there for him:

"An eternal bond was established, a marvel occurred, and my destiny is locked into yours for better and for worse."

Giselle would not lie to others or to herself. She was the most determined and stubborn woman he ever met. She had kept an impossible dream alive for years. She was the one who masterminded their relationship. He also reckoned that he had been in love with her since the day they met. He had never forgotten the powerful moment when their eyes met, her determined naivete, her direct ways that pierced his soul, that charisma that only few possess. He knew that she was not going to disappear as other women had before.

But again, what if he was wrong? What if he had disappointed her? She had barely spoken of love after the first few days. She had been quiet most of the time, sitting or walking at his side. Content, perhaps, or bored.

So, in this egregious example of cognitive dissonance, Paul kept checking his phone, looking for a message, a sign from her, and then shaking his head when the gadget remained silent and indifferent.

Then, as Paul was staring at the horizon, a vibration dazed him.

It wasn't Giselle though. It was Laura instead.

He had not talked to her since he left for Finland.

"Paul, are you still alive?"

"I am fine, what about you?"

"I am fine too. . . but what about you? You disappeared after Finland. What happened?"

"Nothing, everything was fine, nothing special."

"Yes, but you prolonged your stay by two weeks. Did you meet anyone there?"

"Meet whom?"

"A woman, for example!"

Paul hesitated. Would Laura be jealous or hurt? In the end he admitted:

"Yes, I did."

"And who is she? Can you tell me more? Do I know her? Is she nice?"

"She is the one who came to your place and wanted to meet me. The ballerina, do you remember her?"

"Do you mean that woman who happens to bear a name? Like, for example, Giselle?"

"Yes, that Giselle!"

"And what happened between the two of you?"

"Nothing serious, just some good time. She was nice, and we agreed to spend time together."

"Like. . . ? How much time together? What did you do?"

"Nothing special, we just took a trip around Finland."

"Did you perhaps see reindeers and took pictures of them? Or visited Santa's home, for example? Or maybe, ate mushrooms gathered from the roadside, and watched midnight lights where the day never ends?"

"Something like that! How do you know?"

"Paul. . . Giselle has been at my place almost every night since she came back. She is the happiest person in the world, and we are having a great time laughing at your eccentricities. I know everything! And I am happy for you both."

"I am glad that you are not upset with me. She is very young though—too young."

"Come on, Paul! Don't waste time listening to yourself! Listen to your heart instead. Age does not matter when one is in love—it is the least of considerations. Just one day of true love is worth a lifetime of solitude. It is a miracle that only a few fortunate ones are privy to experience. One is never alone after tasting true love; there is no separation and solitude afterwards, and the loved one will stay within one soul forever whether in physical presence or not. With the loved one, one shares an eternal dream, an illusion, perhaps, but it is the only one worth living for, the only one that endures the test of time, that may persist in the universe after we are gone, like the cosmic background is still there, after billions or years, as a residue of the Big Bang. Don't be afraid of loving and being loved.

"Besides," Laura added, "you are not that old."

Then:

"Why don't you call her?"

"I don't know. I do not want to stalk her. I was waiting for her to call me. Besides, I do not want to give her false expectations. I miss her very much, more than anything else, but I do not know if I love her."

"But Paul, do you understand that missing one, longing for someone's company, is the essence of love? How can I make you understand that Giselle is your match, that she is just you in a woman's body? This is your last chance to love and be loved. And she deeply loves you. She understands your puerile idiosyncrasies better than anyone else, she knows how introverted and inhibited you can be and how wonderful of a person you are after the onion is peeled. She understands you even better than I do."

"But then, why didn't she call me?"

"Because she wants to give you time. She told me that she knows you love her and that you will call her sooner or later. But in the end, she is also a woman, who needs to be courted. How difficult can it be to understand women? She expects for you to take the initiative, and you darn will! Whether you like it or not! You better call her now!"

And Laura hung the phone.

Paul looked at the phone. He was in total agreement with Laura. He knew that Giselle was the love of his life, and he acknowledged that it was his turn to call.

As he was about to call, however, his mind grew confused, like being high in the good old times with Crazy Wayne.

Laura's voice resonated:

"She is the happiest person in the world. . . . And she deeply loves you."

He was euphoric, crying of happiness.

So, he conceived something better and more fulfilling than a plain phone call.

Meanwhile emotions kept pouring in. Painful memories erupted to contrast and enhance the flavor of happiness. He thought of the time past, of Turo, Naomi, Crazy Wayne, and his mother. Could all this pain be erased by a joyful moment? Or the sole purpose of years of sufferance was to build a preamble for the appreciation of happiness? Would this moment last and not be ruined like everything else in the past? Was he at the apogee of his life? Would everything decay from now on? Could he bear that risk?

Sure, he could! Till now he had only surfed life. Now it was time to dive into it!

He returned the phone back in his pocket and, breathing the breeze of elation, walked to the margin of the cliff. Paul looked in the distance at the surfers and beyond them the whales, looked up at the seagulls, the pelicans, and the eagle. He felt on his hands the caress of the northern breeze invisible like the ghost of an angel and his arms turned into wings, and he spread them ready, like Icarus, to fly into the sun.

***

The car stopped in front of an unpretentious house in El Granada; hard to imagine it was the residence of the famous composer. Giselle thanked the driver, pulled out her backpack, and walked up the path. A bush of red roses covered the gate of a wooden fence parting the front yard from the walkway. White bougainvillea adorned the entrance on one side, on the other a graceful Chinese lantern plant climbed along the wall and hung over the porch. A light breeze enlivened the tranquility.

Giselle rang the doorbell.

It took a lot of courage to come to Paul's place but in the end, she could not wait any longer.

Just as she had done with Paul, Laura had encouraged Giselle to reestablish the contact. She suggested that Paul was just too withdrawn and insecure of a character to take the initiative. He needed her reassurance. Even the resolute Giselle hesitated, but in the end gave in. After all these years, it was not the time to give up! Besides she missed Paul more than she could tolerate; their time spent together had cemented an already indelible bond.

Instead of calling ahead, Giselle had decided to surprise him.

After a few seconds, the door opened but instead of Paul, a pretty, young woman appeared:

"Good morning, what can I do for you?"

Stunned, Giselle answered:

"I am Giselle, a friend of Paul. I was in the neighborhood, and I thought of dropping by to say hi. I hope I am not intruding."

And then she added:

"I am sorry, I should have called before!"

Then, hoping she was mistaken, she asked:

"Is this Paul Vincente's home? Maybe I have the incorrect address?"

"Yes, it is," replied the woman.

Silence ensued.

"I am sorry, Paul is not here. He left suddenly last night for New York as if something unexpected had come up. I am just a neighbor. He asked me to take care of the kitty while he's away."

And in fact, just behind the woman, Giselle could see a kitten, staring at her.

An awkward moment followed when neither could find a word to say. It was the neighbor who recovered first and suggested:

"Why don't you call him? He did not tell me when he will be back, but I guess it is a short trip. For longer trips, he gives more extensive instructions. He was recently in Finland, and I ended up taking Carina, the kitty, home. When it comes to Carina, Paul can be quite protective. They are very close, perhaps she is his only friend," the lady concluded with a smile.

"I am afraid of bothering him, he may be there for business. He may be in a meeting."

"Let me call him then. I need to call him in any case to ask when he will be back," suggested the lady.

"By the way, I am Carmen, nice to meet you. Please come in."

Inside, the home was luminous, with light coming from wide French doors. The walls were crowded with paintings, photos, diplomas, and awards. There were pictures of Paul with various acquaintances, mostly renowned artists. Among them there was a large poster of Wayne that occupied an entire wall of the living room.

While Carmen was looking for the phone, Carina approached the intruder. Giselle kneeled and the kitten rubbed her head against her knee, while she massaged her ears. Encouraged by the amicable response, Carina tested her new friend by gently nibbling at her finger, while she held Giselle's hand with her front paws and kicked it with her hind ones. As Giselle was about to respond with the other hand, attacking Carina from the back, the latter jumped up, arched her back before sprinting under the couch. From there she peeked to assess the situation, wiggled her butt, and pounced on Giselle's ankle to resume the touch-and-go exercise.

"Hi, Paul. There is a friend of yours here. Can you talk to her?"

"Hi, Paul. this is Giselle. I am at your place. Where are you?"

"I am in front of your door in Manhattan! What are you doing at my place? Are you stalking me?"

"Stalking you? Look who's talking!" replied Giselle. "You are the one in front of my door!"

"I am not stalking you! I just wanted to surprise you! I even have a bunch of roses in my hand. What am I going to do with them now?"

"And I am here to surprise you."

"Okay, no point arguing. So, what are you going to do now?"

"I can wait for you."

"And what if I never come back?"

"Then I will wait for you for the rest of my life, like Hachiko."

"What about waiting till tomorrow?"

"That definitely sounds better."

"Can you take care of the cat?"

"Yes."

"Let me talk to Carmen then."

The phone was returned to the neighbor, who had been listening, amused.

After ending the conversation, Carmen showed the house to Giselle, and, per Paul's request, gave meticulous instructions. As she was about to leave, Carmen added:

"I am glad that Paul found someone who cares for him. He sounded different on the phone as soon as he realized you were here. I have known him for a while now, and that man really needs a good woman at his side. . . much better than a cat!"

After Carmen left, Giselle explored the premises, followed step by step by Carina. It was a very modest place, far from the pretenses of Hollywood homes. Everything was practical and built around music. A grand piano at a corner of the living room, various instruments scattered around including a drum set, perhaps belonging to Wayne, recording equipment, and a small stage at another corner. In the same way, the backyard was set as a stage where friends must have gathered to amuse the neighbors. It also boasted a big professional kitchen that reflected Paul's passion for cooking—a remnant of the childhood years growing up with Turo.

A few minutes had passed before the phone rang. It was Paul.

"Is Carmen gone?"

"Yes."

"Did she show where the cat food is?"

"Yes."

"And what about the treats?"

"Yes, she showed me."

"Do you know how to give them to Carina? You must give one at the time, holding it in your hand, otherwise she does not eat them."

"Okay."

"And what about you? Are you going to eat?"

"Later, maybe."

"There is a lot of stuff in the freezer. But you must take it out now."

"Or you can go to Asian King Kitchen down the road. It's good, not too fancy, but genuine. You tell Alex you are my friend."

"Don't worry, Paul, I can manage."

"And what about your stuff? Where are you going to put it?"

"I do not know. I will find a place."

"You can put it in my room. It's the bedroom upstairs with the big TV. You can sleep there."

And then he quickly corrected:

"Sorry, I meant, you should sleep in. . . our room."

Few minutes later, the phone rang again:

"And since you are there, can you check the mail and water the lemon tree? And the redwood sapling?"

And then again:

"You can find the controls for the audio system under the cabinet of the family room. To the left of the fireplace."

And again:

"Be patient with Carina, she is just a kitten and likes to play. And even if she attacks you, she is very gentle. Don't be afraid. She is needy for attention but she's a good cat."

"I know. She is purring on my lap now. Don't worry, I love kittens."

And on and on, Paul kept calling to offer frivolous instructions and admonitions that were accurately interpreted by Giselle as meaning:

"I am so happy you are there, I love you, and I cannot wait to be back!"

Finally, the phone rang one more time:

"I am in the cab to the airport. I was able to find a flight that arrives in San Francisco around nine tonight. I have a car to pick me up. You go to sleep; I will wake you up when I get home."

***

But Giselle did not go to sleep; instead, when Paul came down the escalator at the arrivals at SFO International, he found Giselle waiting for him. He was still holding the bouquet of roses. He walked towards her and hugged her. A kiss followed, exchanged according to Cupid's standards with a most proper technique mastered during their Finland days. It was a perfect kiss whose flavor persisted for a lifetime.

***

OUR LAST PARADISE

Following the reunion at SFO International, Giselle and Paul lived happily forever after.

***

Time runs fast; yet its flow is imperceptible. It seems only yesterday when Giselle was born. And now, as I condense into an epilogue the decades that followed, I reckon that the essentials rest in the chapters past; life is not about its conclusion but the path that led to it. Therefore, my dear reader, quench your expectations and be content with the morsels that keep life going when the dreams of youth are fulfilled, and the best is gone.

It is now the time to ponder whether a similar account was ever authored, not by writers or poets, but by the actions of people. I would love to know if any among us experienced in person or know of someone who lived anything close to the magic of Giselle's tenacious dream.

This novel explored the hypothesis that true and everlasting love sometime, somewhere, may occur, and a bond between two people, when sincere, can be as enduring as the utmost powers of the universe that defy the boundaries of space and time. It concludes that, at least in Giselle's case, it does, and, therefore, this novel best belongs to the fiction category where it can rest on the bookshelf in peace together with Snow White and Cinderella.

In the real world, there are people important to us, whose existence we verify on occasions.[24] They exist unchanged in the corner of their life

---

[24] This paragraph is a paraphrased from a correspondence with Catterina Coha and used with her permission.

distant from our mind, buried in the depth of the subconscious. This may apply to long gone parents, still staying with us, visiting our dreams, defining who we are. And what about the likeness of one's faraway lover, so far that the real person becomes a stranger, while the only reality rests in one's imagination. In the end, it does not matter. It is the communion of materiality and fiction that sculpts our life, and it is upon us to determine the balance that offers comfort.

Therefore, Giselle's story, fiction, or reality, is important to me. When in bed I close my eyes and imagine, I learn more through introspection than peeking into the real world. For this, I thank my characters, who patiently listen and talk to me, and, whether they exist or not, they stay true to comfort the spirit when it would be otherwise dejected.

Thus, with this novel, I created a dream, most likely, a paranoia, a delusion that, improbable, unlikely, impossible as it may be, is still worth living.

***

Returning to the story, one can assume that Paul and Giselle had children and grandchildren, that they paid regular visits to their respective families and to the other characters that enlivened this novel. It may very well be that Ivanna Yvanova and Uncle Borysko married; that Professor Federico and Signora Maria learned to coexist and enjoy life together under Lori's supervision; that the Maestro bragged for the rest of his life about his pupil, while Madame Petrova recounted for the benefit of younger students the miracle that made a dream come true. And one can also imagine that Laura spent most of her time with her beloved friends, uncertain about whom to adore the most—her big brother Paul or the charismatic Giselle. Giselle and Paul may have also established a charitable fund to inspire little girls from rural areas to pursue untouchable dreams and envisioned other good deeds in harmony with their simple and benevolent personality.

***

I will miss all these characters dearly, but before bestowing the ultimate goodbye, let me recount one among several reunions that they enjoyed during their lifetime.

Giselle and Paul took it upon themselves to host a celebration of their legacy each year at Thanksgiving in El Granada. In this occasion, they even flew in the fiddler and his violin. . .

***

Paul was distracted looking at Uncle Borysko, who meticulously chewed and swirled the wine in his mouth before gulping it down. He pondered over the value of that awkward habit. While listening, Paul grabbed the bottle of wine and poured a generous portion into his glass and drank it. He then swirled the wine to appreciate the prolonged sensation offered by the concoction. Looking at Uncle Borysko and raising the glass, Paul nodded and smiled. It was Thanksgiving after all, time to forget about the world out there and enjoy the emotional overload that casual conversations spiced with alcohol can offer.

The live music at the Princeton Brewery took a break, and Dane, the lead guitarist and a friend, walked toward Paul. "Let's invite your fiddler to play with us!" Dane was saying. "You bragged about him so much! Let's give it a try! We will follow him with drums and guitars when we figure him out."

And so, after the break, Igor the fiddler took the stage and began to tap his foot. The distant music from the steppes was revived in the Jazz Club, and for one memorable evening, Igor's foot and the drummer's beats recounted that levitation of humanity that most unites us—the universal language of music. Giselle's foot started tapping, then the other one, till she soared into the dancefloor to improvise a rain dance that combined the movement of the Cossacks and the Native Americans. Everyone present laughed at the ad-libbed performance.

Turning toward Paul, the Maestro said:

"We should record this! It could be another hit!"

Paul smiled. He was about to answer, but he was distracted by Madame Ivanova, who took his hand and pulled him onto the dancefloor. There she harmonized her steps with Giselle's and even poor Paul had to follow the rhythm. Signora Maria joined, dragging Professor Federico, who, after warming up and to everyone's surprise, was a darn good dancer. And look at Uncle Borysko with Ivanna Yvanova! That's what I call (almost) professional dancing!

While people danced, Paul returned to the table where Laura was sitting. She had been withdrawn and did not care to join, preferring to observe everyone with grace.

As Paul sat close, she mumbled:

"I will never understand how these waiters can carry Martinis filled to the brim across crowded rooms, without spilling a drop, particularly without being drunk."

"How come you are not dancing, Lauretta?"

"I have not been sleeping well recently. I am always tired; I keep counting sheep till there are no more left in my brain. They should create a 'counting sheep' app to help the insomniacs."

Then, changing subject she continued:

"I am so glad for you, Paul, and for your Giselle. You seem so happy, and I feel proud to be part of this story. I hope one day, you will remember your Lauretta, when I am not here anymore.

"I remember when you were a clueless teenager, who could not remember where he left his socks the night before, and I had to go fetch them for you in the morning. I remember the times in the Bronx, and how much we loved each other then, when you took me around with your friends. You were so proud of your little sister. And I continued to adore you and always hoped that you would do the same. And after my divorce, after I returned to America, I was willing to be near you because I was also a lonely explorer of life as you are; I longed for true love and freedom. But I remained a little sister to you, you never saw me as a woman. It has been bitter and sweet. Then Giselle came into our lives. That was when the world changed colors; from rainbow to gray; when the present turned into the past and I chose your happiness over mine. I am thankful that I am part of it. And it is okay. I do not care about the outcome; I just want to know in the end that I did all I could. I have no regrets. But for you, I am afraid, I am just an ordinary person."

Paul smiled.

"I have never met an ordinary person, Lauretta. Each human being is special one way or another. If you are ordinary. . . you are the first one, which makes you even more special."

"Okay, I am special then, but not for much replied Laura. "I have lymphoma, Paul, a bad molecular type. . . Started chemo a few weeks ago. The doctors are encouraging but deep inside, I've already given up. What is the point of living longer? I was lucky enough. I lived a privileged though purposeless life. What's the point of begging for a few more days? Months? When one tastes the flavor of death, life suddenly takes a different meaning. I need to retire; I do not belong to this world anymore. When I look at old photos of myself, my eyes were different, determined at scrutinizing the future. Now they are skeptical and lost, wondering about the essence of that future."

Paul held Lauretta's hand and told her:

"Sorry to hear this, why didn't you tell me before? Don't give up, Lauretta. I love you too, I love you very much. True, I never saw you as a woman but a sister. We were raised together, I held you on my knees when you were just a little girl with curly hair. How could I change my mind? But you are important to me, and to Giselle. Remember what you told me once: "*Life is not meant to be perfect, but it is worth living to the best of one's capabilities.*" Don't give up, I will talk to Giselle after Thanksgiving. I am sure that she wants you to move in with us. Together, we will overcome."

Lauretta smiled and mumbled:

"How much hope can one squeeze out of an empty toothpaste tube? The bulldozer of life: death, the great equalizer."

Meanwhile the dancers were back. Giselle sat close to Paul and squeezed his arm. Lauretta had changed demeanor to play the expected cheerful character. The news was not meant to be spilled to spoil a great reunion. Paul understood and, releasing Lauretta's hand, said to Giselle:

"Laura has not been well recently, but she is getting better."

Giselle scrutinized the depth of Paul's eyes, and she understood. Several questions came to her mind but she knew there was no point asking.

Meanwhile Uncle Borysko was recounting war stories. Paul heard him throwing hyperbolae in broken English, recounting heroic acts in between the wine chewing. It was the remnant of a true Cossack:

"They were so scared. . . they ran so fast that they left their legs behind!"

And then he turned toward Ivanna to gauge the effect of his story. But Ivanna was intent on trying to grasp the meaning of the conversation in Italian between Lori and Madame Petrova. Giselle had been working hard to draw her into her adoptive parents' culture during Ivanna's frequent visits to Milan.

Lori seemed irritated about some pretentious character, telling Madame Petrova in Italian:

"I asked myself, if he is so rich why can't he buy a wig for himself?"

Paul guessed that she was talking about a suitor that did not strike her fancy.

Off to the other side, the Maestro was saying to Professor Federico: "She is sort of a tentative intellectual. She tries hard, one must give her credit. But in the end, she is an intellectual desert." Which prompted, in an apparent non-sequitur, Professor Federico's reply: "In my mind, photography is there only to plagiarize life, but there is no camera fast enough to take picture of deep emotions." To which the Maestro continued in his parallel soliloquy: "I agree, nothing is as loud as stupidity; people can go on and on repeating themselves to those unfortunates who are stuck listening. And the paparazzi take advantage of it, to amplify and eternalize stupidity, to give a story to the press. They do not only plagiarize life, but they distort it: they are Hollywood's Photoshop surgeons. And people around them, critics and journalists, are intellectual cowards who have nothing to offer but rehashed garbage!"

Meanwhile, on another front, the conversation, mixed with vodka, wine, and Martinis was degenerating. The fiddler, possibly recounting events from long gone adventures in perfectly broken English was trying to impress the recently acquired musician friends:

"She was so ugly that I could not have made love to her even if I took a Viagra overdose!"

And we should forgive the medical anachronism that he used just to make a point.

Uncle Borysko looked with embarrassment at the ladies around him and as he was about to reprimand his old friend's comment, the proper Signora Maria interjected: "True, some people can be unappealing, but I hope you would not count me as one of them."

And so, these silly bits of incongruent conversations went on and on during that carefree Thanksgiving evening. Paul's mind collated them into a symphony, to memorize those voices beyond the life of the beholders.

And here is where we leave all of them, in that cheerful autumn dinner.

***

Giselle was by then a Hollywood star. Gradually, from live performances, she had taken more screen roles that allowed a regulated lifestyle. At the same time, the big screen made her visible to broader audiences. She received prestigious awards and, together with Paul, accumulated a fortune that was preserved according to the simple lifestyle imprinted upon them by their modest roots.

Like Paul, Giselle did not bask in success. Popularity contrasted her longing for privacy and frugality. Soirees and big galas were no match to the gratification of feeding the hens, caressing Oldie, and enjoying egg and tomato soup in front of Grandma after a day spent running across the fields. Like Paul, she considered popularity as an imposition over true life. In the end, she aspired to reunite with Paul; anything else was irrelevant.

By then Paul had given up most social commitments and spent his time with Giselle. Giselle and music made life complete, and Jerry had learned to leave them alone, recognizing that the business was doing just as well despite the seclusion.

They still lived in El Granada but moved to a secludedhome, with more land to allow privacy and space for a chicken run. There they hosted friends or spent evenings alone. Paul composed music based on Giselle's ideas, and Giselle danced according to Paul's creations. And every evening, before dinner, Paul, reenacting a routine dear to Naomi in the old Bronx days, said grace:

"My God, if you exist, I am thankful to you today; another day spent with the reverberation of my life, with a companion that makes me real. Thank you for giving Giselle to me. I thank you for her smile, for her eyes, for her heart that listens to my words, for her kindness and thoughtfulness that imparts joy not only to me but to everyone around us. I thank you for today and pray for a tomorrow that is just like today."

***

On a weekend morning, Paul went to the garage and drove out the Ferrari. Despite the frugal life, Paul maintained a strong affection for the luxury convertible he inherited from Wayne. With Crazy Wayne at the steering wheel, they had gone places and accumulated so many memories into the dashboard together with the miles dialed by the odometer. Therefore, on occasions, Paul drove Giselle up and down Highway 1, along the California Coast with the wind fondling her hair.

That morning, Paul announced they were going for breakfast up to La Honda to Alice's Restaurant. With the top down, sunglasses on to protect their eyes from the sun and their privacy from snooping fans, they climbed I-92. At the top of the hill, they turned into Skyline and drove into the redwood forest.

It was early when they arrived at Alice's and parking was open in front of the restaurant. Paul opened Giselle's door, leaving the vintage car for the bystanders to admire. As they waited in line for a table, a couple recognized Giselle and offered to let them skip the line. Paul graciously declined, stating that they were in no hurry and that he was just as happy to enjoy the coolness under the shade of the centenarian redwood: "Every moment spent with my Giselle is just as precious; sitting or standing."

When their turn came, however, there was no separate seating, and the host guided them to the end of a large wooden table occupied at the other end by a young couple and their daughter.

"May we sit here?" asked Giselle with her affable smile.

"Yes, you are very welcome," replied the wife.

Soon, young admirers came to greet Giselle and asked for the customary autograph. When the fuss died down, Giselle noted that the little girl was staring at her, so she cheerfully asked: "What is your name?"

"Sabrina." And then she added: "Are you Giselle? The ballerina?"

"Yes, I am!"

"I am also a ballerina!" said Sabrina. "I have been taking ballet lessons for years."

"I have a question for you Sabrina: Why do you want to dance?"

"Because I love it! I do it by myself and train and train and train. I would never stop no matter what."

"Then you already have your answer to my question; now you know why! You dance because you cannot live otherwise!"

The little girl's face lit up. She giggled and said:

"One day I want to be like you!"

In response, Giselle looked into Paul's eyes and then, turning to Sabrina, she replied:

"No, Sabrina, you do not want to be like me. You want to be better than me and better than anyone else. Never put limits to your dreams."

***

On occasions when he could not join her on tours, Paul waited at home for Giselle. He spent time scanning the walls that kept accumulating old and new memories in the form of posters, sketches, paintings, and awards, mostly about Giselle. He had become dependent on Giselle and detested her absence just as much as he cherished the anticipation of her return.

So, one afternoon, Paul was fussing in the kitchen as he had resumed the old habit of cooking with Turo. Christina, the housekeeper, was helping by meticulously cleaning and cutting a bag of brussel sprouts when they were both surprised to hear the doorbell ring earlier than expected.

Christina went to open the door, ready to discourage solicitors or fans.

Instead, Paul heard:

"Is Paul home?"

It was Giselle's voice. Paul went to the door. Giselle stood in front of him, a backpack at her feet.

Answering his inquisitive look, she preempted:

"Paul, I quit my job!"

"Why, Giselle? What happened?"

"Nothing happened. I just do not want to be separated from you anymore. It is not worth it."

And then she continued:

"Paul, this is our last paradise. Nothing will come after this. Each moment, each second is precious. I do not want to be away from you, not for a single day. We do not need more money or fame. We just need each other. I will not spend a single day away from you from now on."

Paul stepped out of the door and hugged Giselle.

"I did not have the courage to ask, but I have been hoping that you would make this choice on your own."

***

The following decade was indeed their last paradise. Giselle and Paul were at each other's side day and night, coveting the remaining bits of life, capturing each moment as if it were the last one. They walked along beaches at sunset, climbed the mountain trails that overlook the endlessness of the Pacific Ocean, strode the Golden Gate Park end-to-end, listened to semi-professional bands, and visited the Rose Garden where Giselle took pictures of every flower. They watched the Dragon Dance in China Town and ate dumplings for Chinese New Year. They observed children play and, from the distance, listened to the monkeys' hoot at the San Francisco Zoo. They giggled at the penguins' rocking steps, while the mischievous otters chased each other. They empathized with the snow leopard that, from the console of its cage, scanned the horizon searching for something that would never materialize. And they drove the vintage Ferrari to Sonoma, to Mendocino, and up further into Oregon's redwood forests. And further up, and further down in an unending succession of unforgettable moments.

Wherever they went, they held hands because they were alone in a world where all ties, family, and friends, were no more. The two orphans were all that were left, the only survivors of an enchanted tale. In that solitude, they were reborn. In the darkness of oblivion their souls were attracted like moths to the light. They were twin flames that kept admirers at the outskirts of their seclusion to repel distractions that could spoil their intimacy. They never argued because respect was the foundation of their relationship, a perpetual benefit of the doubt that molded a life without regrets. And they yearned to believe that everlasting love exists in this world as a pledge to be carried to the ultimate journey.

***

But, like all of us, Giselle was not meant to live forever. Her abdomen began to swell. A diagnosis of cancer was dealt, and the clock started to tick down.

Giselle accepted the news with grace. She reserved gratitude for a life that had offered all that she could ever want, most of all Paul, the Paul standing by her at the doctor's office. But it was a fiend's verdict for Paul. In front of Giselle, he acted confident, but inside, life was hell. He could not accept that his younger half, his precious Giselle, lived in death row, while he was still healthy and strong. He had always assumed that he would be the first to disappear. He had arranged for Giselle's comfort without him. He dreamed of her revisiting the places of their life, remembering everything and keeping their dream alive. He imagined her beautiful eyes searching for him at sunset, her melodious voice whispering to him over the ocean breeze. But he never thought of a life without Giselle.

***

Jerry visited often during the chemotherapy cycles. When Giselle was in the hospital and Paul could not stay by her, Jerry would take him to Ebb Tide café, in Miramar. On one occasion, Jerry was recounting his older brother Mark's anguish when their dad reached the finish line.

Jerry was jittery more than usual; he was sweating emotions as if Giselle was his wife rather than Paul's and he was expecting support rather than giving it. Just the same, that day was not the best in Paul's new life, neither was it the worst. It was just average. It would have been a horrible day by anyone else's standards. But he had adjusted to the burden of depression.

"Mark is a physician, the one upon whom my dad had always counted on. Dad always stood by him and trusted him more than anyone else. But on the last days of his life, Mark did nothing to save him. Dad's death haunted him, although from a medical perspective, he had made the right choice.

Dad suffered an intestinal infarction as a complication of a surgical procedure. Nothing could have been done to help at that age, in those conditions. Yet, as we were standing by the ICU bed, powerless watching his last few heartbeats, guilt swelled in my brother's heart. . . but it was too late.

"In a deeper sense, letting him go was the finest decision. Life is merciless. At an old age, each day may be the last one, but even worse, it may be one of many that crowds the waiting room of death. Senseless life can go on for years; one can age, get sick, become handicapped, yet life goes on and on. My father wanted to die when he realized he could be no more than what he used to be. But life kept torturing him with nothing to hope for and only pain to fear.

"One day, I hope not too soon, Giselle will be terminally ill, and you will have to make the most arduous choice. She is an angel, whom everyone loves. But then, it will be just you and her. She will be at your mercy and only you, the companion of her life, will share those treasured moments when, at the threshold of the eternal silence, each whisper from the departing will echo into the rest of the other's life. In a few moments, your lives will be replayed. She will look at you for the last time with an inquisitive expression, like my dad did with us. She will hold your hand tightly. She will smile trying to express gratitude for the love she received, pleading for a promise of a reunion in a world with no beginnings or ends.

"Life is a continued struggle to translate what we are into what we do. But at the end of the journey, nothing can be done, and one can only witness, helplessly, its natural course."

And Paul replied:

"I am trying to spend time constructively, but a form of mental depression distances my thoughts from all I care about, as if I am afraid of disturbing the beauty of the memories by contaminating them with the current ugliness. We used to love the pilgrim soul in each of us, but now we can only admire the unspoken sorrow over our erratic faces. I live in the twilight or reality, questioning whether the present is an illusion, whether she is gone already. Yet I cannot let her go, because since we have been together, Giselle has been the blueprint of my life."

***

After a few more cycles of chemotherapy and experimental treatments, Giselle gave up. Water filled her lungs, which needed to be drained with increasing frequency.

That evening, she decided no more. Paul helped her upstairs to the bedroom, adjusted the nasal cannula and the oximeter. He watched her fall into an intermittent doze. He sat by her side, admiring her beautiful hair that had regrown after the last cycle and of which she was still very proud. Her breathing was elaborate. On occasions she opened her eyes and searched around, questioning her whereabouts. When her gaze encountered Paul's, she smiled, reached for his hand, and held it as tight as she could.

A while later, Giselle asked: "Paul, I need my pain cocktail. Please get it for me."

"The doctor said we should be cautious with pain medications if you have trouble breathing. Let's go to the hospital. They can make you breathe better first."

"No, Paul, we are not going to the hospital anymore. These are my final moments and I want to spend them alone with you. Please give me the pain medication."

Paul rose, went to the bathroom, and fetched a pill and a glass of water.

When he returned, Giselle smiled. He tucked the pillow behind her to help her breathe, when Giselle said: "Thank you!" Then she added: "I mean, thank you for everything. For being the reliable companion of my life. Thank you for loving me. I could not have been more fortunate. I remember the day we met when you asked for my name. You were so handsome and charismatic. And your words, your words changed my life."

Paul smiled. "I remember that moment too. I forgot to breathe when you turned your face and stared into my eyes. Without knowing it, I fell in love with you right on the spot! My mere existence had been questionable till I met you; you gave meaning to my life. Thank you, Giselle, my better half. Thank you for every moment, for every smile, every word, every kind gesture. I also could not have been luckier. I am the lucky one!"

Then Paul lost control and, reclining over Giselle's abdomen, sobbed.

"Shh, shh. . . Come on, Paul," interrupted Giselle, caressing his curly hair. "Don't forget, as Turo said, real men aren't supposed to cry even when they chop onions!"

***

A little later, Giselle woke up again and, finding Paul's eyes staring at her, she pronounced her last words: "Say goodbye to all our things for me."

More time passed and Giselle slipped into a coma; her breathing became irregular, alternating deep with shallow breaths. The oxygen saturation declined.

Silently and peacefully, Giselle passed.

***

Paul sat at her side for a while not knowing what to do in that moment and for the rest of his life. He then rose, searched for his phone, and texted Jerry:

"It has happened. Please go ahead with the plan, please take care of everything."

Then he went to the bathroom, looked in the mirror. It was ironic that he did not look that old after all. It was obvious that too many empty days without Giselle lay ahead, too many to bear. He wondered why he did not cry. He tried, but no tears came out. His soul was numb as if he was made of marble.

Turo was right, he thought. "Real men don't cry even when they try."

Instead, he opened Giselle's medicine drawer and grabbed the bottle that contained the narcotics. It had just been refilled. He took it to the bedside. Then he went to the kitchen, found a bottle of whiskey and a glass. He brought them upstairs and sat them on the bedside table. He then hugged Giselle one more time, kissed her lips, closed her eyes, and laid at her side, holding her hand. With the other hand he ferried to his mouth a pill and a glassful of whiskey in turns, till he was about to lose consciousness. He then lay waiting to join Giselle in the ultimate journey.

But things were not as expected. Life did not fade into eternal darkness. Instead, Giselle and Paul walked side by side, holding hands toward an overpowering light. It was as if the sun had levitated into a giant red ball that covered the visible sky and they could look into the glare with impudence. The light though was not from the sun; it was God smiling at them. In him, they saw the face of many. They saw Turo and Naomi, and Uncle Borysko and Ivanna, and Igor the fiddler, and Signora Maria and Professor Federico, and Lori, and Giovanni the Maestro, and Madame Ivanova, and, of course, the sweet Lauretta and her parents. They were all smiling, while a voice emerged. It was a chorale of hundreds, thousands, millions of voices chanting:

"Welcome to the kingdom of everlasting love."

The End

ASIAN KING'S KITCHEN

"Same table?"

I nod while I proceed to my seat. The paper napkin with utensils wrapped in it is already waiting. I am about to ask for chopsticks, but Alex brings them pronto. I take out my computer, place it to the side, and open it. I lean my iPhone over the computer screen as it's trying to tell me something.

I inspect the premises. It's Friday night but in this corner of the Asian King's Kitchen restaurant, nobody sits.

The habitual fly comes to greet me, looking at me with its humongous eyes. I wonder what it's thinking.

"Bottle of wine?" Alex says.

I nod.

"Cheap wine? House? White? The usual?"

I nod.

"Pot stickers?"

I nod.

"Chinese chicken salad?"

I nod.

"Mongolian beef?

"Yes, just the usual," I confirm as he drops the paper envelope with the chopsticks on the table.

"Maybe sweet and sour?"

I nod.

"Maybe. . . rice?"

I nod.

And I wonder:

"Why did I come to AKK to eat by myself? Just two minutes from my home on Highway 1 along the Pacific coast. I could have stayed home, cooked something in my treasured kitchen. Did I really miss the Mongolian beef?"

I realize that what I really needed was a warm welcome, to be greeted by a sweet smile, to be comforted that I need not to be alone this Friday night. And I found it all in Alex, the only waiter at AKK. Reliably there, rain or shine, steady like the cliffs at Pillar Point.

I open the webpage. I try to surf, pretend to be working. . . or perhaps I am just trying to distract myself by reading. Or perhaps I am simply demonstrating composure to the fly that is still looking at me by pretending to be busy and focused on some ethereal project and, therefore, deflect the pathetic image of a hermit who can't find a soul with whom to share his Friday night.

But I am hesitant, not sure what to do. Everything pertaining to my life seems extraneous. I am more interested in something fresh. I feel that what is enclosed in the walls of my existence has been rehashed one too many times already. And the computer and the iPhone are just reminders of that.

"Sorry, laptop of mine, loyal companion; you will not do for tonight. Same goes for you, my dear iPhone. Keep the messages to yourself. I know that nothing will come through that could make a difference tonight."

I look around another time. I want to enjoy the table, the red of the paper lights, the gold of the Chinese characters, the composite fragrances that come from the kitchen. I want to dwell in the anticipation of a good meal just as I felt when she sat in front of me the last time we were here. No need to busy myself with the computer that night.

***

"Boy! But did she keep me busy!" I recollect.

She would say: "What are you going to do about that woman? Why is she texting all the time? Doesn't she know that you are married? At least for a little longer. . . I hope.

"What are you telling her? Or not telling her?"

"Can you send her a message? Tell her to leave you alone?"

***

Alex opens the bottle and pours a full glass of chilled wine.

"Wo shiuan bin bai pigiu," I attempt.

He smiles, pretending to understand.

No ice bucket, of course.

I am sure that if I requested it, he would manage a way to please me with some creative concoction. But, who is going to ask for it? After all, this is not happening at the Ritz Carlton a few miles down the road in Half Moon Bay!

***

I would try to reassure her: "Honey, she is just a colleague, she is inexperienced and checks with me often. You have nothing to worry about!"

She would smile sarcastically: "Yes, she really needs to be held by the hand! What did she get her masters for?"

"Doctorate!" I would point out.

"Now you are defending her! See, you care about this woman more than you are willing to admit!"

And I would try to change subject: "What do you think of the new vases for the balcony? That cobalt blue in contrast with the green of the bushes and the white camellias!"

And she would react: "I don't even understand why you bought them. We have to carry water to the balcony and it's too windy and sunny for the camellias. Why didn't you plant them in the ground like everybody else does?"

"I thought you would like to see them in front of our bedroom. You love camellias, don't you?"

And she would say: "I have other things to worry about nowadays."

***

The pot stickers arrive with the matching sauce.

I recollect how much she liked them. . .

Save for the last time:

"What's wrong with this stuff? They don't taste like the usual!"

"Should we ask for something else, honey?"

"No, it's okay. I am not that hungry anyways."

And I would say:

"So, are you going to take Maggie to Half Moon Bay for the Pumpkin Festival this weekend?"

"No, I am too tired nowadays. You take her, so you can flirt with all the mothers there, they stick around you like flies on soda pops and you do nothing to discourage them. You never learned to keep women at bay!"

"Honey, I am just trying to be polite! If someone comes to talk to me, I cannot be dismissive, it's a small community where we live and—"

And she wouldn't let me finish:

"You can just walk away saying you have to go somewhere or answer coldly with a yes or no! Period! Time is too precious, but you waste it happily when it comes to women! I told you, don't ask open-ended questions that prolong the conversation! But you keep going on and on, you do not know how to put an end to a conversation. . . or maybe you don't want. It has been like this for thirty years! You make me insecure. I begged you so many times! Fortunately, it will not matter soon!"

And I would say: "Honey, I love you! You have nothing to worry about, I am always with you, aren't I? I really do not care about any other woman."

"And what about this one who keeps texting you! The 'Doctor,' isn't she?"

And then she would shake her head and say with a sigh: "Do what you want! I am not here to tell you what to do. I gave up a long time ago!"

***

"Did you book the Hotel for Mendocino?"

"Yes, honey! I booked a suite at the historic Mendocino Hotel!"

"Why?"

"What do you mean?"

"You know that I don't like those old decrepit places—they're pretentious and uncomfortable!"

"Sorry. The room has a great view though!"

"Can you change it?'

"I doubt I can at the last minute, but I can try. Can't you do it? So you can reserve whatever room you want?"

"Why should I? I thought you said you would take care of everything! Or you are too busy worrying about that woman?"

***

Silence.

***

"Lesley invited us to Thanksgiving!"

"Great!" I reply. "Good to have Thanksgiving at your sister's this year! We hosted last year. You need a break!"

"I know you arranged it all with her behind my back! Didn't you? Why didn't you ask me first? Am I completely out of the picture now?"

"I swear it was her idea! I had nothing to do with it! And I think it is good for you to rest during the holidays, you really need some peace!"

"Don't patronize me. I know what I need! I don't like to depend on others, you know that!"

"Yes, but this is just supper! Not a big deal. We can host the night before, for the people coming from out of town! We can take everybody out to

165

Mezza Luna in Princeton By-The-Sea! It's the best Italian food! Great Pizza, the real Italian way! Or at Sam's, or to Monster Chef. What about all-you-can-eat Japanese food?"

"That's going to cost a fortune!"

"Honey, we have all the money we need! We can enjoy a good evening with the family and be proud hosts!"

"Hosting Thanksgiving supper is another thing! You cannot understand, after all you are not even American!"

"Yep, I have only been living here for forty years!" I acknowledge with a grin.

"Can you talk to Lesley and ask if she agrees to host it at our place this year? After all, this may be my last chance!"

"Come on, honey, don't be a drama queen!"

"No! I mean it! Please ask her!"

"Okay, honey, I will"

She looked at ease, finally. I felt relieved but—

"And what if she says no?" she resumes.

"Don't know! What if she does?"

"Are you going to shove your tail in between your legs and let her push you around?"

"Honey, I don't know, do you really want to pick a fight with your sister about this?"

"I am not going to fight with her! You are supposed to do it for me! Do you care how I feel? Can you stand up for me at least once in a lifetime?"

"Honey, I will talk to Lesley! But let's not worry about it for tonight! I promise you: I will talk it over with her! But now let's enjoy our dinner!"

***

"And what if that woman keeps asking you out? Would you give in as you are doing with my sister?"

"Honey, I am not going out with this or any other woman. Trust me. Lesley is your sister, and she just wants to host Thanksgiving! It is not a date! The other woman is insignificant!"

I would then pretend that I needed to go to the washroom to break the unremitting stream of inquisition. I knew through years of experience that it would be hopeless to try to calm her down during her anxiety attacks. No way to comfort her!

When I came back, she turned her face away. She mined her handkerchief from her purse and rubbed both sides of her nose up to the lower eyelids. Then slowly, she fished out her hand mirror to check her makeup without seeming too concerned, out of habit.

"Playing drama queen again?" I asked with a smile, stretching my arm across the table to hold her tiny hand.

"No, I am fine! I will be fine, don't worry about me! I have learned to be fine no matter what. Let's have dinner as you said!"

She remained tranquil for a while, moved around bits of food on her plate, and piled the beef on one side and the carrot strings on the other.

"By the way," she continued, "I checked her out. She did not go to a legitimate graduate program. That was a low-quality program."

"Honey, let it be! She went to local schools, as most people do where she came from!"

"Why do you keep defending her? Can't you just agree with me? Just maybe to humor me. Can't you just admit that it was not a good school?"

"Sure, honey, it was not a good program."

***

She managed to put something in her mouth that kept her busy for a while. I looked at her while she was concentrating on mastication. She was still so beautiful in spite of everything that was going on, with her delicate head covered by the silk scarf elegantly wrapped around and tied with a diamond brooch, and the candid hand, wearing her wedding band, delicately scratching the tip of the pointy nose.

***

"Why aren't you talking?" she asked after managing to dispatch the beef down the food pipe.

"I don't know. I am afraid that I would irritate you more. What would you like to talk about?"

"I don't know?! Maybe about what you will do with the children when you get remarried?"

"Don't worry, honey, they will be fine, and you will take care of them too. Besides, I am not going to marry anyone."

"Do you care for her?"

"Yes, of course! I care a little, she works for me."

"I don't want you to care for her! I want you to hate her!"

"But why should I hate her, she has done nothing to me!"

"She is ruining your family, don't you see? She is just a selfish person! If she cared for you, she would find another job and leave you alone!"

***

Then I would initiate: "Next week is our anniversary! Where would you like to go? I thought you may want to have dinner at Compton Place in San Francisco! We can then spend the night at the San Francis!"

"Why should we go there? You know I do not like Indian food!"

"What about Don of the Bimini Twist!"

"You know I don't care for seafood, and if we having seafood, might as well stay here in Half Moon Bay."

"What about French?"

"I don't know! I am not even sure what there is to celebrate!"

I did not answer; there was no point.

***

Then she looked straight into my eyes. She smiled, hinting complicity, and asked: "Come on, tell me. She invited you for dinner, didn't she?"

168

I would try to buy time. I had no problem confessing the truth but I just worried that the admission would prolong this unnecessary conversation interminably and exponentially raise the anguish. But I decided to admit: "Yes, she did."

"I know, I saw the text message when you were gone. So what are you going to do?"

"Of course I will decline, but there is nothing more to it, it is just a business dinner with other colleagues. In any case, I will decline to make you happy."

"Thanks, but you should tell her that for the time being you are not interested in going out to dinner with her or any other woman, that you are a happily married man. Can you do that for me? Can you text her now in front of me?"

"Honey don't make me look ridiculous. There is no point escalating this, I will just decline! She would think that I am pretentious and may even take it as an insult!"

"See, you love her! You do not want to shut that door, do you?"

"Honey, please trust me. There is nothing between this woman and me. Just let it go, sweetie. Can we just have our dinner in peace? Enjoy a few precious moments together?"

***

"I am tired, I want to go home," she said after a while.

I stood up, took her angora jacket from the chair, and helped her wear it. I led her by the arm, and we walked out of AKK. The breeze was chilly. I wrapped her shoulders under my arms to keep her warm as we walked toward the car. I opened the door and helped her in.

"The food tasted insipid today!"

"Honey, it is because of the chemo, you are having the worse effects now, but you will recover soon."

***

She did not. A few days later, at the nadir of white cell counts, she developed overwhelming sepsis and died. "Which restaurant for the anniversary?" Never came to matter.

"Food no good?" Alex wakes me up.

I am neglecting the pot stickers, I realize.

"No, it is so good. I was just thinking. It's excellent! Bring the rest! I am really enjoying them!"

As I reach for the Chinkiang vinegar to supplement the sauce, three middle-aged men enter the scene to be seated at the table right in front of me.

They are loud; they curse gratuitously with prodigality, and they wear Hells Angels leather vests. Every exposed skin is covered with tattoos. Their scurrility disturbs me. I listen to their vocabulary, and I am disheartened listening to these born Americans who use just a tiny fraction of a vocabulary that is endowed with rich idioms. I figure that we foreigners appreciate the value of communication and spend much effort to earn acceptance; perhaps we overdo it.

I try to distract myself, but the man facing me notices that I have been staring at them.

"Hey, pal! Can I help you?" he says with a smile.

I rouse and answer:

"No, thanks, I was just lost in thought."

"Where you from?" the same guy says. "You a Frenchie?"

"No, Italian! But good guess! I am from Northern Italy and my accent is close to the French. Most people assume that I am French."

"Italy!" shouts one of the two guys who had their backs turned to me.

"I love Italy! My granny was from Sicily!" he says as he turns around.

It turns out this man is in fact a woman, with the paper skin of a smoker, with long disheveled gray hair that turns into a nicotine tan around the face. She wears an American flag wrapped around her neck from which a coarse voice burps out as if she were a disgruntled toad.

She raises the bottle of beer and: "Cheers to Italy!" And leaning forward, she reaches toward me without rising.

I pour wine in my glass and respond to the cheer. Then I offer: "Would you like some wine?"

She says: "Sure thing, cutie!"

I yell out to Alex: "Can you bring more wine glasses?"

Her two companions refuse the wine, only she accepts. I rise and go to their table to pour the wine.

She moves the chair to the side, leaving room for me to sit between her and her boyfriend.

"You don't mind, honey, if we kick it with our new Italian bud, do you?" she pretends to whisper in his ear.

No answer from the guy, who still has his back to me.

"My name is Elpida," says the one who started the conversation. "I am Latino! Comprendo uno poquito de Italiano! Buonasera, buonasera." Stretching his hand toward me.

As I shake it, I say:

"Interesting, you have a Greek name! It means *"hope"* in Greek, did you know?"

"No fucking way! Never knew! Well, never too late, I guess! That's exactly what I need. I am fucked, man! Got married and now I am screwed! Elpida! Hope! That's good! Maybe Elpida is all I have left!"

I tried to empathize by asking: "What's so detrimental about marriage?"

"Detrimental!? You call it detrimental? Other than detrimental: she fucked me up! That bitch married me for the dough! Not that I had a shit ton of it. My sister fixed us up. 'A friend of a friend, time you get married!' she says. She did not know better, bless her soul! The bitch is from Mexico— San Sebastian Bernal, El Queretaro! I married her there, small little town of cobblestone and I put down cash for the wedding. She takes the whole town to the party; they are all relatives one way or another as long as someone else pays for it! I am from Mexico too but ciudadano Americano now.

"The witch could get the green card and move in with me to America, but she says no! 'Me quedaré con mis padres,' she says, 'passa el dinero! Send me the money!' Just to make sure I understand. When she wants her English ain't so shit no more!

"I tell her: 'Ven a pasar unas vacaciones.' After all it is our fucking honeymoon, I think!!! 'Luna de Miel ' I shout! She says: 'Esta Bien!' She comes and next she wants to go to fucking Las Vegas. So, we go there and she shovels my money into the ass crack of slot machines. I get pissed: 'Enough is enough!' I scream. I throw her on the bike and back we come to California.

"'Me duole la cabeza,' she says when we are back and I'm ready to fuck. She goes to sleep on the couch. I go to ruffle her a bit to get what I paid for: 'Gotta bang you darn fucking whore!' I try to convince her all nice like. But she runs to the kitchen and takes out a knife! 'Wow, wow!' says I. 'Take it easy, babe!' Next, I load her on the plane back a su casa.

"Didn't hear from her for a month. Then she calls: 'Dónde está el dinero?' She figures that she gets the alimony 'cause we are married. 'Forget the dinero! Fuck you and the dinero,' says I. Next thing, I get a piece of shit from a lawyer. El abogado says that I better pay, or they sue me. 'Sue me your ass, want the dinero? Ven a busclarlo,' I text.

"'Tu traer aquí'—Traer aquí my ass!—'Me devorcio do ti,' I tell her. Next, el abogado asks to be paid because he is fixing the divorce. I call the abogado. . . there is no abogado! El es su amigo! He's her fucking pimp!"

As I try to empathize with Elpida's misfortune, the lady beside me starts caressing my hair: "You are cute, honey! Soft hair!"

By now she's totally drunk, and nobody cares about her mumbling except for me. I gather that the silent guy on my left may be her boyfriend. He still does not turn to look at me or say a word.

I check him out, worried. The guy is huge! But he says nothing as if he couldn't hear.

I tap him on the leather jacket: "Are you OK?" – I ask just as I recollect that I am not supposed to touch a Hells Angel's jacket!

No reaction.

I turn toward Elpida.

"He's Dan," Elpida says, anticipating my question.

"Dan, are you okay?" I insist.

"He's okay, don't bother 'im, he's okay," says the woman.

Then Elpida says: "Just heard today that his daughter died. . . Took too much prescription." And looking straight at me, continues:

"Do you know what I mean?"

"Yes, I understand. I am a physician. I have seen quite a lot of that unfortunately!" And I persist: "I am so sorry, Dan! I cannot imagine how devastating that would be. I just lost my wife ten days ago to cancer. It has been tough, but I cannot imagine losing a daughter."

Dan does not turn. Then he starts:

"It's all my fault—Never cared for her, that's my first marriage. We were so young. I left them both; not sure why. Don't even remember why. Just needed to move on, jump on the bike, and go! Never saw them again. Then she found me; she came with the Harley, and tattoos all over. 'Look Dad, I look just like you!' And she did! I say nothing. I wonder if she found me for my money, why would she come to me otherwise after all this time?

"I say: 'You are not gonna get my money. I gotta go!' I says. She looks at me, she cries. That pisses the bejesus out of me even more! 'Look,' I say, 'I have no time for this wishy-washy crap; get the fuck back on the road! Go back to your Mom.'

"Next I know, the police calls from Salinas; they found her in a motel, holding a syringe in one hand, a piece of paper in the other. 'What does the paper say?' I ask. The policewoman says: 'It just says: Dad. . . '"

"Funny thing. . . " Dan adds.

"I guess it isn't that funny" He reconsiders: "I never really thought she came for the money. I was so happy to see her, but I just didn't know what the fuck to say after all these years! And why would she want to be with a jerk like me? Better be home with her mom!"

I ask Alex for more wine.

Elpida and Dan join me this time. The rest of my food arrives. I look at Alex, who hesitates, and I nod with a smile. He sets the plates where we are. There is only one table now.

Elpida adds:

"We took him here to cheer him up! He's not as hard as he looks!"

I hear a burst of noise coming from the right as if someone is starting up the Harley.

Turns out it is the Valkyrie clearing her throat. She adds: "You did good!" says she to Elpida.

Impulsively, I corrected her: "You mean he did '*well*.'"

"No, not that good, let's not exaggerate!" she replies with a sad smile, shaking her head.

***

At the end of dinner, I offer to pay, they don't let me. I win part of the negotiation and I get to pay for the wine and beer. But Alex says: "Pay one bottle. *Other me do!*"

"What about the fortune cookies?" asks Elpida.

We have one more glass and we toast:

"Elpida!" I say.

"Elpida!" they say.

My fortune cookie promises: "All your sorrows will vanish."

I return to my table, place the computer into my backpack and the iPhone in my pocket and I move toward the door.

"Say, doctor!" Dan calls. "I am sorry for your wife!"

"Thanks, Dan," I say and pat him on the leather jacket.

"You know you are not supposed to do that?" Dan says and stands.

He is at least six three. He gently punches me in the right shoulder with a curved upside-down jab and says:

"So long, doctor! Elpida!"

***

In the driveway, the Tesla is waiting for me. It opens as I approach and turns on the lights to welcome me, but no illusions. Realistically, it just recognizes my wavelength.

I enter, rubbing my shoulders in response to the chill. I go over the events that night when we last walked together, and I held her against the same chill. I look at the empty seat. I back out the car avoiding the Harleys, and then I stop and take out the iPhone. I write to the woman: "I am sorry, I am recently widowed. I am not ready to date anyone. I miss my wife too much."

Then, I turn the iPhone toward the empty seat. Maybe she can still see it.

***

The point of the story is that if you ever consider going to the Asian King's Kitchen, don't travel there just for the food. Food is fine and so is the service. But you go there because of Alex and because of his smile, and because you do not want to be left home alone on a Friday night. You go there to find people that, no matter how different they appear, are just like you. And their voices, loud or soft as they may happen to be, will mix in a buzzing concert spiced up by kitchen aromas, giving you the momentary illusion that, for no good reason, one may find hope in the warmth of a friendly place, and that illusion will endure just as long as you will rest in its premises.

And when you are there, don't forget to raise your wine glass and say:

"Elpida!"

Do it for me, if not for anything else.

LOCAL NEWS

Folks! Nothing like living in El Granada, California (Population: 3,585 people not including me; I moved in after the census) on the Pacific Coast a few miles south of San Francisco, a.k.a. Princeton by the Beach (Westbound across Highway 1), a.k.a. Pillar Point, a.k.a. Mavericks Beach etc. Some say that strictly speaking they are not part of El Granada, but I do not buy it! Anyways, a mini paradise a few miles from Stanford, Google, Facebook, Apple, Uber, Tesla, Airbnb, etc. They all sit there on the other side of the hill in Silicon Valley, while we are here, with our own ecosystem and microclimate, cooler in the summer and warmer in the winter.

Sure, a few young or aging preppies live here, but mostly retirees with nothing better to do than try to be creative (as we will see later) and then those fishermen. Boy, am I so envious of them fishermen; self-conscious biotech nerds dawdling around the piers, pretending to read the winds out there and gauge the red flags flapping over the Harbor Master! Yet keeping an eye on those sea wolves! You can catch the reverberation of the eighty-foot waves in their fearless eyes. And when you walk by, they barely see you, as if you were just a sardine not worthy of their attention. In fact, they talk over great whites and whales while they set sail! I really wish I was one of them. Anyways, this is just my problem. Nothing to do with the story.

And of course, there are the "penguins" (as my friend calls the surfers in black wetsuits), perpetually waiting for the king wave at Surfers' Beach! Again off-topic, I apologize.

Bottomline, we are a tiny community, but we're rich and autocratic. We even have our own news: "*Next-door El Granada.*" You just have to sign up and you will know, who is missing a cat, a dog or a parakeet, and who found them; who is selling what or who was ticketed by the sheriff for running a stop sign; and you will receive updates with recordings of mountain lions prowling the neighbor's backyard at night, caught on motion-sensor cameras; and about coyotes, and barn owls or barking sea lions, harbor-seal pups, blue herons, golden eagles and peregrine falcons, cormorants and pelicans, and the lady bugs or monarch caterpillars, or the cute but obnoxious gofers. For racoons and skunks, no need for next-door news, the residual mess and the lingering stink let you know they are around.

All you may wish to know (or not) is there. And of course, wonderful pictures pile up each day of spectacular sunsets behind Pillar Point; or of "fogbows" in the early morning.

And these are the local news, reported by anyone for everybody's consumption. . . just in case. Whatever you need. . . just ask!

And you will find out all the things you missed—in fact, I just realized that I don't have a bear-spray, just in case I encounter a cougar during my hikes up the hill. But watch the wind! You may get it all in your eyes and then you are doomed to be at the mercy of the mountain lion!

And we have external correspondents, who read the blogs and reply from far away. My Washington D.C. correspondent Wendy assures us that natural blue chrysanthemums do indeed exist (contrary to what was implied by a recent post of mine). In fact, one can even buy the seeds online:

https://parkseed.com/blue-knoll-heteropappus-flower-seeds/p/03108-PK-P1/

or http://www.anniesannuals.com/signs/h/heteopappus_bk.htm

Now let's walk to Pillar Point Harbor.

There is the black cod man. He goes all the way to the Farallon's islands to get those darn cods. He tells me that when there are too many great whites at the open sea, the sea lions jump on the boat to stay out of their way and there is no way you can get rid of them! And what about the sea urchins and the Buddhist monks praying for them?

And James and his driftwood sculptures. They are all over the harbor outside and inside restaurants and shops!

And there is Jim, the guy with the long hair and a faded beard that runs down to the flanks like moss dressing a redwood tree, who want to start a business with me, in honor of my Italianism:

"Let's spike Prilosec in the Prosecco and call it Prilosecco! Avoid heartburns while enjoying life!" Great idea, but I will leave it for after retirement.

And there's so much more around like Barbara's Fish Trap depicted in a previous blog, the Brewery, Mezza Luna Restaurant, and the funky Yacht Club where sea lions seem to hang out more than people. Each one is worth a story on its own (I'll tell you next time—like I did before for Asian King Kitchen, a few miles down South on Highway 1).

Okay, let's leave the harbor now and go back to El Granada.

The best news are the ones you get firsthand from the neighbors. Take last Sunday. The doorbell rings and here comes Rich (Riccardo) Croce, who lives across the street. Donning the proper mask and glove attire according to COVID etiquette, he offers me his new book! Riccardo is an Italian from the Bevento area; his wife's name is Ara.

Rich wrote *La Guida Divina* (*The Divine Guide*, 2020 by R. Croce) with contributions by citizens of EG, including Roberto Pugliese, the Mezza Luna Restaurant owner, also from Southern Italy, from Paola, a coastal town just a few miles from my hometown Pizzo, in Calabria.

The book starts with opening quotes from Dante, who, like Riccardo for English, played a significant role in replacing Latin with the Italian language. So, it is fitting that the title of the book is inspired by his great work, *La Divina Commedia*. It is his hope that "La Guida Divina *will guide the journey through the hell of proper pronunciation and usage to the heavenly beauty of the Italian language.*"

"*The guide starts with the sounds of vowels and vowel combinations in Section 1, and then shows how the sounds combine, in Section 2. These are followed by hints for proper pronunciation and syllable formation; in Section 3, it should be cautioned that regional Italian dialects may vary and, although one may have trouble understanding them, Italians are used to accommodating different dialects and will normally be able to understand the pronunciations contained in this guide. Section 4 contains guidance for the proper use of the troublesome pronouns "ci," "ne," and "da." Section 5 offers a guide to Italian verb usage.*

Section 6 contains some hard-to-find rules for adjectives and some grammar rules that, although not as hard to find, are often forgotten or not taught. The final section, Section 7, describes the difficulties one may encounter with certain Italian words, phrases, regional dialects, and punctuations, and suggests a couple of things to practice. . .

In Riccardo's self-description: *"I am a student of the Italian language, whose native language is English; although, some people would dispute that I am originally from the Bronx and have never lost my accent. My nonno and nonna on my father's side came from Montesarchio outside of Benevento, Italy; my grandparents on my mother's side came from Stockholm, Sweden. Neither Italian nor Swedish was ever spoken in my home. Over the years I have reached out to my relatives in Italy, and I have become obsessed with being able to communicate in Italian. As such, I often try to talk to my Italian friends at La Mezza Luna restaurant; but I quickly discovered that no matter how well one knows vocabulary or grammar, if your pronunciation is not precise, Italians will simply not understand you. Even worse, unless you know the Italians really well and ask them to correct your pronunciation, they will prefer to talk in English and let your poor attempts go unchecked. . . And so on and on. . .*

***

And just an hour later on the same Sunday, Tom Clifford knocked at the door, this time to collect a few old cameras and lenses he repurposes into the art of optics. Retired from his previous rocket scientist job, he now does many creative things, including useful interactive toys for children similar to what one finds at the Exploratorium; one, for example, is entitled:

"This may be ugly, but it's fragile and does nothing!"

This is his feedback after he went home to dismantle my old cameras, including a sixty-year-old reflex Minolta:

"I've tackled two lenses so far, and have gleaned:
two shutter-action toys,
seven gears,
six big units that will soon yield their precious optics
nineteen big ring items, and
eighty-two tiny screws!

I will attack the other goodies soon and will send you pictures of the results of the bounty."

Tom was born in Texas, one of nine kids into a legacy of academics and engineers! Another creative writer and artist! Tom worked on the birth of space travel including Gemini at McDonnel, the Space Shuttle, and satellites at Lockheed. And so many other engineering achievements in Silicon Valley.

He wrote a collection of short stories, *All this fun, and a paycheck, too?* a collection of short stories from a long and satisfying engineering career; showing how much fun, worthy, and enriching a technical life can be.

And an autobiographical gallery of photographs concentrating on his life experiences: *A day in the life of a rocket scientist.* He is also involved in "green" initiatives and now, retired, enjoys kayaking, fishing, hiking, photography—often from his wife's aerobatic airplane.

As we mentioned, he is now a recovering-engineer-slash-wannabe artist.

***

But here comes the pressing news!

"Goats!!!! Delivered today by Sand Hill beach! Our ecological grass mowers!

Sorry, I have to go take some pictures of them!

A bien tot.

PREMEDITATION

This is a story that began a long time ago, when I was not over my obsession with Edgar Allan Poe yet. But I never finished because I could not think of a gasp-inducing end. Still, I can't! But the story took a life of its own. So, here it is:

***

I was sitting in the porch of my home in El Granada with a glass of chilled wine on the table and a book in my hands, when a neighbor came and sat on the rocking chair. He liked chilled wine just as much as I did and this was not the first time that I had to move my ass, go into the kitchen, and get another glass.

I had not seen him in a while and I wondered where he was returning from. He was sort of a goofy old guy in his sixties, still in pretty good shape, quite talkative when he was not absorbed in some distant thoughts, and keen to open his heart when conversations drifted toward the bizarre. He loved to regurgitate narratives that sounded more like fables, slowly recounting what belonged to his past, whether personal or imported from another life. He confided in me because he knew I enjoyed his eccentricities and that like him, in my retirement days, I had nothing to do between the hours that preceded the sunset through the ones that followed it.

"So, Jack, how is life treating you. . . and your delightful Brett?"

"Well, we are carrying on," I replied. "We are getting old, that's for sure! You know, sometimes I look at her in the evening just before going to bed and I recognize my grandmother in her. And I say to myself,

Oh my God, I married my Grandma! But then I turn off the light and get cozy at her side."

"Well, you are lucky," he replied, "to have someone to keep you warm at night! You have no idea how lucky you are! Not having to wonder what would be if you would breathe your last by yourself in the middle of the night and nobody finding out till days later when someone would send the skunk team to find out where the stink is coming from!"

"Yup! She's been a good companion. . . Tolerant! That's the right word! She has been very tolerant. Gotta be thankful! And what about you? How's life treating you?"

"Same as usual! Tolerant, I would say. Mutually tolerant! I accommodate it and get along with it, day after day just as much as life is still tolerating a few more breaths from this old carcass. Any alternatives? Well, at least the football season is here! That gives me something to worry about!"

So it was that after two glasses of wine and some more small talk, he then began:

***

I am going to share a personal story with you, something that really happened to me not so long ago!

Maybe not exactly a story. . .

But more precisely a. . . nightmare.

I was sitting in bed late at night reading with a pillow tucked against the headboard and the bedside lamp keeping me company.

It was no ordinary novel. Not one of those predictable bestsellers. It was actually an interesting story.

It was, as a matter of fact, the egregious story of my life.

"*Oh boy! How interesting could that be?*" you may say.

Not much. No problem admitting it. Definitely not to a general audience. That's why you are never going to find it in the windows at Barnes and Noble. Nor in the back shelves! Just don't waste your time on that, trust me. But you have the unique opportunity of listening to it for free, compliments of my insomniac nights.

Also, it was interesting enough to me.

As it should be.

Or it was at the start, at least!

But as time passed by and chapters went on, it became ever less captivating—lots of disconnected thoughts, forgotten plots, repetitive actions, languid nostalgia, fuzzy recollections, not what one would call a pageturner! Quite the discrepancy from the earlier chapters.

You may recognize how painful it is to be stranded with yourself. That aging, emotionally unpredictable, and fragile self! Especially when one is not fond of that guy imprisoned behind the mirror, who exclusively reflects disappointment and disgust.

And this is why I wanted very much to get this story over with, once and for all.

But I was also tired, you know? Another never-ending day enslaved by my eccentricities!

Who knows how many times I turned back to check on the shadow of my conscience that was following me incessantly? How many times did I try to chase it away? And accelerated my steps? Even ran. But that silent, imperturbable shadow had been following me all day. A remarkable day indeed as you will soon hear.

Anyhow, I was sitting in bed, the bedside light my only companion, trying to get through the story in one way or another. For a bad actor, who can't follow even the conventional script of life, it's difficult to keep the momentum going and the play soon turns dull. It is at this juncture that the merciful writer needs to step in to compensate for the meaningless existence of his pedantic character with creativity; feed the lost soul with new ideas that could pass the threshold of monotony! But Pirandello has long gone, and I do not know anyone that could improvise a *"Recita a soggetto "*[25] just for me. So, the last chapters of my orphan story sat in my hands, going nowhere, having no appeal even to a soap opera fan.

Therefore, I was determined to get through it as quickly as I could. Yet, lifelong compulsions dictated the terms: stick to the progression of events.

---

[25] "Recita a soggetto (Tonight we improvise)," play by Luigi Pirandello

Sentence by sentence. Paragraph by paragraph. Heartbeat by heartbeat! Do not attempt to circumvent the monotonous flow of life with its haphazard succession of loosely connected events.

In the end, I overcame the uncontrollable compulsion to walk through the book word by word and I turned my brain onto a fast-reading gear: catching the first words of a paragraph and jumping to its end, convincing myself that I wasn't missing much in what laid in between. That seemed to alleviate the problem but, as I progressed, new pages piled up rapidly; faster than I could catch up with, loaded with a disconcerting accumulation of leftover crumbs of life, trivial and inconsequential garbage of no appeal even to a Hollywood screenwriter. A compilation of senseless garbling that never ended, perfectly attuned, I guess, to this stage of my life.

The more I flipped, the more there seemed to be no end at all!

I just needed to get through it and dive into my well-deserved peace. I kept flipping pages faster and faster. Every few paragraphs, I checked how many more pages were left. . . . Do you ever catch yourself doing that? Some people appraise stories by opening pages at random; they do it in the bookstores to decide what to buy. Some even take a peek at the end to judge from the punchline whether the rest deserves their precious time. But of course, one cannot do it with the story of his own life—do you have any suggestions?

I didn't think so.

***

Anyhow, I finally told myself:

"*What the heck!*"

And I jumped to the last chapters.

If I remember correctly, there were only forty-nine pages left! Yet, with each chapter (I am afraid I am repeating myself) the story was growing ever more tedious. It might have had to do with the essence of life, which begins in the fast lane, exciting for a while but quickly slows as aspirations and dreams scale back from flying into the moon to more practical achievements that converge into retirement plans, conservative investments, senior discounts, handicap-accessible facilities, optimization of bodily functions, and so on.

My eyelids were growing heavy. I thought of the monotonous repetition of each day's routine. I needed to rest. I thought with contempt of the sun. What an idiot our star is. Just spending each day hopelessly going from east to west without any aspiration at all! For millions—*billions!*— of years, following the same routine day after day! East to west, east to west, over and over! But of course, what do you expect from a star? No brain there, no *libero arbitrio*!

"My mind is superior to that of the stupid xun's," I thought. "Something needs to be done to break the monotony. If I can't go back, I will jump forward! I will read this story according to my own *arbitrio*!. . . And then. . . let's get over with it!"

***

So, there I was! Into the last chapter of my life.

I found myself in the Maldives flying from Malé to an atoll fifty miles or so south. I was sitting on the back seat of a seaplane. The young pilot talked incessantly about his dream to move to America while a nice guy kept offering sparkling wine and addressed me as "Sir." It was just the three of us. That's because I paid premium dollars for the vacation. An exclusive selection for a "very important person." I bought that package because I had decided that it was time to treat myself with something special. . . exclusively for me! I had kept my existence frugal till then, gilded only with sacrifices: family, career, recognition, acknowledgment, you name it. I had lived in a box, a comfortable package shipped from birth soon to be delivered by a rushed courier to its final destination.

So, it was time to finish with grandeur, light the fireworks! Unbridle the pleasure!

I had booked the trip to the Maldives, this spectacular vacation, to accomplish something extraordinary. Something most would not have the courage to conceive. I planned. . .

Let me explain.

Lately during my constipated nights, I had been watching crime stories. I obsessed over the minutia of investigations, the perseverance of the detectives, the inexorable determination to find the motive, the clues, collect the evidence to frame the suspect, and then the ultimate incontestable step: DNA evidence. I concluded that clearly, there was no crime that the FBI could not solve! There was no such thing as the perfect crime save for those haphazard murders carried out by disturbed minds that bore no logic, no motive and didn't deserve my attention.

But, the well thought out, carefully planned, premeditated crimes would sooner or later be unraveled

I loved watching all of that! I was engrossed and obsessed with it! I spent my empty evenings watching TV series, guessing the resolution during commercial breaks, enjoying the arrests and the judgments. Going to bed, I transitioned into sleep forging my own crime, in turns being a detective and a perpetrator.

And this is how one night, I suddenly reckoned that I could do better than all those clever criminals and I could overcome the scrutiny of the best detectives. I knew that I could create the perfect crime—the inscrutable premeditated murder!

Think about it: the first thing detectives look for is a motive!

But. . . What if there was no motive?

What about a murder committed just for the sake of it? Just a cold-blooded murder without any possible trigger? And what if the crime is perpetrated in a place that bears no ties to the criminal's life? No acquaintances or relatives that could be deemed related to the murderer's actions. How perfect would that be?

This is why I chose to take a trip to the Maldives.

I was enchanted by the idea and kept pondering the details as I was looking through the seaplane window at the passing atolls, little onion rings sprinkled amidst the Indian Ocean. Little brackets of existence, tired of the picture-taking honeymooners, and waiting for something exciting to happen.

"What a perfect setup!" I thought.

***

At the berth, the master of ceremony welcomed me with some sort of exotic alcoholic beverage.

With him was a woman, an acquaintance met by chance during a business trip some time before in a faraway country. I persuaded her to join me there for the luxurious vacation. She was a naïve young woman of egregious beauty and relaxed disposition. Exactly the companion I needed to execute my plan.

She acted as if she was happy to see me.

"What a majestic performer!" I thought. "But at least she demonstrates some gratitude for the opulent vacation!"

Unlimited variations of photos were taken; Her and me; me and her; me and her and the master of ceremony! With flowers, with drinks, with and without the seaplane in the background! Big smiles in the vanguard, big smiles of joy, undefined and unjustified joy poorly masking my depression under the scorching sun.

We were then escorted on a golf cart to a bungalow, a palafitte over the coral reefs. A ridge at the end of the lagoon separated us from the big blue ocean creating a pool of transparent sea where one could follow the tropical fauna swimming and grazing about. It was perfect beauty.

I tipped the master, and we were alone. We sat on the porch overlooking the lagoon that reflected the living postcard in which we found ourselves waiting for the sunset. When it came, it was as spectacular as predicted and a few more photos were taken to commemorate who knows what. After the sunset, we entered the bungalow to dress up for dinner.

The bungalow consisted of a big room with a king bed in the center facing the tidal pool, the reef, and the ocean beyond. We looked at each other in silence from the opposite side of the bed. She opened her suitcase, took the clothes, and organized them in the closet. She then drew a black silk night gown and spread it over the bed. Then she looked at me and smiled.

We walked out.

She held my hand. After a few steps, I freed my hand and supported her arm more formally instead as we walked to one of the resort's restaurants. It was a most romantic dinner. I made sure to act as a cheerful honeymooner. I competed with the waiter in pulling out the chair for her, and unfolding the napkin, touching her shoulder, and squeezing it gently before taking my seat. I held her hand across the table. All had to be perfect according to plan, and indeed it was!

***

Later, in the room, we shared the bed. She had brought protection just in case we needed it.

"Thoughtful of her," I thought. "One could call it professional!"

But it was not going to be necessary. I was done with that stuff. Nothing comes easy with women! I paid for her to keep me company. I was not looking for sex. Besides, the possibility of becoming attached to her unnerved me.

I told her that I brought her there because I wanted a companion. I did not expect anything else. I just did not want to be alone in such a beautiful place.

She reacted by shedding a few silent tears. It was not a sad cry at all, just that feminine outburst that compensates for wordless emotions. When she recovered, she told me that all she had experienced so far was a more or less respectful consumption of her body by men. A trade that had made her life livable, even comfortable, but not particularly meaningful. She was touched that I had chosen her as a companion, though temporary. She asked whether I did this often. I replied that this was my first time. She asked why I did it. I replied that I did not know.

Then she added as she lifted the sheet and got into the bed:

"It's okay. But if you change your mind, I would be happy to make love to you."

We laid in bed. She accosted me and rested her head upon my shoulder, and I placed my arm around her shoulders, caressing the hair of this innocent soul. Soon, she fell into a deep sleep and as her breaths were clocking the night, I looked at the ceiling and went over my plan.

***

As days passed, she grew fond of me, an almost filial love, sweet and devoted. She became solicitous, anticipating and taking care of my needs. Meanwhile, she told me she felt secure with me. For the first time in her

190

life, she was not alone. Indeed, she had a miserable youth and it made perfect sense that she found a home, finally, in the arms of a paternal figure.

I liked the unfolding of the relationship for various reasons. Surely, I was starting to develop a certain attachment of my own for this sweet little woman. But most importantly, I reckoned with gratification that she was following my imaginary script to perfection. She performed, under all possible appearances, as the honeymooner I wanted for everyone to witness.

I asked her to write messages to me stating her affection with the pretense of playing a game of love and leave a track of memories to be cherished after we would part!

"That's a good way to dissuade any suspicion should anyone bother to look into my lines of communication later on!" I thought with satisfaction and a generous amount of pride.

"What kind of motive could a rich old man have to commit a murder in such an idyllic condition?"

Days went by rapidly. I took her fishing, swimming, sailing, snorkeling, scuba diving. I took her for long walks at sunset along the beach, where she caught and held little hermit crabs that suspiciously peeked out of their shell and gently pinched her fingers before running away when she released them while the giant fruit bats hovered discreetly over us. I let her hold my hand, particularly when we were encountering other couples.

We had luxurious dinners, followed by late nights when we listened to live music in the submarine bar. We laughed and cheered while I sensed the envy around me and experienced the perverted joy of showing off this image of perfect love. I was ostentatiously affectionate in public, in disproportion to our private conduct back in the room.

**

The last night came.

We retired around one in the morning. We would have to wake up early to go to the berth for her departure, while I would linger in the atoll for another day.

She was not tired at all. As I laid in bed, she sneaked closer and closer.

"I want to make love to you," she said.

I turned toward her, and I kissed her. A gentle kiss on her lips and I said:

"Not tonight! Maybe one day. Maybe if we see each other again. I really do not want to spoil this beautiful vacation with a last-minute fling! You are a good woman, young, beautiful, and intelligent. Now you know it, and you can thrive with a man who respects and cares for you. When you go back to your country, remember who you are and make careful choices. You will have lots of opportunities, but then, if you still think of me, then, maybe, we can see each other again. And that time, I will make love to you."

***

The morning came. I was the first to wake up at the light of dawn. She was peacefully breathing, her head on my shoulder just as we had fallen asleep.

I started caressing her black hair and her forehead. I whispered her name a few times till she opened her eyes.

"Time to go!" I told her.

She looked at me with the startled gaze of one who is reorganizing her thoughts.

"I know!" she answered.

She stretched her neck to reach my face and kissed me in the cheek. Then she started packing.

At the berth, the seaplane was waiting in the fresh morning breeze. It was just the crew and the two of us. I hugged her tightly, this time without staging any performance. I had grown fond of the sweet lady. I kissed her on the lips gently while her luggage was carried on board. I helped her to the doorway, and I kissed her once more. She immediately ran to the window and waved at me. The door was closed, the plane sputtered, and she waved again. With the camera, she caught one last picture of me, she waved one more time and smiled while the plane departed, leaving a phosphorescent wake behind.

***

Sunrise was about to happen. I took a deep sigh.

It was finally time for me to focus on the main purpose of the voyage. I could finally contemplate without distraction and execute my plan.

The staging phase was completed. Everyone in the island knew perfectly well what a fortunate and happy man I was. In addition, I had gained popularity with the staff and guests, by tipping the former generously and entertaining the latter. Nobody would ever suspect such a jolly character like me of murder.

Only thing left was to finalize the plan.

You see, I am not a bad person. I have a gentle disposition, not a whim of violence ever entered my thoughts throughout my life. I would never hurt a fly and sometimes I even feel ambivalent about hurting mosquitos! Therefore, the selection of the victim had to be done carefully.

First, I needed to target someone with whom I was unlikely to have a close relationship. If you pay attention, you will agree that by dying one leaves the burden of grief to the survivors who mourn the loss. And this can accumulate to a significant amount of pain inflicted to multiple survivors. Definitely not something that my conscience could bear! Thus, the victim had to be a loner that lived in a neglected corner of life and whose death would go pretty much unnoticed.

Second, the victim himself had to be someone who had nothing to lose, who in fact might even appreciate the chance of trashing the senseless routine of life. Someone who had nothing to live for. Someone who struggled day after day waiting for night to come.

There are many loners around of course, but I had always known in my premeditated scheme who the victim would be. The choice had not been difficult at all.

It was obvious that the perfect victim was me.

I lived alone, my only close relative was a daughter whom I barely saw, maybe once a year for Thanksgiving. She left years ago to follow a degenerate guy and only God knows where they lived now. I had a few distant relatives who never called me or checked on me. A few friends whom I had not heard from or seen for months, who would perhaps remember my name when and if they found out. They would say a few customary polite words at best to whomever happened to be around before going back to their businesses. But that would be all, not much to worry about.

And what about myself, you may ask. Honestly, I had nothing to live for. Probably I didn't for quite a long time. So, why should I feel bad for myself?

The only concern I had was that I did not want the occurrence to be perceived as suicide. It would have been unbecoming and ridiculous to work so hard all my life just to end it like this!

"What a moron! Why didn't he do it earlier?" I could imagine people asking. "He could have saved himself lots of trouble and the world some oxygen!"

In any case, it was not a suicide for the simple reason that my motivation was not to kill myself. All I wanted was to commit the perfect murder and the perfect victim just happened to be me!

What I needed to do was to stage an accident.

As I was thinking of the details, my cell phone beeped, and a message appeared on the screen. It was from her:

"My dear, I think I love you and I will forever. I remember what you told me last night and I will try to find happiness somehow, but I know that true happiness will only be with you. I really hope that I will see you again."

I texted back:

"Sweetheart. If you really want, you will see me soon. I promise that I will be there. In the meantime, cheer up!"

And then I thought to myself:

"What a perfect exchange! No motive to kill or be killed! Instead, a promise for a happy future to come!"

***

The day went by uneventfully and evening came.

I treated myself to a Lucullian dinner. I selected the best wines and most extravagant food. I left a generous tip. I chatted with the waitress about the following day and about my departure. How much I would have missed everyone, who had been so kind to me, and I talked about my beloved girlfriend whom I will soon see again. I was sorry that I had to leave but all good things had to find an end! And I had so much waiting for me at home, etc. etc.

I said good night and I went to the submarine bar to listen to live music. Unfortunately, it was some sort of tedious disco music. But it was good enough to justify a few drinks. After about an hour, I was obviously drunk. I could barely find the door and ostensibly I staggered out. Some kind soul asked if I needed help. I expressed my gratitude while I stepped forward. Finally, I reached the bungalow. I undressed, placed my belongings on the bed, and in my underwear I stepped out toward the tidal pool that the tide had filled deep enough for one to drown. I had taken a chilled bottle of gin out of the refrigerator and carried it with me so it could put me to sleep in the warm water.

As I was about to step out of the door into the porch and walk down the steps to the lagoon, the cellular beeped again.

Not sure why, but I stepped back, perhaps driven by the curiosity of finding out what would be the last message I'd ever receive in my life. It was probably my gentle companion from the previous nights who had reached home and wanted to say good night.

"Great," I thought. "I can leave one more trace of happiness!"

It was instead a message from my daughter:

"Dad, I am out of the house, I need the security code for the alarm before I get in. I need to move in with you. I am pregnant and Scott wants me to abort. I told him to fuck himself and left him. I need a place to stay."

And I answered:

"My sweet Julie, welcome back! Keep the baby! You did well! Forget that loser. I will take care of you both. Here is the code! Wait for me. I will be there in a day! I cannot believe I will be a grandpa!"

I felt that one more piece was fitting into my scheme!

"Who is ever going to believe that one would kill himself after such news and such a promise!"

"Meanwhile, Julie would be fine. She would inherit my fortune, keep the house, and raise the baby."

Instead of going into the tidal pool, however, I hesitated and sat on the rocking chair in the porch.

For some reason, I recollected the story of a friend's grandma.

The parsimonious lady had decided that it was not cost effective, after a certain age, to continue living and took it upon herself to find an end when, according to her judgment, the time had come. So, one day, she went to the pharmacy to buy something she thought could help the plan. When she found the potion, she took three bottles and went to the cashier. One can barely imagine her disappointment when she saw the price! She thought it was ridiculous to spend so much to die and figured it was cheaper to live, particularly within her modest means. So, she went back to her routine and lived for a few more decades.

Not sure how truthful the story was, but it made me smile. It was my first unprompted smile in a long time.

"Maybe I can drink myself to death on another occasion. It is getting chilly and besides, Julie and the nipper may need me!"

So, I was sitting in bed, with the bedside table lamp my only companion, trying to finish the book. But still more pages were left. They were empty white pages. I guess even the author had grown sick and tired of the story for the night. I rested the book at my side, I don't think I even had the strength to turn off the light. I closed my eyes and told myself that if I could not finish the story tonight, I would have to wait patiently for destiny to write a few more pages at its own convenience.

***

The neighbor smiled, filled his glass from a new bottle of wine that I had just opened and while he was drinking, I said:

"I guess, the point of your story is that we cannot take control of what happens, not even when we think we make choices about our own life, because we are subjects to the whims of our foolish brain upon which we have no jurisdiction, and just a little nipper can come into one's life and reprogram it anew. And I am glad this happened to you. In the end, I need someone to drink with."

THE SWAN SONG

The silver Swan, who living had no note,
when death approached, unlocked her silent throat.
Leaning her breast against the reedy shore,
thus sang her first and last, and sang no more:
"Farewell, all joys! O Death, come close my eyes!"

The Silver Swan *by Orlando Gibbons*

***

"If an old man speaks in a crowded street and nobody pays attention, does he still make a sound?"

We were sitting face-to-face, a Martini in his left hand and a frozen Margarita in mine, when he continued:

"My grandpa used to garnish the family dinners with his World War I adventures. I still carry vivid memories of those retellings. I was the only one listening. Nobody else did. Neither did he. He spat words out of his mouth mechanically for the consumption of the innocent grandchild. I was the only one naïve enough to care. I remember this one:

It's the third year. We've done our turn, and the company or whoever is left of it is set to go back home. And then the captain says: "We are gonna go nowhere. The country needs us, tomorrow we go out and fight for freedom." We looked at each other and said nothing. Sure enough, the next day, instead of going home we are in the trenches. First thing, as soon as the shooting starts, the sergeant holds up his riffle and snipes at the captain's head. Nobody says nothing. Two days later we're home.

"Grandpa took out his dentures; they were too loose, and a crumb of the *torta del Paradiso* was stuck between them and the palate. Then, he turned his index finger upside-down and judiciously scraped the crumb off. That

199

made him gag a little and so he guzzled a good sip of Barbera. Then, he returned the dentures into their original position, puffed, rubbed is nose, and forgot about the grandson waiting for the next story."

Pretty sure it is an apocryphal recollection, maybe a dream of his, but this and other fantastic stories came out of his mouth after sufficient drinking, only to be dismissed by all and, as years went by, also by me."

After another sip of Martini and a scratch of the head, he continued:

"And Grandpa walked along the streets, arguing loudly with himself. There were no cell phones then, or earpods, and people thought he was just a crazed old man; but he was a visionary ahead of his time. There would be no qualms now.

"But now, just like Grandpa, it's my turn to be a dusty antique; a relic to be displayed in a vintage store, a gramophone with a scratchy voice."

After another sip of Martini, he concluded with an affable smile, turning his dark blue eyes towards me:

"You see? The biggest fear of aging is becoming irrelevant."

His piercing eyes seemed lost, torn between studying my reaction or staring toward the deep abyss of the future.

I had no idea where all of this was coming from. Yet I had no propensity to encourage more of this strange conversation.

Instead, I tried to lighten up the mood:

"Come on! Don't be silly! You are an icon among friends, admirers, fans. You will never be obsolete! And you will never be even close to irrelevant to me. You know that I love you!"

"Thanks!" he replied with an ironic smile. "I love myself too, or at least I used to!"

No point trying harder.

I sat silently, looking at my idol. A gentle soul under the hide of a grumpy old man.

"It is not just about oblivion; it's more than that. While the world fades around me, standing in front of the mirror of my conscience, I see regrets,

I see the treasures that I squandered. Too many ghosts to share the emptiness with. A vague fear of the unknown is my angel of the night. One wants to shout, to tell everyone, to ask for mercy, but who is there to listen? Who wants to be bothered by the whimpers of an old man?

"As a good friend once said: 'An open door always makes you pause, leaving you to wonder which way to go.'

"But what if there is nowhere left to go? Everything becomes purposeless and the distant horizon, far from being a challenge, becomes an insignificant nuance. How many times can I go to bed at night ready to die only to wake up alive the next morning and wait for my next chance? See? This is my curse; the limbo at the twilight of life."

***

We said goodbye. I hugged him tightly. Standing rigid like a flagpole, acquiescent, he accepted the embrace. As my hug lasted too long, he put his hand on my shoulder, squeezed it gently, kissed the top of my head lightly, and said:

"Time to go now. But first I want to give you this."

He took a giftbox out of his pocket and held it out for me. I opened it. It was a pin—a red rose made of coral on a white gold stem with small diamonds adorning two yellow golden leaves.

***

Day passed, then months. Life was neither good nor bad, it was simply empty.

I missed him. He had been my mentor since my post-doc days. I continued in his department as a faculty member. I grew up under his protection. We were very close. I saw him go through difficult times, personal and professional. I saw him jump into retirement. I saw him lose his wife to cancer. Our relationship became intimate, comfortable, even loving. He never expressed any feelings for me beyond what's appropriate for a professional relationship.

But a woman knows; I saw his pride, when I gave a talk, when I received an award; it was more than paternal affection. I knew just exactly how he felt. And I waited and waited till all commitments disappeared, no wife, no children around. He was an aging old me, and I was still young and attractive. Though we became closer and closer, he never responded to my subtle hints. It was just a lovely friendship.

Yet, I never married.

***

Then, he disappeared.

He did not return my messages. No one came to the door when I rang the doorbell. I worried, we worried, we informed the police. Searches began, but he was nowhere to be found; he became a missing person, and with time, nobody cared anymore except for me.

Women have physiological needs, and besides, they are compelled to please their parents. I convinced myself that he was gone. I had relationships, then I married, and I had a daughter, whom I love very much.

Years passed.

As I said, life was neither good nor bad, it was just empty.

***

A few years from the disappearance, I received a letter. The familiar chicken scratch spelled my name and address. It came from somewhere in the South China Sea.

My dear,

Sorry for disappearing suddenly. I had to do it. I love you. I always have since the first time I met you. Your spirit full of life, your uplifting personality, your beautiful smile. But you were the "hope diamond" of my life. I had commitments and even worse, we lived in two different worlds that happened to cross. Forty years separate us. What an irony to meet the right person at its crepuscule. I know that you loved me, and this is why I had to go, give you a chance to find your own life.

I was happy here, living in a medical resort, taking care of cancer patients till I became one of them.

This is my swan song, I just wanted to let you know that I love you.

That night, I talked to my husband, I told him everything and said:

"I have to go see him; I have to find closure."

***

The seaplane landed at the shore of the quiet resort. Few locals came to greet me at the pier. They brought me to the village chief. A sweet old man with very dark skin and very white hair. They spoke English quite well.

I asked about him. The elder looked at me without a word. Then, he walked out of the hut, gesturing for me to follow.

Shading his eyes from the sun with the palm of his hand, he raised the other arm to point toward the summit of a hill close by.

"The doctor is there, resting in peace."

I asked to be carried up there. They pulled out an old Toyota fit for the jungle, and we reached the summit.

Under a tall meranti tree, a pile of dirt surged among tropical flowers.

As I approached, I saw a slate planted vertically at the head of the fresh mound. A rose was carved at the top and, below it, this sentence was engraved:

"I knew you would be here."

***

More years passed. Life is still neither good nor bad. But it isn't empty anymore.

THE STRANGE CASE OF CLARA'S EYES

I Ricordi

Vengono alla mente
Poco a poco
Prendono forma
Lentamente
Ridanno sensazioni già
Stampate nella mente
e
Improvvisamente
Tutto è lì
Vicino e vivo
Come se fosse ieri
Rimangono fino a quando
Ti rendi conto. . .
Non sono il tuo presente
Solo un pezzo del passato

***

Memories

They sneak into mind
Gradually
They take shape
Slowly
Sensations return
Printed in the mind
And suddenly
Everything is there
Near and alive
As if it were yesterday
They stay until
You realize. . .
They are not your present
Only a piece of the past

Giuseppe Masucci, January 19, 2015

A WALK IN THE PARK

On a cloudless April 1st of several years ago, Luca, or more precisely, Professor Leoluca de Mirafiori, was taking a stroll across the Giardini Pubblici[26] of Milan. With both hands in his pockets and it being about five in the afternoon, Luca had nowhere to go, nor did he retain a precise recollection of where he was coming from.

Suddenly, the professor interrupted his meditative saunter. He sat on a bench and, intertwining the last three fingers of both hands, he joined his palms, opposed his thumbs against each other to hold his chin. He then applied both index fingers to gently massage his upper lip all the way to the base of his nose, upwardly dislodging the heavy framed glasses he wore.

Having satisfactorily completed such ceremony, he began to reminisce.

***

We all experience occasions when the past appears livelier than the present itself, which in turn seems breathless and inanimate. In those moments, we witness events that happened a long, long time ago as they materialize in front of us, while we discreetly stand aside as silent bystanders.

Of late, Luca had been living by default as if there were no other practical alternative. It appeared to him that reality belonged only to his mind, while what was out there was just a distraction, a realm breathing an autocratic and autonomous existence that had no impact on his own being. It seemed like he was transiting life as a tourist, who roams a notable place to which,

---

[26] Public Gardens

however, he does not belong; a site from which one accumulates assorted images to be deposited in the baggage of memory for future use. Just as we are unsure about what to do with the heap of photographs that sit on our desk at the end of a journey, he did not exactly know how to exploit that mélange of recollections save for, perhaps one day, conflating them into a disorderly catalogue, a jumbled memoir for a nonexistent audience.

He had tried in the past to apply the power of concentration to trap the ephemeral progression of events. By enhancing life's corporeality, he imagined it would be easier to get hold of its parts. But this effort could not slow the process. This attempt to capture experiences could not stop their motion by turning them into still objects. Unlike photos, life could not be framed, and he eventually conceded that attempting to catch the moment while the present wriggles away and turns into the past right in front of one's eyes was to no avail.

As a consequence, through a process of reverse logic, he had taken to disregarding the flow of current events as if they were just momentary illusions not worthy of consideration.

Yet, depending upon the direction we face in a moving vehicle, we may judge that we are staring at the future when facing forward or to the past otherwise. In reality and independently of our perception, our movement makes no difference to the stillness of inanimate things that, indifferent to time and motion, dwell where they are, save for the imperceptible ethereal motion of the universe by which unwarily, we all abide. But, engrossed in the illusion, we wonder whether we could reverse the course of our own life by simply turning back to stare in the direction from which we came.

Accordingly, Luca, dismissing his skepticism and uncharacteristically engrossed in the moment, scrutinized his surroundings as if what had elapsed in the last decades constituted only a dream from which he was now awakening to realize that his past—in the form of centennial horse chestnut trees orderly aligned along pebble paths, the conceited pigeons, the pond with its boring carps, the lovely mallards, the elegant water striders and the lilies, the monumental fountains, the artificial miniature hills, the Museum of Natural History, the Planetarium, the austere statue of Antonio

Stoppani,[27]—were all still there, completely unchanged. Contrary to the rest of his life experience, time had miraculously halted exclusively in these Gardens, a natural preserve against the extinction of moments. All of it was still there unchanged while, in the rest of his world, several things had come and gone with the progression of time.

**

It was, therefore, natural for him to rewind at leisure the footage of life while resting on that bench. And as Luca was going through these meditations, he looked around, baffled to see that, after enduring many winters and summers, what had been long gone, was still there unchanged, including this old bench where he used to sit with friends when they skipped school during similarly bright days of spring. . . And that old horse chestnut tree oddly shaped like a humongous diapason with two parallel, diverging branches a few feet above the ground so they only reached past the children's knees, where a long time ago, he kissed Sleeping Beauty.

Some coquettish classmates had persuaded him one purposeless afternoon to reenact Perrault's tale by impersonating Prince Charming. Clara, who was acting as Sleeping Beauty, was lying with shut eyes in the embrace of the tree's branches. When the moment came to rouse her from her slumber, he sneaked toward her, and with the gentlest of motions, grazed her lips with his own.

Two immense blue eyes opened in front of him, of an infinite color and of the loftiest freshness; and she smiled and flushed simultaneously. Without hearing the giggles of the girls and the squawking of the immature boys, he lifted her from the tree and, holding her in his arms, walked away bequeathing another gentle kiss that this time, however, resulted in a bit warmer and velvety contact between his two slightly open lips and her upper one.

**

On the following day, as Luca approached the school entrance, a scrawny boy with red hair, freckles and a noticeable pimple in his left cheek placed himself sturdily in front of him with legs spread wide and his index finger

---

[27]The author of *Il Bel Paese,* a bestselling book published in 1876 celebrating the beauties of Italy and decades later becoming the name of a brand of very popular cheese.

pointing straight at Luca's nose. Although it was Luca's fourth year in that high school, he had never taken notice of the minuscule creature, and without giving him the satisfaction of paying any attention, he swerved to avoid him. But the stranger stepped closer and, as Luca was about to overtake him, he delivered a controlled punch right to the side of his left lip that, without truly hurting him, obliged Luca to acknowledge the existence of the annoying contender.

Luca, who was a youngster of athletic build, agreeable personality, and respectable upbringing, abiding by the Milanese upper-class etiquette of polite debate rather than contentious disagreement, did not know how to react against this adversary of miniature proportions but sedulous temperament. Therefore, proactively, he turned his chest toward him, and to avoid further embarrassment, he held the redhead by his arms, lifting him up to look him straight in the face.

"What the hell is wrong with you?"

To which the redheaded boy, shaking by then, answered:

"I was told that you kissed Clara at the park yesterday. . . don't you know that I love her? For you—for you these are just—they are only games," he stuttered.

Luca held the wriggling worm a little closer and with tightly closed lips he kissed him just to the side of the pimple and then whispered:

"I am sorry, do not worry, she is all yours."

Then, he dropped the boy with his legs spread wide, frozen in the same position as before, and left him there with his arms resting flaccidly along his gaunt torso.

Following that episode, Luca noticed Clara more often in the crowded school corridors; with her royal blue eyes shining like sapphires among her unremarkable friends; and when their gaze met and he kindly smiled at her, she blushed. But he never came close or talked to her. An inexplicable pride to honor his commitment to the freckled boy forced him to pretend that he was occupied; he quickly corrected his gaze to look over her as if something behind her was distracting him.

Days and months passed till high school was over, and they both moved on, along the distracting paths of life for which all that was needed was a tiny suitcase to carry one's hopes and dreams.

But her gentle demeanor, her sweet smile, her elegant countenance never abandoned him, and those transparent blue eyes with the clarity of Ceylon sapphires kept staring at him wherever he went and made him wonder what could have been if he had gotten to know her better. Even years later, he thought of Clara with regret, as an omen of lost opportunities, of dreams that do not materialize, of voices fading into echoes in the irreversible mystery of time until. . .

Now, as he sat on the bench, his eyes closed and his forehead resting between his palms, Luca could see her smiling clearly, as if he was at present taking her away from the embrace of the tree and into his arms.

*****

It was then that his trance was interrupted by the voice of a man asking him: "Who do you think invented marriage?"

On his right side sat an aging gentleman of the finest Milanese breed, who had approached the bench unannounced. He wore a tweed jacket with an elegantly folded pocket square, and an azure and thinly striped shirt where finely woven initials, "LM," stood at the left side of the collar. He wore a thick tie that could have been of the Marinella brand.[28] His trousers were of premium wool, and they were short enough to expose two skinny ankles covered by lightly colored silk and cotton socks that connected his body to a pair of leather-woven Moreschi[29] shoes of impeccable elegance. As a result, the stranger's demeanor appeared immured within his own attire although of these constraints, as for most aristocrats, he did not seem to take notice.

The stranger held his left arm along the backside of the bench as if he was about to offer the comfort of an embrace. His hair ruffled under the breeze, and it was of a chestnut color that shone under the oblique sunrays and heightened two green and penetrating eyes with which he inspected Luca

---

[28] Classic fashion brand from Naples producing mainly ties
[29] Top brand of Italian shoes for men

as if he was reading a treatise, while his words melted in the northern breeze to pleasantly caress Luca's cheeks.

Luca had turned to verify the source of the voice. But rather than questioning the stranger about his identity, satisfied after a preliminary glance by his decent appearance, he turned his attention back toward the diapason-shaped tree, relaxed his body over the backside of the bench, furrowed his eyebrows, pursed his lips into a curious shape that resembled a duck's beak and admitted to the tarrying stranger:

"I have no idea!"

Encouraged by Luca's admission of ignorance, the stranger crossed his right leg over his left, intertwined his fingers, and embarked in an impromptu dissertation.

"Plato imagined that humans originally existed as hermaphrodites conceitedly autonomous in reproductive needs. At last irritated by their arrogance, Zeus split them into two parts each complementing the other. This is why humans, now torn in their essence, wander the world seeking to reunite with their match. Thus, love is the longing to retrieve what we lost, the instinct to restore the unity of our spirit. . . . Some may argue that this is the justification for marriage."

"Yes, but how does this myth relate to the institution of marriage as it is inflicted upon us by society? How does this allegory advocate for the exclusivity of a lifelong relationship?" wondered Luca still staring at the empty embrace of the tree.

"According to the Christian faith," continued the stranger, "God instituted the covenant of marriage by uniting Adam and Eve. 'It is not good for man to be alone. I will make a helper suitable for him,' God said and, while Adam was asleep, he removed a rib from his body to form his eternal companion and complete His own creation. Even though Adam and Eve were two different creatures God called them 'one flesh,' therefore, being the Minister of the first marriage ceremony.

"But one could say that the Devil contributed his own part through Eve," the stranger reasoned.

"There was Adam!" the stranger continued. "The poor guy was innocently enjoying a carefree life immersed in the beauties of the Garden of Eden.

Then the Devil, together with Eve, plotted his curse gifting that unfortunate prototype of mankind with a conscience. It was a diabolic deception to bridle him like a draft horse. . . the curse of Eve! To be lashed for the rest of eternity by the whip of guilt, the rules of conventionality that traveled beyond East of Eden to become universal. And from then on, men are expected to follow, among other moral constraints, the rules of monogamy, though they still cannot quite understand the reasoning. In other words, how come we can hold with our fingers as many roses as we want, and we can eat as many candies as we please, or ride as many horses in the big prairie, but we are supposed to share our life just with one woman, for better and for worse. . . and mostly for worse? Who set this rule and why do we have to abide by it?"

It occurred to Luca that the stranger's words resonated, familiar concepts that must have been dwelling in the corners of his subconscious for a long time without answers for he had never managed to articulate any of them.

"Of course, in Adam's time, it was easier to be monogamous because there was only Eve. There were no distractions, no subtle touches of the hand in moments of unhappiness, no understanding smiles, no compassionate eyes to compensate for one man's loneliness. There was nobody to turn to when Eve had her premenstrual syndrome or other oddities of women's behavior that remain beyond any man's ability to comprehend."

As the stranger kept talking, Luca noticed two mallards, a beautiful male and a not-so- homely female silently parting the still surface of the pond, tranquilly paddling toward their future and unwarily leaving behind an imperceptible wake as a fugitive memento of their recent past.

"But the instinct to multiply, to propagate the reach of the human species complicated things. Men became bewildered juggling the instinct to procreate against constraints imposed by their wives. While they generously tried to satisfy as many women as they could, women took the Bible directives literally, turning the covenant of marriage from the original allegory into a firm commandment: '*Thou shall not covet other men's wives!*' Say the commandment! 'Thou shall not covet other women at all save for your proper wife' was the interpretation!

"Why do people get married in the first place? Who started this unfortunate practice? Who invented marriage! Was it a man or a woman? Did insecure women create this covenant because they wanted to preserve their possession coveted by other competitors like growling dogs defending their bone, or did men, just as insecure, invent it to try to guard their wife from predators with a virtual boundary? Who invented marriage? Was it a man or a woman who drove a covenant meant to control the uncontrollable?"

At this point, Luca started to feel kinship for the stranger, who had risen by then to a friendly accomplice.

"But it is understandable for men to view monogamy as a part-time engagement, pretty much like a professor takes a sabbatical from routine assignments. And it can be expected that men can be serially monogamous by having different women in separate and discreet moments to adapt their behavior to societal views. Thus, men can devote themselves wholeheartedly to one woman at a time by looking straight into her eyes and momentarily forgetting about all the other ones. It is like our beloved Italian strikes that are programmed by the hour; you can have a lifelong hunger strike that is planned in between meals! Just the same, men can be comfortably monogamous in multiple relationships by genuinely devoting heart and soul to one woman at a time. Just schizophrenic hermaphrodites with multiple personalities searching for various selves."

"Marriage is not an institution of nature. The family in the East is entirely different from the family in the West. The institutions are society grafts, not spontaneous growths of nature," continued the stranger, paraphrasing Napoleon.[30]

***

"What about those men like me who never learned how to love properly?" interrupted Luca. "Is this logic stipulating a pretext for all of them? Is this all intended to rationalize depraved behavior? Are you telling me that the conduct of all my life was not as debatable but the result of a legitimate rebellion to conventionality?"

"Well, that could be the topic for a whole novel," answered the stranger with a composed smile.

---

[30] Napoleon Bonaparte's speech in front of the Conceil d'Etat on the Civil Code and subsequent quotes from Honoré De Balzac's *The physiology of marriage*.

Then, he cordially shook Luca's hand and departed, stating:

"I hope to see you here again."

"When will I see you again?" asked Luca.

"When the appropriate time comes," responded the stranger with a bow.

***

Following the stranger's departure, Luca also rose and began to walk home distractedly. He thought about his wife, or to be more precise, his former wife as he had been divorced for some years. And that thought made him turn toward the mallards that were still cruising along in harmonious peace:

"Those animals are together for a lifetime! There is no rule or covenant that forces them to stay together; yet they do not part. Have they learned what I have yet to grasp after all these years? Are love and companionship a given for them?"

And at the same time, he remembered a remark offered by a woman once dear to him:

"You are like a leopard. . . powerful. . . beautiful. . . smart, whom we all adore and admire, but whom nobody can own or control because it thrives in freedom."

It was getting late, and the breeze was cooler. Shrugging his shoulders, Luca went home musing over a seemingly trivial question:

"Which is happier, the leopard doomed to follow its lifelong solitary trail or the gregarious mallard? Why was his instinct, like that of the leopard, programmed to dismiss love? Don't leopards ever encounter blue eyes like those of Clara? And if they do, would they take notice? And what about his own story? Would Clara have made a difference by turning the leopard in him into a happy mallard if he only had had the courage to give it a chance? Or, as with Clara, was it in his nature to shut his heart to the joys of a lifelong companionship? What drove him to the solitude that was now bearing down on him with the overpowering weight of regret? What waited ahead for the solitary leopard, now that the vigor of youth was languishing, and loneliness was becoming a reality rather than a choice?"

***

Walking out of the park, he ignored a beggar by turning his gaze to the opposite side of the sidewalk. But after a few steps, he stopped. He put his hands in the pocket and found a few coins. He retraced his steps to deposit the little fortune into the beggar's hand without looking at him and without waiting for signs of gratitude. He did not feel he deserved any; he had done it only for himself, to temporarily quench a troubled conscience, perform an act of goodwill to compensate for the harm imparted to others throughout years of self-absorption.

It felt even cooler in the early evening, and he dug both hands in his trouser pockets hastening his steps toward home. So many memories of women were suddenly flocking into his mind; beautiful, warm, intelligent, and generous companions, who had in turn performed love dances around the path of his life. Women he had misled with temporary attention; with whom he had never been able to establish a reciprocal relationship; a procession of vanished opportunities that had left him ultimately alone as an odd and thirsty plant to desiccate in the rain forest.

And on that cloudless afternoon on April 1st of several years ago, he suddenly missed each one of them including the one who was the most important; the one who used to be his wife, the one from whom he had parted for what seemed to him now to be no apparent reason.

**

Luca lived in an elegant apartment within the meandering streets that carve a path between Via Monte Napoleone and Via della Spiga. It took him about a quarter of an hour to reach home, snaking through the crowd of shoppers. By then, it was dusk, the streetlights gleamed and, together with the elegant shop windows, enlivened Corso Venezia.

Few drops of rain started to fall in spite of the cloudless day, and soon it was pouring:

"Aprile, ogni giorno un barile!"[31] he recounted.

---

[31] "April, each day a barrel (of water)!" – an expression suggesting that rainstorms are common in the month of April.

By the time he reached home, his clothes were sopping. He did not look for the key but rang the doorbell. He needed for somebody to greet him as a reassurance that he was not totally alone.

"Good evening, Mister Luca."

Sabrina came to the door, dressed in her servant's uniform. Luca inherited her from his dad who died a few weeks before. She had no job and nowhere to go. She would stay with him for the time being.

Luca looked at the minute Filipino woman and smiled at her, making her blush.

"At least I am not entirely alone!"

And he recalled the times when the cat came to welcome him before the divorce, before his wife took it with her without any consideration of joint custody. Even that had seemed trivial then.

Sabrina took the jacket and disappeared in the laundry, while he walked to the bedroom to take the rest of his clothes off. He piled them on the bed and redressed. Then, he called Sabrina and handed the pile to her and, while she was attentively organizing it into the laundry basket, he felt warmth in his chest—a familiar sensation triggered by the presence of a pretty woman that had opened the door to so many adventures in the past, a tender feeling that knows no boundaries.

"Sabrina," he said.

"Yes, Mister Luca," she replied.

"I want you to dine with me this evening. . . and, by the way, you can call me Luca."

***

That night, Luca made love to Sabrina, for no good reason at all. He simply did not want to be alone; just as he was when he was a little boy and did not want to be left abandoned in the dark and he sneaked in mom's bed. Since then, he had never been without a woman in his bed for too long; it did not matter which one as long as she was pleasing and with an agreeable disposition and, like a kitten, he would purr in response to any kindness till the flow of life would attract him elsewhere.

Later on, in the silence of the night, as Sabrina's head was resting on his chest and her pretty shoulders were rhythmically rising with each breath, Luca stared at the ceiling and momentarily forgot his solitude, the grieving for his dad's departure, the angst for the lost opportunities that had tormented him that afternoon. Once again, he had yielded to the ephemeral illusion of companionship that the contact with a warm and naked body can offer to a solitary leopard. Then, deeper in the night, as he still could not sleep, he saw Clara's eyes, those big blue eyes of infinite color, staring at him in mysterious silence.

THE STRANGE CASE
OF CLARA'S EYES

THE OLD BOYS ACADEMY

Now, Sabrina turned out to be quite an exceptional woman. Her existence perfectly balanced Luca's needs. She was well educated. She spoke Italian and English fluently besides Filipino, her native language and, whenever she pronounced "Mister Luca" with her purring Filipino accent, his ears pricked up like those of a kitten.

Sabrina took the initiative of answering the phone, taking accurate messages in both languages and orchestrating Luca's personal life with pride. She took care of his wardrobe with zeal and, as if a magic wand had been waved on Luca's life, soon everything around him became well ordered and as meticulously clean as a spinster's closet.

Luca discovered shoes, ties, and shirts in the armoire that had been buried in drawers and cabinets for decades, waiting in vain for his occasional returns to the hometown. He lifted an old pair of shoes dating back to his high school days that had been polished as a vintage Ferrari. He noticed, right on the center of the right shoe, an old scratch that had survived the last thirty years with dignity. After turning the shoes a few times in his hand wondering what to do with that testimony of youth, not having the resolve to put them down to rest for an additional indeterminate number of decades, Luca decided to wear them; in the end, they looked quite the same as his current loafers as he had never changed his preppy style through all those years.

Swiftly, he resumed and even enjoyed the orderly life that had been put aside after the divorce. Without the pampering from his attentive wife, he had discovered that laundry could be hung around the house right out of the washing machine and shaped by his own body at the time of use. Sabrina, meanwhile, ironed everything she could get a hold of, including, curtains, sheets, socks, handkerchiefs, towels, tablecloths, napkins, and ties and she washed them with compulsion after each use without giving them a chance to get dirty. Conforming to the craving of an art collector, she would bolt out of the house in her free time to scavenge for any possible permutation of absorbent, cleaning, softening, moisturizing, refreshing, or aromatizing equipment to be applied to the prince's clothing, and Luca ended up walking out of the house smelling of talc powder like a pampered toddler fresh out of the tub. She would admonish him about correct combing strategies and adjust his tie so it was properly centered, and all of this was done with such a delicate touch that progressively Luca not only stopped resisting but became dependent upon such attentions.

She cooked meals of several variations, thanks to the Internet. And she accepted Luca's criticisms with grace and his recommendations as Gospel. She enacted requests verbatim without needing to be reminded. She had an iron memory and a sharp intelligence that was applied with ardor to all domestic matters as if they were of cosmological relevance without expecting more than a modest check at the end of the month to be sent in total integrity to the Philippines.

Above all, she did not interfere with Luca's life, whether it was about professional or personal matters and she left Luca free to continue his degenerate existence without question. She even served occasional lovers with deference, whom he brought home inconsiderately for a dinner and overnight stay. Afterwards, upon Luca's request, she even offered comments on those guests' qualities that not only demonstrated how much she understood her master's nature but also made him laugh in good humor.

Luca had found in Sabrina the ideal companion to meet his self-indulgent expectations and, after a few weeks of such coddled existence, being impressed by her talents as a servant and as a woman, the professor's subconscious started to recognize in Sabrina some sort of human being. As a consequence, he retained her for the time being as his servant concubine—a reasonable prerogative for a spectacularly pampered person.

***

At this juncture, I wish to warn the readers who may be starting to dislike Professor Leoluca de Mirafiori's character, that we should not hasten to judge others and that Luca was in truth not such a despicable narcissist as this preamble may suggest. Rather, what we are observing in this moment of Luca's life represents a downfall of destabilizing circumstances that coincided to shape a naturally withdrawn personality into an aloof character just as much as our reflection in the mirror summarizes a composite of long-gone events of which the image portrays the outcome.

In reality, Luca, far from cynical, was a profound and decent character worthy of empathy, if not sympathy, when judged from the perspective of the path that had been tossed to him. As we previously mentioned, Luca lived by default and his detachment toward Sabrina, or whoever else was roaming in and out the outskirts of his existence, paralleled his own disengagement with the affairs of life. In the back of his mind, he very much appreciated Sabrina's fervor and even envied her energy. He would be the first to agree that she deserved more than she received. But how could one blame a cadaver for not rising out of the sepulcher to water a thirsty plant?

Yet Sabrina seemed to understand, and no matter how gloomy her master was when he returned home, she welcomed him with a smile, warm meals, and other joys that were only for him to choose. And she did it in good humor since she was thankful for all she received that consisted of a decent salary, a comfortable room in an elegant neighborhood, a few books to read, and an old computer to connect with her children whenever she wanted to. That salary, in particular, was sufficient as she had two young children in the Philippines and a husband, who waited for the monthly transfer that sufficiently took care of so many things in the faraway country.

***

To better appreciate Luca's state of mind, it is therefore sensible to retrace his story a few years back when, still trusting that he had a blissful family and a decent future ahead, he was returning a day earlier from a business trip to his apartment in Park Avenue and was greeted by the bell boy with a handwritten envelope freshly dispatched from Italy.

It was an eccentric note from Tullio, an old friend with whom he had shared the pains of adolescence in high school and with whom he had studied medicine at the University of Milan before moving to America after graduation. Translated from Italian, it said:

Distinguished Gentlemen,

Following an extraordinarily high-level discussion, Prof. Zamponi and I decided to establish the Old Boys Academy (with special emphasis on the "Boys" rather than the "Old" element).

Membership is highly selective, arbitrary, and admittedly self-indulgent.

Currently, the Academy has no bylaws, and none are foreseen neither in the near nor in the distant future.

The intention is to provide a forum for jovial and pleasant exchanges. Professional discussions are discouraged but not completely forbidden providing they do not generate severe spells of boredom measured as yawns or, more flagrantly, snores among the participants.

Gatherings can be held monthly in any agreeable and conducive ambience in the presence of plentiful chow.

In relation to the latter point, we propose to hold the first gathering at my residence in via. . . Milan, on November 15. . .

Wives or significant others (more or less significant that they may be) are not only discouraged but also strictly prohibited!

RSVP directly to me (no assistants need to be involved).

Tullio.

Folding the letter and returning it to the envelope, he smiled, shaking his head, and wondered how to decline politely while the old wooden elevator was still sluggishly climbing toward the thirty-sixth floor:

"Nice of them to remember me. . . I will send the apologies tomorrow to steadfast Tullio. . . I wonder whether Giuseppe was invited. . . Would he go to Italy just for that?" And for a second he entertained the prospect of joining his old friends.

***

Holding the envelope with the left hand and unscrambling the keys with the right one, Luca judged that by then his wife should be home and impulsively rang the doorbell. By the time he had managed to open the door and pull the rolling case through the door, Christina was staring at him, impassive and without attempting a smile. George, the house feline, came to rub his feet, attempted a crowing meow, and dropped belly up expecting some reciprocity. Luca bent and rubbed his soft tummy in silence.

"I thought you were coming tomorrow," Christina managed to say.

"Was done early, caught an earlier plane. I thought you would be happy. We can even go out for dinner, so we do not have to cook and wash dishes!" mumbled Luca, still looking at the cat.

At the beat of silence, he rose and walked by Christina, dragging the rolling case, and he bent to kiss her somewhere in the face. She did not resist but also did not respond as if she was trying to convey some news.

Moving toward the bedroom and passing by the dining room, Luca saw Jonathan, a longtime common friend sitting at the head of the table, with an elegant meal for two in front of him, a bottle of Champagne, and a lit candle to complete the scene.

Jonathan got up and stood motionless, incapable of finding a word. Luca helped by releasing his grip from the case and in apology, stated:

"Sorry for interrupting you guys, I can just go to my room."

Just then Christina came out of the kitchen with a set of plates and cutlery that she placed on the side of the table opposite her and to the left of Jonathan, who was still standing at the head of the table.

Smart people cannot lie, not to themselves not to others, if only out of respect for one's own intelligence. Luca did not ask for explanations and nobody offered any; it was clear that the marriage was over. . . No other explanations were necessary.

The old friends continued with the dinner that had to be consumed for the sake of decency. The recovered Jonathan identified topics to fill the time, and everyone managed a labored conversation heroically.

Luca noticed the food prepared by Christina. It was his favorite meal— rosemary-flavored standing rib roast with baked potatoes. But tonight, it was bland and so was everything else. He shuttled a piece of meat into his mouth, alternating it with a piece of potato and a sip of wine, while Jonathan was reporting on the financial crisis. He was a businessman in Wall Street and Luca pretended to listen with temperate interest, but as soon as dinner was over and the plates were adequately emptied, Luca rose.

"I am tired. I am going to bed. Do not let me bother you any further."

Dragging the rolling case, he reached the bedroom. He noticed that the bed was perfectly done and wondered whether they had already been sleeping together or if it was soon to come. He looked with marvel at himself in the mirror, at his statuary appearance, at the face of a man known for his good looks of which he had been made aware by so many women and pondered:

"What does she find in that plump and bald slug? Only notable thing about him is the flashy Rolex."

It should be noted that Luca took for granted his appeal to the other gender without any special pride, just as a matter of fact as if it had been imposed on him by fate, just as a life on a wheelchair is imposed upon a handicapped person. Yet, with his analytical mindset, he entered his charisma into the algorithm of his existence with objectivity, leading to the proprietary assumption that women existed exclusively to complement his being. But now, what was wrong with his wife?

Poor Luca! How could he have known that Christina had tried so hard to be close to him for all those years! That only in the end, only when she could not bear to compete with the furniture for attention anymore—as a pretty decoration, a picture on the wall—did she fall for the seduction of being pursued, being cared for, being praised for her beauty, her intelligence, her qualities as a caring mother, as a woman, of her entitlement to be loved.

How could poor Luca know? In fairness, he had praised Christina on occasions, but rarely, never spontaneously, only when objectively demanded by a conversation of substance. For a scientist, things do not need to be repeated once the truth is established; when a statement is made it should hold forever; an ascertained truth is a step from which one moves forward. He knew how good of a person his wife was and he had told her once and for all.

But this is not how women's minds work; they need reinforcement to allay their insecurities; they need nurture like an indoor plant; they need fertilizer for the flowers of their heart to blossom, water to keep them alive. But emotions are difficult to express in scientific terms, it was too difficult for Luca to translate feelings into words, it was logic without metrics, calculation without integers. He knew that he should have told Christina that he loved her more often than he did, but that word, that concept seemed so empty, so vague, and so intangible to be used with ease.

"Am I overreacting? Am I over-interpreting?" he questioned as he walked to the marital bed. There, he lifted the sheet, reached for the pillow, put it under his armpit and walked to the den. After turning on the light he looked at the familiar objects and wondered what they witnessed that he did not know. He then rested the pillow on one arm of the couch, took off his shoes and dropped them on the floor, removed his pants, undid his tie, and opened his shirt. He slid out of it and let it fall to the ground. Finally, he lay down, adjusted the pillow, and stared at the ceiling.

Like a cat listening to a mouse behind the wall, he heard the two lovers whisper a few words and soon the latch of the door was secured. Jonathan had the decency to leave, and Christina came right after, looking for Luca. Not finding him in the bedroom, she walked into the den, just as beautiful as she was when they met thirty years back.

Christina did not talk but simply looked at Luca who bitterly smiled and asked:

"Do you love him?"

"Yes."

Luca felt the urge to ask: "Why?"

But at once, he realized that many more questions would follow without answers: questions referring to times past that should have been raised then, not now when it was too late. Instead, he looked straight into Christina's eyes:

"Do you still love me?"

Christina, who had been unnaturally self-contained and distant throughout the evening burst into tears. Without answering, she came toward him, kneeled at the couch, put her head on his chest, and sobbed:

"I am so sorry!"

Luca lifted his ataxic hand from the side of the couch where it had dropped and delicately caressed Christina's blond hair. It was a strange feeling. It had never occurred to him what it would feel like to be deserted by a woman, a companion, not to mention his own wife, and he found himself surprised by the feeling.

Staring at the chandelier, he reckoned that without admitting it, he had loved this woman throughout those many years. In spite of differences and difficulties, unspoken grudges, resentments, misunderstandings, rebellious actions, they had shared so much together, raised beautiful children who had now gone along their successful paths.

He felt no anger, not even sadness, only profound tenderness. He thought of his wife as a teenage daughter searching for new horizons, exploring the unknown, cutting the umbilical cord that had kept them united for all those years whether they liked it or not, and he realized that if he really cared for her, he had to let her go. This is what true love was about. In the end, as he had learned raising his children, one cannot control others' wills; one can only try to understand them.

Eventually, her uninterrupted sobbing distracted him, and he said to his wife:

"Shush, stop crying. All will be fine, do not worry; everything is going to be fine. Go to sleep now, we can talk tomorrow. I just cannot talk anymore; I would not know what to say."

Christina rose and, without turning, hurried to what had been their bedroom for decades. She approached the door while Luca kept staring at the ceiling.

"What a strange feeling it is to be alone," he reasoned.

He realized that he had never experienced the sentiment of truly being alone. Throughout life, he always had a companion at his side, mostly by default, girl after girl, woman after woman, affair after affair till his marriage. Each departure had been just a door revealing the path to the next one. But now, for the first time, he savored loneliness; that immeasurable emotion, so limitless and impalpable, that comes without sadness or joy, without despair or hope, but which is now absolute emptiness, like the eternal motion of stars and galaxies along their solitary journey in the darkness without hope for encounters in the millions and billions of years to come.

About to close his eyes, Luca remembered Tullio's invitation. He thought it such an odd coincidence, an omen. Far from believing in supernatural powers, he perceived the note as a forewarning of change, a harbinger of resolution, and a leap into the future by retracing the old. He took it as an invitation to revisit the dated path to search for the crossroad that led to the wrong direction, to restart anew if it wasn't too late. Thus, he told himself:

"See you, Old Boys, see you in Milan!"

***

It was still early when Luca woke up and the light of dawn penetrated the room just enough to let him explore the surroundings and recall the events of the night before. He recognized the den and that vision reminded him of the new predicament. Luca scanned the familiar objects that enlivened the room in the past, while now they were framing its emptiness. He thought of the quote: "If a tree falls in the forest and nobody is there to hear it, does it still make a sound?" And he recited: "If a man cries in the forest and nobody is there, does it really matter?"

Indeed, for the first time he finally understood what it meant to be alone, to be on his own, not just for that day, that week, that month, but for the years to come.

He rose, tiptoed to the bathroom to wash up and shave without disturbing Christina. In a rebellious act, God only knows against whom or what, he snubbed to shave and by seven thirty he was walking out of the house with a free day ahead. Before leaving, he returned to the den, picked up the note from Italy, slipped it in his pocket and repeated:

"See you, Old Boys, see you in Milano!"

***

The air was crisp under the canopy and Luca, exiting the building, subconsciously aligned his spirit to it. He discovered that he was just as free as the breeze that was lifting his soul, and he felt relief from the burden to please, if from nothing else. He considered that throughout life, he had been limited by the fear of upsetting others: his parents first, then his wife, then the relatives, particularly those on her side, even his children. Averse to confrontation, he avoided arguments and conceded to the will of a strong woman, nevertheless pursuing his wants in subterfuge according to the tenet that, when caught, it is easier to ask for forgiveness than for permission beforehand.

This wariness led to confusion and distrust, mostly for petty reasons: coming late from work, finding excuses to avoid family gatherings or dinners with boring acquaintances, performing otherwise innocent activities that she disparaged. All behaviors innocent in their motivation but that lead to suspicion at the receiving end.

The more Christina reacted with rage to the subterfuges, the more he, like a reproached cat, withdrew. He mastered progressively deceitful talents, figuring out how to avoid being caught the next time. He persuaded himself that Christina would never accept the truth, no matter how innocent. Everything happened instinctually, subconsciously, without a good reason, with the naïve maliciousness, the deceptiveness of a child who does not want to study or a puppy that stole a cookie. But these actions were not perceived as such by his companion and gradually, almost inadvertently, this misbehavior dug, an abysmal valley between the two, and the only relief in the relationship progressed to rely exclusively on solitude.

But today he was finally free! He owned the world, with all its prospects, and he had nobody to please or be accountable to.

As the fresh air was seeping through the skin of his forehead and refreshing his mind, he crossed Park Avenue in high spirit and proceeded to Fifth Avenue in search of a place to buy a cup of coffee: the first accomplishment of the new life! And that elation. . . that refreshing joy lasted indeed for a while. . . but a very little while, just until the middle of the crosswalk.

As he approached the other side, looking at the countdown of seconds by the stoplight, he felt sadness. He reckoned that what he had been misrepresenting as relief and freedom was a reaction to profound anguish, and that the momentary happiness was only sugarcoating a rotten apple.

By the time the sidewalk was reached, happiness was replaced by bereavement. He reckoned that the momentary relief was harbinger of hopeless loneliness, while his existence was turning into a meaningless vegetative state; nobody to please, nobody with whom to share successes or seek comfort. Luca wondered what life would be about now. What was the purpose of it all? Did he really care that much about his profession? Or were his achievements solely aimed at impressing his wife, at making her proud? Admittedly, his profession was useful and, therefore, in some sense important, but now his existence had changed flavor, his own identity was gone; now that his wife of so many years was not in the picture there would be no mirror to reflect the fruits of his own success, no smile to compensate for the unending stream of frustration. In truth, he was the tree falling in the deserted forest where no one can hear, see, or care.

Yet, his determined logic did not intend to concede to emotions. He turned to an objective analysis of the current predicament, and he questioned himself:

"How did all of this happen? How could it have happened?"

Not finding a clear-cut answer, as he crossed Madison coming from Sixty-First, he resorted to more tangible reflections—

"She is unhappy with me. I love her, and I want her happy. Ergo I must let her go! This will be my purpose from now on and my only source of contentment!"—thus recovering, with such contorted formula, a vestige of purpose to his life.

By the time Fifth was reached, he had pledged to sacrifice his life for his wife's happiness, and this resolution gave him peace. . . for a while. . . just until another thought arose:

"Wait a minute!" he said to himself. "Why should I worry about her happiness? I did nothing to deserve this. I worked hard all my life. I provided for the family just as much as she did, if not more. I worked weekends and nights. I did not play golf or fool around with friends, no nights out, nothing of what I was accustomed to as a bachelor. Why am I sorry for her? I should be angry!"

But even the concocted wrath did not last long. No matter how hard he tried to picture his unfaithful wife lustfully enjoying life at his own expense, his imagination kept carrying back those moments when they met decades ago, the first communications in broken languages, that mélange of Italian, French, and English. And the same vexing imagination could not be controlled and kept dumping a plethora of unnecessary images from the time when the children were young, and life was joyful and enriched by unbridled expectations and sweetened trepidations.

In the end, he concluded that there was no reason to bear resentment toward Christina just as much as there was no reason to blame himself. To every action there is a reaction, any effect derives from a cause but too often causes are vague and mishaps are downfalls from remote and negligent choices of which we bear no memory. Yes! Uncountable had been the wrongs from each side, reactions to poor choices that spawned chains of counter-reactions, an endless stream of mistakes to which there was no determinable beginning, whose initial perpetrator was hidden within the oblivion of time.

There had been many circumstances when she could have acted in a suitable way to save their relationship. But just as many chances had been given to him to do better. . . to hold her hand instead of walking away, to look into her eyes instead of turning them away, to listen and respond considerately instead of dismissing her worries with superficial accusations or patronizing comments.

A well-known defense mechanism called remotion came to assist Luca in this predicament when circular and unproductive thinking overtook the conscious mind. Incapable of finding closure by solving the quandary in which he had been thrust so unexpectedly, Luca reframed his thoughts on the Old Boys Academy. And he fancied his old friends sitting around the poker table at night. Some of them focusing on the game, others annoying the players by introducing distracting thoughts about the Vietnam War, Bob Dylan, Woodstock, The Band, the cultural revolution in China, and other notions that professors did not discuss in class but were in their minds at those intense times when they were youthful and in so much want for adulthood.

He thought with a smile of Gramsci's[32] *"Lettere Dal Carcere"*[33] and his Cultural Hegemony theory; so much debate around lofty topics that he could barely remember now. Heated discussions while Tullio attempted to focus the herd on the game to quench the juvenile wrath of the friends. But they all cared about distant events, remote in time and so far away from their town, where they were cozily sitting around the table in cold winter nights, with hosting mothers, who could not refrain from checking on the guests at the cost of irreparably embarrassing their respective sons.

And those preferred evenings when safe sex was anticipated as they converged to a friend's home whose parents were out of town; those evenings when girls were allowed to decorate the room as three-dimensional holographs.

With a smile, he recalled the time when one of them observed: "The best safe sex I know of is when my parents are out of town."

He recalled "La Candela,"[34] so called because she stood on top when she made love, like a candle on a stick. She spent the night in the guest room passionately hosting in turn the ones who needed a break from the game or had become weary of politics. And she was so proud of such privilege to serve! And she loved them all, thankful to be accepted like an abandoned bitch that has found a home.

"Boy, was she fun," he smiled. "What happened to her? I wonder; I wish I could see her again."

And he thought of the alcohol. It was hard liquor that they drank to be like the grownups: whiskey, vodka, and Cognac, taken out of the parents' cabinets. He recalled the crystal chalice of Cognac held by the handsome Tullio, who had given up herding his friends into the game and had retreated to the armchair to pose in mockery of his distinguished ancestors' portraits that were hanging on the walls just above him; a pantomime could not be appreciated by his friends because by his own nature, Tullio, whether pretending or not, somberly looked just as stale and stiff as his departed relatives did a century before.

---

[32] Marxist theorizer and founder of the Italian Communist Party
[33] "Letters from jail"
[34] "The Candle"

***

Along Fifty-Second, Luca noticed a street artist who was painting a portrait on the sidewalk with pastels. She was a pretty Oriental woman, focused on the ephemeral work, barely aware of passersby. That vision of the beautiful stranger toiling so hard early in the morning distracted him further from his current predicament. That vision of youthful enthusiasm offered a serendipitous albeit temporary relief to his loneliness.

Luca approached and his own shadow covered the art, effectively distracting her for a moment. She turned to look at him and smiled—a beautifully simple and innocent smile. He wanted to talk to her, to tell her about his current predicament, of his pain, his guilt, his remorse. . . of his certainty that he would never repeat the same mistakes, that he would be a better companion from now on, and that he needed somebody to believe in him. He wanted to tell her that her petite body reminded him of a sparrow sipping the water from a puddle created by the recent rain and that her smile forecasted a beginning; it was the first sunray after the storm.

But those chaotic impulses clogged his throat and he said nothing. He reciprocated the smile and went on along his path.

After a few steps, he turned and saw her still busying over her decidual masterpiece meant to last till the first rain and he thought:

"Is she portraying with her decidual masterpiece the meaning of life that, no matter how beautiful, will soon be gone?"

He almost went back to introduce himself politely, to offer to buy her a cup of coffee, but instead he shrugged and moved on:

"I can always talk to her when I come back."

***

Several miscellaneous and disconnected thoughts, emotions, and arguments continued to crowd his mind in the following steps—from the infatuation with the pretty artist to the resolution of sacrificing the rest of his life for Christina's happiness, to rather despising her and all members of that gender, to avenge his pain by turning against Jonathan and telling the banker's wife about the affair.

Finally, he considered the ultimate drama: a suicide that would make both perpetrators repentant for the rest of their lives. In the end, he got bored of all those nonsense, figuring that none of those contemplations yielded any actionable resolution worthy of an academician on the account of their lack of originality. Therefore, he decided that life, in its multifactorial essence, was way too complicated to be repaired with simple measures and, incapable of balancing with logic the thrust of his emotions, he once again shrugged and moved on toward the Plaza.

By the time Luca arrived at The Plaza Hotel, he had forgotten about the troubles with his wife, he had forgotten about the Old Boys and forgotten about the street artist, and instead he thought to himself: "Why not? I will treat myself with a cappuccino at The Plaza. Why not?"

In the end, this was the only sensible action he could find the resolve to complete.

***

Entering the coffee shop, he noticed a rather minute woman of remarkable contours, dressed more like a cowgirl than a New Yorker, who stared and addressed him with the sweetest smile:

"Howdy, partner, what's up with you?"

Stupefied by the comment, unconcerned about its sincerity, he looked straight into her eyes, and reached out to gently squeeze her right shoulder as he answered: "Don't know. Actually, to be frank, I feel just a touch lost. . . just a little bit more than a touch in fact, sort of dumped if you please. . . not that you would care anyhow."

"Why shouldn't I care? Don't we all feel lonely most of the time? You looked distraught indeed!" she replied, following him with her big eyes as he proceeded to the counter to order a cappuccino.

While waiting for the cup, he turned around and noticed that she was still looking impertinently at him with a mischievous expression. As she moved closer toward him, he asked: "Do I know you?"

"Probably not. . . but I do know you, Professor!" and nodding her head, she added thoughtfully: "All women in campus with a good vision know you for sure!"

Then realizing that her cheerfulness did not steer much of a reaction in the Professor, she touched his right elbow and, turning pensive, her forehead creased and she asked:

"What makes you so lonely? I am sorry, I was jesting before!"

Flattered by the pretty woman's praises and in dire need of examining his thoughts through a conversation, Luca impulsively opened his heart to a total stranger:

"My wife is cheating on me. . . after thirty years."

Then, listening to his words, he thought it better to temper them with: "She is in love with someone else."

The pretty woman did not say a word. Her stern look turned into a tender smile—a maternal act from a woman's dexterity.

"I came home a day earlier from a trip, and I found her having a romantic dinner with a common friend. Candles, prosecco. . . or maybe champagne, standing rib roast with rosemary. . . whatever! All the nine yards! And when I asked her whether she loved him, she simply said 'yes.' What bothers me the most is that the guy is bald and fat, and to be honest I do not think he is that smart either. . . . He is just a businessman."

"Do you still love her?" she asked at the first break.

"Don't know! I wonder if I ever loved her to start with, but I spent all of my life with her, all that I can remember. I never asked myself whether I loved her. . . I guessed. . . I assumed that I did. But now, to be sincere, I miss her regardless if I love her or not. Isn't it what love is all about?"

"Did you tell her?"

"Tell what?"

"That you miss her."

"Why should I? Why would she care? She loves somebody else!"

"Oh dear! I guess you really do not understand women, do you? Besides, aren't you jealous? Don't you want to smash the lover's face? Just curious! Not a suggestion!"

"Never been jealous! I always believed that one's love should be earned each day anew, not taken for granted. If a woman does not want to be with you, what's the point of cursing, yelling, and screaming? In the end, if she deserts you it is because you failed to make her stay. I have no control over a woman's feelings. The only thing I can control is myself! I could have tried to improve if I knew. . . but I guess it is too late now.

"This is the way I feel. But I do not understand what it is I did—I thought I was a good husband. Maybe she just grew bored of me. Perhaps she just grew bored of me... by the way, can I get you a coffee or something ... my name is Luca, what's your name?"

"Valentina," said the pretty woman and with overstated affectation, added:

"Extremely honored to meet you, Professor de Mirafiori!"

Luca talked a lot that morning and Valentina listened thoughtfully, looking straight into his eyes with her own that barely blinked, crossing her leg occasionally and arching her back to emphasize her bosom that was admittedly remarkable.

Suddenly, Luca remembered that he had planned to call Giuseppe, who by then must have been awake in California. Therefore, after exchanging contacts, he excused himself by thanking Valentina for the patience prodigally offered to a serendipitous encounter.

"No problem at all, Luca. I enjoyed talking to you! Your wife is a lucky woman. You are a good person., Not a good communicator maybe, and definitely a little too self-absorbed. Amend the past! Open your heart! Go back home and talk to your lovely wife and you will see she will forget about the chubby banker!

"But in case she does not. . . you have my number!" she added.

To that last comment, Luca responded by approaching the petite woman, circling his arm around her waist, lifting her up, giving her a hug, and kissing her gently on her closed lips.

"Thanks," he said and away he went toward Central Park.

***

"Hey Luca, what's up? It's been a long time since I heard from you!" answered Giuseppe.

"I am getting divorced," said Luca impetuously forgetting that he had called Giuseppe for an entirely different purpose. He wanted to ask him whether he was planning to go to Milan for the Old Boys' get-together.

"Congratulations! It was time, finally!"

"What do you mean?" said Luca, totally dumbfounded.

"Come on, you two have been the oddest couple for a long time. You acted as if she were a dentist about to pull a tooth as soon as you opened your mouth. We all wondered when Christina would get tired and leave you. Who wanted the divorce? Do not tell me that it is you because I would not believe it. You would simply be too spacy to even think about it."

"She is having an affair with Jonathan, you know, the banker. You know who I am talking about, that fat guy with the Rolex. And how do you know she is the one who wanted to break up?"

"Because she told me the last time I saw her that she was unhappy with you. That you couldn't care less about her! That you had completely dissociated your life from hers, always away, not involving her with your work, avoiding vacations together, and fooling around with women. She is not a stupid woman; in fact, she is a great woman."

"What does she know about women? And how would you know?"

"I do not know, but Christina is not stupid. Women have a sixth sense! And you are so naïve on these matters! When will you ever grow up? We are not in high school anymore! That was decades ago! You cannot have one affair after another, no matter how insignificant you may deem it to be, and expect your wife not to sense it."

"Then what about you and Shirley?" Luca retorted vindictively.

"That was long ago and, in any case, I guess I am better than you at keeping my affairs discrete! At least I do care enough about my wife to make sure that she does not feel completely neglected and does not look around for other men. . . that I know of, at least. Anyways, I am not the one divorcing."

And noticing silence from his friend's side, Giuseppe added:

"Come on, man! Cheer up! You must have sensed what was going to happen. Don't tell me you are completely surprised? Are you? Or not?" And because there was still silence on the other side, he added: "I can't believe this! The guy really is surprised! Come on! This guy really is the dumbest self-absorbed son of a bitch I ever met! Come on, Luca! Cheer up! You can find as many women as you want. Otherwise, just go back to Christina and tell her to forget about that hot air balloon and that you will take good care of her from now on!"

"This is not why I called you," interrupted Luca, who by then was confused to the brim and worn out by the stern logic of his friend.

"I called to ask you whether you received any messages from Tullio recently."

I should note at this juncture that Giuseppe, a fellow that some of my readers might recollect as the main character of my novel *The Wise Men of Pizzo,* was not from Milan but from a little town in Southern Italy. Therefore, not being originally part of the old high school clique, he had been adopted by the Old Boys, who appreciated his skeptical demeanor and ironic wisdom. Giuseppe had befriended them by spending long stretches of time in Milan during college breaks when he needed a respite from the American life.

Hence, Luca meant to tactfully test whether Tullio had included him in the reunion.

"Yes, I did. That old archimandrite Tullio! Of course I got it! What a crazy idea but you know what? If you go, I will go too. We live only once! Don't we?"

And before hanging up the phone, Giuseppe concluded: "By the way, my regards to Christina."

***

On the way back, Luca retraced his steps towards home and walked to the place where he had left the street artist. But the object of his infatuation was not there anymore. Her masterpiece was completed, and a few casual admirers were standing around it. But she had collected her belongings and she was gone forever. The sparrow had migrated to a more welcoming land, and, in her flight, the sunray of her genuine smile had dissipated after piercing momentarily through the clouds. Luca felt a pang in his heart, a forgotten feeling that came together with the vision of Clara's beautiful blue eyes of infinite color that had been fated to follow him silently for the rest of his life.

And he wondered: "What is that ephemeral semblance of hope that a smile and two caring eyes can impart upon a soul, like a promise for something beyond the selfish boundaries of our lives, an evanescent glimpse of a beauty as eternal and infinite as the universe that does not belong to us."

***

"Christina, are you up? Sorry for bothering you. I wonder if you are busy today."

"Of course I am up, I did not sleep all night! Then I could not find you and I was worried. You did not even leave a message, nothing! How are you? Where are you?"

"I am okay. I just went out for a cup of coffee. You busy today? Are you going out with Jonathan?"

"No, I decided to take a break, I am confused. I need some time alone. What about you?"

"Nothing. . . I mean, not much. . . actually, nothing, I mean completely nothing to do. I guess I could work. I do not think I could focus. . . . What do you think? Should we go for a walk together? I am still in Fifth. I could come to get you, or I can wait for you."

***

The river in which one steps is not the same. More and yet more waters keep flowing on.

Into the same rivers we step and yet we do not step, we exist and at the same time we do not exist.

After all, one does not step into the same river twice. Waters disperse and come together again. . . they keep flowing on and flowing away.

In the end, there is only flux, everything flows,

Everything is in flux and nothing rests,

Everything flows and nothing remains,

Everything constantly changes and nothing stays the same.

—Heraclitus, *The River*

***

Thinking about Heraclitus' poem, Luca roosted on the familiar bench in Central Park—the same bench, where he used to wait for Christina when, coming home from work, they would go grocery shopping or would instead look for casual dining before wrapping the evening up. It was an ancient routine that lasted for decades and intensified after the children had moved away. A bench that, like a pebble in the river, was indifferent, letting the flow of life run over its smooth surface.

So, he settled on that bench once more, waiting for his Christina, rehearsing the most sensible strategy to confront her.

As a matter of fact, there was no strategy at all; what Luca was imposing upon himself was a pretense of logical considerations that unconsciously reflected the simple desire, even fervor, to see her again. Instinct had compelled him to call her in the first place, a need to come to a resolution either through forgiveness or anger, but a resolution, nevertheless. He feared belligerence and prepared with angst for the worst because he could not cope with the swiftness of her arguments in moments of wrath. He just wanted peace. He had to convince himself that decades of living together could outweigh any challenge brought by the current predicament.

Or at least. . . he was hoping for a truce. He recollected Valentina's admonishment that reverberated in Giuseppe's words:

"Amend the past! Open your heart! Just tell her that you care and that you do not want to lose her."

He also vowed to be a better listener, to listen with care and empathy. He wanted to acknowledge her. Perhaps for the first time in his marriage, he willed himself to understand Christina for the sake of love. . . or at least this is what he contemplated.

But even such noble resolution came in Luca's style. His apathetic mind had finally identified Christina as a problem, an interesting problem worthy of investigation, and he gave his heart permission to lucubrate and dissect. It was a primordial form of affection, a difficult one to explain in comprehensible terms to those who live a normal life—those who experience the freshness of spring water when they submerge their hands in it and do not have to explain to themselves why they should sense and perhaps even enjoy that simple sensation.

Luca was not like them, he was not familiar with spontaneity, and he experienced only second-hand sensations; he was scared of emotions, particularly happy ones; perhaps a Christian remnant of repentance for guilts that could not be identified. Often he remembered his stern grandmother who never laughed except in rare occasions when she cracked grandchildren jokes:

"We laugh now, but who knows how much crying is waiting for us tomorrow!"

He processed and fabricated into emotions the messages imported by his senses, a contorted exercise that demanded explanation for things that could not be explained. It was the best he could do because it had never occurred to him that there is no reason to explicate everything, that humans are impetuous, and their deeds are irrational. Rationality is of use only retrospectively to justify one's own actions.

Resignedly waiting for Christina like a defendant awaits judgment, he held the empty cup of cappuccino, turning it clockwise and counterclockwise over and over. He observed the assortment of park dwellers distractedly, and tightening his grasp on the cup at intervals, he found reassurance in doing so as if he was keeping hold of a handle that connected him to the pragmatism of existence.

Realizing that he had been tormenting the empty cup for more than an hour and that such occupation had no intelligible purpose, he stood and walked toward a bin to dispose of it with satisfaction, after carefully selecting the appropriate container, a token of a deliverable that could be completed in defiance of the overbearing apathy of the morning.

Mission accomplished; he looked toward the direction from where Christina was expected. Not seeing her, he returned to the old bench. But it had already been occupied by a young couple tenderly holding each other's hands and basking under the occasional sunrays that descended from an otherwise self-absorbed sky occupied with churning and digesting strata of grey and white clouds in its turbulent stomach.

***

Christina came with a light gait and approached him with a smile. Luca walked toward her, touched her left shoulder, and kissed her on both cheeks, the Italian way.

"Should we get something to drink?" he offered.

"Sure!"

They walked aimlessly up and down the park without managing to get to the point of the conversation. They reminisced about distant episodes that had nothing to do with the current predicament and they laughed. They walked off the path and through the grass. Then, he climbed a small hill as the children used to do and waved at her from the summit. They admired a few reminders of the late fall in the shape of colorful leaves that carpeted the grounds. They stared at policemen riding the horses and asked a passerby to take a picture of them under an ancient tree, to immortalize. . . what? They would not know. He attempted to wrap his arm around her shoulders, but she declined politely. He grazed her hand with the back of his, but she withdrew it hastily. When they sat on a bench, he tried to kiss her, but she said:

"I do not think it is the right thing to do, Luca!"

Then he asked her: "Are you happy with Jonathan?"

"Yes! I have not been this happy in a long time. We spend time with each other whenever we can, and he does all he can to be with me. He has given me back the self-esteem I lost waiting for you day after day. . . . . He makes me feel like I am worth something."

And then she continued: "I do not know what happened! You know, I loved you so much, I did all I could to make you happy, hoping for you to want to be with me. I could have never imagined a life without you. But then, I realized that it was not up to me; that you were not happy with me no matter what I did, that you were with me because you did not have the courage to leave me and there was nothing I could do to change it. I had to do it for both of us. . . ."

"What about his wife?" interrupted Luca; mostly to deflect the sequitur onto something he could not confront. You may call it dismissive but, he truly did not know what to say.

"He told her last night after he left our home. He moved out. He already has a flat downtown. He had it for a while."

"And our kids?"

"They are grown, they will understand!"

"Do they know? "

"Of course they don't!"

"Who is going to tell them and what are we going to say?"

Silence. Christina was turning stiff. Her ease was gone; she assumed a defensive posture by settling her intertwined hands in a crevasse between her knees and looked into the distance.

"So, are we divorcing?" asked Luca mechanically, as if he was about to summarize a scientific discussion at journal club.

"Yes!" pronounced Christina.

Luca looked toward the pond at the lovebirds, those mysterious monuments to eternal love. He remembered the reason why he had asked Christina to come. He thought of the intent to ask her to forget about the whole thing, to forget about the bald banker with his fancy watch. He thought that it was time to tell her that he loved her, that he cared more than anything else, that he was sorry for his dismissiveness in the relationship, that he was repentant for all that had gone wrong no matter whose fault it was. But, he did not say anything. Her words "I have not been this happy in a long time!" had created an insurmountable barrier.

He told himself that he had no right to interfere with her happiness. How could he expect to deliver what he had failed to give her for decades?

And he gave up.

This time he surrendered not for a vain principle of martyrdom, but because he genuinely felt that he did not deserve her.

"Okay," he said then clasped his hands against each other and rested his mouth over them. . .

"Okay," he repeated. "I guess this is the right thing to do."

Practical as usual, Christina had already worked out all details. The divorce would be easy. The children were independent. They both had similar assets and made about the same amount of money. They could have gone to a mediator and have it executed civilly. Soon they would both be "free" to pursue their happiness.

At the word "free," Luca looked at a hawk hovering over Central Park and wondered about the meaning of the word. Are those unbridled creatures free? Aren't they slaves of their own nature? Is freedom something we can take advantage of, or is it just another way to subdue ourselves to our instincts?

His subjection encouraged her to talk, and she vented what had been interred for years. She confessed, as if she was talking to a brother, that she had another affair before Jonathan, a brief and casual relationship some time ago when he was gone for a business trip. She narrated that the relationship with Jonathan had been going on for months. She explained that it had started with a casual comment after a business party that she attended alone because once again Luca was out of town. Jonathan had invited her out for dinner afterwards and said that he was in love with her, that he had been in love for a long time, that of course he was not expecting for her to act on it as long as she was happy in her marriage, that he just wanted to let her know. But she, under the seductive fumes of alcohol, confessed that she was unhappy, that her husband did not love her, and he was having affair after affair. Jonathan listened with empathy and while she talked, he took her hand. Not long after, they slept together, and they did it again and again with passion whenever Luca was out of town or during the day in Jonathan's flat.

Luca listened to all this in awe. He could not imagine Christina, his proper wife, mother of his children, to behave with such creativity and rebelliousness. She appeared to him as a different woman. He listened attentively, trying to imagine the scenes that she was describing and wondering what was he doing in those moments. He did not say a word till a sudden thought interrupted his train of thought: "But then, what is going to happen to us?"

It had occurred to him that this was not just an academic discussion! It was not journal club! He reckoned that fate was knocking at the door, that his life was about to be turned upside down, and he continued:

"As far as I am concerned, I just do not care about all of this. You are still my wife, and you will be forever. We can divorce. You can get married again and sleep with whomever you want but I do not care. In my heart, I will be your husband forever, and one day when you need me, I will be waiting for you. See those mallards out there? They live together without need for covenants; they are bound forever by their own natural disposition. I do not know what law of nature keeps them loyal to each other for a lifetime but there they are, united forever!

"Christina, I will be your lovebird and you will be mine no matter what we end up doing for the rest of our lives. My dream is that there will be happiness when we think of each other, that there will be pride for all we have achieved during these years and, when possible, that there will be love and not hate nor resentment, that there will be intelligence and understanding.

"In the end, what else is left but hope, through the knowledge that there will be respect among the characters of our precious story? I think we have lived long enough to know that mistakes are nobody's fault but the consequence of careless choices whose accumulated burden cannot be reversed by regrets. I do not know what is ahead of us—for me, a lot of solitude, and in the end perhaps this is what I deserve and need. Solitude, like silence or darkness, enhances the senses and makes you feel and see what you could not see before."

It was Christina's turn to listen silently. And she listened voraciously with tears in her eyes till the tears turned into sobs.

"You see? I love you so much, I miss you already, but you, you already sound relived, you already look at the future, you are doing nothing to gain me back, you are not fighting for me!"

And Luca did not understand. He wondered:

"What have I been doing till now? I listened to her, I tried to tell her that I love her forever and she told me that for a long time she has not been as happy as she is now with Jonathan? What should I fight for? To make her unhappy?" and he told her:

"You just told me you are happy as you have not been in a long time. Why should I change that, what right do I have to make you unhappy again?"

Christina looked at him, admiring her husband, whose passion and resolve had awoken lost emotions:

"Would you want to go back together? Would you really want me to leave Jonathan?"

That question completely confused the already perplexed Luca, who was sitting in front of a wife who had turned from the faithful long-term mother of his children into a vibrant, sexually-active, and romantic person. He lightly questioned what it would be like to go back to her and whether it would be possible to reassemble a broken crystal from thousands of pieces. But he saw no impediment to giving it a try and he said:

"Of course, I am open to it. Let me think about it. What you just told me about yourself confused me quite a bit, but I am open to the idea."

Poor souls! Why did she miss the fact that what he actually meant to say was:

"Yes, of course!" only tempered by an instinctual tinge of caution meant to preserve a façade of dignity. And why didn't he simply answer:

"Yes!"

That was all she needed to hear from her handsome husband of so many years.

I am puzzled myself as the author of this story and I wish I could change the events with a simple stroke of the pen. But that would be unrealistic. There is no such thing as benevolent authors, who can correct the course of actual lives, who can suave with wisdom the faulty logic of our choices and temper with the pastels of hope the wilting canopy of solitude.

I wonder why we cannot recognize the root of our feelings till it is too late. Why we entangle our decisions with the twisted logic of a conversation that dissipates our will, while we forget to listen to the depth of our soul. I do not know how to answer these questions. Perhaps, somebody else could. Yet, these few misinterpreted words had a determining impact on these two decent people's lives.

"See!" Christina almost screamed. "You do not really want to get back together. Enough with the bullshit about lovebirds; you have no clue what you are talking about." And without another word, she stood up and left.

Luca watched her disappear in the distance, wondering what had gone wrong. Trying to summarize in his mind the various pieces of a puzzle he could not assemble, he told himself:

"I better let her go, she would never be happy with me!"

***

Pigeons are not known for their intelligence but perhaps they are not as stupid as we think. This particular one landed just at Luca's feet and stared inquisitively at him with its left eye first and then, twisting its neck, with the right one as if to get a second opinion. Was the pigeon questioning his acumen? Wouldn't it be great if in moments like this, a pigeon, an angel, a God, or whoever is up there could descend to reprogram our thinking? To tell us what we should do? To make us notice what is standing right in front of our eyes when we are too confused to see? Perhaps, the pigeon was trying to tell Luca something with its perspicacious stare as it circled around, bending and bobbing its neck. Finally, it gave up and walked away with dignified steps.

The instinct of self-preservation comes within the enclosure of one's ego. One wants to perpetuate that collection of embodiments through which the identity mirrors. But at that moment, Luca had lost any sense of belonging. Nothing that he could recognize in his visual field or beyond it was familiar. The world around had nothing in common with him; it was a world that belonged to another person who was now gone; a married man with a family and a future ahead, a person whose soul had walked away following Christina's steps. It is in those moments that a person gives up.

Luca rose to leap out of that torpor. Mechanically, he walked home. But then he realized that it was not home anymore. He then turned hundred and eighty degrees toward the opposite direction where the rest of the world was waiting. But that seemed too overbearing in its boundlessness. He then turned ninety degrees to the left as to halve that infinity and indeed he saw something concrete; just a few yards away there was the pond with the lovebirds. . . and he walked toward them. . . and he observed them for God only knows how long till he realized that companionship did not apply to him—not now, not for the time to come. And so it was that Luca began his journey as a solitary man.

***

Odi et amo. Quare id faciam, fortasse requiris?
Nescio, sed fieri sentio et excrucior
I hate and I love. Why do I do it, perhaps you ask?
I don't know, but I feel it in me, and I ache
–Catullus, Carmen 85

"Time flows. So does everything else. Only I persist; dammed to judge into Eternity what's evil and what's not because of the Omnipotent's wish. . . but I question why. I judge petty human affairs in their ephemerality, and I wonder why should I care. People are reactive, their decisions are casual, and one gives them too much credit for believing them capable of willful sin. They do what they do out of compulsion, sloppiness, and instinct. There is no premeditation even when it may appear so. Why would one kill the lifelong companion to collect life insurance? Does this comes from a well-thought-out, compelling, and logical decision? Or isn't this action an excellent example of absolute madness? Believe me, they are all uncontrollable base instincts. Only instincts govern human actions, and their deeds result from egotistic subjection to their chaotic fate. One's life story is a prolonged struggle at mastering the pseudo-logic of rationalization.

Yet, I must judge the indecipherable enigma of the human mind and, when all is gone, when only memories remain to witness a purposeless life, I am sentenced to eternity. I judge based on memories that will be obsolete in a generation or two! Life flows and soon it's gone; yet I judge, from the perspective of eternity, the perpetrators of this tedious and insignificant flash of existence. I judge the path of lightning, questioning why it struck one tree rather than another, as if it is the result of willful causality rather than a combination of chances. What is the purpose of all?"

A lanky and gaunt gentleman of elegant composure was standing beside Luca talking to himself, yet cognizant of being heard. When Luca turned toward him, he twisted his neck like an eagle, without other motion from the rest of his body, and looked through Luca's eyes as if he was staring at his mind. Just the same, Luca saw through the gentleman's eyes, beyond a crystal gate, an impenetrable abyss.

"Most misdeeds committed by humans come from thoughtlessness, but the worst come from false morality. Some humans are compelled to justify their actions with a sort of distorted logic, and they become masters at this. Most atrocious choices are made because the faulty mind asserts control. In fact, most dangerous are those with strong beliefs, the moral among humans, those that rationalize their impulses with faulty reasons," the gentleman continued, emphasizing the world "moral."

"Now I ask you, what kind of human are you?"

Luca shook his head and guessed: "I do not know, perhaps a little of both?"

"Yes, correct answer! Most humans are."

By the time the intrigued Luca was ready to pursue the conversation, the stylish gentleman had vanished, and he was left wondering.

Meanwhile a new sentiment was dawning:

"A tree falling in the forest, that's what I am. I carry this weight in my chest! I would have never imagined that it would hurt so much! But does it matter in the end? If nobody can share my pain, does it really matter?

"Solitude quenches everything by making one feel irrelevant. And the gentleman was right, it's our moral part that judges the fruit of our instincts that cannot be judged."

This time he earnestly fancied to end his life.

"It is easy for a doctor. It can be done inconspicuously."

But then he thought: "Not worth it! Too many people would hurt because of my stupidity—my dad, my children, maybe even Christina. . . . Not worth it. Sadness is subjective. I should not take my feelings personally! Better stay silent like the tree in the forest. If I am the only one to know, my desperation may not be true, it might just be the fruit of my imagination."

So, arguing with himself, Luca shrugged and strolled along, thinking about the lanky gentleman: "Who was he? Why did he question what kind of human I am? What did the question have to do with what was going on in his current predicament?"

As he walked further, sadness turned into wrath. For the first time in his life, he experienced anger. Till then, all had rolled peacefully. Day after day, life had been still in its motion, and the slow flow of time reaffirmed its stillness; yes, the children could have won a few more soccer tournaments, and definitely, reviewers could have been more lenient about his science. They could have saved a little more money if Christina had been more frugal, they could have even bought a little cottage upstate. But overall, he had been very lucky. Nothing ever shook his privileged and fortunate experience. Years after years, building a block after the other, he had erected a palace of apparent professional and personal achievement. But now, all of a sudden everything had crumbled.

It wasn't just about Christina. It was about all that she represented. It was the vicarious life he had breathed through her. Luca realized that his life had been a charade, a castle made of cards, and a drama put up to please those who could not accept the emptiness of his soul. He also reckoned that he had never been sincerely happy, even once in his life, particularly on those moments of youth when he should have been. He truly did not know what true happiness was, but he had learned to fake it in physical appearance. He had learned to cope with the emptiness of the spirit by manufacturing emotions.

Christina with her constructive attitude had naturally guided him through the murk. She had been the lighthouse in the stormy darkness. Perhaps, more than a lighthouse, she had been a docile firefly in the depth of the night with the reliable reappearances of its placid glow.

He reckoned that he had loved her through the good and the bad times, and what she had interpreted as disengagement was only fear to displease; it was embarrassment of sort, an impression of inadequacy in front of the beautifully opinionated and strong-willed companion. Like cats often are, he had been misinterpreted. Cats are social and affectionate animals, but they respect other's territory and do not intrude. They approach only when they feel unquestionably welcome.

He did not feel welcome by Christina. He had learned to observe her from a distance, from the corners of life, fearful of unpredictable bursts of anger, as she was capable of. Christina had never understood that those moments of impatient wrath only distanced him from her because like a cat he could not understand her words or appreciate her motives; he could only sense the rage.

But now, Christina was gone! She had abandoned him; for no good reason, just out of an impulse, like the gentleman said, an arbitrary decision rationalized by a faulty logic. And he—he was left impotent; clasping the winds of his vanishing past like a child thrusting a hand toward the balloon that inexorably climbs the sky.

And he hated Christina, he hated her and loved her, he hated all those preposterous rationalizations of loneliness and neediness, but he loved all the rest. Once again, he thought of the gentleman, and he thought: "Nothing we do comes from selflessness, and we rationalize our impulses to deceive others and ourselves, while nothing we do originates from a sound reason."

Then, recognizing the tastelessness and vulgarity of his turmoil, his embarrassed id forced him to camouflage the anger as indifference for the future to come.

***

As we previously implied, Luca, perhaps to compensate for his instinctual detachment, had no familiarity with physical solitude. From the nurturing arms of his mother, he naturally transitioned to the arms of one girl after the other, and then a woman after the other. He barely knew what it was like to be in bed alone without a warm body to comfort him through the night. Women were transitional objects toward which he held profound affection. So, one at a time, each woman temporarily carried the baton of his hollowness till they were drained by the apathetic character and unloaded it to the next one. And this reaffirmed Luca's impression that relationships are transient and thus justified his casual attitude toward the other gender.

The day ahead was still long and without his wife to tell him what to do, Luca did not know how to organize his next steps. So, he did the most obvious of all things. He pulled out the piece of paper where Valentina's number was waiting and dialed:

"Hi, it's Luca. . . "

"Well, it did not take too long!" answered Valentina. "Do you want to come over or do you want to meet somewhere?"

***

Valentina's studio was tiny and luminous. There was a miscellaneous collection of art on the consoles and on the walls: photographs and paintings, little statues, and colorful marionettes from all over the world; an obsessive collection of lighthearted beauty that probably compensated for a harmonious melancholy. And Valentina described everything with forceful enthusiasm that made everything appear more tangible.

"I did not come here to make love to you," preempted Luca considerately, to break the ice. "I just came here because I could not think of anywhere else to go."

"I know," replied an understanding Valentina with her mischievous smile.

"In any case," she continued, "everybody knows that a proper girl would not make love on the first date. First date: one exchanges pleasantries; second date: the first kiss; only on the third is she supposed to yield. This is my resolute etiquette!"

Needless to say, within half an hour they were making love. Luca could not resist the beauty of her delicate and athletic body capped by the most flirtatious poses. He sat on the couch and drew her to him. After a preliminary kiss he started to fondle her to which she replied: "I am not very good at saying no!"

"Sorry, I cannot resist touching your butt."

"Am I stopping you?"

"I thought you said you do not make love on the first date!"

"Yes, but if we count this morning. . . this is already the second. . . one and. . . by the way. . . you kissed me this morning. . . so that anticipated. . . the second date! It can be argued that. . . this is in all practicality. . . the third one," said she in between kisses.

It was so mechanical, technically proficient, and irreproachable. So, they made love. Luca concentrated on her beauty, on her passion and responsiveness, on her orgasms. Luca tried hard to focus on what a man should focus on in similar circumstances. And he tried even harder to forget Christina, and not to think about how she might have enjoyed Jonathan's attentions. He tried to repulse the image of himself impersonating Jonathan making love to Christina. He tried very hard, also in respect to Valentina's sweetness, but in the end, he turned upside down in the bed, looked straight at the ceiling and did not say a word.

Valentina rested her head on his shoulder and gently caressed his hair. Then she ran her index finger along the contours of his silhouette, from his forehead to his nose, his lips, his chin, and further, further down. She kissed him a few times and then she told him: "Do you know that I love you? I have been in love with you for a very long time. You have always been in my dreams since the first time I saw you giving a talk. You were so handsome under the dim lights. Your eyes were so bright, and your pupils dilated, your words so passionate, your person so charismatic.

"But I know you do not love me. I was just lucky to have you here for a fleeting moment and I thank you for this," she added.

"I want to go!" Luca said impulsively. "I am sorry, but I need to go." And he began to put his clothes on with determination as if he was in a rush. But as he was about to leave the room he turned back, walked close to Valentina, sat beside her, and kissed her gently on the forehead, stroking her hair.

"Thank you. You offered shelter when I needed it. I will not forget it. I am just not ready for you or anybody else. You are sweet, and you are so beautiful! Sorry if I leave, I just need to go, not sure where, but I need to be alone."

"You are like a leopard. . . powerful, beautiful, smart, whom we all adore and admire. But whom nobody can own or control because it thrives in freedom. You can only follow your instincts that are solitary. Like a leopard you can only share love momentarily before moving toward the next catch. But I love you for what you are, for what you can and what you cannot give, because I know that deep inside, against all your instincts, I know you are a decent and caring human being."

As he was about to exit, Valentina called him: "Luca, I want you to know that I love you and I will be here for you whenever you need me."

***

That evening at home, Christina was waiting for Luca with a simple dinner and a bottle of chilled wine. So, they ate silently. Then Luca thanked her and went to sleep in the den while Christina washed the dishes and dignified herself with a few more chores. When he was about to fall asleep, Christina tiptoed into the den, bringing an extra blanket. Believing him asleep, she sat close to him; she caressed his hair and murmured: "Be well, my Luca, you deserve to be happy. Who knows who will snatch you. Do not fall for any woman. You deserve a good person, someone better than I was."

And as she was saying this, she started sobbing but Luca did not move. He pretended not to hear. Once again, he just did not know what to do or say. This is simply why he pretended to be asleep.

***

Tullio came to the door wearing his preferred attire for casual events which consisted of a wool vest, the customary velvet trousers, and soft leather loafers. Standing stiff like a flagpole in a peculiar aristocratic posture, donning the usual charming smile best suited for toothpaste commercials, he opened his right arm to greet Luca. Nothing had changed in those decades! Truly, nothing had changed!

Luca smiled and offered his right hand. Then, he changed his mind and thrust his arm around his friend's waist and lifted him up in a tight hug that lasted longer than necessary while he revitalized the past through the embrace.

As he was about to say something, Luca felt a punch in the back and heard Roberto's jovial voice: "Look who's here! The little scoundrel! The ladies' man! Hey, Luca! Any virgin left in the USA?"

Roberto, who was even taller than the other two, piled on the embrace sticking a bottle of chilled Prosecco in Luca's neck that gave him goosebumps and a refreshing sensation of the disordered and unpredictable ways in which things evolved in the good old times.

Then, Tullio's mother, who had managed to resist the not-so-subtle encouragements by her son to vacate the premises, came at the door eager to once more play the role of the magnanimous Mamma-host. In fact, just like decades before, the dinner was planned at Tullio's parental apartment partly in respect of history and partly to circumvent potential disputes with his better half at home.

Tullio's mom always retained a maternal affection, if not an obsessive infatuation, for Luca and she had been anxious to see him again after so many decades.

"Dio Mio![35] You look even more handsome now than you used to! What a distinguished gentleman! But still with those *biricchini*[36] eyes!"

The mom took Luca by the hand and, utterly disregarding Roberto, the little woman carried her catch to the sofa in the living room. "Accomodati, accomodati, bello mio![37] Tell me, how are things with you in America? *Nuova Yorka,*[38] isn't it? How is the family? Did you ever marry? Who is the lucky woman? Do you have children? Do they look like little Luchini?"

That was not exactly how Luca had intended to start the evening. As he was about to offer the standard "all is fine" answer and a few generalities about the children, Giuseppe had arrived and was coming out of the kitchen with a few pieces of Grana Padano[39] in one hand and a little plate with slices of soppressata[40] in the other. He deposited the goodies on the coffee table and, sitting close to Luca, put an arm around his shoulders and stated: "His wife is giving him trouble; she is getting rid of him!"

Why would a smart man like Giuseppe violate any sort of privacy rule by making that blunt statement? Well, that was the point of the Old Boys

---

[35] My God!
[36] mischievous
[37] Make yourself comfortable, my handsome boy!
[38] "New York" in some sort of Italian!
[39] Brand of Parmesan Cheese
[40] Spicy sausage from Southern Italy

Academy: no beating around the bush, "*unus pro omnibus, omnes pro uno,* "[41] they were just there to share their lives for better and for worse like in the good old times.

"I think I am divorcing!" Luca admitted, and that confession, for unclear reasons, took five hundred kilograms off his chest.

"Because his wife has a lover," added Giuseppe free of charge.

"That is no problem at all! I can find you a lovely woman any time," interjected Roberto's mouth — a mouth that, like its owner, always bore a paternal instinct toward his friends.

"There is an abundance of good-looking young chicks around, who would love to make your acquaintance! Milano has become cosmopolitan! Lots of models from all over the world! There is just l'imbarazzo della scelta. "[42]

Wearing his imperturbable smile, Tullio interrupted: "Come on, Roberto, if there is somebody who does not need your help to find a woman, it is Luca!"

But it was Tullio's mom who took control of the conversation and, waving her tiny hand to demand silence, she posed the last word on this: "Luca, that woman, I mean your wife—whoever she is and whatever her name is— does not deserve you! How can a woman leave you unless she is a complete fool?"

"It was partly my fault, I guess. Christina is not a bad person," whispered Luca, looking elsewhere to find a diversion away from the topic.

"The divorce is very painful to me. Although I have not been getting along with Christina, it is difficult without a person with whom one lived almost all his life. She got tired of my apathy and found somebody else. He is an old friend, and they are happy now. In fact, she told me that she has never been that happy. And I am happy for her but still I feel desolate thinking about the past. All seems to have vanished all of a sudden. It is a strange sensation! It is like a fog that hangs over the rice fields and erases everything. One wonders whether everything is truly gone, or if it is just out of our sight, as a momentary illusion. But then when the mist dissipates one

---

[41] One for all, all for one
[42] The trouble of making the right choice

realizes that indeed all is gone! And I wonder whether even I will disappear into the haze. Maybe, I myself am the fog."

And he continued: "You know, I feel exposed now as if I am walking on a tightrope without a balancing stick. Christina was my balancing stick! She is the only woman who truly knew and understood me!"

"And this is probably why she left you!" Giuseppe interjected sympathetically.

***

At that juncture, the intercom rang and Tullio announced: "Enrico is here!"

"Is he still a communist?" questioned Giuseppe, affecting some interest on the subject. Giuseppe carried an inborn antipathy for those who identified themselves with any ideology and, as much as he respected Enrico as a friend, he felt contempt when it came to politics.

"Is he going to bore us to death with his Gramsci rubbish or did he finally get over it?" continued Giuseppe who was starting to feel comfortably at home.

"Of course, he still is!" proclaimed Roberto. "But no more Gramsci! He made a career out of it but now he has real problems to deal with! He is now the mayor of—and he goes *pappa ciccia*[43] with all the politicians, whatever their colors are."

"And they say he is even good at it!" intervened Tullio. "They even say he is 'honest'! As if honesty has anything to do with a politician's prerequisites. Wouldn't you rather go for somebody who is effective and can solve problems than for an 'honest' guy? Who cares if he gets a cut as long as the trains run on time? But Enrico still carries a monastic life breathing the socialistic spirit. He lives in his one-bedroom apartment with his wife and drives the same old Fiat that you probably remember from before you went to America with all the stickers attached to it that are probably the only thing keeping it together! His favorite hobby is adding cold water to the engine before it melts! But anyways, there is nothing you can do about Enrico; boring but honest! He really can't do without integrity! It's not his fault, it's in his genes and there is nothing you can do about genes, isn't it

---

[43] Hand in hand

true, professor?" Turning toward Luca: "Any gene therapy to correct the 'honesty' problem?"

"Well, perhaps he is both; just because he is honest does not mean he cannot be effective!" concluded Giuseppe, who was starting to regret his original outburst in consideration of Enrico's preeminent appearance at the door.

But in all events, the conversation took another turn before Enrico's arrival. The mom had not fallen for the diversion and, keeping focus on her prey, she did not relent. Holding Luca's hand, she continued:

"Luca, listen to me. . . you have always been the sweetest among all of your friends. They are all wonderful, including my son. . . but you. . . you are special. Since I can remember, you were always humble and even shy, with so much inner depth. You never believed in yourself, and you always looked for affirmation. Handsome and smart, you never had a tinge of arrogance. You were so charming in your simplicity and just looking at your eyes, I know that you still are. But no matter how many girls loved you, you never learned to understand women. I remember those times when you confessed your affairs to me! You were always so panicked about those who loved you! The more a girl loved you, the more scared you were and the more you ran away from them! Why was that? Did you ever figure it out?"

***

Enrico came in and after the customary hugs and handshakes, he sat at Giuseppe's side. He was the image of Saint Francis—not an extra gram of fat, simple but ordered attire, piercing eyes mitigated by a sweet smile, and no words to accompany his presence but a genuine inclination to listen.

The mom continued: "Luca. . . "

Tullio came to his mom's side and, gently tapping her on the shoulder, invited her to leave as she had promised. But the mom waved him away: "Just one more word and I will go; let me finish!"

"Luca, listen to me: you deserve to be loved! Stop running away from those who love you and believe a woman when she tells you that she loves you. Women do not use this world as lightly as men do!"

At this point, Tullio took the bottle of Prosecco from the table, poured a glassful into his mother's crystal glass and gently, lifting her by holding the fragile body under the armpit, he walked her away while she received hugs and kisses from each of the Old Boys along the path, pretty much like the statue of the Madonna is venerated in Southern Italian processions. As she was about to disappear behind the fixture, she turned around and, waving at the Old Boys, she concluded:

"Thank you for coming! I missed all of you during these very long years! You are one of the best memories of my youth and your presence makes me feel young again!"

***

"I guess your mom still has a crush on Luca!" smirked Roberto after she disappeared.

"Maybe you should take her to *Nuova Yorka* with you!" smiled Tullio. "She would definitely love it!" and then he added: "I love my mom; she has been both a mother and a sister to me! And after my dad passed away, she clinged to me and my sisters, spending all her energies convincing us that she is the luckiest of women; telling us how wonderful her husband was, and how great her children and grandchildren are. I never heard her complain of anything in all my life and in so many ways she is much more of a companion to me than my wife. This is why we have the reunion here. . . . So, I guess what I am trying to say is forgive me for her intrusion but I did not have the heart to keep her out completely. She really wanted to see you all."

"No problem, Tullio! Of course we love her! We all remember how hospitable she was! No apologies needed," reflected Giuseppe, who was gradually returning to his natural disposition as a moderate and not judgmental wise man.

"Yes, nice woman!" confirmed Roberto. "A little too intrusive sometimes. . . like the time when she walked in on Luca with La Candela on top of him while we all thought she had gone out to La Scala!"

"You mean Luisa! What happened to her?" Luca suddenly awakened from his trance at the mention of his old girlfriend: "What a nice woman she was! I never met anybody sweeter than her!"

"She is married now with two children! She is a different person now!" answered Tullio defensively. "Don't get any wrong ideas! Besides, she aged! She is not the way she looked."

"Her husband is sick; he has terminal cancer," interrupted Enrico who was the only non-physician in the room.

"What cancer?" asked Giuseppe who was the expert on the subject.

"Don't know. In the liver, I believe."

"Most cancers go to the liver eventually! Do you know where the primary was?" Then recognizing that it made no difference for the purpose of the conversation, Giuseppe added: "Sorry, never mind, he is probably in good hands at the Institute and in any case, I barely know Luisa. I guess she goes back to your depraved high school days, which I did not have the privilege to witness! Anyways, maybe Luca should consider revisiting the relationship! She may need some support and Luca needs somebody to talk to! Maybe he can take her to *Nuova Yorka* together with Tullio's mom!"

"Maybe Luca should have married her to begin with instead of going to America!" added Tullio sarcastically, who was getting bored of the conversation and sported a portentous yawn.

"She would have cheated on Luca just as much as she would have with anybody else!" commented Roberto, who had been silent way more than he could bear.

"Don't be so cynical," intervened Tullio. "You never know women! And in any case pretty much all women cheat on their husband at one point or another! And this is good! The ones who don't become a pain in the neck with their righteousness and they are generally, and not surprisingly, the ugly ones!"

"So, your wife is cheating on you? Isn't she?" surged the friendly Roberto.

"None of your business," intervened Giuseppe but Tullio calmly and aristocratically stood up, towering over his friends:

"She is! So what? With all the times I cheated on her, how can you blame her? Since she found this guy, she is leaving me alone and this is good enough for me! Cheers!!!!"

And the old boys lifted the glasses of Prosecco for a toast:

"To our wives and their happiness!" exclaimed Tullio, staring at Luca and expecting a positive reaction from his phlegmatic friend:

"Come on, Luca, loosen up! See, we are all on the same boat!"

"You see, Luca? You should learn from Tullio! If you lose your wife, you can just take it easy and compensate with high-class young lovers," concluded Giuseppe.

***

"I am going to call Luisa," interrupted Enrico but once again the intercom rang, and Marco was announced.

"Let's wait for Marco," said Tullio. "He is the last one we are expecting."

"What about Mario? Is he coming?" asked Giuseppe.

"No, he is having troubles in Rome where he is now. He called to say he cannot make it."

"What kind of troubles?"

"Not sure. Marco knows since they are colleagues, and they are quite close."

"Well, let's call Mario then, at least to say hi."

The doorbell rang and Marco came, carrying a load of bottles and dessert boxes!

Marco was the most jovial and wittiest of them all. He was a short, skinny character with a composed and dry demeanor. He wore formal but not elegant attire independent of the occasion, so much so that it was whispered that he would go to bed wearing a tie. Even worse, the rumor was that he wore calf suspenders to support his socks, which he did not take off till he was in bed. However, such debasing gossip had never been substantiated since none of his friends had ever seen him naked nor had any relevant woman ever offered to testify on this delicate subject. Thus, since nobody could prove otherwise, the Old Boys assumed for practical purposes that indeed Marco was the kind of guy who would wear calf suspenders even in the shower. Just like his posture, dry was his humor; sharp like a Chinese knife that could cut through bones as if they were butter.

"Hello, everybody! What a pleasure to see my Old Boys again! Where have you been all these years while this poor guy had to take care of all your relatives!"

In fact, Marco, among his various talents, was the doctors' doctor. With terrific common sense, he was taken advantage by all his friends, in particular those living abroad, who made sure that he would intervene whenever a problem arose among their relatives.

Turning toward Luca, Marco gave him a big hug: "How is your dad doing? How is his heart? Is the A Fib[44] controlled?"

"Fine! Thanks for taking care of him. Yes, he takes his Coumadin and Digoxin religiously if not for anything else but to make sure that you do not scold him. Thanks for checking on him often."

"So, what happened to Mario?" asked the impatient Roberto.

"Don't know for sure! I believe he has some problems with the administration in Rome. I have no idea why he left Milan and his unbelievable cardiac surgery program to go there!"

"Obviously, it must have been for a woman!" interjected Roberto, receiving unanimous assent from the audience.

The phone was put on speaker mode and after a few rings Mario answered:

"Hey! It's us, the Old Boys! Sorry you couldn't make it!" opened Tullio.

"We wish you were here," added Marco. "Everybody is here! Including The Americani! What is going on with you? I heard a lot of bad rumors! Did you get in trouble for taxes?"

"Sort of! Well, guys, it's a long story. . . You know people are jealous and they would do anything to get rid of a successful guy. But I did my part to help them on this! In the end it is always about women! I used some grant money to pay for a pied-a-terre where we could meet and then deduct the payments from taxes as a business expense—at least this is what my detractors say! Now they're forcing me to resign to avoid a bigger penalty! You know, it's a Christian place! So, they worry more about the image than facts! Who can blame them?"

---

[44] Atrial fibrillation in doctors' slang.

"Wow, is she beautiful at least? Is she worth it?" asked a fretful Roberto, who was earnestly more concerned about this latter aspect of the problem; how could somebody blame Mario if the prize balanced the cost?

"Of course, she is! How can you even ask something like that? What do you think? That I lost it? She is amazing, her skin is so smooth, you see. . . not that cold and frigid slickness of marble, but the grainy smoothness of silk that sticks to the pulp of your fingers and penetrates the skin into the blood, if you know what I mean! You can go up and down her body with ease and yet, you feel you are touching an angel who is made of real flesh!"

In the silence that followed, several heads nodded their endorsement:

"How could anybody argue with such a well-presented and compelling argument?"

"Is she Japanese?" asked Enrico suddenly, interrupting the meditative moment.

"No! Why do you ask?"

"Japanese women have that kind of skin!"

Well, that was unexpected. Everybody wondered how Enrico could come up with that conclusion. It was Roberto who recovered first and asked:

"I think you are thinking of their kimonos! And in any case, how on Earth would you happen to know anything about Japanese women's skin, or, for Christ's sake, any woman's skin?"

"I heard it in a movie!" answered Enrico truthfully.

"Ahh. . . now that explains it! Anyways, sorry for the interruption, Mario; so, what are you going to do?" resumed Marco.

"I think I will have to resign!"

"Well, you remind me of Al Capone. After killing all of these people with your cardiac surgery, they finally got you for tax evasion!"

"Wow! With a friend like this, who needs a mother-in-law!" exclaimed a disgusted Roberto.

The proper Enrico had to add his part: "I am sorry, Mario. Is there anything we could do?"

"No, don't worry, guys, I will be fine, and I can always make a lot of money by going private. I know this is not what you want to hear but you know what? Lovers are expensive!"

And even the prude Enrico assented with a smile.

"Do me a favor, guys! Keep me in mind for the next time and I will be there for sure. . . if I am not in jail!"

***

"Wow, that was interesting! Are we all this rotten? Is any of us straight at all?" commented Giuseppe, not without a subliminal sense of pride.

That was a good question and each of the Old Boys considered it thoughtfully. As they were going through this introspective moment considering their existence and wondering about their friends, all eyes converged toward the honest Enrico. If there was hope for redemption among all, he was the one who could save the pack of wolves from perdition. So, Enrico saw a myriad of eyes staring at him over this very special kind of inquisition:

"Come on, Enrico! Do not tell us that you never cheated on your wife! Got to be some woman who loves your pimples!" attacked Roberto.

Now, you ought to know that Enrico did not smile that often; nor did he frown easily or exercised in extravagance any connection between the frontal lobe and the mimic muscles of his face . Most importantly, he did not blush at all or behave like octopuses or chameleons that change colors in response to environmental pressure. But all of this happened at once as the aftermath to Roberto's question. While the honest man was blabbering some disconnected excuse, everybody understood that even the honorable Enrico failed to carry the lantern of purity for his profane friends, and they all lost interest in the matter:

"Yes, obviously we are all rotten! So what? Let's move on with dinner!" concluded Tullio. But this caused Roberto to claim proudly:

"Wait a minute! I am the only one who never cheated on his wife!"

"Of course; you have never been married!" Marco pointed out.

"Well, whatever works!"

***

Dinner started with a clap of hands and Tullio announcing:

"Que la fête commences!"

Simultaneously, a blond woman of the kindest manners and a charming smile emerged from the kitchen with a steaming bowl in her hands. The latter emanated a fragrance reminiscent of Alpine forests and contained a consommé of Porcini mushrooms.

Upon first inspection, tacit exchanges conceded unanimously that the woman was endowed with a great body! This first impression was confirmed by subsequent inspections carried discreetly with the corner of the eye by each member of the audience that was obediently taking position around an ancient mahogany table. A tablecloth laced by the hands of some grandmother a century before and concealed by all sort of hors d'oeuvres covered the latter. There were typical Northern and Southern Italian cold meats such as Prosciutto di Parma wrapped around breadsticks and hot soppressata reposing over dried tomatoes. There were grilled vegetables drizzled with balsamic vinegar and virgin olive oil and decorated with fresh rosemary twigs, bruschetta with basil and vine-tomatoes, chunks of parmesan cheese, baccalà[45] soaked in pomegranate-vinaigrette topped with black olives and ginger flakes, smoked lox with capers and lemon cloves, goose liver pate and, right in a middle, a big bowl containing gigantic prawns that sat prostrated toward the center in reverence to a porcelain basin from ancient China filled to the brim with cocktail sauce. Such cornucopia was sprinkled with delicious, though often underappreciated, pickled gherkins. At the center of the table also sat a crystal bowl, where colorful and fragrant camellias floated on rose water—an elegant touch emblematic of Tullio's mother, who wished to remind the guests of her tactful presence.

In the absolute silence, the woman approached the table, deposited the soup close to the crystal bowl and, progressing guest by guest, she held a ladle with her right hand and lifted a plate with her left, pouring a generous amount of consommé. All was done without spilling a single drop on the tablecloth. At last, she reached Tullio, who, as she was pouring the

---

[45] Dried and Salted Cod

concoction, put his hand around her waist, just on top of what technically should be referred to as the junction of the gluteus maximus to the iliac wing but is more widely known as rump. Tullio smiled at her and softly stated:

"Grazie, Martina."

Martina responded with a submissive smile and a subliminal bow of the head and for the first time she looked around. When she sighted Luca, who was also staring at her, Martina, as most women did at such occurrence, radiated a graceful smile while Luca appropriately pretended not to take notice.

As soon as Martina disappeared in the kitchen, Giuseppe asked:

"If Luca takes your mom to *Nuova Yorka*, is Martina going with them?"

Simultaneously, Marco interjected:

"Let me say this to you, Tullio, if you do not mind: did you really have to screw up the dinner with this woman? Nobody is going to focus on anything else now!"

"Come on, guys! Grow up! She is just my mother's help! A woman from Ukraine! She just offered to help!"

"And what was that caress to her butt about? Come on, do you think it went unnoticed?" added Roberto. "Be honest! Tell us the truth! Did you do it with her?"

"What kind of question is this?" intervened the proper Giuseppe to protect Tullio, who did not seem the least fazed by the comment and, continuing to smile enigmatically, lifted the cup of Prosecco for a toast:

"Welcome, all of you! Welcome back to the Old Boys Academy! *At Maiora*! I already see that in spite of the decades, little has changed in our spirit! *Unus pro omnibus, omnes pro uno!*"

As they all raised their glasses and gulped down the nectar, Luca nodded and thoughtfully offered his expert opinion:

"She is indeed a beautiful woman!"

"Thank you, professor, for pointing it out! We would have never noticed!" added Roberto, while Tullio interjected:

"Guys, let's forget Martina! Can we just move onto something more interesting?" This left the audience wondering what could be more interesting than the aforementioned miraculous apparition.

I forgot to mention that sitting at the table, as part of the Old Boys ensemble, was Tommaso. I forgot to mention him because frankly he was the least notable creature. He rarely spoke and, therefore, all his friends fondly regarded him as part of the furniture, taking no further notice beyond such generous concession. He was a stocky and buff figure, exaggeratedly tanned, donning gold watches, bracelets, and heavy necklaces that shone over the hairy chest from the open shirt, in utter dissonance with the subdued elegance of his friends. Yet, he had been a legitimate constituent of the Old Boys Academy since high school simply because his congeniality deflected any questions about his upbringing. He studied briefly in America accumulating just enough credentials to elevate him, upon his return, to a prominent gynecologist with mixed academic and private practice. He was seen consistently with spectacular women hopping in and out of his red Ferrari—women in miniskirts exposing stunning legs veiled by black stockings and supported by laced garters . Allegedly, he was married; and in fact, a plump and unrefined woman introduced as his wife appeared on a few occasions at his side. But, like him, she never took the initiative to begin a conversation, and nobody ever felt compelled to compensate for that shortcoming.

As the Old Boys were about to move away from the subject of Martina, unexpectedly, Tommaso pronounced:

"I agree with Luca, she is really beautiful, she is just perfect!"

This further disheartened Tullio, who had been trying to elevate the conversation just a notch, .

Meanwhile, Giuseppe, overtaken by a philosophical attack, shared this hypothetical scenario:

"Think about it! Luca goes back to America with your mom, Luisa, and Martina. What a trio! Maturity, affection, and attraction! Commitment, companionship, and passion! The perfect relationship built around three women!"

"Yes. . . till the three of them start plotting against him! Then the poor Luca is kaput! *Unus adversus omnibus, omnes adversus uno!* Excuse my Latin!" reflected Marco.

"He can then find a nice, fourth woman!"

"Till she also joins the pack!"

"It will end like Christopher Columbus, who had to run out of the Old Continent! Believe me, he discovered America by accident; the issue about the Earth being round was just an excuse. He was just in trouble with a bunch of women and needed a pretext to get out of town and reboot in the New Continent!" mentioned Roberto.

"And where did this notion come from?" asked Giuseppe, who was the most versed in historical matters.

"I read it in Wikipedia."

"Didn't know you were a Wikipedophile! Great for you to keep up with high standards!"

"That Wikipedia sounds good till you look up topics about which you actually know something about. Then you will appreciate how inaccurate it can be!"

"Glad we are moving away from the Martina subject!" sighed Tullio in relief just before Martina returned. This time she was carrying a copper pan filled with steaming rice colored by saffron and smelling of the white truffle that had been freshly grated on top.

Martina, in addition to the consommé, offered to grate extra truffle from Alba or Parmesan cheese on the rice, with the premonition, however, that truffle alone should do for taste.

As she approached Tullio, all eyes gawked at his hand, but the experienced Tullio, preempting the inquisition, maintained composure, leaving this second passage uneventful.

A few bottles of Barolo that had already been opened and vented were brought in and the friends generously poured it into each other's crystal glass. Roberto took the bottle from Tullio's hand and studied the label.

Then nodding his head in approbation, he returned it to Tullio, commenting:

"Wow! You must have put some overtime for this stuff! Hope the quality does not compromise the quantity! You know, these 'Americans' suck wine like sponges when they get a chance to return home!"

"Speak for yourself!" grunted Giuseppe. "Come to Napa sometime and you will be on all fours within an hour!"

Tullio reassured him that a rich patient donated a case of the precious Barolo and added that there was plenty of white wine in the cooling cellar and of liquor of any color and vintage dispersed in his mom's home that had been waiting for the Old Boys' return.

Again, Martina smiled at Luca, and again he pretended not to notice. But after she left, he reinforced his previous statement: "She truly is a beautiful woman!"

In answer to this comment, Roberto sighed loudly and in agreement with Tullio, mumbled:

"Okay, let's get over this!"

But Tommaso muttered:

"Yes, she is just perfect. . . Just like my wife."

I admit that it would be an exaggeration to state that a clank caused by the Old Boys' jaws dropping on the floor could be heard from miles away. So be it! It still provides the reader with an approximate idea of the magnificence of the Old Boys' reaction! After Roberto had a chance to recover his own jaw from the floor and reattach it to the temporal-mandibular joint, to test his regained verbal skills, he asked:

"What do you mean your wife looks like her? If I remember correctly, your wife looks. . . looks. . . looks just. . . different, I will say. Maybe a different kind of beauty?"

"You are talking about my other wife," reacted the inflexible Tommaso, while he shoveled a forkful of rice in his mouth and raised the glass of Barolo to facilitate the progress of his chewing.

"Sorry, I did not know you divorced!"

"I didn't."

"I am sorry, let me get this straight—and I'm sorry again if I sound brash, but—did your wife get a total body replacement recently? Is that what you mean by your new wife?"

Tommaso was not only quiet but also exaggeratedly slow. He could make a sloth look like a cheetah. But eventually, as everybody was about to give up, he mumbled:

"I am talking about my other wife!"

I assure you that this is what emerged from Tommaso's munching mouth, to everybody's disbelief!

The friends looked around to confirm consonant reception. Then, they waited for a volunteer to carry the sequitur of such strange conversation. Nobody came forward and the curiosity mounted. Finally, Tullio reluctantly felt the responsibility, as the host, to initiate the interrogation:

"Tommaso," he calmly opened, "we do understand that this is none of our business, but we are friends and we do care for you. Did we understand correctly that you have two wives?"

Trying to coordinate talking with munching, Tommaso answered: "Yes. I know that you do not consider me a genius, but you should concede that even I can figure out that one plus one equals two!"

"But do you understand that at least in Italy, no matter how permissive our beloved country is, polygamy remains illegal?"

"This is why I shared this information with you guys in confidence, and please keep it to yourselves." Then he added:

"It is not the law that I am concerned about. I do not want Isabella to know about Jasmine. . . and vice versa. I would not want for either to be hurt."

"Now, this is what I call being considerate!" commented Giuseppe. "We cannot take good care of one wife and this guy here sports the energy to worry about two!"

"And how did you even get married? Don't you need a license or something?"

And Tommaso started telling his story:

*

Listen, guys, I know that it is none of your business, but I am still compelled to share the story with you all. I met Jasmine at a strip club. She was a stripper, and I had a dance with her. Next thing I knew, she tells me that her husband is a drunkard and abuses her and their child. What's a man to do? I felt bad and decided to marry her. The husband comes to beat me up and kill me. He was the bouncer at the same club, and he was huge; he could kill an elephant with one stroke, but I tell him: "Listen, she is not happy with you, and you have a lot of debts. I will pay them off and you let her go." We both agreed that it made perfect sense. We shook hands and from then on we became good friends. . . . We jumped on a plane to Las Vegas and we married on a chapel decorated with bouquets of plastic roses. She was moved and cried and she fell deeply in love with me. She wants kids from me. I want them too because Isabella can't have any. God knows how much we tried! Later, during a romantic dinner, I got drunk and when I do, my imagination unleashes. I tell her with tears in my eyes (not sure where it came from) that my Isabella died a year before in a car crash and Jasmine cried in empathy—isn't she sweet? And we both cried though I reckon some part of me cried in relief that Isabella is alive and well. We ended up enjoying the sweetest honeymoon. Now she is pregnant with my first baby! It's going to be a girl! She wants to call her Isabella, but I think it would be too much."

"And what about Isabella?" interrupted a suddenly interested Luca.

She is happy. She doesn't know about Jasmine. I have never been as kind to her as I have been since I married Jasmine. I spend two weeks with one wife alternating with the other for the other two weeks. I tell them that I took a missionary project in Rwanda requiring two weeks on site each month to help women with difficult pregnancies. I learned everything about endemic problems there! You won't believe how primordial the conditions can be in that beautiful country devastated by fratricide! I feel ashamed for the way we carry our life of entitlement! How can we complain about anything? Sometimes I feel like I should go to Rwanda for real, but then, how can I if I have to rotate between two wives?

They both admire me for this Rwanda thing and now I am addicted to it. I am a victim of my own success. I go from one to the other and narrate great stories about rescued pregnancies and miracle babies and, as I polish them, I start to like the stories myself! I know that they are fictional but so what? They seem to enlighten and mature them into better persons! After all, does is really matter what's real or what's imagined? Isn't it the intention that counts?

*

"God save the King!" concluded Giuseppe, lifting a full glass of Barolo. "As long as you can deal with it! It certainly takes a lot of planning and coordination; not for everybody. Your next job might as well be an intelligence agent for the CIA!"

But the usually reticent Tommaso, under the influence of Barolo, was relentless and could not bridle the mouth from its momentum:

*

Well, it wasn't always that simple! This is when a friend's help is critical. . . Once, I was almost exposed to Isabella. I was in a faculty senate meeting when I get this call. I go out of the room and it's Isabella:

"Why is there a photo of you on the Internet marrying another woman in Las Vegas?"

"Marrying what?" I say, pretending to be surprised. . . and I was! My dear gentlemen! What did Jasmine think? Why did she post the photo without consulting with me? I cannot tell you how much I hate social media; they just complicate a poor man's life. Anyways, I say in a whisper as if I could not talk:

"Can't talk to you now! I am in a meeting. I'll call later!"

But as I go into the room and I sit down, I can't focus and keep shaking and tossing on the chair till Professor Salimbeni, who was chairing the session, notices and asks:

– Something wrong? –

I cannot stop myself! I keep shaking and I have no idea what to do. I am not concerned about the faculty senate. I care about my wonderful wives! And how could I be blamed? How could I have predicted that my little

Jasmine would do something so naïve in her sweet spontaneity? This is what I recounted in front of them!

Anyways, Professor Salimbeni listens pensively to my story, nodding his head at intervals and in between scratching his temple with a pencil, which otherwise he kept twisting in his nervous hand. Promptly, the astute academician reckons that this is no ordinary faculty senate matter; this is a real problem! Therefore, he says:

"There are a lot of superbly practiced men in this room, who survived the turbulent waters of academia, which are almost as bad as dealing with two wives: any suggestions from the audience?"

Professor Gasparoni, who is the Chair of Ethical Studies in the Department of Philosophy, has no doubts:

"Buy a luxuriant bouquet of red roses and go home. There, you tell your wife. . . – Then upon reflection he specifies: –I mean the wife, who just called. . . tell her the truth and plead for her pardon! We all make mistakes, but true love should overcome minor setbacks. Tell her that you did it out of generosity for an abused woman. Women like candor; she will forgive you if she loves you. If she does not forgive you, then it means that she does not love you and then. . . forget about her!"

"With all due respect for my distinguished colleague, I would have to humbly disagree. Philosophers are often naïve in practical matters," – explains Professor Lentini, Chair of Civil Litigation:

"Never admit any fault unless you talk to a lawyer first. You must understand the extent of the consequences of confession in the court of law!"

"Then what is a poor man supposed to do?" say I.

"I know what you are going to do!" says Professor Leoni, Chair of Humanistic Studies, who had recently published a treatise on the aftermath of the feminist revolution in the Western world, demonstrating that he knew just enough about women to possibly endure them.

"You tell her that this was just a prank! A set up to protect the poor woman from an abusive boyfriend; that you pretended to marry her to discourage him! But it was just a farce, a joke pretending to be in Las Vegas, thanks to

Photoshop. Kind of thing anybody would do with friends when drunk! In the end she knows that you have. . . an active life so to speak. Only thing she cares about is reassurance that you do not leave her for another woman and, most importantly, that you keep bringing the dough home!"

I turned to look at our chairman Professor Salimbeni wondering whether he would call for a vote. But he simply nods his head and says:

"Great idea! This is why we should support humanistic studies or, as they call them now, Science of Antiquity! It is the evolution of civilization, the survival of the human species against the odds, the fortitude of manhood before feminine hurricanes. If I were in the same predicament, I would follow Professor Leoni's advice. Any further suggestion?" Nobody says anything.

"Okay then, you proceed and let us know how it went at the next meeting. Let's move ahead with the agenda. By the way"— he says turning to the assistant—"it goes without saying that this confidential matter does not need to be included in the minutes!"

*

"And so, what happened?" asked Roberto.

"Well. . . Isabella was touched by my generosity. She told me that she always knew I was a good man and that she was proud of me for helping the poor woman, and for the Rwanda thing as well. Both corroborated each other as evidence of my compassionate metamorphosis. She cried, even apologized for accusing me. I gave her a big hug and forgave her. She never talked about it again and never looked me up on the Internet."

"Wow, there is always something to learn from those scholars. I guess it helped that Professor Leoni spent most of his life scratching his head over Macchiavellis, Ciceros, and Descartes! *Cogito ergo sum!* And it was really something for him to figure that out in the spur of the moment! A tribute to the senate of our glorious university! Sometimes something of substance can come out of it!" said Tullio raising and drinking another glass of Barolo in immediate succession.

Silence followed. Then Giuseppe, who in spite of his successful career held a grudge against the academic system and its overbearing bureaucratic aspects, lifted the impasse.

"Perhaps, the faculty senate of the University of Milan is more practical than in other places. Academia in America is now under the hands of bureaucrats. So much posturing about doing 'good' for people's health but little support to move forward with programmatic studies that could fulfill the promise! Bureaucrats run the show—people that justify their existence claiming a need to solve problems that would not exist if they didn't create them in the first place. A bureaucrat is somebody who can find a problem for any solution! But for sure cannot find a solution for any problem! Bureaucrats will do anything to convince you that you do not know what you are doing and that they are the only ones who can help you fix problems they know nothing about. They will drive you crazy with 'strategic planning' trying to package creativity and intuition into a box! What kind of strategy do you think Heraclitus, Socrates, Plato, Pythagoras needed? And what was Newton's strategy? Keep walking under an apple tree till something hit his head and teach him gravity? What about Copernicus, Galileo, or Einstein? What about Vera Rubin, who described dark matter? What was her strategy besides sitting for endless boring nights taking notes behind a telescope? And what strategy followed Beethoven when he composed Moonlight. . . and Albinoni composing the Adagio? Did any of these creators need a strategy or they simply needed to be left in peace without interference from idiots?"

"In the institution where I work, for example," continued Giuseppe, "there was an escalator from the ground floor to the second-floor cafeteria. I took it each morning for my regular cup of coffee. . . each morning except for when it was out of order, which was not so rare of an occurrence. The poor escalator was out of service every other day and one could observe two or three maintenance guys musing over the dismantled steps in awe as if they were Japanese tourists facing the Grand Canyon. It vexed me so much, but I sucked it up, mumbled something about raising a complaint about it to some unknown entity while I climbed the stairs and, by the time I was up, I would have forgotten about it. Then one day, I received the honor of being invited to be part of a prestigious panel of scientists assembled to discuss strategies to advance the treatment of cancer! It was indeed a great honor to be included in this distinguished group of experts put together by our administration with the specific purpose of demonstrating that they were doing something to earn their salary. But it was also utterly boring to trail all day along pompous presentations that emphasized how,

274

coincidentally, the protein, the mouse model, the new gadget that each expert happened to be working on stood as a portentous solution to the cure of cancer and perhaps anything beyond that including possibly global warming. Therefore, money should be thrown at it! By the end of the day, everybody around the big table was worn out. Some were even dozing off except for the bureaucrats, who were frantically typing notes to justify their existence, pretending that they understood anything that was discussed. It was then that a ruinous idea assailed me: I switched on the speakerphone that reached up to my mouth like the leg of a big daddy spider and, when my turn came, I said:

– Maybe we should consider a feasibility study. We should try to fix the first-floor escalator in this building once and for all! Then we can worry about curing cancer! I mean, Macys, Bloomingdale (for the Italians, UPIM and Rinascente) and all other big department stores manage to assure their customers that each day stacks of escalators reliably elevate common people to the altitudes of consumerism while we cannot even get one to work for our scientists to get a cup of coffee in the morning! If we cannot match that, how can we deal with complex problems like cancer? Conversely, we could ask Macys' managers to help us here! –

It was obviously meant to be a lighthearted comment at the end of a draining day, but it did not go well. Even from the twentieth floor, where the meeting was held, one could hear the crickets chirping cheerfully from the gardens below! Nobody laughed!"

"And then what happened?" Roberto asked eagerly.

"You mean to cancer or to the escalator?" Marco asked sarcastically.

"Well, a few days later, my Chief summoned me to his office after he heard of my unsolicited remarks and warned me to watch my tongue in the future. Meanwhile, the escalator was removed forever from the premises and that took care of it! Of course, cancer is still there for the next strategic panel to contemplate."

"Yes, sounds exactly like our administration: feed the bureaucrats with chatter and they will be content, but do not challenge them with real problems, except of course for Tommaso's case which, after all, was handled by bona fide academicians!" summarized Roberto.

"Well, it must have been quite embarrassing. I hate when I throw a joke, and nobody gets it," commented the astute Marco.

"Tell me about it! But it can be even worse! Talking about embarrassing situations in academia—" interjected Tullio, "Do you know what happened to me? I was at a stage of life when I was happily trailing along my existence on the passenger seat. Wherever life wanted to go, I docilely followed. My only goal was to inconspicuously carry a lifeless body around in the form of flesh wrapped around a beating heart. . . and that was fine with me. But my wife insisted that I should see a shrink."

"That's called depression, nothing that Zoloft can't take care of," interrupted Marco who, like Tullio's wife, was rather inclined to turn philosophical matters into practicality.

"That's exactly what the shrink prescribed! But only after I dropped five hundred Euros in his piggy bank. Next time I will come directly to you, Marco! Anyways, I started taking the pill that did almost nothing except for forcing me to produce enormous yawns! You have no idea what kind of stretches of the jaws were involved! They would last a minute and I was at constant risk of dislocating my mandible. I could barely breathe in between yawns, and I had to wipe tears from my eyes! It was embarrassing! It was the worst nightmare. . . like when one dreams of having a boner in a public beach while wearing those 'dental floss' swimsuits so popular in the Riviera! I'm sure you can empathize with me.

"Anyways," he continued, "it was a minor token to pay to restore one's sanity, one would say! That was also what I thought till I had to listen to a presentation from Il Rettore Magnifico[46] of the University, who gave a forecast of the strategic development of our research program, a highly selective audience, pretty much like Giuseppe's panel for cancer! Well, I sat right in front of Il Rettore forgetting about the Zoloft and its side effects. Few minutes into his talk, I was overtaken by a yawning attack that was completely incoercible. As I became unnerved, I started yawning more, with small enough pauses in between to wipe my eyes from the tears and take a deep breath. The problem is that yawns are contagious and mine must have been particularly compelling since in a short while the whole audience was yawning uncontrollably with mouths as big as those of caged

[46] The Magnificent Director (name used for the Provost or President of the University)

276

lions at the zoo. Our Rettore Magnifico, as you know, is a very experienced person with infinite public speaking practice. Therefore, he courteously pretended not to notice and carried on, trying to finish as soon as he could till he himself was overtaken by a yawning attack that was just as incoercible. Fortunately, the speech was meant to be short and at the end, he thanked all for enduring the wearying presentation. He, more than anybody else, was well aware of the unpleasantness of strategic mumbo-jumbo though it's a tenet in academia. In the end, Zoloft had a group therapy effect, a pharmacological peer pressure on our Rettore Magnifico to keep the BS to the minimum! Unfortunately, I am quite aware that this episode did not help my career and my prospects in our esteemed faculty senate. . . "

***

"It is heartbreaking to see how funny life can be sometimes. It is deceitful; it makes one believe that it is worth living just because of these rare exceptions springing occasionally along an otherwise meaningless existence!"

Luca's comment interjected amongst tearful laughs like a cold shower. Everybody realized how dejected the friend's mood was. But nobody reacted.

"Well, talking about yawns and embarrassing situations, I will tell you what happened to me. I would love to know what you would have done in my shoes," mended Marco, who was trying to recover the good humor for the benefit of the gloomy friend.

"Of course, needless to say this is highly privileged information that cannot go beyond these walls!" he continued.

*

There was a young intern at the hospital. She was petite and pretty. She had a reserved personality that a radiant smile, like a pulsar in the deep sky, dependably enlightened. Often, she sat by herself at the cafeteria in between surgical cases reading a manuscript or a book with delicate eyebrows that when furrowed looked like little exclamation marks. She wore nerdy spectacles that were bigger than her face and made her look just irresistible. One day, after a long case—I believe it was a hepatic resection, in which she helped me as third assistant—I noticed her at the cafeteria sitting by herself as usual behind the spectacles with the corrugated eyebrows, munching chips. I asked for permission to sit beside her, with the excuse to gather her thoughts about the case that we had just completed. She smiled and after a little while we were talking about anything but medicine. Turned out she was recently divorced and lived alone. To make it short, we sat in the cafeteria together a few more times, then we started to go for walks in a nearby park and eventually we ended up having dinner on a night when my wife was going to be late due to her own commitments. It came after a romantic rainy afternoon. We had walked in the park and visited the museum of Natural History. There was nobody there save for the stuffed creatures that looked resignedly at us with their glassy stares. When we walked out of the museum, it was still drizzling and she rested her weight on my arm that was carrying the umbrella, pressing her little body against me. We went for dinner at a bistro close to her place and we had a bottle of good wine. When it was time to walk her home, the rain had subsided, but my arm was still warmed by her embrace. At a red light, I kissed her, and the kiss lasted for a few cycles of greens, yellows, and reds whose reflections took turns on the wet street. We walked for a little longer and we kissed again. . . and again till after a few more stop-and-go we reached her place.

"Do you want to come up? I live by myself. It is a small but cozy place; we can have a drink before you go home."

Her apartment was more like a studio! It had a kitchen-dining-living room unit and an adjacent bedroom in which a matrimonial bed peaked from the open door with enticing warmth in that cold night. Needless to say, it did not take long to adjust to the coziness of the warm embrace and soon we were making love while the rain was tapping at the window. With astounding efficiency, within a few minutes, she reached a spectacular orgasm. That encouraged me to persist on my duty to provide further opportunities for pleasure. But she appeared excited no more. You very well know that it takes delicate moves and gentle persistence to go over the refractory phase of a woman. So patiently, I rocked my body with grace and continued to kiss and caress her till I noticed a periodic huff. The latter progressively turns into a clearly detectable rumble till it matures into a flagrant snore! The gentle soul had fallen asleep and, while I was still inside of her, she was detonating thunders that were worthy of my late grandpa, who was relegated in exile by my grandma to the basement in safeguard of her sanity.

Now, it had never happened to me before and I felt both hesitant and embarrassed! What is a man to do in such a circumstance? Have you ever encountered such case in any textbook? Never knew that narcolepsy could affect pretty women! Or maybe it wasn't narcolepsy at all; it was just my uninspiring presence? Good news, for the sake of my ego, that at least she did not yawn away like Tullio! Anyways, I could not lie down to sleep beside her because I was mindful of my wife waiting at home. So, I tried to wake her gently, just to say good night, let her accompany me to the door, and lock it from inside. But to no avail. Sleeping Beauty was resistant to any attempt from Prince Charming and I am glad it was not she in the fable because I am sure the poor Prince would have had quite a hard time fulfilling the happy ending! Anyways, I kissed her, and I shook her softly! I repeated a little less softly. I even checked her pulse that was beating regularly in restful rhythm while she lay like a baby who had fallen into a solid sleep after gorging on a bottle of formula. In the end, I gave up and I left her sleeping. I walked out the door and walked home with my tail between my legs, not knowing what to think. I am sure it would not have happened if Luca were there instead of me! So, Luca, do not complain that life isn't beautiful, and although you worry about Christina, remember: each end is nothing more than the beginning of a new journey! Be happy, my friend. There are lots of Sleeping Beauties out there that are waiting for their Prince Charming to awaken them!

***

Needless to say, at that point, everybody was wondering whether Marco on that occasion had been wearing his infamous calf suspenders that certainly might have had something to do with Sleeping Beauty's detachment. But nobody dared to ask.

Instead, at the conclusion of the heartfelt confession, another round of wine refreshed their throats.

This not-so-hilarious story conformed to the calando of the friends' mood in an increasingly somber atmosphere.

Then, Roberto offered:

*

Well, I will tell you my embarrassing story! It's not so bad, actually, but interesting! It shows how semantics can change lives. . . . In my bachelor routine, I frequently invite pretty women for dinner at my place. I let them enjoy a meal and a good bottle of wine, then, a seat on the sofa where we fondle each other a little till we progress to the bedroom. Believe me, guys, with the right selection criteria it works just about ninety-five percent of the time. But this time, I invited this middle-aged spinster who had an interesting body but who turned out, as the discussion evolved, to be a virgin! Who knew they still existed? That, of course, in some ways excited me even more! But also enthused my sense of responsibility! I wanted her to experience a memorable first time! So, I took it slowly, letting her relax according to her pace. Of course, meanwhile I was thinking to myself:

"How can a woman with such a great body still be a virgin?"

Meanwhile, little at a time, intercalating between "Oh Gesù e Maria," "Oh Madonna Mia," and other such pleas to a greater authority, she let herself be fondled at relevant trigger points. She held my wrist as to control the progression of my fingers along her legs but without demonstrating any earnest intention to halt the inevitable. Instead, all of a sudden, she was taken by abrupt resolve and with crazed movements she stretched her arm toward my crouch, opened the zipper, and extracted from the underwear my masculine attribute. She started caressing, rubbing, stroking, squeezing, and ravaging it, as if she was a witch manhandling a ladle into a boiling potion. Then, she suddenly froze and looked at me with glazed eyes. In complete embarrassment she questioned:

"I do not know if I can handle this!"

What a strange selection of words! In fact, she was doing a great job at handling the aforementioned object. So, I reassured her:

"Dear, I promise that, having quite a lot of experience on this matter, you are doing a fabulous job!"

Well, that was just exactly the encouragement she needed ! Maybe before that night, nobody took her as literally as I did!

*

The Old Boys cheered again and again as they got drunker and drunker.

"Yup, semantics can be crucial," added Marco. "I recollect this young woman, whom I examined in the emergency room. She came with belly pain. I asked her if she was sexually active and whether she could be pregnant. She sternly denied but the pregnancy test came back positive.

"'Why did you lie to me?' I asked empathetically. 'You should trust your doctor! I am not here to judge but to help.' I said.

"' I did not lie to you," she replied. "You asked if I was sexually active, but I am not! I lie passive in bed and let me boyfriend do his part!'"

More cheers ensued and wine washed their throats. Then that Jiminy Cricket, Enrico, had to ask:

"Why are we doing this? What is this obsession? Why do we have to run after women who do not belong to us? Why do we have affairs? Why do we enjoy recounting them so much? Are we ever going to grow up?"

"Why should we?" exploded Tullio. "Aren't we beautiful people ninety-nine percent of the time, perfectly fitting into the cage of conventionality? Why can't we be childish at least when we get together? Life has taught us a lot of lessons but above all we learned how dull it can be! We all know how to harmoniously cradle in the arms of high society and its expectations; we can go through its conformities smoothly but. . . is it really us? Where did the spontaneity go? Why did the mischief of youth abandon us? Can wisdom be derided at times? Are there ways in which a man can feel alive simply by rebelling against the predictability of a prefabricated life? We are not bad people; we pay our taxes, take care of our families, stop at red lights, and obey speed limits. So, should we talk about our perfections tonight? Should we discuss how we could be better than perfect? Or should we just forget about it for a night? Should we rather follow the Peter Pan's spirit that is still in our hearts?

"I don't know, maybe it's just boredom dumped upon us by conventionality. Some people rob banks or drive drunk. Others take drugs or do crazy things just to feel different from their neighbors, that they are colorful pawns in the chessboard of life. To play with consenting women is safe and legal. What is the harm if they enjoy our caresses? And it is interesting too. I have affairs because I like to hear the women's stories, particularly those of the married ones. Why do they cheat on their husband? What do they think of men, who cheated on them? Maybe I will learn something about myself," concluded Tullio.

"You remind me a lot of Alessandro," interjected Giuseppe. "He was like this. For him, women were just a learning experience, a curiosity. The closer we became, the least I could understand this part of him."

"Oh yes, Alessandro; your compare [47] from Terronia Beach! What happened to him? Didn't he die of AIDS? I always thought that he was kind of weird—was he gay?" remembered Roberto.

"Yes, he died of AIDS, but he was not gay. He got it from an infected woman, does it make any difference?" asked an annoyed Giuseppe. "Alessandro was the finest man and he ended up where all of us could end up one day with our degenerate existence, except that for us it is more chatter than reality, for him, promiscuity was a modus vivendi."

***

The shift from momentary exhilaration into depression is a well-known aftermath of excess alcohol consumption. After inciting euphoria and excitement by dampening the restraints on our behavior, ethanol subsequently reaches our mood centers, converting unbridled joy into gloom. So, it was to be expected that from the playfulness of the early dinner, the evening landed in a sedated atmosphere.

To restore the mood, Tullio resurrected the inspiring idea of calling La Candela:

"If I recall correctly, this is the moment when La Candela lifted our mood with her cheerful personality! I wish she were here now! I should have invited her. She is part of the Old Boys. Who cares about her husband or the fact that she is not a man?"

So Enrico extracted his phone and dialed the number.

***

---

[47] Compatriot

"Luisa, it's us! The Old Boys! We're having a reunion. We wish you were here!"

"No way!" the Old Boys heard from the speaker. "Why didn't you tell me! Really? All of you? Even. . . even the bratty boy? Even my Luca?"

"Yes, everyone, except for Mario who is having some troubles in Rome! And yes, Luca is here! Come on, Luca, say something!"

"Hi, Luisa, your voice hasn't changed at all. . . I hope you are well. . . . Your husband is sick?" came out of Luca's mouth as he was searching for something to say.

"Yes, it's sad. I can tell you all another time. A good man, I love him dearly, but nothing like my love for you all. You filled my life with excitement. Those times were magic! And I was the only girl that you allowed in your circle! All of you so handsome and smart, unconventional, crazy, inspiring! I miss you all. And I miss my Luca, so gentle, kind, insecure, needy, and yet, the most autonomous of all; a tiger that roams the forest camouflaged among the leaves and invisible to the eye but whose presence anybody can sense. I miss you, my Luca! I think of you every night, my prince. I hope you are well!"

"His wife is cheating on him! He is available now!" offered Giuseppe magnanimously.

"I wish we would have invited you here," added Tullio, "but honestly I did not think of it. I guess I felt in my subconscious that you are a married woman and that after all you belong to the opposite gender. I guess we still think of a married woman differently than of married men! And I'm sorry, we didn't know about your husband. Enrico just told us this evening."

"No, don't worry. Perhaps it's better that you did not invite me. It would have been too much of a temptation. I would not have come, though. Nothing to do with the fact that I'm married but just because I am an aging lady, a faltering gardenia. You would not care for me anymore; I do not want to disappoint you with my gray hair and wrinkles."

"Don't say that, sweet Luisa! You are always going to be the same for us! You are the nicest woman I ever met," interjected Luca, who had finally managed to find something appropriate to say.

***

After the phone was silenced, Luca commented:

"Life resides in the impalpable essence of a future and past that are tenuously stitched together by the thread of the present, which distracts with its permanent illusion of corporeality. Each end marks the path toward the beginning of a new journey, you say. But what I know is that I had a wife and now I have none! I had a family and now I have none! I had a dream and now I have none! I had a future, which is now buried in the past. Luisa was sweet, beautiful, and creative, it was the embodiment of our future then, and that's gone like Christina is gone and like everything else. What will be the next to go?"

"You know, she still loves you!" Enrico interrupted Luca's soliloquy.

"She may, as many women claim they do. But I do not believe that love exists in the end just because nothing else exists save for the permanent illusion of the present, as I just said. This is why I do not like to talk about love. I avoid telling a woman that I love her. Funny thing is that when I told my wife that I loved her, just once or twice in my life, just one crazy time, I really meant it! I felt a lifetime commitment that was inspired by an incoercible hope springing from a person's heart. But she didn't believe me. Why should she anyways, with my track record? But I swear that I did, just once, only once or twice in my life, and I meant it; but that was not enough for her. And now. . . now I just miss her. We have been talking about affairs and sex all night. But in the end, sex is just a distraction like most other things; perhaps real life is made of love, and you realize it even more so when you are alone, when you dream of it, and you miss it.

"I wish one could craft emotions, tune them up or down at will. But that is not possible!" continued Luca. "We can describe how we feel but, in the process, we cannot change what happens inside of us. Semantics do not help in my case! For an artist, graphics is about geometry, music is about mathematical harmonies, photography is about light and angles, poetry about verbal consonance, narrative about dynamics of flow because the content is wrapped in form and that is what the artist cares about. The emotions that the artist bestows, and admirers covet are a given reality shared by all humans upon which the masters base their work. They are the dough that allows the chef's masterpiece. We all can experience at times

284

fantastic feelings, emotions, and thoughts. They are no different from what a poet experiences, but we do not know how to translate them into a universal language as well as the poet can. The reason why we can relate to great artists is because they describe just exactly what we are feeling. Artists do not invent emotions; they cannot create or change them! They can only describe them better than most. I am no artist, and I wish I could better explain to all of you what I feel tonight but perhaps you could imagine it if you ever went through the same. And I wish I could be empowered to change my emotions together with my semantics but how can I if even a poet can't?" Then he added: "And I am sorry if I am spoiling this beautiful party."

"Dear Luca," interjected Enrico. "We do understand! In fact, what is unfamiliar and new to you is common knowledge for most. You never had to conquer a woman—no flowers, no poems, no good words, or gallant gestures. For you women have been a given, apples that wait to be picked from the tree when they are ripe. Who can blame you? We can only be sorry for you because in the end you never had to work hard enough to covet your prize. It's only now, when for the first time you lost what was bequeathed to you by fate that you are discovering what most of us have always known."

***

"I need to go pee." Luca had regained color and initiative, at least when it came to bodily functions. So, he stood tall, turned around sporting a controlled gait and walked over to the direction that led toward both the kitchen and the guest washroom while his friends continued to chat.

As he disappeared behind the door leading to the services part of the apartment, Roberto questioned:

"Should we trust him? I think he is going to 'make friends' with Martina—il lupo perde il pelo ma non il vizio!"[48]

"He's just drunk and sad, he's not even thinking of her," stated a defensive and confident Tullio.

But as time passed without Luca's reappearance, the suspicion grew.

---

[48] The Wolf sheds its fur but not its habits (A leopard can't change its spots)

"I think we should go check on him before your mom finds him with Martina on top of him," suggested Roberto.

As the friends were inquisitively looking at each other waiting for some resolve, Martina appeared with a big platter in which a Tiramisu Milanese style filled with true Mascarpone cheese was standing.

"Where the hell is he then?" Marco jumped up. "He cannot have been peeing for a quarter of an hour." Leaving his friends, Marco rushed to the rest room and from there the friends heard him knocking at the door, gently at first and then more vehemently.

"Luca, what are you doing there? Come out, it's no time for jacking off! You are too old for that."

But still nothing could be heard. By then, the other Old Boys were assembled around the door.

"What is going on? I swear to God, the guy waited to come here and kill himself in the embrace of his friends. He was in that foul mood all night and we kept jerking him around with our stupid comments! Come on, you idiot! Open the door!" called out Roberto, summarizing the thought that was in everybody's mind.

"Or maybe he's just having a heart attack. We aren't that young anymore," rebutted Marco optimistically.

"Luca!" screamed Marco again. "Get out of there!" Then turning to his friends, "We should do something to open this door!"

"I will take care of it," and, as Tullio was about to kick the door, it opened, and a wobbling Luca came out:

"Sorry, guys, I fell asleep on the toilet. The jet lag, I guess, or the wine. I haven't slept much recently."

Tullio sighed and hugged his friend. Then, holding him by the arm, he helped him to the couch. There in turn each friend approached, touched his forehead to check his temperature, read his pulse, and look at his pupils.

"Luca has more doctors than he needs here. Just let Marco do his job! He knows better than any of us," exclaimed Giuseppe.

"Maybe we should give him a thorough check up since we are all here. Tommaso may even give him a gyno exam. We should at least give him a rectal exam! And with two fingers," offered Roberto.

"And why that?" asked a perplexed Giuseppe.

"So, we can offer a second opinion!" exulted Roberto for catching a sucker with his joke. "Don't they teach those things in America?"

"That is an old and disgusting joke," retorted Tullio, while Roberto and the others started to leave. They patted Luca, who was by then laying semiconscious on the couch.

"A bien tot. . . and till the next time. Next time at my bachelor place!"

After the Old Boys left, only Tullio and Giuseppe remained at Luca's side:

"How are you? You better sleep here tonight. Martina can keep an eye on you." And turning toward Martina, who had been observing the scene from a distance, he said:

"I will call his dad, and you take good care of our prince!"

"How are you, Luca?" asked a concerned Giuseppe. "You are not going to do anything stupid, are you? Remember, you have kids, you have your friends, you have your dad, and, after all, you still have Christina. She loves you, you know that, and she needs you more than ever."

"I wish I could use better words to describe my feelings in the hope that a different connotation could quench the pain, but in the end I am just a sad and lonely man no matter how I label it. But do not worry; I am not contemplating anything that would embarrass any of you. I am fine, I just need to sleep."

"Be well, my man. If it is of any comfort to you, consider that you are getting what you deserve: you have been a real bastard with your wife and you are now receiving the just punishment. But look at it as a new start, a catharsis that will make you a better person. This is healthy sorrow, the bitter pill that will cure the ailment. I will go now, and you sleep in peace. Nothing is ever lost in matters of love. Trust me. Sleep well and we will check on you in the morning."

And having so spoken, both Tullio and Giuseppe left, while Martina closed the door with care and locked it from the inside.

***

Around three in the morning, Luca woke up in the profundity of darkness. He realized it was dark because his face was squished against the back of the couch, and he felt obscurity in the mind because he was lost in space and time.

"I wonder if this is what afterlife is like—awareness of emptiness," he thought, while he endeavored to reposition himself within the coordinates of existence.

As he turned his face away from the couch to facilitate breathing, specks of light appeared through the curtains, compliments of the streetlamps. Luca recognized the surroundings and recollected the latest events. He also noticed that he was wearing only underwear and that a flannel blanket snugly covered him. He rose and walked. In doing so, he stepped into a body. Her legs were stretched from the armchair to the coffee table, where her naked feet were resting on a pillow. In the silence and among the shadows, Luca identified Martina, who was sleeping in restful peace with her head reclined to the side and with half of her body exposed from a dropping blanket. Before continuing, Luca seized the blanket and readjusted it to cover the beautiful woman.

A few hours later, Luca was awoken by a soothing massage to the shoulder. When he opened his eyes, the morning was tentatively trying to break through the curtain and the light was just sufficient enough to recognize the face of Tullio's mother smiling at him:

"Martina slept at your side all night because she worried about you. I just sent her to bed. How are you?"

Luca appreciated the maternal attentions, but he had no intention in engaging in an early morning conversation and thus responded:

"Much better! Thank you so much, but I am still sleepy," and pretending to be still in the twilight of consciousness, turned around, pulled the blanket over his head and fell asleep again.

Two hours later, his shoulder sensed a soft tapping. The day was by then irrevocably established and his eyes could see the brightness of Martina's eyes:

"La Signora went out shopping and she asked me to keep an eye on you. Would you like coffee?"

Luca pulled himself up, resting his back against the armrest of the couch. He bent his knees, resting his arms on them, and massaged his eyes to wake up once and for all. He looked at Martina with curiosity at first then with affection.

What a nice woman! he thought. "Yes please, I would love coffee."

After Martina left, he put his trousers on and after refreshing in the powder room, followed her to the kitchen. Martina was fretting with the aftermaths of the chaotic night that had been mostly cleared to restore the luster of a pristine kitchen. Luca walked to the kitchen table, drew a chair, and sat waiting for the coffee and staring at Martina.

"So, your wife left you!" started Martina, continuing her chores without turning.

The espresso mumbling on the stove appeared to assert its opinion about the predicament in displeasure and, for a few moments, Luca listened to it while waiting for inspiration.

"Yes, she did!" he finally spewed. "Believe it or not, she said she did it for me! Can you imagine? She said I did not have the courage to leave her, and she had to take the initiative to break the marriage, to relieve me from my unhappiness! How convenient! Don't you think? Would anybody leave their companion for love?"

Martina did not answer but instead she poured the coffee into two cups with meticulous care, brought them to the table, returned to a cabinet, took out a sugar bowl, opened the refrigerator, and poured milk into another bowl. Then, she came to sit, placing them in front of Luca. Suddenly, she startled, rose, went back to the same cabinet, opened it, found a colorful box, unwrapped it, unloaded the content on a plate, and returned carrying the biscotti to the table.

"Yes!" She picked up the conversation. "A woman would do anything for the person she loves. This is exactly what I did."

Luca put a spoonful of sugar in the coffee, and then some milk, stirred the mixture pensively, raised his eyes to encounter those of Martina, and offered:

"Would you like milk or sugar?"

Martina shook her head.

"Okay then, tell me your story, Martina. I want to know about you."

"I was married once in Ukraine. I married my high school sweetheart. We loved each other and we married as soon as we were old enough. He was a handsome, hardworking, gentle, and cheerful man. Life was paradise for us. . . for a few years. But then we dreamed of children. We fantasized, talked about them, imagined them, counted them with our fingers, and he could not stop smiling. He would push me from the back of the swing, higher and higher in the sky, and when I would finally scream, he would laugh and say 'You are such a baby. Our child will be fearless!'

But the children never came.

"Finally, I went to see a renowned expert in Kiev and after a lot of tests he told me plainly that I would never bear children. I went through all these analyses by myself in secret, hoping to surprise my husband with wonderful news but instead, when I came back that evening from the big city to our little town, I could only hide in the kitchen. As I was cleaning the dishes from the previous evening, I reckoned that I needed to tell him the truth, plain and simple, as the doctor had done with me. When he came in from the field, I set in front of him and opened my heart.

"He had tears in his eyes, but he told me 'Do not worry, Martina; it is not of the essence. We will be happy anyways if this is our fate.'

"But things changed after that day. He continued to be the same handsome, hardworking, and gentle man, but the cheerfulness was gone. So, one evening I prepared a pleasant dinner. I served all the delicacies that he liked. We ate and drank cheerfully, we smiled and we laughed recollecting the good times. But, after he went to bed, I left the house forever. . . . And I came to Italy. And here I am now, a few years and a few jobs later!"

"And what happened to him?"

"I asked for divorce. He could not understand, and I did not want to explain the reason. If he had known that I was leaving him for the sake of his ability to become a father, he would have never agreed. Eventually, when he finally believed that I did not love him anymore, he agreed to divorce and two years later he married another woman from the same little village, a very nice girl in fact, and now he has a little daughter. My friends tell me that his beautiful smile is returned to his cheeks and that makes me happy. So, you see, one can leave somebody for the sake of the other person's happiness. Your wife might have been earnest when she said that."

"And what about you? What's next for you?"

"I have been going from job to job because sooner or later somebody tries to have sex with me. It is the course of being beautiful. But I am happy here now with La Signora and, when he visits, with Tullio, who is a true gentleman. I am a very low maintenance person. I do not expect much, all I want is respect and a tad of care."

"At least you did not run away with somebody else!"

"Does it really matter? Maybe for your wife it was easier this way. It would have been too painful otherwise!"

Luca rose, took the cups, brought them to the sink, and rinsed them.

"I better go now! Thanks, Martina, for last night. Thanks for caring for me; your husband lost a wonderful wife. . . . You know, you are a beautiful woman and, just looking at you, one would imagine quite different stories in your past. Isn't it strange how different we are from what we appear to strangers? Thank you for sharing your story."

"And you are a very attractive man. Not just handsome—attractive! There is something about you that sets you apart. You deal with women with spontaneity. You seem sincere in each gesture and word. I can see why women love you. I heard so many stories about you from La Signora. She also loves you! You very well know that!"

"And what about you? Would you love me one day?" jested Luca, smiling.

"Maybe I would! This is why I would not sleep with you! You are too special for that. I would not want to trivialize what could be. . . one day."

"I really think. . . I better go!"

And after putting on the rest of his garments, Luca hugged Martina, lifting her up from the waist, and left:

"Say goodbye and thank La Signora for me," he yelled from the stairs as Martina was carefully closing the door.

***

The rest of the morning, phone calls poured upon Luca from all his friends who were checking on him save for Tommaso, who, recovered from the fumes of alcohol, had resumed his verbal parsimony. However, when Luca arrived home, he found a bouquet of white roses at the entrance and a note from the Tommaso that said:

"Be well, my friend! You are not alone!"

Luca's dad welcomed him in good humor and, with some ancestral pride around the masculine attributes of his son, he mumbled:

"I guess you are still young! The wee hours of the night suit you best like when you were a man apprentice! You have good genes, and you know whom to thank!"

"Did anybody call?" asked Luca without preamble, pretending he did not hear the distasteful comment.

"Yes, the cleaning lady did, she will be late today because she has to take her son to the doctor."

"Great to know! That's exactly what I was wondering about!"

Luca went to his room, sat on the bed, and began to read the walls as if he was there for the first time visiting the childhood home of another person.

"Something wrong?" asked the dad.

"Yes, Christina and I are divorcing!"

And sensing his father's shock, he explained:

"She found somebody else, a bald guy with a Rolex."

The dad recovered his composure and approached him. Placing his soft hand on his son's curly hair, he said:

"Well, if you think that's all it takes, you should shave your head and buy a golden Rolex too!" Thus extracting a smile from his prodigal son.

"She didn't even bother to call! She knew I was coming here! She could have called! Just to know how the trip went!"

"Why don't you call her?"

"No, I don't want to make her feel stalked! She's probably content with her lover! Why should I bother her?"

***

In the afternoon, Luca received a call from Martina:

"Say, do you want to go out for dinner this evening? La Signora gave me the evening off. I can show you around Milan! It will be my treat. No expectations, just some fun. It will be amusing to go around the Centro, just the two of us. With a hunk like you at my side people will think of us as celebrities!"

"No, Martina, I'm sorry, I'm not in the mood today. Maybe another time? Maybe before I go back to New York?"

***

Later that night, Luca and his dad were sitting at the table after a simple and cozy dinner. It was not a talkative moment and the two sat side by side with the television in front informing them about irrelevant events occurring somewhere out there in the vast world.

The Dad did not initiate any conversation of substance because he knew his son. He knew that he did not like to talk about failures and that he considered the divorce a letdown. In the end, they were Catholics, weren't they? An eccentric version of agnostic Catholics destined to carry guilt without hope in their subconscious! For sure his mother would not have wanted to hear about divorce. Thank God, she had graciously departed a few years before! Of course, Dad wanted to know more to provide comfort, but he let his son take all the time he needed.

Indeed, after dinner, Luca seized the remote and silenced the television.

"Dad," he whispered, "of our existence, days are like leaves shedding one by one from the old horse chestnut tree. . . lying on the ground wherever the wind scatters them as testimony of an irrevocable past. The rain, the wind, and the sun mark the passing of the seasons, where the trees can sprout more leaves for them to fall to the ground in this meaningless cycle. I am perplexed about what lies ahead. But I will accept what's to come: the joys and the sorrows, day after day, as I am expected to do. I will follow the path you showed to me, just as other good men did before. I will, but I suppose that it won't be trivial, and I need your guidance. I ask for your blessing before I embark toward the unknown."

And the dad replied:

"The future! We all obsess about the future and do not live the present! Your Mom ate only rotten fruit to save the good ones for the next day, when it would be rotten, and she could eat it without guilt. The same goes for bread; she never ate the bread that I bought that day, but the stale one from the day before. In a lifetime, I could not make her understand that it made no sense! That she could break the cycle just by skipping a single day. When she died, there were so many beautiful dresses left in the closet that were never worn waiting for the right occasion. In the country, we had two dogs. One came and waited at the gate whenever he saw my car arriving, he waited till the gate was open and I drove all the way to park at the end of the path. And he followed me, wagging its tail day after day for all its life. The other dog, after a few repetitions, figured the pattern, and when he saw me, he ran to the end of the path where he knew I would step out of the car and greet him. Which one was right? Which one understood the difference between the present and the future? Which one was happier? We will never know.

"In the beginning, life is a journey crammed with hope. Without it, there would be nothing, not even the memory of your childhood so full of fragrance. As a youngster, I had no time to worry about the future. My present was hard enough to distract me from other worries. I just tried to survive the miseries of the war and its damage to our family. Besides, I had nobody to talk to. I had no dad, my mother was too busy making ends meet, and my brothers had either died in the war or had gone far away to build a new life. . . and you, of course. . . you were not there yet. So, I learned to carry on without asking anyone questions, not even myself. But now, you ask your father's advice. You ask questions that I never dared ask myself! What can I say? Maybe I could tell you what life has been for me.

I remember that life begins as a dream when as a boy one plays around the mother's skirt. But soon it turns into a troubled battle, and one soon realizes that, being a child no more, he is walking a solitary journey of fear for what's to come. And, while one fears the future, nostalgia of the past hovers like fog upon a deserted path.

It is toward the end of the journey that I suddenly see my son in front of me, pensive and hesitant just as I was then, and I wonder what his future will bring. Why would it be any different than mine? One would not know. When I observed you as a child and listened to your loquacious dreams, I said to myself: 'Perhaps I accomplished something!' But now that your life is gradually equating to mine, now that your dreams are resting in the casket of memories together with mine, I ask myself: 'What did I do?'

"But listen at least to this advice: Life goes on at its own pace and it will continue to do so. You do not worry! Live in peace as much as you can, do not hurt anybody and hope for the best. What is to come is beyond your control and, therefore, the future is not your burden. Soon a day will come when your own son, in a quiet night like this, will ask the same eternal questions. I cannot guess what you will say, but I imagine that you will recollect this night. . . . Enjoy the moment now, the quiet night appears still and yet it will soon be gone. Observe carefully because one day you will relish each gesture. . . each word of mine.

***

In his room, Luca sat on the bed, connected his phone to the charger and as he was about to place it on the bedside table, he checked the list of missed calls one more time, just in case. He checked the mail too, just in case. Then, he took a deep sigh, turned off the light, and lay in bed watching the dancing lights from passing cars.

A few hours later, Christina sat on the bed, connected her phone to the charger, and as she was about to place it on the bedside table—and we will never know if out of curiosity, or perhaps out of nostalgia, or perhaps sadness or even despair—she checked the list of missed calls, just in case. She checked her mail too, just in case. Then, she took a deep sigh, turned off the light, and lay in bed watching the dancing lights.

SABRINA

(Or where Luca inadvertently finds himself entangled in a thorny conundrum of women's wisdom)

Piano piano, little by little, delicately, tactfully, tacitly, and perhaps even a touch insidiously, Sabrina turned into what Professor de Mirafiori never had: she became Luca's soul.

As the majority of Filipinos, she was a Roman Catholic. Yet, she nurtured her own interpretation of what the illustrious religion stands for. For her, religion was rather an overture toward a dialogue with a confidant that would patiently listen to her monologues in the comfort of the penumbra of a church. Therefore, Sabrina spent a significant portion of her free time in a Romanic Basilica, talking to a painting of God that hung in a recessed transept or, for more sensitive matters, to a statue of San Francesco standing at its side and sporting an empathetic smile that trembled over his lips at the mercy of some impertinent reverberations caused by the flickering candles.

Such conversations progressed without need for verbal validation by the listeners, who in turn, having been dallying at the site for the last few centuries, had no precise business to attend to on their own and, therefore, held no specific qualms against prolixity. Neither was Sabrina expecting their endorsement, as she was confident that whatever she proposed was of obvious consequence. Therefore, it did not need formal ratification and their silence could be interpreted as assent. Fortunately, Sabrina was a most sensible and practical person and, therefore, her assumption was correct most of the time, and I am sure that if you were God or San Francesco, you would have also regularly agreed with her resolutions and supporting corroborations.

The substance of the matter was largely practical, since Sabrina judged that she lacked adequate sophistication to talk about anything that transcended daily routine. Initially, her conversations pertained to distant family matters, but gradually, her attention turned to Luca. Within a few months of coexistence with her master and commander, Sabrina reckoned that his perfection overshadowed what others would refer to as imperfections. And about those, she felt the obligation to debate in the presence of an objective third party, circumventing the impropriety of confronting the master directly. Therefore, she confided to God or San Francesco according to the sensitivity of the subject to return home with the presumption of confronting Mister Luca in accordance to a mandate conferred by a higher authority. As a consequence, while he was at the university giving lectures or listening to others' views about the future of mankind, the oblivious professor had his existence dissected, judged, and readjusted in the eloquent silence of a church.

A vexing and recurrent quandary addressed Luca's recklessness in abiding to a dressing code proper for his status. No matter how compulsively Sabrina fussed to perfect his attire for the morning, Luca could always figure out creative ways to alter the masterpiece. Ties not properly centered or loosely tied, ruffled collars, inside-out pullovers, mismatched buttons, and respective buttonholes in the placket of the shirt, belts skipping loops, insufficiently tucked shirts were of the order. Worst of all, incompletely zipped flies became frequent accidents that stressed the poor woman. And no matter how mundane such consternations might appear to the unaware, they carry legitimate significance for those who, like Sabrina, devote their life to the appearance of their beloved masters and retain a chauvinistic attitude toward tidiness.

She was also concerned about Luca's reserved demeanor. Often, she observed his gloomy days, particularly during weekends, when he walked aimlessly back and forth in the living room, sat amorphous on an armchair staring at the ceiling without saying a word till he fell asleep even though he had just woken up.

From the the door, she would ask: "Mister Luca, are you okay?"

He would reply, waving his hand:

"Of course! I am fine!" or sometimes he would not reply at all.

Sometimes, he would take her for a stroll in the park as if she was a bitch that needed to be walked, but even then, he would not talk much. He would pace at her side, supporting her arm, opening doors, and paving the way or summarily brushing off leaves from a bench where she was about to sit. But no conversations of substance ever came out of those moments.

And she would ask God: "What should I do?"

Receiving no answer and having none to propose on her own, she sighed and lit a candle.

For San Francesco, she reserved more sensitive flaws that would not be properly conveyed to the Omnipotent without informed consent from the master. She felt that the experienced saint could oblige as an ambassador by conveying those matters in confidence better than the muttering of an unsophisticated woman. Not to say that God wouldn't understand in any case! God forbid! But surely the saint could unearth better words to sugarcoat the message!

Such sensitive issues related, for instance, to excessive consumption of alcohol. Not that Luca was an alcoholic! But for the abstemious woman, even a glass above the ordinary raised a flag! She was also stressed by Luca's refusal to go to church on account of the persuasion that any matter related to religion was a superlative waste of time. Luca told her that he was an agnostic! And when she figured out what that meant, she considered that in the end she also did not know for sure whether God existed or not. Yet, there was no reason not to pay Him a visit, talk to Him and ask for advice! What was there to lose? In any case, it was up to the saint to figure out how to present this quandary to God because she did not want to hurt His feelings, particularly in the case that He did indeed exist.

In other words, the poor woman was trying hard to deal with the inconsistencies of existence, when one wants to follow some sort of logic that resonates within oneself and at the same time wants to protect the logic of one's loved ones and respect it without totally understanding it. Luca's agnosticism was, in her practical estimation, just a preference, a fad, perhaps just a fondness for a particular flavor such as one would choose linguini over spaghetti at a restaurant; and who was she to argue against it?

But the most serious of all matters deserving the highest of the saint's discretion pertained to Luca's affection for women, particularly for two of them: an aging pretty woman whose name was Luisa and a beautiful young woman called Martina. Both of them had increasingly taken a dominant role in her master's life, alternating their presence at home at the expenses of other occasional mistresses. Both of them in turn sat at the dinner table on the same chair to the right of Luca, unaware of each other's existence, while the discreet Sabrina would serve warm dinners and clean after them. Of the two, Martina was self-conscious and could not restrain from fighting with Sabrina for returning dishes and serving plates to the kitchen, and it was only Luca's imperious gaze that forced Martina to sit beside him while Sabrina accomplished her duties undisturbed.

Luisa spent long evenings sitting on an armchair in front of Luca or cuddling with him on the sofa, but rarely had she crossed the threshold of his bedroom. Not because she would not wish to, but because most of the time Luca did not seem interested in moving in that direction.

Luca rather kept extracting from his friend all that she could tell him about how women think. It was an obsession, and he would often bring up Christina with the lame excuse that she could serve as an example. Luisa, in turn, listened patiently and empathetically to the childhood sweetheart with the maturity of an experienced woman and she reckoned that her beloved Luca was still, even after all these years, the same insecure boy who, in spite of all the fortune that had been bestowed to him by destiny, particularly in gallant affairs, had learned nothing about women and, perhaps, even about life. So, night after night, a maternal instinct overwhelmed her and all she wanted to do was hold that handsome, lonesome, and clueless man in her arms.

In time, Martina and Sabrina grew closer. Not that Luisa was an insensitive concubine! Not at all! In fact, she was the warmest of creatures, but, belonging to the Milanese high society, she had a proclivity for giving Sabrina presents and giving her gratuities substantive enough to be appreciated by a woman who had a family far away and could use each penny to make her loved ones thrive till she could one day reunite with them. But Martina had taken Sabrina's affection because she was a servant just like herself and she could empathize by admiring in her what she could never be: the enchanting Cinderella worthy of Prince Charming.

Martina, who spent nights sleeping at Luca's side more and more often, seconded by the encouragement of her Signora, reserved the mornings, when the professor had left for the university, to confide in Sabrina. It should be clarified that Sabrina was the most selfless among people.

Therefore, the saint had to worry not about comforting her feelings or emotions over this strangest of predicaments. Moreover, Sabrina had never confessed to the saint the extent of her relationship with the master, particularly the carnal details, and although implicitly she talked about Luca as one would represent a lifetime companion to a marriage counselor, she never put her personal relationship on the table for discussion and, therefore, at least officially, San Francesco could tactfully disregard this facet of the matter.

Rather, the saint was summoned to worry about the potential effects that such dissipated life could bear on Luca's wellbeing and furthermore, on Martina's. Sabrina in fact was increasingly more concerned about the latter. She felt that Luca did not appreciate the depth of Martina's love for him or the beauty of her loyalty to him.

Others shared Sabrina's concern. Tullio had approached Luca with a benevolent scolding:

"I think Martina is getting too attached to you! I believe you are misleading her, and you should let her be unless you really do care for her. But I doubt it! Not to be a snob, but why would you want to tie yourself to a nice but unsophisticated woman, who has nothing in common with you?"

Tullio's mom bore another opinion in line with her resolve to find the perfect match for the prince once and for all:

"Martina is the perfect woman for you! She is beautiful. She is nice, hardworking, and capable of attending to all your needs without judgment. You do not need another Christina or another high achiever. Those women go their own way eventually and you will be left alone in your old age! Martina will take good care of you just as she has been doing for me!"

Then Luisa broke the camel's back.

"I heard," she said with a mischievous smile as she was sitting one evening after dinner on the sofa in Luca's arms and looking toward a turned off television, "I heard that a beautiful woman has been spending quite a lot of time in your arms on this same sofa."

Luca did not answer but rather caressed Luisa's black hair dyed to perfection.

"I know everything about this Martina; Tullio told me, and Sabrina confirmed. Do not be mad at them; they did not mean to betray you. They are both concerned about you and certainly also about Martina."

"It is none of their business," mumbled Luca who, taken by surprise, had otherwise no deeper words to package into a cogent sentence.

"Just as it is none of my business either!" replied Luisa calmly. "But still you better listen to those who love you." And rising from the sofa, she went to sit on the sofa's armrest, put her delicate feet on Luca's abdomen, and looked straight into his eyes as she continued:

"My dear Luca, you cannot do this to Martina. I do not want to sound like a snob but we—I mean you and I, and the Old Boys, and the people you are used to—belong to another social status, another cultural background. No matter how liberal we think we are and how sensitive to the world we pretend to be, we have been raised by the cynicism of sophistication! Words like love, commitment or care are just concepts to us, an intellectual exercise. We are like politicians sitting at a table to discuss the pros and cons of commencing a war. They drink coffee or tea around the table and do not smell the stink of rotten bodies, they do not hear the cries of mothers for their shattered lives, they do not see the dust of destruction from the falling homes that were familiar surroundings for thousands just moments before. It is just a game for them no matter how thoughtful they pretend to be.

"And it is the same for us. We can filter words according to modern or ancient philosophies; we can coat them with existentialistic shadows and stick them against nihilist walls as two-dimensional graffiti. We can dissect the meaning of any word and turn them upside down, interpret its impact on our or other's existence, wonder about the weight of its relevance in the context of universal truths, the big scheme of things! We are trained to look at concepts as if they, in the end, meant nothing at all in relation to our daily life.

"But people like Martina are different; they come from the countryside, where culture has not spoiled their dreams yet, where they have not been indoctrinated by skepticism and cynicism and it will take a long time for their souls to be proselytized if ever by the cult of futility, pointlessness, senselessness in which we comfortably thrive. Martina carries dreams that are as fresh as the spring water from her mountains; she believes in suns that are meant to shine for the benefit of people; in crisp autumn breezes; in the whispers of the night. If you ever told her that you loved her, trust me, she hung her life, her future, every drop of her energy into a dream that you cannot even conceive of from your nihilistic bubble.

"Let me ask you something that may seem trivial to you, but means a lot to a woman: Did you ever tell her that you love her?"

"Yes! I did. As you said, I am not sure what I meant, but once she asked me. I did not think too much about it. I just simply said yes! We were making love and I felt a deep affection for her then. How could one spoil such a moment? I do not think that this should count!"

"But it does not matter what you think! By the way, do you know that you never told me that you love me in all these years? And do you know why? Because I never asked you if you did! You would probably have said yes! Just the same to me, in a sweet, intimate moment. But in my case, you would have known comfortably that I was well aware that it did not count! And this is why I never asked you."

"So, what's your point?" interrupted Luca, who was listening attentively to Luisa's sermon. He felt that there was something in it that transcended Martina's issue and had more to do with Luisa's ability to articulate the roots of his emptiness; what could be seen as a self-centered and narcissistic existence.

"I think you should choose. I think you should leave the poor woman alone or commit to her. You know that you will always have me as your off-the-shelf, platonic soulmate, and you know that you will always have the harem of women who care for you, but you have to learn to make at least one of them happy! If not for any other reason but for your own edification! Women will sacrifice a lot for the one they love particularly if their sacrifice will not go wasted. But it is not rewarding to take advantage of them without returns. If you love her, marry her! If you do not, don't mislead her any further!"

"I was already married once! I thought I was a good husband and look where it went. Truth is that I cannot make any woman happy. Truth is that I am not meant to be a good companion. I am a leopard, as somebody told me. I roam the Savannah without any purpose, hunting when I am hungry and finding a mate when I need one; but besides those moments, I wander without purpose hopelessly listening to distant calls and searching from scents of novelty, harbingers of deeper meanings that transcend the futility of our existence. You are right! Perhaps education has spoiled our life! We cannot take anything seriously and what may appear grand to others means nothing to us! How could Martina understand any of this? How can Martina comprehend our unspeakable secret?"

***

A few days later, Sabrina was lying in bed in Luca's arms while he was staring at the ceiling and caressing her shoulder. Luca gently pressed her shoulder to make sure she was awake and asked:

"Do you think I should marry Martina? Everybody seems to want me to marry her! Am I missing something? In the end, you are the only one whose opinion I care for."

For the oddest reason Sabrina, who had concocted in her dreams a positive outcome for Martina's story, felt a deep pain, an overbearing weight in the depth of her chest that stopped her breathing. When she could talk again, thinking of San Francesco as a beacon in the middle of a stormy night, she gasped: "I do not know; I think I will have to think about it."

***

The next morning, the temperature was biting in the basilica and the saint's smile wasn't welcoming. In fact, on closer look, Sabrina noticed that the saint wasn't smiling at all and that he probably never was. She recognized that all along his benevolence had been an illusion produced by the flickering of the candles.

To persuade herself, she approached the statue from the side and looked at it carefully, squinting her eyes. The saint continued to display an austere expression as if he already knew the terms of the imminent confession and was already considering the elements of the extreme quandary. It also occurred to Sabrina that the saint was well aware of the unspoken truth, that he knew about her affair with the master and that, likely, he was disgusted by her promiscuity.

Perhaps, he was looking down at her as a vulgar prostitute, an indentured servant for sale to support the family! Wouldn't it be just exactly what anybody would conclude? How could the saint swallow the pretense that she truly loved Luca? What a convenient conception! Was it really love or just convenience? The saint was right to look down upon her: she had no right, no entitlement for sympathy and she reckoned that she should return home without wasting more of his precious time.

But she also considered the tenets of Christianity that include forgiveness, charity, and compassion. She recalled that a preacher told her when she was a young woman that Christ listens rather than judge. Turning to the painting of God, she sensed the same. She recognized very well that she was far from perfect, as most people aren't perfect and that her sin was grave, but courage rose out of despair, and she began:

"Dear God and dear San Francesco, I am talking to you both because I need all the help that you can offer! I am an unsophisticated woman. There I was it seems so long ago—just a schoolteacher! But the money was not enough to raise my family. I came from so far away because I could not take care of my children in the Philippines. My husband was lazy and a drunkard. He lost job after job. He would not show up at work when he was supposed to. When he did, he argued with his boss or the coworkers till he was fired. I left my boys with my parents. They are good children. They want to study so they will have better lives than their parents. They want to become respectable people, people whose words matter in society. Children now know that there is a big world out there, a world of opportunities, and they want a chance to be part of it. . . I came here and worked hard. I never asked for anything more than what I was offered.

But then Mister Luca appeared in my life. I never dreamed of being close to him. I was just his father's servant. When he visited from America, he seemed such a gentle and quiet man, a devoted son. He was patient with his dad and nice to me. When my master died, he decided to move back to Italy, to his childhood home, and he retained me. He said he did not have the heart to leave me without a job. I stayed with him because he was a good man and he respected me. He was a quiet man and he looked sad and solitary. He barely talked and whatever I did, he thanked me for it. Never criticized, never upset, and his few words were always encouraging. Sometimes he would say soothing words like: 'Sabrina, can you please make sure that next time the wine is chilled for dinner?' Because I had put it out too early when a friend visited; and that was as bad of a criticism I ever received.

"Whenever I wanted to go somewhere, mostly go shopping for the house, he never denied me. And I was so grateful to have a safe job, with no expenses in such a comfortable and luxurious apartment, warm in the winter and cool in the summer. I was even proud of belonging to it as if it were part of my own life. Meanwhile, I could save the entire stipend for my parents and the children. And I came here regularly to thank you both for my blessings. . . and I could not think of anything else to hope for. At least this was what I told you and repeated to myself, but. . . inside of me. . . deep inside. . . I loved him. I wrestled with my mind to keep the thought away. I kept telling myself: 'Sabrina, Mister Luca is not for you. He does not even see you; he is surrounded by all these beautiful and smart women. . . and such elegant and smart friends. . . "accomplished," as they say. You simply do not exist!' –

"Yet, I waited all day long for him to come home, and rushed to the door when the bell rang hoping to catch a smile. I would prepare meals the best I could, anticipating his fancies, and I wished to be his servant for the rest of my life. I was so happy to be at his side. No matter how many women came and went, I was the one who took care of him day after day, and he showed me his gratitude.

But then one evening, he came home and asked me to call him Luca. He made me sit at his side at the dinner table. He held my hands after dinner and took me to his bedroom. I should have resisted, I know, my God, but I could not. I loved him so much and I knew that I would do anything he would ask me to do. . . then and now."

She stopped to consider her own words and anticipate the icons' reactions, and then she continued:

"How could I say no when he took me by the hand? How could I say no to my dream? I did not even know whether what was happening was true or the fruit of my imagination! I was living in actuality what I had lived so many times in my fantasies. I am not ashamed to tell you that I love him ever more now. I love him with the unconditional love of a woman who wants her man happy. I want you to know that I am not here on my behalf. I am here for him. I am not asking for your forgiveness or understanding. I am not asking for your support. I just came because I need your advice. He asked me. . . he asked just me. . . his humble servant. . . he asked for advice. He wants to know whether I think that he should remarry.

"They all want him to marry Martina, a lovely and beautiful woman, much prettier and younger than I am. She is a servant just like me, but she is tall and of natural elegance. She has a beautiful smile and a sweet voice. She is nice to everybody including me. She tries to clear the table and help me with the dishes when she is a guest for dinner. She talks to me, and she asks for my guidance as if I were her older sister.

"And Mister Luca asked me, as I said, if he should marry her. He told me that he cares about my opinion most, more than that of anybody else! Do you understand? He said that he wants my advice—the advice of a humble servant counts more than those of doctors and professors! Do you see how great my responsibility is? I ask you both, what should I say? How would I know what's right for him?"

Sabrina paused, waiting for an answer. In turn, she queried the painting and the statue. But nothing happened. The silence echoed within the recesses of the basilica and only a soft litany could be heard from a few benches afar. Gradually, Sabrina reckoned that there was not a thread of communication between her and the icons. And that she could sit there all day and night, and the following day and night, and no word, no movement, no suggestion would come to appease her anguish.

So, she looked at her hands resting on her fragile knees. She stared at her feet reposing on the footrest in a pretty pair of red moccasins that she had found on sale a few months before. She rubbed her calves with her palms to provoke a resemblance of purposeful dignity, buying time while she was deciding how to extract herself from that impasse. She looked back toward the origin of the litany wondering what she was doing there. Was this all a superlative waste of time, as Luca would have sentenced?

A few benches afar sat an old woman with a rosary in between her thumb and index finger mumbling Ave Marias. Farther apart there was a young man, likely an expatriate like her, kneeling in front of another statue of an anonymous saint; another pariah that could find acceptance and comfort only in the darkness of a church.

It appeared to her that those two, like her, were talking to a mute listener and she concluded that this time she was on her own; that, as for when she made the decision to leave her children in the Philippines, it was solely in her hands to choose the path. It was for her and only her to decide what was good for Luca, for Martina, and for herself.

So, she turned around, walked out of the church where the sunshine blurred her eyes, and resolutely walked home. She had made up her mind about how to proceed.

***

That evening came on a Friday and Luca retired late after dinner with the Old Boys. It was not particularly late. Yet, he did not ring the doorbell but quietly unlocked the door of the apartment, did not turn on the lights, and held his breath so as not to disturb Sabrina. In his hand was a handwritten envelope addressed to him that he had collected from the mailbox. He removed his coat, draped it on a chair in the entry hall, quietly moved to the den, and sat in front of the computer.

A few minutes later, Sabrina knocked at the door, sneaked her head through the opening, and asked:

"Mister Luca, may I come in?"

Luca raised his face. The dim light coming from the screen drew a ghostly appearance on his features and from A distance his eye sockets seemed recessed and empty like those of a cadaver.

Luca stood up and walked toward Sabrina, who had turned on the lights to return Luca to a human state.

"Sit down, please!" said Luca, in the meantime taking his place on the armchair in front of her.

Then proffering a gracious smile, he said:

"Sabrina, Sabrina, how many times have I told you to call me Luca?"

Sabrina did not answer. Instead, she kept staring at her knees. Then she spoke:

"I came to give the answer to your question."

"What question?" Luca asked distractedly.

"Last night, you asked me whether you should marry Martina."

"Oh, yes! I see. Sorry, I sort of forgot about it! So, what do you think?"

"I think you should!"

Luca furrowed his eyebrows and looked straight into Sabrina's face to engage her eyes, but she stubbornly kept looking at the floor.

"Sabrina, do you mind looking at me when we talk?" and he continued: "And why do you think I should marry Martina?"

"I am not sure! She is beautiful, she is considerate, and I believe she really loves you. She told me so many times! She is very loyal to you, do you know? She is an honest woman! I do recognize that she is just a servant! Just like me! She has no proper education but why would you care about it? You have plenty of that and you seem bored of it. She could take care of your needs, she could anticipate your desires, she could stand by you unconditionally, without questioning, just wait for you and love you. She could take care of your clothing, of your meals, of the house. . . Or maybe, she will not! When you marry, she will need a servant for herself, and she will just be your devoted wife. Maybe she would retain me. I could serve her just as I do with you! I don't mind! I am a poor woman with children far away who need to survive. I will continue to serve the two of you, but please, do not ask me to continue our relationship. I am asking not only for myself but also for Martina. I could not do that to her. I know how painful it will be for me to sit in my room at night without hope of being close to you. But at least there would be the comfort of knowing that I did the right thing. Otherwise, it would only be wrong, and painful for us all.

"I don't know what makes you happy, Mister Luca, but it seems to me that, when she is around, you are as carefree and playful as I have ever seen you. But I agree with Signora Luisa: you should either marry Martina or let her be. She really believes that there will be a future between the two of you. . . maybe even children and. . . a new life for you, Mister—I'm sorry—Luca."

"Martina cannot bear children! It is a long, irrelevant story. In any case, I do not want more children. I love the ones I have, and that's it," said Luca, waving his hand off.

Sabrina raised her face that had gone back to staring at the ground while she was talking to scrutinize Luca, wondering what he knew. Then she lowered her head again and continued to stare at her knees.

"So, you really think I should marry her?"

"Do you love her?"

"Well, love is a vague concept to me! I am not sure about what the correct definition is! It is more like the air in the sky. I do not know where it starts and where it ends, where it comes from and where it goes. I loved and I was loved once and where did it all go? What did I mean when I said 'I love you' to my wife? What did my wife mean when she whispered 'I love you' to my ear at night? Do I enjoy being with Martina? Yes! Do I like to hold her in my arms? Yes! Do I think of her sometimes? Sometimes I do! Could I live without her? Yes. Do I love her? Probably not! I don't know what you mean by love. What do you mean by love, Sabrina?"

"I do not know, sir! I am not the one who should speak of love. I am just a humble servant, who never had the chance to meet love! I was married very young. My mother liked the son of a friend of hers. So, he became my fiancé. Once, he forced himself inside of me while I was taking care of the laundry and my mother was in the other room. I did not have the courage to scream. And I became pregnant. I had to marry him. I married that man, who said that he loved me in front of my parents. I just did what was expected of me and after that I kept working and working. He got me pregnant again; I had another child and I continued to work to support the three of them till I had to abandon them all because I could not make enough money to pay our debts. This is all I know about love."

"So, you never loved anybody?"

"No, sir!"

A mischievous smile appeared on the face of Luca, who impertinently asked: "Not even me?"

Sabrina's ears burned under the orderly tucked hair, but she did not answer.

Luca sighed profoundly, rose, walked to the desk, and said:

"Anyway, Sabrina, thank you for your advice, but I am afraid it is not needed anymore."

From the desk, he fetched the letter unfolded over the hand-written envelope.

"Here, read this! See? People still write letters nowadays!"

Sabrina looked inquisitively at her master and hesitantly took the letter:

My beloved Luca,

I am sure that of all people, you will understand my decision because you are the only one who knows my secret. As you know, I do not want to become a burden to anybody and most of all to the one I love. I sacrificed once for someone I loved, and I will do it again for you.

Yesterday, I told my Signora that I needed to go back to Ukraine to take care of my parents. It is not true of course, but it was the only story that would not hurt her feelings. I will go elsewhere instead where nobody will know, not even you, to restart all over again. I am doing this because I love you and I know that you need your freedom. I know that they all want us to marry. But for the wrong reason! It is all out of pity for me. Nothing to do with mutual love!

My dear Luca, I know that your heart is not with me. Your heart is with your Sabrina. I am a woman, and I can sense things that only a woman can. I can see how you breathe her. I can see how you feel her when you do not see her, how unconsciously you search for her. You have been so kind and wonderful to me, but your smile is not the same as the one you reserve for her. And I see how she looks at you. No matter how much the poor woman is trying to hide her feelings, I can see how she burns of passion for you. She looks at you with the devotion of a dog. She can anticipate all that you might think and desire without the need for words. She answers even before you ask. This, my friend, is love! It is exactly that love that you dismiss as a meaningless word.

A few nights ago, I found a thick Asian hair on your pillow, just like Sabrina's long and beautiful black hair. Trust me! I am a jealous woman! But I am not jealous of Sabrina. She is just a servant like me. A woman that for whatever reason had to leave her family, her life, her familiar places to gratefully serve as a second-class citizen in your country. She was a teacher, you know. She is more educated than I am, and she is a servant just because she lives where she does not belong. She is a smart woman.

And for me, I know when to make a dignified retreat. I want you to know that I loved you very much and I will probably continue to love you forever. You are a much better person than you give yourself credit for. But you need to follow your heart! You need to be happy. Maybe Sabrina could one day give you the children that I could never bear for you.

Good luck, my loved one. Be well!

With all my heart,

Martina

Sabrina was flushed all over and her hands were trembling. She put the letter on the coffee table and ran to Luca's bedroom. She pulled out the blankets, scattered the pillows, and searched with frenzy everywhere, even under the bed; not a single hair could she find! How could she have missed that one? She! The one, who fussed so hard to keep things flawless!

When she turned around disheartened, Luca was looking benevolently at her from the door.

"I am so sorry! I have no idea how this could have happened! I always change the sheets every time a new woman comes! I am so sorry." And she started sobbing.

"Do not worry, Sabrina. I never really intended to remarry; to be specific, I never intended to marry Martina. I just needed to know how you would react to the idea."

Luca approached Sabrina and held her in his arms, and she surrendered to them for a few moments. Then she wriggled out of the embrace.

"I'm sorry! I'm confused! I need to go to my room! I hope you understand, Luca! Mister Luca! I mean Luca! I really need to go." And she left.

Luca sat on the bed. He took his shoes off and at the same time he realized that the evening could not be over that simply. He remembered the comfort of the prayers' routine in his childhood. A routine dictated by his despotic grandmother. Kneeling at the side of the bed, he hastily susurrated a Pater Noster, an Ave Maria, and a Credo before jumping into bed in peace, relieved at having accomplished simple and concrete duties. He fancied to kneel and revive the comfort of that obsolete routine. But he smiled instead and thought:

"The power of habits! The addition to conformity."

Still, he could not figure what else could take him to a placating closure of the day. Barefoot, he walked to the kitchen and opened the refrigerator to do what any man would do in such a circumstance. But when he held the cold bottle of beer in his hand, he felt no interest in it. He returned it to the refrigerator. Walked to a cabinet and took a crystal glass thinking that something stronger would do. He went to the ice dispenser and released a few cubes. Holding the glass, he proceeded to the bar in the living room to pour some Cognac. But as he was about to dispense the liquid, he sensed that even this gesture was pointless, a deception to distract oneself, an act to dignify one's misery. He reckoned that he did not like to drink alone and that he was, as a matter of fact, completely alone just as he was the night when he found Christina with Jonathan. He was alone in the vast silence of life.

He returned to the kitchen, dropped the cubes in the sink and rinsed the crystal glass. Then, he deposited it on the table and placed his hands on its smooth edge resting all his weight on his stretched arms.

"What am I going to do next?" he wondered.

And he meant it literally! It was not about what he would do for the rest of his life, or for the next year or month, not even what he would do the next day. He could not figure out where to launch his immediate next step. He was paralyzed. Maybe. . . go the restroom to release the extra fluids, a remnant of the party with the Old Boys? He felt no urge! He wished to go to Sabrina's room and lay close to her. But she had just run away from him, and he had no right to disturb her. Maybe go to the balcony and jump into the night? That was ludicrously dramatic, a pathetic hysteria, an unbecoming ending for a dignified existence! Perhaps he should retire into the study to read Martina's letter once again. Why not call her? She still must have kept her phone with her. No! Martina was right. He did not love her. At least not in the way women think of love. He could tolerate her easily; he enjoyed being with her, and that was a lot to ask from a solitary man who still missed his wife!

But love? What is love? What do they all mean when they use this word? Perhaps Martina was right! In spite of his reluctance to admit it, perhaps he did love someone! A humble soul, who cared for him unconditionally! Who waited and loved! Perhaps Martina was right that he cared for Sabrina more than he would admit it! He reckoned that when evening came and it was time to go home, he eagerly anticipated Sabrina's smile at the door. He recognized that he looked forward to the fragrances coming from the kitchen and the warmth that they aroused in his heart; lost memories of lives lived long ago when his grandmother was waiting for him, then his mother, then his wife; all those women whose only purpose to their existence was to serve him; all those simple joys that had been taken for granted day after day. What was there left to live for, now that they were all gone? What was left for him? He thought of Sabrina's fussing around him to scout little imperfections that she could proudly fix, the little Tinkerbell who worshipped an aging Peter Pan.

And he recounted the eagerness of her accounts about insignificant events of the day that were still important to her. And he thought of her tiny and nervous body that trembled in his embrace when he hugged her because he was in a good mood. He thought of those who would scorn him for mingling with a servant! But why should he care? Nobody of consequence in his life was there to judge him. A pro of being alone is being free. And who was he to judge her status looking from the throne of privilege? What would Sabrina have become had she had all the opportunities that he had? Such a smart and thoughtful woman!

Again, he thought of going into Sabrina's room to find warmth in her embrace. But he could not. He realized that he had taken advantage of the poor woman all along, of that impotent subordinate whom he had carelessly harassed and he felt embarrassment and regretful.

"I should leave her alone. . . What am I doing? Why am I harassing a helpless woman? What's become of me?"

314

Where else could he go, then? The apartment was too small to run away from the embarrassment and the anguish. It was just a miniature reproduction of the boundaries of existence from which there is no escape. Finally, he succumbed to the comfort of routine and progressed toward the bedroom. There, he hooked his cell phone to the charger and took all of his clothes off. Finally, he lay naked in bed waiting for merciful sleep.

***

But in the middle of the night, Luca woke up to sense a warm weight pressing against his right side. It did not take much to reckon that the object was Sabrina's curled body wrapped in the simple flannel nightgown and glued to his right flank. Gently he wrapped his arm around her and pulled her even closer. Sabrina murmured something indecipherable, probably in Filipino, and turned to the opposite side, pushing her back against Luca, her cold feet against his knees and she continued to sleep. Luca, in turn, wrapped his body around hers, with his left hand, he unbuttoned the familiar openings of her nightgown and thrust his hand over her tiny breast to massage it gently till he also fell asleep, and in that sleep they became one.

***

And on that same night, in the basilica, the impertinent candles with their flickering lights restored the smile on San Francesco's mouth.

THE STRANGE CASE
OF CLARA'S EYES

"In the solitude I observe my own image reflected by thousands of mirrors. I am chased by anonymity while above hover Clara's smiling eyes, staring at me. She was an angel who stayed just for a day, like a dragonfly. Yet, in those moments, so many Claras transpired. I observed multiplicities of smiles, hints of cries, myriads of misgivings and hesitations. . . and of hopes and joys. . . and of sorrows. . . all shining, like stars in the sky, in the depth of her eternal eyes. . . "

Thus was Luca garbling in barely coherent terms at the White Truffle Bar in Corso Venezia, locking his yearning gaze toward the interlocutor, who was in turn impassively staring at him with glacial eyes.

"My life is a splendid tale of lost opportunities," Luca continued, "like those nightmares when one brawls to escape but the feet don't follow and stubbornly stick to the ground. When one wants to climb the mountain, where on top shines the statue of hope, but the arms and legs do not obey; when one wants to catch the colors of a butterfly to no avail because all it is. . . all it is. . . is just a vaporizing mist.

"Like the butterfly, Clara never happened; it was a delusion born out of an accidental encounter that never recurred. When she opened her eyes at the Giardini Pubblici and mine were drawn into hers, I took a glance at a world not to be encountered again. I can't explain what it was. Perhaps it was the revelation of love, the reunion of the split hermaphrodites, and the fusion of two bodies into a single soul. In her silent eyes I saw my own reflection reverberate for a few perpetual moments.

"Her eyes looked straight into mine as if they were searching for my soul and it seemed to me that they were inspecting with empathy and gravity all at once, as if they were trying to retrieve their lost self, that separated from her a long time ago, in times so far away that they were impervious to any memory and echoed only in the cosmic background of the unconscious.

There was a heavenly calm in their warmth. There was the patience of resigned sorrow, a strained optimism in the melancholic smile that accompanied her gaze in an attempt to obliterate the anguish of sleepless nights spent in solitude and despair. All of those I recognized in that glance, and all seemed familiar to me.

As the night loomed at the end of that momentous day, I could not sleep, but in the darkness I continued to meet her inquisitive eyes that stared at me, and I imagined a speechless love that thrives on desire and hope while seeking assurance against the fear of abandonment.

"It was a scrawny boy who broke the enchantment and deterred me from pursuing her. He wanted her more than I did—or so I believed. . . then. The little thing challenged me! He even punched me with a girlish but determined fist! And I thought: who am I to fight this? Would I have ever been able to love a woman that much to reproduce this impulsive act? Would I ever have the courage to confront not this minuscule rival but the ridicule in front of my peers for arguing over a petty skirt? Why would I risk the laughter to win a girl when so many of them are longing for me out there?

As a youngster, I was taught self-control, insightfulness, and introspection, something that the grownups considered "maturity." I was jaded over spontaneity and passion: all childlike feelings, unsophisticated emotions suited for the masses. . . And love! What was love? True love comes with maturity, it will come one day, some unspecified day, when a child turns into a man, when all dreams vanish, conformity takes over and the suitable companion is chosen to proceed toward the predetermined path where the script of life demands for an unimaginative wallpaper to decorate an otherwise perfectly pointless existence. True love cannot yield to spontaneity but should be planned ahead to pursue a lifetime covenant of commitment.

"But on those days, I could have embraced my impulse! I could have stepped away from the programmed script! I could have chosen the beautiful Clara and respond to the call of her eyes.

"But I did not do it! Unaware, I gave up the most precious thing!

"In the public gardens one is forbidden from picking flowers. It is against the law. So why should one stray and pick the flower of all flowers, following the breeze of the moment? How could I have known that a lifetime would go by, a consumption of days would flow interminable and leave me wondering incessantly about Clara and her eyes, that Clara, who was not. . . who simply wasn't just another girl?

In the days that followed, I noticed her frequently during the last year of high school, standing out among all her friends. But consistently, as soon as those eyes encountered mine and stared straight into my soul, I turned my gaze away. Why? I don't know. It was the scrawny boy, his passion, that defeated me. He carried something I had been deprived of by my sophisticated upbringings. And I waited, I considered, and I reflected while the train was leaving the station, the gazelle ran, the butterfly flew away, and the falcon hovered unreachable in the blue sky. By the time I reckoned what Clara meant to me, she had long vanished. And from then on, I have been searching for her."

***

"We sacrifice our existence at the altar of conventionality. We are the heroes of emptiness, the crusaders of lost battles, getting to the battlefield when the war is over. . . . And all of this suits us just as well because we never learned the value of earning through sweat, by dirtying our hands and wearying our bones with hard labor. So, we do not cherish what we take for granted. It is the entitlement to happiness, which makes it trivial and hollow, and when the magic happens, we cannot recognize it, soaked as we are in the comfort of habit. Just as well, we do not take risks because we believe that we have all that suffices, and we do not consider it prudent to gamble such privilege against the pursuit of the mirage of happiness.

"We'd much rather avoid the embarrassment of failure by walking the beaten path, where risks are abated, and successes are predetermined. We follow this in every aspect of our life. . . including love. And I conformed too. . . and this is why I lost Clara. I confused her for an ordinary poppy among thousands that peek their head barely above the grass along anonymous streets. I did not appreciate that she was the one and only; the one to pick against the orthodoxy of conformism.

"I should have recognized early on what Clara meant and I should have had the courage to stray from the beaten path. . . to trespass the forbidden barrier, just like the botanist managed to follow the homonymous analphabet Clara in Capek's story; the Clara who found the exotic blue chrysanthemum in the forgotten valley missed by all because of the discouraging *"do not trespass"* sign. But Clara, who could not read, reached with ease the treasure that sophistication had banned others from finding.

"And now Clara's eyes and their memory are all that is left; those eyes, her inquisitive eyes keep staring at me as a memento of lost opportunities, of the chance I had to embrace love, the companionship of a lifetime, the soulmate that legitimizes our existence.

"That's how I missed the chance of my life! Perhaps Clara was not the perfect companion, but I regret the opportunity to know! I will never know.

"Do you know what I mean?"

The interlocutor pithily assented:

"Of course, I know what you mean! I know the human soul better than anybody else! I listened to stories like this millions of times."

***

Then Luca asked:

"What is that feeling that bears upon the chest as one squints the eyes toward the balloon that escaped one's grip and climbs the sky unbridled to join the passing clouds? Or when one examines the shards of an unrecognizable crystal vase that fell on the marble floor, or when for the last time one catches the eyes of the beloved disappearing behind the window of a moving train? What do you call that sensation? I can't think of the precise word."

And the interlocutor replied:

"It depends; it is called 'loss' at times, when one reckons that what is gone cannot be retrieved, not now, not tomorrow or in the days to come. It's lost forever and ever no matter how far eternity may last. But it is called 'regret' if, while mourning the departed object, deep inside one reckons that the loss was, at least in part, caused by his action.

320

"In your case, it is as muchloss as it is a regret. While inevitable, it resulted from your actions. . . and this is why you can't find the right word—no word satisfactorily embraces the anguish of the remorse for lost opportunities; strangely enough indeed, since it is such a common occurrence among humans!

"Yes, you admit to yourself that in an impulse you released the grip to let the balloon escape, and that you are the one who opened the cage for the songbird to fly. But it wasn't totally your fault. You should blame yourself only to a certain point. It was not a deliberate choice; it was a compulsion that came from the recognition that you were clinging to an impertinent dream; a caprice that possessed you to let go of that which did not belong to you and had to be freed. You could not reach the determination to act but your instinct did it for you.

"And powerless, you stared at the hesitant bird that rested on the nearby branch one last time before departing forever, and you smiled at her while your heart was crying inside. But you know that you had to let her go, because like the bird, she did not belong to you but to a bigger world out there, where, in the breeze, untouched dreams still whisper to her ears narrating tales beyond your imagination.

As you said, at that critical time, you felt that Clara did not belong to you.

So be happy with your regrets and imagine the colors of the new symphony that only she could hear wherever she might be. Ask your memories to recount her smile in those magic moments when the two of you were one soul and enjoy that memory that is worth a lifetime."

***

Then, the stranger continued:

"Now tell me of your encounter with Clara—the real Clara, who could have changed your life but, like the first one, you managed to lose. Isn't what you were hinting at with your question?"

Luca lowered his gaze and with meticulousness inspected the contents of the plate in front of him: the golden grains of Arborio rice tinted by glorious saffron and the shaved truffle on top. With the silver-plated fork, he reached for a taster and mechanically shuttled it into the mouth. For a while the mouth was busy chewing what could have been swallowed whole, giving its owner time to think.

"Yes, there is a Clara in my story, a real one made of flesh and bones!" Luca reflected as if was talking to himself. The he continued:

*

You may think of me as a coward, an indecisive apathetic figure, a joker who enjoys sorrows that could have been prevented. But this is not the case! Yes, I lost the real Clara again, and this time there was no excuse, no naiveté of youth to blame, just my ineptitude in matters of love.

I am a good person, I believe. Throughout life, I took care of those who depended on me—my parents, my wife, my children, even my lovers later on after the divorce. I loved them all, even when I didn't. Yet deep inside, I shunned my own feelings. My mind was paralyzed by fear, a fear that goes back to earliest memories, of being left alone. I recount how terrified I was when my dad locked me up in my room as punishment, or my mom declined to stay when I begged her to tuck me in at night. I struggled to overcome those interminable nights drenched by the fear of the mysterious darkness, listening to moving shadows while the echo of furtive sounds crawled under the goosebumps of my skin. In those days I learned to find my own balance, for my composure to depend on no one.

I learned to quench the fear and I dissociated from the emotions that haunted me in those frightening nights. As I hated those nights, I also feared the days when I was left alone in the empty and dark home. I longed for a kind gesture, the touch of a loving mother, the warmth of a hand caressing my forehead. But that never happened. I envied my friends, who had parents and siblings and told me about lively interactions. It did not matter whether they were joyful or quarrelsome. Either way, it was better than loneliness.

I never knew how it felt to be touched by a caring hand. My mother was a good person, but cold like a caryatid. She never spanked, nor caressed or kissed me. She could spend long and peaceful moments talking to me for she was a teacher. She patiently listened to me; she made me develop contentions with rationality. She discouraged emotional appeals. She just could not empathize with passion at all, leaving me entangled in an impassive labyrinth of loneliness, where the only exit rests upon rational reasoning; that became my prison.

So, I did not taste the melodiousness of affection till I fell in the arms of a girl. I was still quite young then, maybe fifteen. The first kiss, the warmth of the first embrace, was so revealing. . . I had finally found a home in the arms of a woman, whom I barely knew and had no particular reason to like. But that soft and tender feeling was addicting, that sensation of loving care craved for so long could not be resisted. And I became obsessed with the desire of those speechless moments of physical reassurance.

But women want more than warmth; some may want pleasure, some may want attention, some commitment. And I would do anything to please them in exchange for that ephemeral contact. I just did not want to be in a bed at night alone anymore, I just needed a body close to me. . . that was all! But that tainted my understanding of love. Love was just a nightly event; a mushroom-picking adventure that temporarily satisfies your palate, while during the day I sheltered within my cocoon.

It does not mean that I bear no emotions. In fact, overwhelming emotions paralyze me. I am afraid of releasing Aeolus's bag for the winds to scatter uncontrolled. At night, with the woman sleeping peacefully with her head on my chest, as I caress her hair, I am overwhelmed by tenderness and by a longing for a few whispered words and tender promises. But my mouth can't open and the magic word, '*love*' never comes out, not even to practice in front of a sleeping witness. And I stare instead at the moving lights from passing cars that juggle into the ceiling.

Perhaps, love is about unfastening the windbag, and letting the gusts go free in all directions, till the storm settles and a new peace is attained by the soul. But I am warned by the previous blunders, and I do not dare to unlock the casket.

Yet, I realize now that ironically my mistakes were not the result of impulse. My faults come from omissions. I regret not what I did but what I didn't have the courage to do. My errors resulted from compromising and choosing conformity over spontaneity. I question why I lost all that I built. Why is my life dissipating in solitude when I had a family and a loving wife? My friends believe, just as she did, that I was not faithful, that passion made me roam around like an unbridled beast. They assumed my behavior from my dissipated and confused youth and from my looks. But that was not the case; I lived a very simple life. Like everything before, I lost my wife because I could not open my heart wrapped as I was in the delusional cocoon of work; trading professional achievement with the significance of a warm gesture, a hug, an unsolicited kiss; that delusion that makes one believe that happiness can be perpetually postponed as a mirage residing in a remote corner of the future, while the present is a transitional entity that can be neglected.

But the future never comes, and those around become impatient and move on. I offered the gifts of conformity to the one who asked for a gesture of courage, and when she reacted with rage against my disengagement, I retreated deeper and deeper into my shell.

I closed my mouth because I was afraid of arguments, of her passionate pleads and emotional outburst, all things that, as with my mother before, I had learnt not to empathize.

So, I chose loneliness of the spirit while I accepted the warmth of physical contact. And I tried to open my heart by giving her physical pleasure. I tried to communicate by looking into her eyes, hoping that she would understand through the exchange of a smile. But she did not see and the cocoon grew thicker and thicker.

As time passed, I missed Clara's eyes evermore. I sought at night the comfort of compassion, of unconditional love, of deeper scrutiny that does not require words. And when I dropped into bed after an argument with my wife, I imagined Clara.

After I caught my wife with Jonathan and we separated, I felt that destiny had given me a chance for a new beginning. It was perhaps a rationalization to help me move on. I do not know, but I started to search for Clara, the soulmate that could see into my eyes! I envisaged her in a street artist, who was drawing with pastels bent on her knees in the pavements of New York. I tasted her in a wonderful woman with whom I slept just the day after I discovered that my wife cheated on me. Her name was Valentina. I became vulnerable and addicted to kindness, like when I was a teenager; I believed that any good deed by a woman was a sign toward the path in search of Clara. And I reciprocated with the only thing I am good at in matters of love: I offered sex, a concrete payoff in exchange for kindness. When I was making love to Valentina, I searched for Clara's inquisitive eyes. But neither the street artist, nor Valentina's eyes penetrated my soul, nor did I recognize Clara in them.

But then, I met Clara."

***

Yes, I encountered Clara again, in the flesh!

It was when I came back from Milan after the Old Boys Academy reunion, and I dealt with the divorce papers. It was so strange to amicably sign off a lifetime for no specific reasons; just a succession of trivial events that accumulated like pebbles till the landslide. I am not sure why I felt relieved by the divorce. I felt validation of my lifetime philosophy that one lives alone to die alone. It was a complacent, self-indulgent pity that kept me going. I kept telling myself: what does love really mean when after decades of marriage everything can vanish for no good reason? Just a languid fall into emptiness, like a leaf of autumn distractedly floating in the arms of the winds till it reaches the ground.

You may say that those were vulnerable times, but I do not think so. I was content in my loneliness. I knew that I could have all the women that I wanted; it has never been a problem for me. But I just cherished being alone. I did not want accountability for anyone about trifles irrelevant to me, no more interminable explanations and rationalizations like before! I just wanted to act without having to offer a reason. Liberate myself from the lifelong scrutiny by my mother, by my wife, by my peers, and most of all, by myself! Liberated at last from that daunting feeling of being chased by high bright lights in a moonless night when they mercilessly glare in the rearview mirror. I became a rebel without a cause in my middle age!

Do you know what I mean? I can live a pretty innocent life, but I do not like shackles. Someone compared me to a leopard once, and I agree, I cannot be told what to do. Not by my parents, nor by my teacher. I can obey only my instincts under the veneer of logical thinking. I wanted to go for what I felt without having to explain to anyone. It was only my dead mother who could still chain me with her logical manacles by inveigling me into the delusion that I was making decisions on my account while instead I was obeying the rehashed laws of conventionality, of cushy adaptation to societal commandments at the expense of any primordial instinct. But even against that I was finally mutinying.

In truth, I was not rebellious! Distraction governed my actions more than willful insubordination; as they say, a short attention span. This is why I never belonged to a church, a party, or a club; I rebel to it by default, by not paying a penny of attention to the rhetoric. I could not relate to, and even less could I abide by, covenants. Surely, if I were to confront Adam's dilemma, I would have grasped the apple without hesitation for the simple reason that I was not supposed to. And this conflict between logical acceptance and intolerance for boundaries governed my life, making a liar of me at times because I could not explain my doings to the dullness of others. I would rather tell them what they wanted to hear. I accepted conformity at the surface while the magma of a volcano churned inside of me, and I finally felt liberated after the divorce. Perhaps I confused emptiness for freedom. . .

I was finally living a content life on my own, without accountability to anyone, with occasional escapades with Valentina, who accepted the boundaries of our rapport.

But at a professional meeting, during a break, sitting in front of me, I met her. She appeared in front of me from nowhere on that round table. I remember that moment as if it were the first memory of my life, an awakening from the torpor of existence. She smiled and I asked for her name.

Her name was Clara.

We did not talk much.

But I could not refrain from staring at her eyes that stayed wide open like those of a squirrel and blinked so fast that they appeared still. They looked straight into mine with inquisitive innocence: the audacity of candor. In her black eyes I recalled the depth of Clara's blue eyes.

I fell in love with her instantly, pulled into the charisma of her gaze. I drowned in those eyes. I searched for my lost soul inside of them.

And her eyes reflected the essence of an unbridled creature, who never met compromise, who grew up of her own without being taught limits untainted by the frivolous moralism to which most of us have been subjected. She lived with the strength of the one who had to create her own principles through the salty path of experience. In her kindness there was the power of a tiger.

Till then, I had thought of myself as an independent thinker. And definitely I was, according to customary standards. But compared to her, I was just a sheep wandering in an anonymous flock; I was just a number in the mob.

Yes, as a scientist I had trained myself to think out of the box. But that was just an exit from one enclosure into a slightly bigger one along an infinite repetition of nested boxes, like the Russian dolls. But for her there were no boxes, only limitless horizons.

Her smile was overpowering and unpredictable, like the sunray piercing the moving clouds. She had thousands of expressions, more than the Chinese characters. Each one reflected a whole new world that unceasingly erupted in its beauty.

I forgot about everything else. There was no world around anymore: What happened to Africa and the Savannah? What happened to the Arctic glaciers? To the immaculate altitudes of the Himalayas? To the spirals of the condors in the depth of the princely skies of the Andes? I became oblivious of it all, or rather, I lived it all by listening to her words and watching her expressions. And so, time went on, a very precious time, without anything else but her presence.

You see, each second, each night, each day was a surprise. Nothing could be predicted if it came from her. Everything was beautiful and natural; everything made sense in her world, which became our world while anyone else would have considered it madness: une folie à deux. Yes, she was mad according to any conventions.

And that challenged me. You cannot teach an old dog new tricks! I tried hard to embrace her beauty, but it went too fast! As I adapted, the bar rose higher and higher. She became intolerant. She was young and she needed to move on. I was just a burden, I realized it bits at a time. Her eyes became defiant at first and even worse, they turned impenetrable. It appeared to me that the infinity of their depth had morphed into emptiness; her jarring stares reflected in reality a lack of expression. She looked at me, but she did not see me. I loved her for what she was. . . and I hated her for what she was. . . but above all I loved her then, as I love her now, for what she was.

Things got bad and things got worse. I am not sure what really happened but, as it had started, within a few months it was all gone. It was like the short season of the desert. A few rains changed the landscape in a blink, returning all to the emptiness as soon as they were gone. I recall those times with wonder: that sense of stupor that follows the wakening from a beautiful yet improbable dream, when one struggles to sort the truth from the imaginary.

One day I had an incoercible impulse to go to the beach where we used to walk holding hands. I have no idea what drove me there after such a long time. I walked up the hill and reached the ridge that overlooks the ocean. And there she was! Her tiny body standing straight against the wind, her eyes querying the horizon as if it were a surrogate for the future. I walked toward her and touched her shoulder. She turned and we stared at each other for a long moment. I held her tiny hand while the wind kept blowing her black hair in between us. Then she smiled. A sad regretful smile as she retracted her hand from my grasp and silently walked away.

I never saw her again.

I hated her for a while, probably just as much as she hated me. She had been reckless and selfish, she had no sense of empathy and consideration for others, and she was bipolar! An angel and a criminal in a fraction of seconds!

*

The interlocutor waved his hand, as if to slow down the flow of words and at the same time reserve his judgment:

"You see! You are judging now! You are becoming me! You are the Devil now! But leave the judging to me when it comes to others' lives. *Let him who is without sin cast the first stone!* You have trouble enough encompassing yours! You can barely account for your own sins and can hardly explain them to yourself. Why would you want to condemn her? How would you know which contorted path brought her to sit in front of you at that table on the day that fate decided to join you? How can you criticize others when you barely comprehend yourself? Just let her be because you have no rights upon her, only gratitude for the time she dedicated to you."

Then Satan leaned across the table pointing the pulp of the right index finger close to Luca's eyes. He stretched out his middle finger, making a V, and sharply twisted both fingers around almost touching each of Luca's pupils. Then, he slowly retracted his hand toward his own eyes to draw into them Luca's gaze.

"Tell me; what color are my eyes now?"

"Blue like the infinite sky," Luca replied.

"Look deeper, what color are my eyes now?"

Luca hesitated; he saw only an immeasurable black.

"Black is the lack of color. It is the color of nothing!" Satan stated and continued:

"Black is the color of the universe, where dark matter and dark energy thrive."

"You are staring now into Clara's eyes because Clara is me! You wanted to travel East of Eden because you could not be content with the privileged life bestowed to you by fate. Like Odysseus you had to challenge the limits of the world and you fell for Clara and her eyes.

"Clara's eyes are nothing else than the reverberation of your conscience. You query them but cannot reach inside of them.

"Since the early years, your existence has been daunted by solitude. But it is not the perceived abandonment by your parents that is to blame, nor the separation from your wife or the loss of those who departed life prematurely. None of them is the foundation of your lonesomeness. Your seclusion is independent of the vicissitudes of life but stands as the fulcrum of your being. The gravitational pressure of doubt squeezes you. No one, no Satan or Gabriel, no philosophy or cults, nothing will change that. Clara's eyes and their depth were the open sesame and the ultimate hope to share forbidden questions in unison with another creature. But that also vanished because in the end, no one could liberate you, not even Clara, from your self-imposed imprisonment.

"You miss Clara because with her your only hope, an illusionary hope if you allow me, is gone and you know that no one will ever take her place. This experience cemented the foundation of your cynicism and despair perpetually.

"Clara's eyes are the gates to hell, or to heaven, whatever you can make of the rest of your life and beyond. You see, Satan does not really judge! It would be too merciful. Satan makes each soul judge for itself in front of the mirror of one's conscience. There is where the anguish rests. This is the essence of hell; no fire or forks and monstrous devils with horns and hoofs; just infinite emptiness and darkness, with nothing to do but listen to your own conscience without any opportunity to amend.

"I am not here to judge you, my friend. I know that mortals assume that this is all I do. This is not the case! I am here to listen and perhaps help if I only could. Even Satan may empathize, not on account of his own experience but because of the innumerable stories I witnessed in the course of time. Your mother had the clear mind of Satan. She used the logic that I use and like for her, it is difficult for me to forgive what occurs among humans out of this realm: Satan cannot appreciate emotions firsthand. Most humans don't live according to a logical process but follow their instincts that they rationalize with logic. It is difficult for me to judge what does not belong to my own essence, but I try to understand. So, I can only compare and empathize.

"You see, I suffer a bad reputation because of a grave misunderstanding. When I appeared to Adam in the Gardens of Eden, I had my own reasons. Man needed to deserve the Heavens. God soon realized that it was superfluous to enjoy the fruits of creation without having to make quotidian choices. If all were to be served on a golden plate, what would be the purpose of all?

"Man needed free will, temptation, and restraint, to earn his own right to exist. God recognized it first and this is why He sent me in the form of a snake. What would a king do surrounded by herds of sycophants? Why listen to 'yes men,' who could not distinguish Him from an apple? What is the value of flawless beings, who" never question and follow the herd like sheep day after day? Are they humans or instinctual beasts?

"Satan's job is simple; it is about posing questions to humankind and letting each choose. Most cannot or do not even want to hear the questions, or simply do not care. They run away afraid of an insignificant apple. But those are not the chosen ones. Those whom God listens to are the ones who question, not out of arrogance but of incoercible struggle for knowledge. Those are the humans that He created, who keep faith to the mandate of the Genesis, those are the true progeny of Adam, who will continue to question the value of an apple over that of the Garden of Eden and who may one day rejoin Him of their own choice.

"Satan is not a separate entity from God, it is part of it, like the dark matter is just as part of the Universe as the shiny stars. None would exist without the other, there would be no good in the absence of evil, the would be no forgiveness if there were no judgment.

"You humans live in a boundless prison within which time and space cannot be trespassed in a lifetime. But some among you rebel. Some act out against the eternal imprisonment, as they know that there will never be parole. Do I understand you well? Some rush out in space when the soul is finally freed from the body, and they turn into the dark energy that expands the universe and, as more and more join day after day, the universal expansion will continue to accelerate into the hopeless despair of infinity.

"On this Earth, the clock builds the time through a mechanical process invented by man to validate an illusion of materiality for what does not exist. And all moving things around produce the same deception to maintain that illusion. But this fallacy is for the consumption of the human eyes because above all God watches impassive and without motion. All is simple up there as time is of no essence. That's why eternity is a misguided idea! Eternity is a superfluous concept in heaven because there is no time up there. And infinity is a measure that implies a line that goes on forever. But there are no lines in heaven and no one who would bother to follow them. There would be no reason. Things there are that simple, in fact so simple that they can be hardly explained to the contorted human mind.

"And Clara's eyes are the gates to the unknown, to the precipice of existence that attracts by a brutal gravitational force, which warps your soul. A fatal attraction toward the darkness of what you refer to as infinity and draws you into a maelstrom without return.

"Clara meant everything to you because she was the opening to the unknown; that abyss where sits the only hope for that ultimate truth so dear to you! She was your last hope to find a companion with whom to share the wonder of the mysteries of life from the inception to the end. "Who could hold your hand while listening in unison to the silence of the night, the deep silence of your nights? But at the same time, you could not handle her because you could not jump into the free fall of her love. Something stopped you and you will regret it for the rest of your life."

***

The plate was untouched in front of Satan. The glass of wine was full, and the smell of truffle was dismissed. With a crazed stare, Luca reached for Satan's glass and asked:

"Do you mind? I need another sip and you don't seem interested in either food or wine."

Luca felt an impulse to touch the interlocutor hand. It felt cold like ice, and he wondered whether he could catch a pulse if he would only dare to check.

"Are you truly here or am I just drunk?"

For the first time the interlocutor smiled:

"I am here just as much as you want me to! You said you do not believe in God or the Church. You are an independent thinker; like a solitary leopard you cannot join a community or cult, yet you talk to me! Do you only believe in Satan? Well, I am here if you believe I am! It is your choice."

***

Luca found himself walking toward the crystal door to exit the Truffle Bar. As he was slipping into his jacket, he encountered a young girl staring at him with deep royal blue eyes of infinite color. For a few immaculate seconds, he froze, entranced by her gaze, till she smiled. Then an impertinent woman's voice interrupted the spell:

"Come on, Clara! Leave the old man alone!"

***

As that was that. . .

On a cloudless April 1st of several years ago, Luca, or more precisely, Professor Leoluca de Mirafiori, was taking a stroll across the Giardini Pubblici of Milan. With both hands in his pockets and being about five in the afternoon, Luca had nowhere to go, nor did he retain a precise recollection of where he was coming from. . .

(Continued in *"Walk in the Park"*)

THE SEASONS OF TIME

"Do you miss Sabrina?"

It was August. It was the beginning of August. But it wasn't hot, it was dry, and a crisp breeze weaving around the passersby and the patrons of the Savini in the Galleria, to gently ruffle Tullio's shiny black hair. It was one of those glorious summer mornings that vindicate those citizens who dwelled in Milan to share with the city its downtime or, putting it less romantically, those who couldn't think of anything better to do for the summer vacation than sending their wives away to crowded beaches and remaining home to enjoy a well-deserved period of truce.

"Now and then, I do!" admitted Luca distractedly and then, shaking his head rather pompously, he continued: "But she had to go! I. . . made her go! She had to be with her children, maturing, good children! With the money I gave her, she will be fine in the Philippines and the children will benefit from a proper education."

Luca was talking automatically, humming a timeworn litany while observing the passersby with more interest, as if he had rehearsed the answer a million times, perhaps to convince himself more than anyone else.

"So, what's next? I have never seen you without a woman around! I cannot even imagine you sleeping alone. Who is going to sing you a lullaby, or fetch the pacifier when you drop it from your mouth?"

Luca turned with a dumbfounded stare toward Tullio, who was grinning at him with his toothpaste-commercial smile. Evidently, Luca was not prepared for that sort of inquisition. At other times, he would have simply ignored the question, deflecting the conversation toward a less challenging topic with aristocratic elegance, while calling the waiter to order another cappuccino. But this time he took the bait and reflected:

"What's next!? Why should there be something next? It is fine the way it is. . . watching the time pass on a ticking clock! Worrying less about the future now that there isn't much left ahead. What is the future but a harbinger of apprehensions? Finally, nothing to worry about, nobody to be accountable to; no more explanations required!"

Tullio persisted, sporting an impertinent smile for the occasion:

"So, what's next then?"

To which Luca responded with a non-sequitur:

"Long ago, I mused over the future; that uncharted territory stirred the excitement of anticipation. But now, most of the future is buried in the past, what else could lie ahead worthy of notice? What mystery could be solved that has not been rehashed a thousand times already? Best to let it all flow naturally toward life's estuary, spending time in the company of memories and regrets that keep me going.

Meanwhile, the continuum of life is approaching its conclusion—a meaningless conclusion. What is the takeaway message? A big goose egg. I am not even sure whether I earnestly tried to learn anything along the path rather than passively follow my own steps. I remember that as a boy, I roamed the deserted rooms of our palace to find peace in the silence. It was then that I began to favor the voices of imagination over the triviality of existence. Ghosts and witches, aliens and monsters became my pals. The more they endeavored to terrify me, the more I chased and howled at them in return till there were only laughs echoing in the silence of those empty rooms. And I remember those walls, decorated by crowded bookshelves where centuries of human troubles were preserved inside dusty books, gatekeepers at the borders of reality and imagination. And reading those books, I turned into a mirror that could absorb and reflect emotions but couldn't generate any of its own."

Luca was, under the effect of the caffeine that propelled his dialogue forward:

"I don't think I ever connected with reality, rather living a life of illusion in a virtual three-dimensional play. I am not sure if those who adorned my life were actual people or characters in a novel and I am even less clear about whether the distinction matters; they are all gone in any case, buried in the past to render memories and regrets almost irrelevant. And I am not sure whether my regrets are legitimate since my choices were not determined by a logical process. "Superficially one could admit that man shapes his destiny, the free will! But the truth is that our choices emerge from the abyss of the subconscious. Maybe they spring from curiosity, the impulse of musing about the consequences of our actions as if they had no bearing upon our existence but just sculpting a novel for others to read.

"You see, irony is what saves us, a way to look at things simultaneously from the inside of our soul as principal participants and from the outside as independent observers. It is this dissociation that makes us see even the most dramatic and tragic events with paradoxical objectivity as if they didn't belong to us. It may be a blessing or a misgiving leading us to question who we are and which part of us is true, the inner one or the one that we observe from the outside of our shell.

"Relationships stand on the ground of insightfulness, at the brink between empathy and judgment. My dad used to say when I questioned my choices as a youngster: 'You have to be honest with yourself, you should be the harshest judge when examining your mistakes to mend them, but beyond that, you should be the most forgiving among fathers to move on and take advantage of what you learned.' And a very dear friend once told me that 'happy memories should be recorded on stone, bad memories should be recorded on the sand to be washed away by the tide.' But instead, even bad memories shall not be recorded on the beach to be forgotten, but rather written in gold on a special jade stone, that makes them shine and be cherished as catharsis to resurrect ourselves by learning from our faults. And by learning to forgive ourselves, we won't be weary of the rigor of judgment.

"Yet, what comes next then? There is no next beyond good or bad memories! Just pure naught! We act alone in the play of life, with an appearance of camaraderie. We all do, but it seems that I am the only one to notice. As a fisherman, I look apathetically at the inexorable beauty of the setting sun knowing that none of it can be reversed, staring out of the window with the disempowerment of a cat admiring things that it will never touch.

"So, what next? How many next are dealt in a lifetime? I wonder if there has ever been a next in my past besides a chaotic sequence of actions, over which I exercised little control. I cannot restrain myself from thinking that the present is nothing more than a preview of our past. If we look back, how many futures began each morning that didn't turn into inconsequential evenings? What's next? I don't know.

"Time partitions into three seasons: the past, the present, and the future, which together shape the illusion of life. The future never incarnates, and we keep going after it like the donkey vainly chases the carrot. And while it turns into past right in front of us, we keep looking ahead waiting for something that will never concretize. And soon one realizes that all is gone with all the contraptions that came with it and only memories are left. I have to disagree with Salvucci here; the past is indeed nothing more than "the product of our memories."[49] And the present? It is where everything converges for a few moments before it disappears into the past while we still wait for the future. Some equate the seasons of time to aging with spring at the beginning and winter at the decline. I am sure that something of this sort is also represented by numerous Chinese allegories about roots, trees, and falling leaves. Personally, I like Santucci's allegory where lifetime is an undefined mixture of past and future observed from the perspective of the present. Like some physicists, I might even argue that time does not exist at all. I would argue that we live in a fixed moment in space and time, and everything spins around us in relativistic motion. Like Heraclitus' foot that stands still in the river while everything flows around in an interminable 'catch me if you can' game between cause and effect. Perhaps life is not as dynamic as it may appear and, as beautifully sung by Otis Redding, 'sitting on the dock by the bay' day after day, powerless, we watch the tide roll away.

"Yes, time is an illusion that surrounds us, to give the impression that something is happening in an otherwise meaningless existence.

"My contention is that I never existed, not in the present, not in the future and, God forbid, in the past. And as for everything else, all my women are

---

[49] Quote from Luigi Santucci's *"Orfeo in Paradiso"*, first chapter

also gone! My mother has long gone! We see mothers as disposable. . . till they die; then we understand!

"Christina is gone forever. Before meeting her, I was a blind man walking alone in the crowd. Following her steps, I thought I saw the light through her eyes. But that also didn't last. Quickly I realized that she was just as blind as I was. As soon as we stopped holding hands, we lost each other in the jungle of life. Now she is gone forever. . . together with her Jonathan to the pastures of heaven. Perhaps, if she stayed with me, that crash would have never happened. I would have taken better care of her. I would not have driven drunk over the speed limit and hit a tree like he did. I never liked Jonathan to be honest. He had the arrogance of the immature, he talked too much, more to convince himself than the interlocutor and he left no time, in his frantic thinking, for listening. He had much more to say than I had the patience to listen and did a good job at convincing only himself at the end of the oratory. You should have seen how proud he was of his own arguments. I never understood what she saw in him, and God knows how many times I doubted it!

"Why did she have to die instead of me? That's the irony! Those who care to live, die leaving those who stagnate in the runway of life. But even before dying, she became a stranger to me as if nothing ever happened between us in the decades before. Whenever we saw each other for whatever reason, she barely acknowledged my presence, treating me with indifferent cordiality that one reserves for strangers.

"And why did we part to start with? It was all because of her foolish jealousy; her distrust only distanced me from her. The irony is that in all those years I never cheated on her no matter what all of you think. But she kept hunting for clues, while she was having affairs of her own. *La gallina che canta ha fatto l'uovo.*[50]

"Nothing could convince her; 'it is difficult to prove a negative,' as they say. And projecting her behaviors onto me, she went on and on with her assumptions, till I gave up trying to cope with it. Nothing makes me feel lonelier than those who do not listen to my words. Even you, my beloved friends, always assumed that I was a philanderer just because of my youth and finally I realized there was no point arguing. I stopped caring, just let

---

[50] The clucking hen laid the egg"

everyone assume whatever they wanted! I resented it but I kept it to myself at the cost of distancing from everyone else. It is intriguing to see how unnatural it is for most to simply believe in what someone says rather than search for some alternative truth behind the corner. I guess it is a human instinct not to trust. But this attitude is the foundation of our solitude within the crowds. I detest assumptions particularly when they are not required to make practical decisions but only directed at the gratuitous judgment of others."

"But then, what is it that you believe in?" asked Tullio, perplexed by the flood of words springing from the mouth of his usually reserved friend.

"I believe only in what I can directly observe; that is the curse of the scientist! And I accept as truth what people tell me unless proven otherwise. Whether it is true or not, is immaterial. One will never know in any case. Only what we can observe shapes my reality; it is the basic principle of contemporary science, what the physicists call *model dependent reality*. It is the only way to communicate constructively among beings. Creating walls of mistrust does not help any conversation. Who am I to judge? And why should I, particularly when there is no practical reason affecting my own life? And why should I be judged for things that do not matter to the ones who scrutinize my existence? This is why I can only relate to the supreme judge, the Devil, which, like God, is the only one who knows the facts. I am not afraid of being judged for whom I really am and what I truly did. But I cannot stand justifying by denial. Perhaps, we should only be judges of ourselves and not be judged by anyone else.

"You may wonder what all of this has to do with your question—what's next? It means that there is no next because I lost faith in human relations. I lost faith in compassion among souls while we mostly dwell in petty grievances. God knows how many times a woman told me 'I love you' just to invariably see the same one take me for granted and become obsessed with the supervision of an invisible territory, struggling to tame a wild leopard by creating a cage around the instincts of nature. And it has nothing to do with loyalty but rather control that suffocates the fresh breeze of freedom.

And it was that corrosive feeling of mistrust that marked the boundaries of my solitude. This is why, Clara's eyes conquered my heart for all these years.

I remember that unassuming and scrutinizing gaze, straight into my soul. It was a wordless dive into each other souls not meant to judge but solely comprehend and empathize. I felt in those brief moments that I could see without seeing, hear without hearing, understand without knowing, just for that glimpse within a lifetime."

***

"Valentina is married to a rich New Yorker. Love has its limits in time and space, and who could blame her? Didn't she need to move on?

"Martina is a stripper in Paris, and we communicate at times. Recently, she wrote to me: *You do not want to be loved; you do not want to love. You suffered the pain of others thinking they were yours and you wanted to distance yourself from all. Now should be the time for you to live for those who love you, but you do not know how to start. You do not have the strength to whisper that word. . . And it's probably true, I do not want to be loved. It is just too suffocating! "Contentment comes at a cost, and it is easier to be satisfied with what one has, even if it is nothing. The secret is not to be ambitious in matters of love, otherwise one will pay sooner or later.

"And in the end, what is this vague concept called "love"? Isn't it just fear of being alone? Just expect nothing, and you won't need love. As my father used to say: 'one lives alone to die alone. . . ' And this is just the way it should be."

"Well, you can recoil under Luisa's skirt and make her a happy widow!" pronounced Tullio, grasping for something to say.

"I see her sometimes, but she only reminds me of the past, that past that does not exist anymore save for the dusty memories that she insists on bringing back. There is no future for the two of us, except friendship."

"Can I tell you something, Luca? It seems to me that you have always shied away from relationships, ever since your beloved Clara. The stronger the feeling a woman had for you, the faster you ran away. Why are you so afraid of them? Ironically, this may be the root of your charisma with women. We all loved and love you, men and women. You were a man's man in high school. But women kept chasing you. You attracted them like flies with your apathy: a strange ladies' man, who knows how to please women without believing in them or understanding them.

"For you, relationships came and went like rainfalls in the monsoon season, forgotten as soon as the shirt dried at the warm breeze. In my modest experience, I had to get rid of women at times. We all know the trick: act like a jerk till they get tired of you. But for most of us, it is not natural. In the end, we are decent people, who care about the way we are perceived; it is just a matter of ego! It is not easy to deceive a woman by making her believe that you are rotten! But you are a natural. You do not have to pretend; you are the embodiment of an ass. You can't even appreciate how aloof you can be. This is why all women in the end leave you, particularly those who are truly in love. They don't know how to handle your ways—slippery as soaked soap. And the absurd thing is that we all admire you.

"You are right that sometimes we create our own castle of solitude to protect ourselves from the burden of accountability. But it is not that difficult to overcome those barriers that you described. You are doing it now with me against your natural instincts. Maybe, there is something for you still to learn, and with it a future worth living."

Tullio paused, staring with affection at his long-time friend, and then continued:

"The difference between an optimist and a pessimist is that the former most often is disappointed by outcomes while the latter is more likely pleased since the expectations were low! I am a pessimist by nature and, therefore, I can't complain about the way my life turned out to be. I know plenty of foolish optimists who wonder why they never won the big jackpot. In fact, most people are like that. But you are neither. Walking lonesome in the crowd, never surprised either way, fatalistically accepting any outcome as if you had no control over the whole process, like we have no control over a thunderstorm! And you are indifferent to criticisms or praises, condescending to them as if they were directed at someone else.

"We have known each other since I can remember and I have never seen you happy or sad, just an enigmatic, apathetic fellow. You passively accept whatever happens as if you had no hope or interest in changing it, as if you were a writer and your own life was just a source of material for a novel. This is also what happened with your beloved Clara, isn't it?[51] Are you sure that she ever existed? Or perhaps she is an inflated memento of a trivial

---

[51] Please refer to "A walk in the park"

moment that you have been brooding over for a lifetime, a cocoon of past regrets you use to shield yourself from present emotions.

There is no role for happiness or sorrow in your life. Perhaps, this is why Christina could not bear to be with you anymore and jumped at the first opportunity. And God knows how many times women stayed loyal to you above and beyond any expectation, waiting for you to ask them to stay. But you never did, you never whispered the right words, you called their love a 'vague concept.' They did not leave you on their account, they left you just to let you wander free in the prison of your bubble. Martina loved you and probably still does, Sabrina would have stayed if you asked her to. But don't blame yourself, my dear Luca. None of your choices was made intentionally as you said. They were the product of confusion, the fruits of the seasons of time, never ripe till they are rotten."

But Luca replied:

"Clara did exist, and she meant a lot to me! My heart lived in her, I couldn't stop thinking of her. I sensed and felt her in everything I did, in any thoughts I had. She has been part of me all along with a lure of wonder enclosed in her image. It is a melancholic feeling of wishful eternity that transformed my existence from disposable to rather precious or at least bearable. And I know that she is still somewhere. I can sense that she is, and I wish that I could look once again into her inquisitive deep blue eyes. I remember her eyes searching inside of me, looking for the bottom of my soul like no one else ever did before or after. I wish I would have asked her then: Clara, what is it that I don't know? What is it that I will never know?"

Tullio listened calmly to see, by the end, tears in his friend's eyes, senseless tears over a woman that like a dragonfly lasted only for a day in Luca's life.

"Wow, you are becoming quite soft in your later years," he mumbled with a smile, and then continued:

"Luca, the truth is that you are lying not only to your friends but to yourself. This is not an assumption since I know it for a fact. Be honest, Luca, why did you let those women go? Why did you send Sabrina away? Why are you avoiding the dinners with the Old Boys? Why does Luisa have to call you over and over before you bother to answer? Why did I have to come to your home today to drag you out for a coffee with a friend? Luca,

I know the truth, we all know about your condition. I know that it is not professional, Marco breached any privacy rule and told me about it, your heart will not last long and you do not follow any therapy. And Giuseppe also knows. He calls me from California at least once a week to ask how you are doing. Luca, why do you distance yourself from all of us? Why do you want to die alone in spite of all the friends and women that you had and still have; men and women, who genuinely love you?"

Luca didn't answer. He moved his chair away from the coffee table, rested his elbows over his knees, and with his hands, covered his face for a few moments. Then, he raised his head, looked into Tullio's eyes, and said with a radiant smile:

"So, you already knew what's next!"

And then he added:

"I need to go; can you take care of the bill? I will see you later."

As he was navigating his path around his friend to leave the Savini, he squeezed Tullio's shoulder; then he bent to whisper in his ear:

"Sorry for the assumption, but I believe you are dying your hair. Aren't you?"

As Tullio smiled and shook his head, he disappeared in the crowd.

***

When he was about to exit the Galleria toward La Scala, he saw the statue of Leonardo da Vinci, patiently posing for the tourists. A fresh breeze pressed on his face and made him feel alive for a few moments, likely for the last time in his life. With embarrassment, he reflected on the quasi soliloquy to which he had subjected Tullio. He thought of what he said and realized that it had been a senseless outburst of repressed emotions that he had no time to conflate into a cogent argument, such a despicable act for a trained scientist. He wondered what the meaning of all that blabbering was and, smiling, he told himself:

"Well, I will let Tullio figure it out!"

***

A few days later, he was walking alone from his home toward the Galleria. As he was passing by the statue of Leonardo da Vinci, he writhed in pain, trying to lift the weight off the middle of his chest that did not let him breath. Leonardo da Vinci started to spin. A lady looked at him and came toward him. Then, everything disappeared.

***

"They resuscitated you, you almost died. You stopped taking your medications, didn't you?"

Luisa was sitting at his bedside, smiling and holding Luca's hand.

Luca kept his eyes on her, admiring her still pretty face, but he said nothing.

"Your children called, they are coming to visit you from America, they will be here tomorrow at the earliest. Meanwhile, you have to listen to the doctors, do what they tell you to do."

"Say bye to them from me." And then he added with a conspiratorial smile: "You know, just in case. . . "

Luca looked around, at the beeping cardiac monitor, the intravenous drip, and touched the cannula that carried oxygen to the nostrils. The oxygen saturation was acceptable according to the monitor and, in fact, he noticed that the shortness of breath was not there anymore. He ambitiously tried to lift himself up, but that was too daunting. Luisa jumped from her chair and hugging him around the shoulders pulled his chest toward her and moved up the pillows to give him support. As he tried to move around in bed, he realized that more contraptions were weighing on him. He had a urinary catheter and a few wires connecting him from under the gown to a few more gadgets. He realized that he was perfectly geared up for the long journey for which he had been waiting for.

"Do you want something to eat? Something to drink? You can have some fluids; they gave you plenty of diuretics and your heart is compensating."

And since Luca was still not saying anything, she continued:

"Luca, you had a massive heart attack, the cardiologist thinks that you will need a lot of rest and then some kind of procedure to avoid heart failure. He will tell you more when he comes for rounds. Marco was here, so was Tullio. They will come back later. Roberto called, so did Enrico. Tommaso sent you flowers, see them? Mario also called from Rome, he is coming to see you. He is the cardiac surgeon! He said that he can fix you anew and told me to tell you not to make any decision before he sees you. Even Giuseppe is taking the first flight from San Francisco. He told mee to tell you to wait for him!"

Luca was getting tired of the tidings as if they had no bearing on the future ahead, so he pretended to doze off, hoping Luisa would desist from such annoying attentions but, unintentionally, he did fall asleep.

***

When he woke up, the stranger was standing in front of him in his affable elegance, sporting attires of exquisite subtle elegance as only a true Milanese can produce. Seeing Luca open his eyes, he pulled a chair close to the bed and talked.

"Luca, as I promised, I am back now that the appropriate time has come."[52]

Contrary to that day in the Giardini Pubblici, he had ditched the joviality but rather maintained the austerity of a captain hovering upon a map to plan the route of his ship toward a tormented transoceanic journey.

And he continued:

"Now you listen. You will be me, another version of me, you will roam the afterlife judging the living. By judging others, you will forget about yourself, and you will find relief in comparing the weight of their sins to yours. You will find a way to condone yourself by understanding the anguish of others. Your sins are venial, even trivial in the big scheme of things, and bordering on dull no matter how much you like to make of them. Your biggest sin was to let life pass without trying hard enough to make anything of it. But even then, how could you have done any better entrenched as you were in the cloud of nihilism that obfuscated your thoughts? So, maybe one day, you will seek the pardon that now you think you do not deserve, and only then, it shall be given to you in the form of relief from those self-flagellating thoughts.

"In your apathy, you had courage and, in contradiction to your instincts, you overstepped and disregarded many *do not trespass* signs because you

---

[52] Reference to: "A walk in the park"

simply could not read them as you never learnt the language of conformity. Sometimes, you paid for it but most of the time you learned by experiencing in the darkness of your thoughts what most would never dare to imagine. Conventional wisdom is not your thing. Not because you are a rebel, it's just in your nature not to pay attention to the rules of life. As Valentina told you long ago, you are a leopard that roams the freedom of the Savanah, unaware of boundaries. This is why, you will make a great judge, because you have no preconceived ideas, because you do not like to judge. The awareness that you have no right to judge will make you the ideal judge.

"Everything flows, as Heraclitus said. Everything flows and nothing persists, including the laws of humans and you know that. A fortunate man you have been indeed. You had all one could ask for and there is nothing more for you to gain on this Earth. There is nothing else ahead for you to learn or live for. It is time to depart. This evening you will sign a DNR[53] order, and at some point, I will come to take you to the kingdom of mystery where darkness turns into light and silence into the refreshing murmur of a torrent. There you may find peace."

A few moments later, the nurse came to the room responding to the call and Luca said:

"I want to sign a DNR order."

***

Around midnight, the door was cautiously opened, and a gracious woman's figure slipped inside. Luca saw Clara, the long-awaited Clara, approaching the bed with a smile. She was just as beautiful as then, just the same gracious girl that had dominated his fantasies for so many decades. And those deep, beautiful, irreproducible eyes were staring at him once again.

Luca smiled and told her:

"I knew that you would be here."

That night, finally, for the first time, Luca saw the seasons of time, the past, the present, and the future converge in the singularity of the soul. He had

---

[53] "Do not resuscitate" order

no fear searching Clara's eyes, those beautiful, deep, limitless dark blue eyes. He dove into them to see. . .

And what did he see? My patient reader will ask.

I am sorry to report that. . . he saw nothing.

The End

THE PEACH

By Yao Lu

*Did you know that there is a profession called the City Management Police?
They will "clean up" those people who do business on the roadside. These
people have no formal jobs. . .*

*Her tricycle was filled with fruit under an incandescent lamp. When I bought
peaches at such a roving fruit shop tonight, the police appeared. The aunt who
was selling the fruit shouted: "The police is coming."*

*In two seconds, she drove away and disappeared from sight. The people
around the grill also disappeared. I was holding a peach for which I didn't get
a chance to pay, and I was in a daze.*

I ate the peach and it tasted good.

THE WAITING ROOM
AT GRAND CENTRAL STATION[54]

by Catterina Coha

It was a glorious morning, with clear skies and a delicate rosy light announcing the sunrise behind the black of the naked trees and the infinite white of the snow. The blistering cold wind of the night had subsided leaving thin sheets of ice that wrapped around the rocks along the river. They looked like presents given by the river to the earth. The river surface was now smooth and clear like a mirror, and mostly covered by ice.

Walking hurriedly toward the car, Julie noticed how light her bulky jacket felt in the deep cold. Despite a familiar sharp pain up her nose, caused by the blood vessels rapidly reacting to the low temperature, she felt energized and optimistic. She had a lot of work, but she was ready to get it all done, while she looked forward to the dusk. This was a special day, when she would finally meet her lover, a very special person with whom she had spent a few perfect moments a long, a long time ago. At the thought of him she felt warmth in her body, a deep bond, like an imaginary embrace. But she kicked the thought out of her mind, it was too distracting, and she could not waste time daydreaming with the risk of being forced to delay because of unaccomplished work in the real life.

They were to meet at the station. It was a nice building, with indoor cafes and a waiting room, a place Julie couldn't wait to get to, and not only to escape the cold of the darkening streets. Although she was a few minutes early, when she entered the waiting room her heart started to beat faster as her eyes searched for him. To counter her disappointment with a

---

54 This is a reference to the short story "Lovebirds" by F. Marincola, published in the collection "Cat Behind the Window."

comforting reason Julie checked the watch; it was still too early. Surely he will be there soon.

To distract herself she sat down and looked at the people in the room. There was an interesting, although not unexpected, difference among the people most dictated by their age: All the young people were wearing earphones and listening to music, or texting, or both, clearly unconcerned with their present surroundings; it was just a place with a good wireless network. Most of the middle-aged people had laptops or e-pads and were either working, watching movies, or reading e-books. Older people were sitting quietly, some looking around to break the boredom; others, usually groups of two to three neatly dressed ladies, chatting cheerfully among themselves. Old couples appeared less cheerful; the wife was most likely talking, in a nagging tone and low voice, while the husband looked invariably around, annoyed. Then, there were a few old women seating alone, keeping their distance from others, advertising a deep loneliness, despite their stern attempts to hide it. Unconsciously, she perceived them all as if they were her mother, and felt empathy for them, perhaps a subtle remorse.

Julie suddenly realized that almost twenty minutes had passed, and he was not there. She anxiously searched in her handbag for her phone, he surely must have tried to call her, and she did not hear the ringtone. There were no messages, no missed calls. Perhaps he was on his way. He will appear in the waiting room in no time, that's why he did not call her. Somebody walked in, approximately his size, and Julie's heart jumped in expectation, but it was not he. Anxiously, she fixed her gaze toward the door entrance, where people were constantly walking in and out of the room, screening each man's face. A couple of times she was ready to stand up and run toward a person who proved to be a stranger, and who was so different from him that she could not understand how she could have almost made that mistake.

Another fifteen minutes had passed, and Julie gathered the courage to call him, feeling already slightly wounded and starting to be concerned that something had happened. The phone was ringing but nobody answered. She did not leave a message. Almost compulsively, she checked his last email, wondering if it was possible that she was wrong about the date, the time, the place where they were supposed to meet. She sent him an email hoping he would see it; maybe he was still in a meeting and could not answer the phone. There was no answer to her email either, at least not right away, not in the next five minutes, or ten minutes, or twenty minutes. Julie sent a text message over the phone. No answer.

After an hour, Julie realized that the crowd in the room had changed. None of the people she had been distracting herself with in the beginning was there anymore. The people sitting there now seemed to her less friendly, almost unpleasant. The room had transformed into an unwelcoming cold place, and Julie felt really uncomfortable. After checking the watch, her phone, and email one more time, she stood up. The weariness of the long, busy day descended on her and she felt a pain in her stomach. She was wounded but did not want to let go of hope. She racked her brain for a reason for him not showing up, tried to stay rational, to keep in control.

She reasoned that her pain was probably hunger since she had no time for lunch and it was getting too late even for dinner. She desired real food but could not force herself to enter one of the restaurants where she had planned to go with him. Instead, she went to a bakery and bought a bagel and a bottle of juice, mostly because she could not think of anything else. The food helped calm the deep sense of anxiety that she was experiencing, and she decided to call him once more. No answer. No reply to her email, no reply to her text message. In a last effort to deny reality, she walked back to the waiting room, looked carefully inside, one last hope, which she recognized was absurd.

The way home was like a tunnel, dark and suffocating. Julie's clothes, carefully chosen in the bright morning, now looked ugly and she would never wear them again. Eventually, she fell asleep. The next morning there was a short email from him:

"I am sorry, something came up, I really could not make it, Love, C…"

And she thought how the word "love" has many meanings, and for some people it is just a salutation. Yet, there was hardly any reason to be angry at him, the relationship she was leaving with him was entirely a lovely creation of her fantasy, of which he might not even be aware, despite her genuine and passionate outpourings of love and affection when they had been together.

Of course, she could find a thousand pieces of evidence to convince herself that he loved her, but then another million to prove he really did not. There is love that lasts forever, and does not need to be fed, but romantic love, the most captivating and intense one, is ephemeral. Like all beautiful things, it cannot live but, in the moment, like the ice wrapping the stones by the river, it makes you wonder at the incredible circumstances of an unlikely creation.

Trying to make it through the day, feeling deeply lonely and worthless, Julie thought about a short story she had read, about a man named Dave who fantasized about being loved by a sweet, wonderful, and caring woman for a day, and this fantasy changed his life.

Perhaps she was like Dave, only her day of love had been real, but even this did not matter, as she understood that our emotions blur the borders between fantasy and reality. There was a river in the story along which Dave used to stroll and watch the lovebirds. Julie's river was frozen and there were no lovebirds, only a lonely eagle circling high in the sky in search of prey.

THE PERSISTENCE OF MEMORY
By Catterina Coha

OBJECT PERMANENCE

It was the first clear day in late April after a couple of weeks of almost constant rain. The window of my son's bedroom faces west and since we live on Riverside Avenue, near the corner with 145th Street, the view is open over the Hudson River and the mellow light of the sunset was basking the room. The five-month-old lying in the crib was delighted with the soft yellow rabbit with long ears, easy to grab by a developing human still struggling to master his motor coordination. In a failed attempt to pull the rabbit towards himself he ended up pushing it on the floor. A loud cry came out of his little mouth, and his eyes were wide open with an expression of surprise and sorrow that seemed to ask "Why did the rabbit disappear?" Being a professional psychologist, I could not help but observe my son to see if he was making an attempt to look for the toy. He wasn't, leading me to conclude that he did not understand yet that objects exist even when out of sight.

I was aware that my wife resented it when I treated my home as if it were my office, and my family as if they were my patients. I stopped analyzing the baby when I heard her footsteps down the hallway, because she was very perceptive towards my shortcomings, which escalated my irritation. She paid me no attention. She rushed to hug the baby and settled down to breastfeed him. I walked out of the room, relieved that I could have a bit of time to myself.

While I was warming some leftovers in the microwave and opening a bottle of beer I started to think about the man I had seen in my office that day. It was not clear to me if he was truly seeking help or just trying to validate a preconceived idea that he could not change. I had overheated the food, so I had to wait to avoid burning my tongue. My mind was running in circles, going nowhere, until suddenly I realized that there was a funny similarity between my son and this man.

"Object permanence means knowing that an object still exists, even if it is hidden. It requires the ability to form a mental representation of the object."

Why would this grown man have the same problem as a baby? The thought made me smile. While sipping my beer I went over our conversation.

"Good morning, doc, I am Jeremy. No need for formalities, please just call me Jeremy."

He was a tall mature man in good physical shape with a confident demeanor and casual sophistication in his manners. It was clear that he was well educated. His joviality was almost excessive, a common behavior for people who feel uncomfortable with the idea of going to a "shrink." I let him run the show for the first few minutes, to give him the opportunity to define his territory and get an idea about his persona. After some casual conversation about the horrible New York traffic, the trouble of getting a cab during rush hours, and the great Yankees game last Sunday, I looked at him with a smile and invited him to tell me his story. I deliberately avoided asking about "his problem," I knew it would be a term eliciting a defensive response. The strategy worked, and we started to talk like old friends meeting at the bar after work. The story that follows is as accurate as my recollection of it can be.

A WONDERFUL DAY IN LAS VEGAS

Well, where should I start with my story? I guess I can say that I am a successful man—professionally, I mean. I lead a large group in the developmental program of a pharmaceutical company. I have a Ph.D. in biomedical sciences and a master in business, and I trained at Stanford. I have always been at the top of my class, and did not have any problems finding jobs, so I could actually help my parents financially when they needed it. I spent a few years doing research in academia, then I moved to industry, and I can say that I am satisfied at my current position. Of course, the money is good, which always helps, but it is really the ability to steer the development of new drugs and have an impact on patients that motivates me. I like comfort, but I was raised in poverty, so I remain somewhat uncomfortable with luxury; I do not like waste, I am not greedy.

You would say that I am the type of guy a woman should like to settle down and raise a family with. I like kids and. . . yes, I always thought that I would have my own family. I was never concerned about finding the right mate, but now that I am getting older, I start to doubt that it won't ever happen. This concern surfaced when my mother died two years ago. I started to feel that my life was empty.

I am not the type of guy who panics, of course. I decided to be rational about it, to do as I do in my work: look at the "available data" from my past relationships, identify the problem, and make plans to address it. This strategy should assure success, or at least it usually does in my professional life. This is where I got lost. I do not usually need help analyzing the facts, but I guess analyzing yourself is not that easy, we probably lie to ourselves far more than we do to anybody else. This is why I am here.

To answer your question, what I learned by thinking about the problems in my past relationships is really concerning to me. But I do not want to influence your thinking by telling you what my interpretation is, I would rather just tell you the facts as they are.

I started my job with this company in December, about fifteen years ago. There was a young woman in another team to whom I was very attracted. Our interactions were professional, of course, until a Christmas party where we danced together. We started to talk and we could not stop. I felt happy. I thought I was in love. She definitely was in love with me. She told me a thousand times. We spent weekends together, did many fun things, and after a few months we were planning to move in together. But it never really happened. I was offered a promotion that I could not refuse, and that required me to move from San Diego to San Francisco. She was sad, but sure that we could see each other often anyway. On our last weekend together, we walked along the ocean. It was a perfect evening with the most beautiful sunset I have ever seen (you see, I do remember details!). It was so romantic, and I was totally in the mood for dreaming and making promises that (now I realize) I could not keep. I told her that we should get married, that it would make it easier for her to join me in San Francisco. We made a vague plan to get married in the following few months, and I left.

I am not so good at communicating by email about personal things, and I do not like to talk on the phone. This is just. . . the way I am. I loved to talk to her when I could look at her in the eyes, or hold her hands. But the phone, it was so contrived, and I could not retrieve a mental image of her that would make me desire to call her. She would call me, of course, looking for intimacy, I guess, hoping to feel my loving voice through the phone. . . but I mostly felt distant and eventually irritated by her frequent calls. She was confused and, maybe, she was wounded. She switched to emailing me instead, thinking this was a less intrusive way to communicate. I largely ignored her emails. I would read them, but often did not make the effort to reply. I was so busy in my new position, so totally absorbed in the work, that time went by and I did not miss her.

I am telling you this, about her being hurt I mean, because I realized it later. At the time I was not thinking about it. As I said, I was so busy that a few months went by and we did not see each other. She wanted to come visit me, but I always had an excuse to justify why I was not available. I could not think about her, I hardly remembered her face. Then, one day, at a business meeting in Santa Monica I was looking at the podium and there she was, presenting some data.

I looked at her, noticing that she was attractive. During lunch, she realized that I was there. She looked at me with inquisitive eyes, perhaps not knowing what to expect. I felt the impulse to hug and kiss her, but it was not the right place. We agreed to meet after work was over and went to walk along the beach. She wanted to talk, and ask questions, and understand, but I just kissed her and the rest of the night was, as you can imagine, wonderful. Every time she would go back to her questions I just smiled and kissed her. It became like a game, and the many important questions became pointless. Did I love her? How could she ask after my passionate lovemaking?

No, it was not just lust. I see your point, but I believe that I was honest, in the moment. I told her the truth, that I was really very busy, the work was intense and exciting. She thought that if she would make it easy for me, we could get married. It could be done during my business trip to Las Vegas, just an extra day. As you say, she was almost behaving like a kid who is afraid of losing a teddy bear and holds it tight. . . . She could have had any man, she was beautiful and smart and funny, but she was really in love.

Well, here comes the worse part of this first story. I myself do not know how to explain it. A couple of months passed. I do not recall exactly my communications with her during that time. I asked my assistant to answer her questions about some details, but—I swear—I think I somewhat forgot about the wedding plans. This is the only explanation. When I was leaving for Vegas my assistant gave me an envelope with a big smile on her face, but I did not open it.

I was there for two days and there were a lot of networking events organized by my company. I met a fascinating woman—I do not recall much about her, to be honest—and we had an affair. On the last day, once the work event ended, we were strolling around Vegas and I met Lauren—yes, finally, her name came to me! She was dressed as a bride. . . She had been waiting for me for two hours at the place where we were supposed to get married. She looked at me with an intensity I had never experienced before, but her beautiful eyes were not full of love but pain and contempt.

Her intense look. . . it came back to me in my dreams, for several months. I had never experienced such a depth of disappointment—reaching inside me all the way to my soul. She spoke almost no words but her eyes spoke for her with so many emotions. I did not know what to do, I felt powerless. I could not accept the responsibility for what happened—I had totally forgotten. So, I never tried to ask her for forgiveness, and never saw her again. Because of my recurrent dream—that every time made me feel unsettled—I decided to seek the first opportunity to move to a different job in the East Coast. I could not bear the idea of meeting her.

Yes, I suppose you are right. Considering that I could not think about my commitment to Lauren when she wasn't physically present, I seem to remember these events in far greater detail than you would expect, after so many years. In fact, after I moved to the East Coast I never thought about Lauren or her eyes again. I was comfortable with myself. This entire story would not be so vivid if it wasn't for a weird dream I had shortly after my mother died. In the dream I saw my mother—she looked young, as when I was still a child—and she had Lauren's eyes, looking at me with disappointment!

MY TRUE LOVE

My wife entered the kitchen and looked at me:

"What were you thinking about?"

"Nothing, I mean, I was thinking about a patient I saw today. I know you do not want me to talk about work."

She shrugged and with quick and skilled movements made herself a milkshake with strawberries, mango, and a spoon of vanilla ice cream. After pouring the fresh drink into a large glass, with a satisfied expression in her face she declared "Good for nursing, and tasty!"

Then, with a smile, she came closer, mussed my hair with her free hand, and said in a loving and slightly mocking tone:

"Okay, I do not mind listening to your patient's story, if it is not boring. . . but only if we can sit in the couch!"

After telling her Jeremy's story, I paused for a moment, and to check if she was still fully awake, I asked her: "So, what do you think?"

"Jeremy is a regular egocentric jerk, and Lauren was lucky she did not get stuck with him. . . "

"That is a little harsh," I protested.

"Yes, you are right. Lauren was a bit pushy. She kind of got herself what she deserved. Who would want to get married in Vegas, anyway? And what would she gain by such marriage? Did she think it would make him more committed?" Briefly interrupted by yawning, she continued:

"Your Jeremy just cares about his own pride and never felt guilty. If he had felt even a tiny bit of affection for this woman, wouldn't he want to know that she was fine, rather than running away?"

She sipped the last drop of her milkshake and with a thoughtful expression added:

"Know what I think? Jeremy's problem is that he feels guilty towards his own mother. Lauren is just a sort of trigger."

She paused for a couple of minutes and closed her eyes, just to reopen them with a visible struggle, and kissed me good night.

"I am going to sleep. My true love will wake up at three a.m. hungry!"

I could not help but feel a little jealous. *Her true love?* And what about me? Didn't I mean anything anymore to her?

While brushing my teeth I realized the absurdity of my jealousy and felt slightly ashamed but forgave myself for the reason that I was already half asleep.

RAIN
by Catterina Coha

I was concerned about the rain. The forecast was predicting heavy rain and wind. I knew what that feels like in New York City. Countless times I had been walking from the subway station to the building where I worked; just a few blocks, but far enough to get soaked despite the umbrella, despite the hooded coat. Nothing could resist the brute force of the wind.

I was supposed to look "nice" for the dinner and reception that night, and did not know how to make sure that I would not get completely messed up. No time or place to change. With some difficulty I found a dress that was decent and practical enough to be worn under the lab coat all day, and possibly appropriate for the occasion. Shoes and make up were more of a problem. When I was younger I could walk and stand for twelve hours in high heels—but now my feet started to hurt when I walked for too long wearing those fancy shoes. I hardly ever used any make up, but the passing of time and the many challenges had hardened my features, and chronic lack of sleep was showing up as dark circles under my eyes. I had little time to decide what to take, or I would miss the train and be late for work. I quickly packed a few make up items and threw them in my backpack, together with the umbrella.

During the day I was so busy that I had no time to worry about the evening. When I realized that I was feeling dizzy, it was too late to go fetch something quick to eat, I had to get going. It was raining, but the wind had not picked up yet, so I rushed out into the street without hesitation. All of the yellow cabs passing by were busy—it is always difficult to get one when it is raining—so I decided to use the subway. There would be more walking to do, but at least I would not be stuck in traffic.

When I emerged from the staircase of the subway station into the darkness of the late autumn evening, illuminated by the flashing lights of the off-

Broadway theaters, I realized that I did not know where to go. The piece of paper where I had written the address was not in the pocket of my coat. A burst of anxiety, aggravated by the lack of food, invaded my body. I searched for the address on my phone but could not read it without my glasses. The wind was strong now and it was impossible to search for the glasses in my backpack while trying to shield myself from the rain with the umbrella. A few well-dressed people walked towards a nearby building and entered. A couple of them looked familiar, and I felt relieved that I could just follow them to the right place. Two young women in the lobby were directing incoming people to the reception hall. I thought that it was curious that the pink ribbon that they usually wore looked slightly different in shape and it was of a darker color. Perhaps it was the way the Foundation acknowledged a new generous donor supporting breast cancer research? I patiently waited in line for the wardrobe and, having freed myself of the backpack, the wet coat, and the umbrella, I entered the hall. I was handed a glass of prosecco and went walking around looking for colleagues and socializing with the donors. I wanted to find a friend, who was supposed to be there, but I got constantly stuck in small talk with strangers, who were invariably delighted to describe their wonderful vacations in my home country as soon as they found out that I was born in Italy. I was slightly annoyed that nobody showed interest in my research work, I felt that I was not doing my job in representing the awardees. Then the crowd moved towards the dining hall, and I followed.

I was lightheaded, probably as a result of the prosecco, being tired and starved. The tables were not numbered, and no names were posted. Very unusual. . . I was not sure where to sit. I must have looked visibly confused because a tall gentleman standing near one of the tables gestured an invitation to sit there. I thought that he must know me. Thus, I was embarrassed that I did not recall his name. He introduced himself with a warm smile as "Julian," and I was then sure that I had never met him before.

I smiled back, told him my name and, trying to get clues about what was going on, I said:

"They usually assign us to a table; I was not sure where I should sit. . . "

"But of course, you have to sit near me. . . " he replied with a deep and sensual voice, looking so penetratingly into my eyes that I had to avert them. My heartbeat increased for a moment. I needed to break the charged silence that followed and recover the "professional" conduct into our interaction.

"Is this the first time you're attending this event?" I asked.

"Yes, but I will come again if you do," he continued in the same sensual tone.

"Where are you from?" I replied, trying to divert the conversation towards an acceptable topic.

"Out of town," was his short reply. "Would you like some wine?" And before I had time to reply, he poured wine into one of the glasses in the table and handed it to me. I should have refused, drinking more before eating would definitely make me tipsy, and it did. I do not remember what I said next, but the topic of our conversation was irrelevant. I started to feel relaxed and comfortable.

Once everybody was seated and enjoying the first course, a speaker went to the podium. As he started to talk, I finally realized that I was at the wrong event. It was not a fundraiser for cancer research but a "dating event." This explained Julian's manners. The person acting out of place was me. I had failed to show up at the important fundraiser and there were probably a few angry people. This was my first thought, the second one was a deep embarrassment. I had never considered a dating service or whatever this was. I felt an incredible disappointment with myself, mixed with suspicion that I had an emerging dementia—how could I go on for so long without realizing what should have been obvious within the first few minutes?

Julian might have guessed what was going on in my mind, since he was respectfully quiet for a few minutes. He then sported an ironic smile, and told me softly:

"I knew you did not come here on purpose. I mean, you were not looking for a date. That is what made you so attractive, in addition to your looks, of course." He paused briefly to give me time to speak, but I did not know what to say, so he continued:

"I hope I did not offend you in any way."

Instinctively, I took his hand and answered, "No, not at all. I actually think you saved me from making a fool of myself. Other people here might not have been such gentlemen!"

He smiled with relief and kissed my hand. Then he offered his arm. "I will walk you out, it is late, and I am sure that you are tired and eager to go home."

I was tired, true, but did not think of home as a welcoming place. I followed Julian, and he helped me with my coat, and offered to carry the backpack to the station for me. I did not want to part from him, so I accepted. We walked in the rain, but it was not uncomfortable. He kissed me in the cheek when we reached the train tracks, and said "I hope to meet you again." Then he walked away without leaving me time to respond.

Once in the train, I realized that I was not wet, even my shoes looked fine, despite the pretty strong downpour we had been walking through. I closed my eyes, exhausted, and savored the magical feeling that Julian left me with. I was almost asleep when the train stopped, and a loud voice came through the speakers announcing that the train had a problem and we needed to change the equipment at the next station. Another train would come in ten minutes. The weary crowd of late-night passengers poured into the platform, squeezing under a small roof that partially protected them from the rain. I was too slow coming out and there was no room left under the roof. I opened my umbrella and waited for the new train, shivering in the wind. I could not think of anything; all the energy I had left was necessary to withstand the moment until the incoming train would provide a shelter. I noticed that I was not getting wet, yet under the lights it was possible to see how much water was coming down. This was odd, but not something to complain about, on the contrary, "this rain is well-behaved," I thought, and the absurdity of it made me smile.

Finally, we boarded the new train. But after about ten minutes the train stopped. The same loud voice came through the speakers announcing that due to the wind a tree was down on the tracks and the train had to go back to the same station we just left in order to change tracks. The process of going backwards was inexorably slow, and when we finally reached the station, it became apparent that the train could not be shifted to another track. We had to get out again in the cold rain. An express train that was on its way would stop for us and take us north. Some of the passengers were calling friends and relatives asking them to come pick them up by car. Others were arguing that it was not possible that another train will make it through. I looked up at Uber's options on my phone, but the closest car was thirty minutes away, so I decided to wait for the train. The rain was unrelenting; it was difficult to see anything a few feet away. I must have been lost in thought or half asleep when the train arrived. There was no announcement, and the train was on another track. To reach it I needed to climb up the stairs and cross to the other side. I think the few other people waiting with me had done it already. I was alone and by the time I ran up the stairs, it was too late—the train had left without me.

I felt a deep despair. It was now past midnight, and I had no idea when another train would come. This was a small station where only the local trains stop, and there is only one every hour, at best. I checked Uber again, but there was no car available. It was probably too late. I took a deep breath to calm myself down and searched for the train schedule online. Reception was bad, the page would not load. Then, my phone died.

I have no recollection of what happened next, I do not remember exiting the station, but I found myself walking without a clear direction in a dark street with nobody around. My mind was blurry, and I was possessed by an incomprehensible determination to keep walking, almost as if I could just run away from the bad situation in which I was. Maybe it was a way to keep my mind focused on coordinating the movements and prevent the building anxiety. Why did I leave the station—the only place where eventually I would have found a form of transportation to go home? Where was I going?

Suddenly, I found myself in an old and shady-looking pub. Only a few people were there, and it seemed that they had not noticed me. I inspected the walls searching for an outlet to charge my phone but did not find any. With some hesitation I approached the bar to ask for a favor to let me charge the phone. The bartender was a heavy-set middle-aged man with mustaches and such a stern expression that discouraged asking for a favor before ordering something. I asked for a glass of Port wine, but he did not understand—perhaps because of my accent, I thought. I looked at the bottles lined behind him hoping to recognize something I could drink. It was mostly gin and whiskeys. I had been so sick the last time I had a drink containing gin that I could not even stand the smell of it. I reasoned that this was not the place where I could ask for cognac, so I ordered an Irish whiskey. He mumbled a list of names, and I picked the only one I had recognized and could repeat, "Jameson, please."

The bartender turned his back to me to go fetch the Jameson, and another man sitting nearby turned towards me and asked, almost casually, "Are you French?" For some reason my accent was often mistaken for a French one, so I was not surprised by his question. I quickly pondered what to answer and decided that it would be wise to give him the satisfaction of guessing correctly. "Yes, how do you know?" I smiled. Although I did not like whiskey, a couple of sips helped me relax and forget that I was in a nowhere land in the middle of the night and I would have to come back to reality and go to work in just a few hours. The man who had mistaken me for a French woman introduced himself as Julian, and I thought with amusement that this was the night of "Julians." He was very different from the first Julian. He did not have the sophisticated gentlemanly manners, but a simple and direct way of talking. He told the bartender that he will take care of my drink, and then asked me how I got to this pub, a place "forgotten by God."

The situation was so out of my routine, expectations, and control, that I felt as if I were acting in a movie that happened to also be my real life. Unable to come up with a more interesting and believable story I told him the truth, that the trains kept breaking down and my phone died and I went looking for some help. He looked at my shoes (or perhaps my—unfortunately—very visible legs) and remarked, in what sounded to me as a slightly sarcastic tone, "So you walked for quite a while in this heavy rain. . . The station is not that close by." I looked at my shoes, and my leg, and my dress, and they all looked perfectly fine. I reckoned he did not believe me, on the account that at least my fancy shoes should have been wet, after walking in the rain.

How to enlighten him about the well-behaved rain? I realized what his sarcastic tone implied, and decided that my only hope was to address it immediately. I told him, keeping my gaze straight into his eyes:

"I am not a hooker, Julian. I really need to get home so I can sleep and go to work tomorrow. If I can charge my phone I will call a taxi, or an Uber."

He looked at me intently and then said in a soft but firm tone:

"Lady, I will drive you home. You will not find a taxi at this time around here."

I protested that it was quite far, but he just said:

"If my wife or daughter were in trouble, I hope they would find a man to help them." I had conflicting thoughts in my head: Was he a family man or just pretending to be one, to convince me to trust him? Overtaken by a sense of fatality I followed him and got into his pickup truck.

The night was dark and the rain falling on the vehicle so strongly made a constant noise that was lulling me to sleep. But I resisted, although I must have blacked out for a few moments because at some point another man appeared in the pickup truck. I was afraid to look at this new face, and could not ask Julian who he was. I had an ominous feeling about the situation. I would know for sure that their motives were bad the moment I opened my mouth; I had no chance to ask for help, no way to get out of the car. My fate was to end up as a headline on the county's newspaper: a doctor found dead in mysterious circumstances. I saw the sign pointing to the exit towards my hometown and opened my mouth to alert Julian to take it, but I could not produce any sound, and the car kept running fast on the Taconic highway.

At that moment I woke up screaming, in my bed. It took me a while to realize that I was home, and the rest was just a dream. I turned on the light and saw the party dress lying on the chair, still slightly wet. My confused mind was trying to sort out what really happened, and what was part of the dream. I had attended a reception, but I went to the real fundraiser. It was raining and windy and the train broke down, twice, but eventually I got home. I probably had a drink at a bar with somebody after the reception, but was his name really Julian?

THE PASSING GAME
by Catterina Coha

I left early. I packed a few clothes and disinfectant wipes, a bottle of water. The rental SUV was easy to drive, and I quickly got used to it. It was a clear morning, one of those mornings when the blue of the sky and brightness of the sun fill you with hope, but today it felt different. I needed to stay focused, concentrate on the long journey, make it on time. It had all changed so quickly.

The road was running along the river and the hills were embracing it. The familiar scenery and memories of driving that road a thousand times with her kept me company. We would talk and sing and listen to the radio. It was our special Saturday trip up the valley for her rehearsals at the theater. I still marvel at the recollection of her performance as the Shakespearian Ophelia, credibly mad, so naturally transformed into a person different from the one I knew. It was magical, yet unsettling.

The exit to the bridge came up, I had to cross the river and abandon the valley to go in the northwest direction. No more daydreaming, I had to pay attention. I glanced at the directions on my phone, making sure not to miss the signs for route 84. At a narrowing of the road, due to unfinished construction, there was some accumulation of cars. I was annoyed, but it cleared after a couple of miles. As I took the exit to merge on route 84 Siri coldly stated: "Go straight for 156 miles." Flat fields and woods with occasional wrecked farms run along the road, a monotonous landscape of no significant beauty. Every so often a sign indicated a rest area. The speed limit of sixty-five miles per hour seemed to reassure everybody on the road that it was safe to go eighty. The traffic was light; mostly commercial trucks were on the road. I turned on the radio to keep me company and found a good station, playing light and pleasant music that did not rouse any emotions but filled the silence. After about an hour, I lost the station and started to search for another one, unsuccessfully. Only fifty miles left to go before the next road. I glanced at the gas indicator, it was down below a quarter, so I decided to stop at the first gas station. Few minutes later I saw a sign "Food and gas in 25 miles."

It seemed to take forever to reach it. I was not hungry but desired getting out of the car to stretch my legs and after getting gas I drove up the side road towards a mall, hoping to find a Starbucks. But the entrance to the mall was blocked. I was disappointed but did not make too much of it and went to a nearby McDonald's. The parking lot was empty. I got out of the car and walked towards the door, which was closed. I read the sign on the door "drive through only." Of course, what was I thinking?

I got back on the highway, with a sense of anticipation for the next step, another exit, another road to take, going in the right direction, getting me closer to the final destination. Only ten miles to the change, eight, six, four, two. . . now! An imperceptible change, but Siri assured me that it was the right road and in the usual emotionless tone directed me to "continue straight for 272 miles." I couldn't help but yawn. There were woods on both sides of the road, somewhat more interesting nature than the prior landscape, and I passed near a little lake. Occasional clouds in the sky.

"Maybe something interesting on the radio," I thought, but there was poor reception. "Of course, who is there to listen?" There were no more than ten houses in a hundred miles!

Finally, I found a song that I could listen to, but the music in my head was better than the one on the radio, so I turned it off. What I really wanted to hear were news, but not local news, I wanted to know how many people had died today in Italy, I wanted to know if the curves were flattening or if they kept climbing, and the breakdown by region.

Damned, I yawned again, twice, and seeing the sign "Next rest area in 15 miles" I told myself loudly, "I need to stop."

The parking lot of the rest area was almost empty. I walked into the small building happy to have access to the rest room. An old lady waited patiently, at some distance, for me to get out before she walked in. The vending machine was not working, leaving me frustrated that I had spent a few minutes trying to choose a snack. I went back to the car, opened the back door to pull out something to munch and my water bottle. The sun was still strong but so was the wind. It was cold. Maybe a good thing, I thought; some cold air to wake me up better than the coffee I did not have. I looked at the phone, checking if any text message had appeared that needed my attention. None from her, and I decided not to bother her, and went back on the road.

It was then that the orange Volkswagen passed me, positioning itself at a safe distance in front of my car. I do not know why I felt the urge to overtake it, maybe it was the carelessness in the color, or the fact that it dictated my speed, which was above the limits anyway. I guess it was annoying to have to follow the cheerfully insulting orange car. Even more annoying was the fact that another car prevented me from moving to the left lane; the silver-colored hatchback took a very long time to pass both of us, at least this is how it felt. Finally, I did get my chance, and while passing the orange Volkswagen, I tried to glimpse the driver, but they were concealed by the dark glass of the window.

I was now positioned between the silver hatchback and orange Volkswagen. I could have taken over both, but I did not want to take the chance of triggering a speeding fine. It had happened to me once before, and I had learned that it is better to be careful in roads that you do not know, the troopers could be hidden anywhere.

A few minutes later the orange Volkswagen appeared in my left side mirror, coming up at full speed and passing both me and the silver hatchback. Without much thought, I felt it was my turn and did the same, getting ahead of both cars. The silver hatchback went next, and we continued the game for about a hundred miles. Occasional interference by other vehicles made it more interesting. At one point, when it was my turn to pass, I got stuck behind a big truck passing a smaller truck and blocking the way. The heavy truck struggled to pass the other, which had increased the speed to hold its ground. For a while it seemed that I would be boxed there for eternity. Finally, when the larger truck moved back into the right lane, I was able to speed up but could not see the orange Volkswagen or the silver hatchback at the horizon. I felt abandoned, like a kid playing a game of hide and seek, who realizes that the other kids already left the playground and went home.

After a few miles, however, I saw my friends. The orange Volkswagen was easier to spot, and it was the same car because I recognized the yellow bumper sticker. I felt strangely happy. I passed it mainly to let it know that I was there and check if it was still in the mood to continue the game. The silver hatchback was hidden in front of a bus but came back into the game as well when I passed it on my way to take the lead. So, we continued the passing game, until the silver hatchback suddenly moved to the right lane and took an exit I had barely noticed.

Now, just the two of us, which became a little less interesting. We passed each other a few more times, until the time came for my SUV and the orange Volkswagen to split. We had reached a major intersection and went in opposite directions. No parting gesture, we were just two of the many cars in the road, like strangers, who had never shared a playful moment of their journey. It made me wonder if the game was just the mere product of my imagination, and the driver of the orange Volkswagen had never noticed me. Regardless, I felt lonely.

I was on the last stretch of the road, last hundred miles or so to go, the sun starting to settle down, when I got her text: "Can you come pick me up tonight?" I had reserved a joint nearby to sleep, planning to go the next morning, not to deprive her of the chance to spend the last night with her friends, in her dorm. The decision to close down even before the spring break had been made in such haste, nobody was prepared.

When I arrived, we did not even hug, it was understood that it was better to restrain emotions and focus on the practicalities. We went up and down the three flights of stairs carrying boxes and pillows, blankets and books, her flute and her sax. Other kids were doing the same, packing their things in the parent's car and going away without saying anything. Freshmen were trying to absorb the reality, the fact that the promised land was slipping away abruptly, in such unreal circumstances, just when they were preparing for concerts, dances, parties, and finals to come. Older kids, especially the seniors, were hugging each other, some were quietly crying while saying goodbye forever to their peers and effectively ceasing to be college students without the closure that comes with a celebratory graduation.

Mrs. Nancy, a middle-aged woman with a strong built and warm smile— whom my daughter referred to as the "dorm's Mom"— was there to help and support the kids, to make sure that they were picked up. I thought that she would probably lose her job, yet she was projecting optimism and energy, and she had bought pizza for everybody the night before, to cheer them up.

Before leaving we went to her favorite café. We both needed to say goodbye to the beautiful college town, a parting gesture. Little less than a year had passed from the day when we first visited, after acceptance, before the final decision, full of excitement. There was a cold wind, the table section was closed but it was still possible to get a coffee. The bartender was one of the college kids, and I thought: "Where will she go, and what will happen to the cafes around here without their main customers?"

We drove away, in the fading light of dusk, ready to go home.

ALMONDS AND GRAND MARNIER

by Catterina Coha

Reality was so painful that I tried writing, as a form of catharsis. But I could not write anything, so I started drinking instead. Some evenings I made it through by working, but others I was restless and ended up trying to poison myself with almonds and Grand Marnier. But there is too little cyanate in almonds to kill you, at least in the almonds I bought in the Turkish store at the corner. The liqueur just helped dissolve the nutty stodge in my stomach and made me sleepy.

For the most part I did not have trouble sleeping. My dreams were confused and confusing, but at least they were there, and this was reassuring. Getting up in the morning required motivation, which was fading a little more every day. Some weekend mornings I slept late enough to see the sun rise but it just made me feel like a prisoner looking out of the window at a world that no longer belongs to me.

As plan after plan got cancelled, I stopped making any. Life was passing as a continuum of monotonous hours, days, weeks, months. Desires previously so vivid were muffled by a sense of worthlessness. It was not just the desires that became meaningless, I did.

It was odd that I became more efficient in accomplishing important tasks because I stopped caring for them. It was almost as I was compelled to take care of unfinished business before I departed. Nevertheless, I was painfully aware of being a phony. I suspected that the people I tried to deceive realized it, but I could not force myself to care about what they thought about me. Once you accept your ugliness you stop trying to look nicer, since you know it is useless.

When I think of this time, the best moment I had was when I was sick. The feverish body demanded attention to my life, providing an excuse for being useless, at least until I recovered. I recall waking up in the middle of the night completely drenched in sweat, having to change in silence as I was feeling cold, the fever starting to rise again. I remember lying in bed one afternoon and feeling that my body was too hot to touch. A breeze from the open window felt like heaven. Oddly, the forced separation from everybody was easy. Maybe it was because it made me feel important, or it was the ultimate way to feel empathy with the masses of people who had been and were sick, to participate in this historic moment. "If you cannot help them, join them!"

In retrospect, it was a stupid death. Lost in the statistics of so many deaths, without even a proper funeral.

ESCAPE
by Catterina Coha

We went skiing, just to break the boredom of the gloomy winter days and get out of the confined spaces we lived in. When you cannot meet new people, you are stuck with whoever you happened to have around when the restrictions started. It does not feel like a prison, but it does not feel like freedom either, stranded with co-inhabitants and not exactly by choice.

The second time we went was the best. She was in a good mood, maybe because a lot of fresh snow had fallen recently. Crowds were sparse even in the weekend, as compared to normal times, due to the restrictions. It was a Monday and there were even fewer people. We went up and down the slopes so many times that I lost count.

She felt more confident than the first time, and mastered the black slopes without problems, so I easily relinquished my caution. At one point I stopped at the top of a really steep double black slope. It was so inviting, I was drawn to it, and the fact that there were no skiers adventuring there made it even more attractive. I asked her if she minded if we split and meet at the bottom. She was silent and I understood that she did not like the idea. Had I been with anybody else I would have jumped down to enjoy a moment of excitement, but with her I just felt like a pathetic bragger. So, I dropped the idea without speaking a word and we continued in the easier slope.

Towards the end of the day, while sitting in the lift going up the mountain, we saw a squirrel jumping erratically in circles in the snow between the trees. She was so amused at the little squirrel who seemed to be searching without success for nuts buried in the fall. "Squirrels often forget where they bury their food," her friend who knows everything about all animals had told her. Her childish amazement was so captivating. Her big brown eyes were smiling through the ski googles. I felt like caressing the lock of her curly hair that had escaped out of the ski mask but refrained from doing it. In that short yet infinite moment our surroundings transformed into an enchanted place. The sun, veiled by clouds, pretended to be the moon, making us laugh at it, while the icicles hanging from the rocks below glittered like the wand of a fairy.

I know that if it weren't for the circumstances, she would be somewhere else. She will return to the life she longs for as soon as it becomes possible. The memory of a squirrel jumping around in the snow, her sweet laughter, and the magical winter afternoon will stay in my heart forever.

HALLELUJAH
by Catterina Coha

On September 11, 2001, in response to the shock and horror for so many lost lives, people in the city responded with solidarity and humanity, although for a brief time. These days things are different. Many lives were lost at the peak of the pandemic last year, long lines became a common sight outside COVID testing centers and, later, vaccination centers and soup kitchens. Homeless people briefly disappeared from the empty streets, but new ones took their place and seemed to be growing in numbers and desperation. Expensive department stores reopened for business, but small stores selling cheap clothes closed for good. More people ride bikes and cafes all have tables outside. Children are back playing in the park in front of the hospital. Theaters and museums reopened, subways are getting crowded, and everybody sports a face mask when riding.

Things are getting better and perhaps it was necessary to reboot the society—changes do not happen without a crash. We all kept working frantically, nursing the fantasy that we have no time for the most important problems—we are too busy meeting deadlines, managing deals, buying stuff that is largely useless and we do not know how to properly discard, planning vacations we will never have time to take, plotting pathetic power struggles at work to win yet another meaningless title of "director" of something.

When the running wheel came to a sudden stop, people had nothing to do; so, they started to think. Because they were not used to thinking, they became scared, and some went mad, buying into irrational conspiracy theories. Others felt so insecure that they believed anybody telling them reassuring lies—lies about their country being the greatest country, which seems at odd with the harsh reality of what is happening in it—and thus, they willfully chose a soothing narrative in complete disregard for the truth.

Others felt reassured by their guns, and by shooting at innocent people who symbolize what they fear. Finally, some recovered a sense of identity and started to protest, to go on strike, but not enough. Not enough to catalyze real change, which means that it all will return to an ever uglier and more destructive way of life, a growing dust ball, much bigger than the past ones, painful evidence that we have actively refused to learn from mistakes in the name of greed.

This is the stage and the setting in which I walk through every day on my way to work, to find a better way to treat cancer. I feel bad for not having cash to give to the countless beggars, yet I rarely remember to put some in my pocket. I feel easily irate when the subway doors close right in front of me, even if a few minutes will not make much of a difference. I walk through the streets without seeing what is around me, gone is the sense of curiosity and wonder that had accompanied me for most of my life, the cheerfulness of seeing all sorts of people. I feel guilty, for my generation is responsible for destroying the planet: we were given unprecedented possibilities, and we largely misused them.

My hope is that the young people will take over as soon as possible, but they may have to kill the selfish, stubborn, narcissistic, and idiotic old farts, who do not want to give up the power. And lock up the worst representatives of the next generation that produced some of the most maniacal egos, of Napoleonic ambitions, who lost sense of reality and think they can own the universe—real or virtual—and have yet to meet their defeat in the frozen plains of Russia, or rather the flooded golf courses of Florida, burned down forests of California and, soon to be polluted, orbit around the Earth.

It is really painful to see (thank God they are not that frequent in the city) young people sporting a MAGA hat—probably genuinely believing that because "they are white and blond and have a good job they cannot go to jail" (quoting from a tweet of a participant in the January 6 attack on the Capitol). These youth are backward leaning, not paying attention to what is happening, overly concerned about feeling good about themselves, walking through life with their eyes covered by empty symbols and brains ruminating falsehood in the form of slogans.

But this morning was different, something happened: I heard *Hallelujah* by Leonard Cohen. A tall young boy was playing it in Grand Central subway station. I did not stop to listen but could still hear it from the tracks before the train came screeching. For a few minutes the world was a better place and the people standing around waiting for the subway changed; they were no longer just individuals, they were part of something bigger, something beautiful, something meaningful: humanity.

TAKE-OFF

by Catterina Coha

"The thing you are looking for is not in there," said the uniformed man in a stern voice, noticing my frantic scrolling and tapping on the iPhone.

I did not want to consider his intrusive remarks or accept such assertion, but I was paralyzed for an instant and stopped moving my hands on the screen, without raising my gaze from the device.

I had been jumping from two email inboxes, WhatsApp and other apps—looking for a signal that someone I cared about was alive communicating with me.

But all was silent, plenty of stored stuff. Nothing happening "live." He was right, the thing I was looking for was the equivalent of a hug. All of a sudden, the iPhone lost the status of a comfort object, almost an intimate friend, becoming a meaningless inanimate tool.

I felt uneasy, my body started to ache and the idea of sitting for many hours in a plane was unbearable. What an uncomfortable seat! Or perhaps it was my back or my stomach that were not well. I closed my eyes, hoping to cancel the reality, unable to think about anything to look forward to. I tried to relax, telling myself that this was an opportunity to get some rest after a frantic day of work, meetings, and running around. But I couldn't, my mind kept wandering in oppressive spaces, while my tired body seem not to even belong to me.

"The cabin door has been closed, at this time we request that you switch your small electronic devices to airplane mode and store larger devices under the seat in front of you or in the luggage compartment."

I gasped at the thought that I was going to be in limbo for many hours, unreachable to others and without control of my fate. I recalled the panic attack of a friend, who felt that something ominous was about to happen in the flight and wanted to get out, alas, too late! She survived to tell me.

Could my restlessness be a premonition? Then, I thought of the adventurous sense of excitement I felt when the plane was taking off. Now, in the best of circumstances, I doze off and wait for the flight to be over. Is this what happens in life? We get to the point when we just wait for it to be over. I had an impulse to switch off the airplane mode just for a second while the plane was taxiing in the runway. Like magic, a message appeared:

"Mom, I had to use the credit card for a college expense, is it okay?"

I quickly answered that it was okay, before returning the phone to airplane mode, with a smile in my heart.

ABOUT THE AUTHOR

Francesco Marincola is Chief Scientific Officer of Sonata Therapeutics, Boston, Massachusetts (2023 to present). Previously, he was Global Head of Research at Kite Pharma, Santa Monica, California (2021-2023), President and Chief Scientific Officer at Refuge Biotechnologies, Palo Alto, California (2018-2021), Distinguished Research Fellow in Immune Oncology at AbbVie Corp. in Redwood City, California (2017-2018) and Chief Research Officer at Sidra Medical and Research Centre in Doha, Qatar (2013-2017). Prior to joining the biopharma industry, Francesco was a tenured senior investigator in cancer immunotherapy at the National Institutes of Health (1990-2013).

Francesco is the former President of the Society for Immunotherapy of Cancer (SITC). He is the founding editor and editor-in-chief of the Journal of Translational Medicine and Translational Medicine Communications and the author of more than 700 peer-reviewed publications. His scientific work has deepened the understanding of the mechanisms leading to tumor rejection, transplant rejection, graft-versus-host disease and autoimmunity. Francesco received his M.D. from the University of Milan, Italy, and completed his residency at Stanford University, California, USA.

He published his first novel in 2013: "*The Wise Men of Pizzo*" which was awarded the "Corrado Alvaro Award for Literature" in 2016. The novel written originally in English has been translated into Italian and Mandarin. He also published two collections of short stories: "*The Leopard and Other Stories*" and "*Cat Behind the Window*".

His site can be visited at https://authorfrancomarincola.wordpress.com
and the published collections at MeiGuiLu Publishing:
www.meiguilupublishing.com

***

Cover Image: Midnight at the riverbank. Photo by F. Marincola,
Sodankyla, Lapland, August 2015.

Organizer: George Patriarca and Paraules Organization

Copyediting: Nicole Arianne Velasquez

***